The Lime Juice Chronicle

Rock on!

The Lime Juice Chronicle

A Novel by

Daniel A Reece

The Lime Juice Chronicle
Copyright © 2023 Daniel Reece

Though this story incudes many factual events, it is a work of fiction, not a history. Names, characters, places, and incidents are either the product of the author's imagination or are used fictitiously.

ISBN-979-8-3901663-4-5

Printed in the United States

This story is dedicated to M.A. Bud Reece and Marion Reece for instilling the values I hold dearest. They and my sister, Marty, showed me more patience than I deserved.

Table of Contents

Prologue

The 2021 Sienna minivan still had its fresh-off-the-assembly-line scent and it was brimming with the latest technology, a pre-collision warning system, 360-degree exterior camera views, radar activated cruise control, lane departure alert, with steering assist and lane trace assist. Despite the Star Wars looking cockpit, it was deadly boring to drive. A lemur could pilot the thing. Tim did appreciate the safety features on his son's family assault vehicle though, given his precious cargo of five eleven-year-old girls.

The girls had hit the wall after playing four soccer games in two days at a regional tournament three and a half hours drive from home. Sean and Ellen were overwhelmed at work, so Tim agreed to chauffer their oldest daughter, Addie, and some of her teammates. Addie was riding shotgun. The other four girls were sprawled out in the back, the sound of the road lulling them into a deep slumber. Tim used to love road trips, but his aging ailing back robbed much of the pleasure. The chance to spend time with Addie was well worth the discomfort.

Tim needed a tutorial from Addie on how to operate the advanced entertainment system which included a satellite radio subscription. Addie was lethargic and seemed indifferent to the radio, so Tim flipped it to the BBC World Service. They were reporting on the disastrous withdrawal of US forces from Afghanistan and the tens of thousands of Afghan civilians desperately attempting to flee with them. It was a tragedy of massive proportions. Tim's depression about it was compounded by its familiarity. It was all so predictable, a policy doomed from the outset. *"Had we learned nothing?"*

Tim switched to a classic rock station, and he was immediately spooked to hear the Crosby, Stills, Nash, and Young, anthem "Ohio." It was as if Sirius Radio was channeling his flashback.

1

Addie was resting her head against the window with her eyes half open. She listlessly asked, "What are they singing about, grandpa? Who are the four dead in Ohio?"

"They were four young people who were shot by the National Guard while protesting against the Vietnam War at Kent State University in Ohio. What do you know about the Vietnam War, Addie?"

"Not much, I know it happened a long time ago, around the time when you were young. I've seen pictures of the Vietnam War Memorial in Washington D.C. Did you fight in the war grandpa?"

"No Addie, I was very fortunate not to have fought *in* the war, but I did fight *over* it."

It was hard for Tim to fathom how something so profound, something that defined a period in his life, in the life of the country, could now be so obscure to so many people. Then he did the math in his head. It had been 45 years since the war ended, the same length of time between when he was eleven and the end of World War I. If he had been asked at Addie's age what he knew about the "War to end all wars," he would have only known there were monuments for those who died, and that it happened a long time ago, when his grandfather was young. It was yet another sign of Tim growing old, when the events from his youth fade from collective memory. He wondered how much of it was fading from his own memory.

Addie perked up when the next song came on. It was one of the most iconic blues-rock numbers ever recorded, The Rolling Stones', "Gimme Shelter." It was like a shot of espresso. Tim and Addie danced in their seats. "Who's playing grandpa? Are those The Beatles?"

Tim's initial thought was, *"Can this be happening? Have we now entered an alternative universe?"* He regained his composure and found his grandfatherly voice, "No honey, those are the Rolling Stones. They're British, like The Beatles, but they had more of a reputation for being bad boys. It's remarkable that they're still playing concerts around the world.

"Which band did you like more grandpa, The Beatles, or The Rolling Stones?"

"Well, I liked them both a lot, but I'd have to say I liked, no I loved The Beatles more."

"Does that mean you were more of a good boy than a bad boy grandpa?"

2

"To be honest, Addie, I wanted to be a good boy, but there were many times when I wasn't nearly good enough."

Chapter 1
The World on a Wall

As 1967 unfolded in the world, it also unfolded on Tim McIntyre's bedroom wall. A slowly spreading collage of the people and events that were fueling the development of his adolescent synapses. Perhaps it seemed to Tim like the world was awakening, second guessing itself, confused and uncertain, because at fifteen, he was becoming more self-aware, second guessing himself, confused and uncertain. Every era has its share of tumult and youth must always grapple with their place in time, but hey man, this was the 1960s! A new culture was blossoming. Old conventions were being challenged and new mores were being defined. The oppressed were stirring. Old political alliances were unraveling. Campuses were erupting. Cities were seething. Southeast Asia, Latin America, Africa, and Eastern Europe were bleeding. Changes were happening everywhere, all the time. It was a time magnificently aligned with being a teenager.

Just as baby boomers rode their demographic crest through a sanguine 1950s childhood filled with Saturday morning cartoons, "I Love Lucy," and "Leave It to Beaver"; dining on a cuisine concocted just for them, Twinkies, Coco Puffs, Pop Tarts and Cheez Whiz, the disruptions of the 1960s were painting the perfect backdrop for adolescent angst and acting out. World events inspired young people, handing them a meta permission slip to break free. Questioning authority was the mantra of the times. Everything seemed up for grabs. It was exhilarating, but with an undercurrent of anger and terror. It didn't feel like history as usual. Tim wanted to capture it, absorb it, and naively, make sense of it.

The primary sources for collecting vivid images from around the world back then were glossy magazines, so Tim ransacked and devoured them. Time, Newsweek, US News, Life, Look and the National

Geographic were capturing the world on Kodachrome, printing large format images in extended photo essays by world-renowned photojournalists. He scavenged drugstore newsstands, libraries, coffee tables and the dentist office waiting room to collect visually powerful moments of race riots in Newark, Boston, and Detroit; the counter-culture scene in Haight-Ashbury and London's Carnaby Street; brutal fighting in Vietnam, Nigeria, Israel, and Nicaragua; scenes from ground-breaking movies like *Bonnie and Clyde*, *The Dirty Dozen*, *The Graduate*, *Cool Hand Luke* and *Guess Who's Coming to Dinner*. You know how aggravated you get when you're reading an interesting article, then discover some jerk has ripped out the photograph that was likely the best one to bring the narrative to life, well, Tim was that jerk. He wouldn't pilfer indiscriminately, but he was prolific. His raids on these publications were strategic, looking for a blend of emerging cultural phenomena, political upheavals and whatever struck him as disturbingly bizarre.

Back in his room, Tim played with various combinations of images, putting them together around themes, looking for both common threads and unsettling contrasts. He juxtaposed a close-up of Janis Joplin belting out the blues next to a black civil rights protester screaming in agony while being pounded by the spray from a firehose; the smiling TV sitcom character Pfc. Gomer Pyle, looking up at scenes of Vietnamese villages ablaze; the Maharishi Yogi face-to-face with Pope Paul VI; Bonnie and Clyde being riddled by machine gun bullets next to hippies handing-out flowers. Week by week his montage spread further across the wall over his desk, opposite his bed. He'd lay there meditating on this wildly absurd state of affairs. He thought it was mind-expanding to lose himself while meditating on that wall, albeit he had not yet experienced getting stoned, but the notion of expanding one's mind had been introduced into the mainstream lexicon.

As eclectic and chaotic as Tim's wall appeared to be, there was one common context, a theme, that for him was strikingly apparent and deeply annoying. Not one of those places, not one of those occurrences, not one of those people depicted were even remotely in proximity to Tim and his life. It was his fate to be planted in the middle of the vast agricultural plains of the upper Midwest, underscore plain. His life to that point was centered in a middle-class neighborhood, in the mid-sized, gritty, industrial city of Waterloo, Iowa. The scope of his life had an outer perimeter that reached to Gull Lake Minnesota in the north,

5

Chicago to the east, and a singular Scout trip to New Mexico in the Southwest. Tim had never met anyone pictured on his wall. He never met anyone like those people. He never had any of those experiences. He didn't know anyone who had. He existed in a separate universe from the one portrayed opposite his bed.

Tim wondered if his life would ever provide opportunities to experience the broader world. Would he ever be able to embark on great adventures, take risks, confront danger, and test his abilities? There was no hint that these opportunities were right around the corner, almost within his grasp. If he knew what was looming, he'd be watching that wall from underneath his bed.

There were two additional sensory components that enhanced Tim's sober contemplations. He installed a blue light bulb in his bedroom's overhead fixture that cast an other-worldly tint over the room. He later upgraded it with a swirling multi-colored shade, that when spun, created a psychedelic strobe effect. But the feature that most impacted his bedroom experience was the sound system, which rivaled any Cinerama movie theater.

He'd been frugal with his meager income. He was too young to get a job that paid legal wages, but his dad, Mac, paid him to clean his insurance agency office on the weekends. He also had a few steady lawn mowing clients. Most fifteen-year-old boys would have saved for a car to buy as soon as they hit that long anticipated magical maturational milestone of sixteen, which was only a few months away. Although he would have loved the emancipation that came from having his own ride, he had a higher priority. The development of high fidelity (hi-fi) vinyl record playing systems was rapidly accelerating. Lots of brands were entering the market. Kenwood, JBL, Sansui, Hitachi, Pioneer, Marantz and Akai all had panache and they projected sound quality heretofore unimagined. He landed on a more mundane brand, Motorola. Its specifications were similar to the more prestigious makes, but it was more within his meager budget. It cost $400 at Sears, which was a fortune for him, even more than what he paid for an old Chevy a few years later. The external speakers were decent, but his primary means of listening was through over-the-ear headphones, while lying in bed, mediating on his wall. It created a total immersion experience.

Every generation has their soundtrack, but hey man, this was the 1960s! There was a burst of musical creativity that had never been heard before. You can't describe the adolescent experience in the 60s without the context of music. Music influenced teens' world view and how their brains were being wired.

Tim enjoyed some of the top-of-the-charts pop-rock records his older sister, Beth, had piled up in her room before she left for college at Marquette. These were 45rpm discs, with the wide spindle holes. Most of them were by acts he would see on Dick Clark's American Bandstand, like Bobby Daren, The Beach Boys, Petula Clark, The Kingsmen, and Trini Lopez. They were fun, musical candy bars. Tim had more respect for the Motown soul sound, particularly Little Stevie Wonder, the Supremes and Marvin Gaye. Their records had unmatched production quality and their performances were always impeccably executed.

Everything changed in 1964. Along with the rest of North America, Tim met The Beatles on a Sunday night, watching the Ed Sullivan Show on CBS (one of only three television networks). Images of The Beatles' introduction to America are filled with young girls screaming hysterically and crying uncontrollably. Tim found this phenomenon fascinating. It was a window into what was a total mystery to him, the minds, and emotions of girls. He was fascinated by how The Beatles could evoke such powerful reactions. It was more than the music, it was those four guys up there playing, and there was clearly a sexual component. It indicated that perhaps girls were experiencing emerging sexual desires like boys. That was an exciting prospect.

The Beatles had a significant impact on most boys as well. They admired The Beatles' charm and good-natured sassiness. The uproar over their hairstyle can't be overstated. For many years, the crew-cut had been the standard for clean-cut American boys, with the pompadour being preferred by rockers, or those referred to as "Greasers." The Beatles' mop tops seem tame in retrospect, but at the time, it was a radical look to most Americans. The Beatles' hair prompted strong reactions from adults, from bewilderment to revulsion. You would've thought these fab four fellas from Liverpool were the greatest threat to western civilization since Chairman Mao. Tim loved them for it. Almost every song on their first US album, "Meet the Beatles," were hits and completely dominated the radio airwaves. The album debuted at #1 on the Billboard chart and sold over 4 million copies the first year. The early

Beatles records were right in line with the formats of most American hits, i.e., catchy melodies, with light lyrics about familiar teen themes. Yet beyond being exceptionally good songs, there was a difference. They had taken what was essentially American music and reflected it back on America in a new way, with a new vibe, and a new accent. There was a sense that they were taking everyone on a ride to someplace new. The journey didn't last all that long, only another five years, but The Beatles took their fans far beyond where they could have imagined.

From 1964 to 1969, The Beatles evolved in ways that both mirrored the changes that were occurring across almost every aspect of society and served as a beacon towards an ever more creative future. You could hear their evolution with each successive album. The pace accelerated with *Rubber Soul* and *Revolver*. The Rolling Stones gave the British invasion a harder edge, with their rock version of raw roots blues. The Stones appealed to young peoples' more raucous nature, and some thought they might overtake The Beatles as musical spokesmen for a generation. Then in 1967, the music world erupted when *Sgt. Pepper's Lonely Hearts Club Band,* was released. The Beatles took contemporary music to a higher plain. It was the compositional equivalent of going from analogue to digital. Nothing close to it had been done before. Producer George Martin and The Beatles used the recording studio as a musical instrument. *Sgt. Pepper's* provided the perfect soundtrack for Tim's wall.

Lucy in the Sky and Tim were looking at the swirling blue tinted world on his wall through kaleidoscope eyes, when the bedroom door burst open. "What the heck are you doing in here Timmy?"

Tim sprang upright in bed and ripped off his headphones, "Whoa mom, what's going on? You startled the heck out of me,"

Audrey, hands on her hips, was exasperated. "I've been yelling and yelling for you Timmy. You're going to be late for the last mass at 11:00. I should have woken you up earlier and made you go to the 8:00 mass, with the rest of the family."

They were about to engage in a ritual they'd been having for months around his attendance at Sunday mass. "Jeez mom, to be honest, I'm just not feeling up to it this week. I don't think I can be fully present at mass today. God deserves more than what I can give him this morning." His response marked a new line of resistance. His mom had become skeptical of his earlier protestations about headaches and stomachaches. He needed a more sophisticated argument, but his new tactic bombed.

She stared at him for a few moments with her mouth half open, then she said, "Are you trying to be a smart aleck? You don't go to mass only when you feel like it. You particularly need to go when you *don't* feel like it. You go so you can feel the presence of God. Besides, the Church says you have to go on Sundays, so you're going. It's a sin if you don't."

He modified his approach, "But mom, I'm feeling the presence of God right here. Listening to music is a very spiritual experience for me, more than what I feel in church."

"That's blasphemous Timmy! It's like praying to false idols. What are you listening to?"

"The Beatles, *Sgt. Pepper's.* It's incredible."

"You're saying The Beatles make you feel closer to God than going to church! My goodness Timmy, I heard them talking about that *Sgt. Pepper's* album on The Today Show. Gene Shalit liked it, but the snippets he played sounded creepy to me. He called parts of it psychedelic, which means drug music. It's not healthy! I used to like some Beatles songs, but I think they've gone off the deep end. You're not going off the deep end with them Timmy. Get your rear end in gear and get to mass." His mom paused and stared him down for several seconds, her lips pursed firmly together, her cheeks becoming slightly flushed. She could see he was wilting. Once she was convinced he would succumb to her righteous furor, she briskly walked out.

Tim picked up the turntable tone arm and laid the stylus down precisely at the beginning of the last track, "*I read the news today oh boy…*" He picked it up again and laid it down on, "*Woke-up, fell out of bed, dragged a comb across my head...*" He picked it up again and laid it on the warbly, "*I'd love to turrrrrn… youuuuu… ooooon…,*" followed by a growing cacophony of white noise and the final pound on one piano chord that slowly waned as he took off the headphones, headed for the door, and onward to pay his respects to the Lord.

Chapter 2
Who's A Good Boy?

When he was younger, Timmy McIntyre embraced his Catholic identity, and he couldn't imagine not being Catholic. He was bewildered by why anyone would choose to be a Protestant. Wasn't it obvious that the Catholic Church was founded by Jesus and that he told St. Peter he was the rock on which the one true church would be built? This mishmash of Protestant churches were all started by guys, just guys. How could they think they could compete with Jesus, Peter, and the popes? Apparently, these guys were all pissed-off about something, but he was never taught exactly what it was that irritated them so much. It didn't matter anyway. They were just wrong and probably damned to hell for it.

Nothing could compete with the Catholic Church for sheer gravitas and flare. It was loaded with elaborate rituals that were performed in wizard-like garments. Timmy was particularly impressed by the incense. During high mass, if the procession came right next to him, with the priest swinging his smoldering censer filled with incense, he would be enveloped in thick, pungent smoke and he would actually get a little buzz on.

Catholics had an elaborate poetic liturgy wrapped in Latin. Protestant churches seemed so bland by comparison. Tim couldn't figure out the difference between a Lutheran, a Methodist, a Presbyterian or Baptist. He had neighbors who were Baptists. His parents said Baptists thought singing and dancing were immoral. *Music is immoral? What kind of an existence is that?* Later, he heard Presbyterians believed everyone was predetermined to either go to heaven or to hell. There was nothing people could do about it. That seemed screwy. Why would anyone bother feeling guilty? Guilt was a core dynamic of Catholicism. It's what makes the world go around. Without guilt, there

10

would be no motivation for confession, no means for redemption. The stakes for repeat offenders would be too high. There was enormous solace knowing you could confess and then repeat offend. Recidivism was hardwired into the theology.

Catholic theology is steeped in mysteries. Catholics don't run from mysteries; they revel in them. The more bizarre, counter-intuitive, and just hard to wrap your mind around Catholic tenets are, the better. The earliest one Timmy was introduced to was the concept of the Holy Trinity. The idea of three distinct entities existing as one unified being seemed designed to teach children about the true meaning of faith. You didn't need to understand God, you just needed faith to believe in God. The need to understand, to question, could actually undermine faith and might be the result of temptation, the sin of pride. The need to understand could be the devil whispering in your ear. Many years later, Tim would learn about quantum mechanics and how sub-atomic particles could exist in more than one place at the same time. Ironically, his desire to understand physics made the notion of the Holy Trinity seem a bit more plausible.

Tim hadn't yet come to grips with the Holy Trinity concept when he was introduced to the miracle of transubstantiation, turning bread and wine into the actual body and blood of Christ! He had to pause and ponder that one every time it came up. It's not that he didn't believe it. It was more, *"Do we really have to go there? Is this really necessary? Now you're saying we have to eat it?"* He was less troubled by the proposition of the virgin birth of Jesus, but as he got older, he found it increasingly annoying. It just reinforced the whole Catholic attitude about sex and the virtue of avoiding it   If Catholics had a slogan for sex, it would be, *"Just don't do it,"*

The first time Timmy had a serious question about a Catholic teaching was in the third grade. It wasn't so much a question about an article of faith, as much as a concern about fairness, which is not surprising, given a sense of fairness is the first ethical instinct most kids develop. "It's not fair," is an almost visceral, instinctive emotion.

Tim attended the nearby parochial school, St. Ignatius. Almost all of the teachers at St. Ignatius were Franciscan Sisters. They wore the classic, "habits," with their faces framed in white cardboard, covered by a long black veil draped over their white cardboard crown. They had wide white cardboard collars and black tunics that dropped down to the

11

top of their black shoes. The Sisters' habits had a powerful effect on their students. They conveyed an aura of authority and sanctity that was intimidating. The Sisters didn't walk, they swept about and hovered above almost everything that happened within the walls of their domain. Whether they were standing in front of the class or patrolling up and down the aisles between the desks, Tim always felt their presence on his shoulder.

Timmy's third-grade teacher was Sister Barbara. He didn't know for sure, but he thought she was about one hundred and fifty years old. Her passion for teaching must have kept her going. She was a stern task master, totally committed to stuffing as much knowledge into her students as their malleable brain matter could absorb. None of her students left the third grade without knowing all of the United States presidents, all of the states and capitals, all the times tables and, most importantly, without everyone in her class buying at least one pagan baby. You heard that right, they were all expected to buy a pagan baby. We'll get back to that in a moment.

Timmy's third-grade sacred world can best be described by a graph with concentric circles. Of course, God would be in the center. He (always He) would be the color of the sun, glowing bright and warm. The first band around God would be the angels, twinkling like diamonds. Angels are the only things pure enough to be right next to God. The next circle would be the saints, virgin white. They might not have all been virgins, but they all would have preferred to be. Next would come Catholics, dark purple, representing grief and guilt. The really cool part about being Catholic was that it was like being born on third base. You could mess-up and sin your entire life, but if you confessed at just the right time and never sinned again before you died, you'd sprint home to heaven. It was just as good as a home run in God's grand game, but timing was everything. Protestants would be the next circle away from God. Their circle would be sort of a blah grey, like the stone walls of the Presbyterian church down the street. Protestants believed in the bible, but their interpretations were all over the map. Protestants could go to heaven, if they were especially good, but it was a big handicap to overcome.

Jews would be the next circle, probably black, but not black in a bad way, just because some of them wore black coats and hats. Timmy's family did not harbor anti-Semitic sentiments; however, they did tend to stereotype Jews. They respected that the Old Testament was Jewish, and that Jesus was a Jew. They didn't blame the Jews for killing Jesus, but they did think they made a big, big mistake by not recognizing him as their Lord and Savior. The McIntyres didn't really know any Jews. They knew people who were Jewish, but they didn't know, know them. Timmy's parents' primary stereotypes about Jews were that they were good businesspeople and that they tended to say whatever was on their minds. Timmy's primary stereotype about Jews was that they were really funny. That's because the only Jews he knew were on television and they all seemed to be comedians. Jerry Lewis, Milton Berle, Sid Caesar, Alan King and Woody Allen were Jews. The circle representing Jews would be black, but with yellow smiley faces.

The Muslim circle would be next. Timmy didn't know anything about Muslims, but they were sort of kissing-cousins to Jews. His only image of Muslims came from stories about Alibaba and Aladdin. They wore turbans and carried huge, curved swords. The circle for Muslims would be red and filled with flying carpets. The circles beyond the Muslims would really be getting out there. Timmy had barely heard any references to Hindus and Buddhists by the third grade, but based on what little he knew, their circles would be filled with elephants and dragons. Finally, in the outermost circle, there would be the pagans, a colorless empty space. Pagans were lost souls, but more importantly, some pagans could still be saved.

"Bow your heads children," Sister Barbara would start each day guiding her students in prayer. "We thank the Lord for all of our blessings, for our homes, our families, for all the love and good food they provide. Most of all, we thank God for our home in the Holy Catholic Church. We pray that we can be worthy of God's love and live by the teachings of His Church. We pray for all the people of this world, but most of all, we pray for the poor pagan babies, so that one day they can find God's love and be saved."

The Franciscan order of Sisters' primary mission was to teach. Some were attached to missions in Central America, Africa and Asia. These places were just busting with pagans. Some of the missions had orphanages filled with babies that were born pagans. So, technically, most of them were not born pagans at all. Most were probably born to parents who were Christians, Muslims, Hindus or Buddhists. The larger point being that they were all born into very unfortunate circumstances, in places that were mostly non-Catholic, and they needed to be saved. In order for the missions to save these pagan babies, they needed money. The Sisters came up with a brilliant fundraising strategy. Students in their US parochial schools would have the opportunity to save a pagan baby by buying their own. In later years, they would use more politically correct terms like, "Sponsoring," and it became a technique used by many other international relief organizations. But the notion of buying pagan babies resonated with Catholic school kids, and it was such a bargain. For a mere $3 per-month, students would be assigned their own pagan baby. They received a thank you letter, with a short baby biography. Best of all, they would get a certificate, suitable for framing, with a head shot photo of the baby and the baby's name of the students' choosing. That's right, they could choose the name of their own pagan baby! Below the photo the certificate would read, "Blessed be (baby's name) who will walk in the path of Our Lord, thanks to the love and support of (buyer's name) who will be graced by God because of your generous heart." The certificate would be signed by, "His Excellency (bishop's name), The Archdiocese of Dubuque. Some kids thought the certificate amounted to a bill of sale.

Naming rights is one of the most awesome adult powers. Some kids took the responsibility seriously and they would struggle to come up with the best possible name. Others, not so much. It was a hot topic in the cafeteria. Timmy and his friends were elbow-to-elbow around the lunch table, savoring their meatless Friday entrées of fish sticks, French fries, and a side of mac and cheese. Jimmy was a pudgy kid who usually started and ended their conversations. He reached over to snatch one of Timmy's fries as he tried to distract him with a question, "Hey Timmy, what are you going to name your baby?"

"Hey!" Timmy smacked his fork on the back of Jimmy's hand. "I'm naming him Damian, after the priest Sister Barbara read to us about. The guy who worked with the lepers in Hawaii. I bet he'll be the only baby named Damien. Everyone will think he's pretty special and holy. They'll hear the name Damien and they'll start looking for a halo over his head.

"Damien, that's the dopiest sounding name ever," Jimmy snorted. "It's dorky, not holy. If anything, it sounds like a devil's name."

Jimmy's assessment was prescient. Years later, Damien was the name of the devilish boy in the horror film, *The Omen*.

Timmy's witty third grader retort. "The heck with you Jimmy. He'll get even more respect then, and when he finds out you called him a dork, he'll stick his pitchfork up your butt. So what smart-ass name are you going to give your baby, Jimmy?"

"I'm giving him a name he can be proud of, Jimmy Junior. He'll be named after someone he can look up to - me. Also, if he's Jimmy Junior, that makes me Jimmy Senior. That sounds like the respectful name I deserve. Matter of fact, I think you guys should start calling me Jimmy Senior, or maybe Gentleman Jim or Mr. Jim, or better yet, Sir Jim."

"Right," Johnny Joe said sarcastically. "But how 'bout we just call you Jimmy the Jester."

"You should name your baby Bugger," Stevie cracked, "cause you have the runniest nose in school." Stevie was a good-natured kid, and like the rest of the boys he reveled in dishing out insults. Stevie reflected, "I thought about naming my baby Elvis, but I don't think Sister would like it. I heard her say the way Elvis moves is sinful. So instead, I think I'll name him Prince Albert. You have to respect a kid named Prince Albert. He'd be treated like royalty."

"Where'd you come up with Prince Albert?" Timmy asked.

"It's the kind of cigars my dad smokes. His picture is on the box and on the bands around each cigar. He's a really classy guy, with a full beard."

"You should send him a phony beard along with his name," Johnny Joe laughed. "He'd look dignified. Even the nuns would respect a baby with a beard."

Johnny Joe was a sharp kid and quietly cocky. He was brilliant at putting together intricate model cars, ships and statues of comic book characters, like the Creature from the Black Lagoon. His skills far surpassed most third graders. He was a better reader than everyone else too. He would read more advanced comic books out loud to the other kids, explaining words they weren't yet familiar with. "I'm naming my baby Einstein," Johnny Joe said with conviction.

"What kind of name is Einstein?" Jimmy asked.

"Einstein's the smartest guy that ever lived. He's the guy who thought up the bomb."

They all knew what "The bomb," was. It was the atomic bomb. It's what they practiced defending themselves against by going through nuclear war drills at school. An announcement would come over the school intercom telling them to quickly get away from the windows, duck under their desks and put their hands over their heads. These techniques would be more effective protecting them from plaster falling from the ceiling than a nuclear blast. There's been a lot written about how the threat of nuclear war during the fifties impacted people mentally and emotionally. But it didn't rattle most third graders that much. It just wasn't something they could realistically comprehend; even though they would regularly see images of atomic bombs exploding on TV. Boys love explosions and they're impressed by anything that makes things blow up. Atomic bombs make the biggest, coolest explosions. The guy who thought up "The Bomb," commanded their respect.

"Baby Einstein," Jimmy nodded approvingly, "Now that's a neat name."

After lunch they were back in the classroom, filling out their pagan baby order forms. Sister Barbara was patrolling the aisles. She looked down at Susan McElroy's form. "Mary, that's a beautiful name, Susan. Your baby will be grateful to be named after the Blessed Virgin."

She looked left, "What name have you selected, Johnny Joe?"

"Einstein," he said proudly.

Sister Barbara cocked her head and shoulders back. "Johnny Joe, you can't name your baby Einstein. That's a Semitic name, not a Christian name. Also, Einstein is a surname, not a given name. Scratch that out and think of something else. How about Edward? Yes, put down Edward."

She slowly paced to the back of the aisle and stopped at Mike Russell's desk. Mike was a fun-loving kid, spry, mischievous, but good-hearted. He suddenly sat up straight, with his eyes darting up at Sister, then side-to-side, then down. His hands were folded over his form.

"What do we have here Michael? Give me your form." She held out her hand and Mike slowly passed it up to her. "Bozo!" Sister swiftly brought her closed fist down on the top of Mike's head. You could hear her knuckles on his skull from across the room. The class tried to stifle their giggles. Mike winced and you could see a slight tear in his eye, but he didn't make a sound.

"Michael, how dare you try giving a baby a name like Bozo! What are you thinking? I have a notion to send you back to the corner for the rest of the day."

"But Sister, I like Bozo. He's my favorite clown. He's a lot of fun. I watch him on TV every afternoon after school."

Sister knocked him on the head again, although this time a little lighter. "Don't give me that Michael." She quickly walked to her desk, grabbed a form and a pen. She filled out the form and went back to Mike's desk. "Your baby's name will be Ignatius."

Mike reflexively looked up at her with a bewildered expression. *She wants to exchange Bozo for Ignatius?* Mike blurted out, "You want his name to be Iggy?" Iggy was their nickname for the school and a term they wouldn't dream of using anywhere near the sisters.

This time Sister just flicked her finger against the back of Mike's ear. "No, not Iggy, Ignatius, it's a respectable name that will garner respect," she said solemnly.

The curious thing about Mike is that he knew naming his baby Bozo would get him into trouble. For crying out loud, his own name was on the form. The thought of getting into trouble at some point in the future, say 20 minutes later, after he turned in his form, didn't bother him, or maybe he just didn't think that far ahead. What threw him off was getting caught right in that moment and suffering a knuckle knock as a consequence. It's the kind of thing Mike would do regularly, and it made everyone wonder what was up with Mike?

Sister walked around the back of Mike's desk and up the next aisle, examining everyone's form and nodding her approval. She paused at Timmy's desk. "Damien, that's a lovely name Timmy. Is he named after Father Damien?"

"Yes Sister, but I have a question." Timmy wasn't aware of it at the time, but he was about to question a core tenant of the Holy Catholic Church for the first time in his life. He was about to publicly reveal a crack in his faith. The question had been slowly percolating and troubling him for days. Here's the rub. Here's what he struggled with about this whole baby buying business. How was it that he, Timmy McIntyre, would have the good fortune to be born a Catholic and be saved, at least after he was baptized, while little baby Damien was born a pagan and needed Timmy's help to be saved? What if Timmy, or someone else, didn't purchase Damien? Would the little tyke be damned to hell? On a matter of such profound and eternal consequence, it didn't seem fair. It just didn't seem right. The randomness of it all hinging on where and how someone happened to be born, the luck of the draw aspect of it unnerved Timmy.

"Sister Barbara, what would happen if the babies were not at the mission and they were not baptized? Would they never be able to go to heaven? Would they have to go to hell?"

"Oh no Timmy, God would never send an innocent to hell. Unbaptized babies would go to limbo. It would be very unfortunate, but it's nothing like hell."

"What's limbo Sister?"

"Limbo is neither heaven nor hell. It's just a place to be."

"But how is that fair Sister? Damien can't help where he was born. He can't help it if someone buys him or not. What if he couldn't stay at the mission and be baptized. It scares me to think he would have to go to someplace like limbo."

"Timmy, you don't have to be troubled by this. It's all part of God's plan. This is how God works and you have to have faith that God always knows what's right."

There it was again – faith. The discussion ended at that. It was not a very satisfying answer for Timmy, but he accepted it, along with the nagging unease.

Chapter 3
Performance Anxiety

In the fall of 1966, at the beginning of Tim's sophomore year at Regis Catholic High School, he had no reason to think he was not fundamentally a good person. By the end of the school year, how he thought of himself and what it meant to be a good person would begin to evolve.

Tim had been an unremarkable student, i.e., slightly above average grades, no significant disciplinary problems, cordial relationships with teachers and those administrators who knew his name. His extracurricular activities were virtuous, but equally prosaic. He continued to be an altar boy until midway through his freshman year. He progressed from Cub Scouts to Boy Scouts to Explorer Scouts, achieving the rank of Life Scout. His enthusiasm for scouting waned during his freshman year, but he stuck it out long enough to fulfill his ambition to attend the Philmont Scout Ranch in New Mexico. The chance for a kid from Iowa to trek across the Sangre de Cristo Mountains was worth earning a few more merit badges, but he quit Scouts immediately after returning home. Achieving Eagle Scout status would be out of step with his drive for mediocrity. At his core, he was a middle-class kid, from a mid-sized town, in the middle of the country, born in the middle of the 20th century. In his mind, he was the personification of ordinary.

Tim was a middle of the pack track runner as a freshman, and he didn't have the pain endurance necessary to get much better. He ran out of gas and bagged it after one season. Wrestling was a huge sport in Iowa. Wrestling meets would fill high school gymnasiums as much as basketball games. Elite wrestlers were renowned throughout the state. Tim appreciated that wrestling was the only high school sport that calibrated for different sized athletes. If height was measured like a golf course, Tim would be a par 3. He was a shepherd boy in the second grade Nativity pageant. He was fortunate they didn't put him in the manger. He was cast as a leprechaun in the fourth grade St. Patrick Day program. Playing Santa's elf was also in his repertoire. He was in the front row of every class photo. For years people would encourage him by saying he would hit a growth spurt, but he was waiting for Godot. Wrestling rules were an equalizer and offered him a potential path to glory. He decided to give it a shot at the beginning of his sophomore year.

Tim looked forward to being paired with wrestlers of comparable weight, but he quickly learned that the wrestlers his size were a different breed. Most were animals on the mat. Like him, they were enthusiastic about competing with guys their own size, but they attacked the opportunity with more vengeance. They trained like fanatics. Iowa high school wrestlers in those days were inspired by the legendary wrestler, Dan Gable, who was from Waterloo. Gable was only a couple of years older, but he was already gaining a national reputation as a fearsome and unbeatable opponent. He trained and competed like a madman. Tim's teammates wanted to match Gable's intensity. The lighter weight wrestlers on the team were the angriest. In addition to their torturous training, they starved themselves to qualify for lighter weight classes, while Tim suffered from trying to add bulk by drinking chocolate shakes. His teammates approached each match seeking to inflict revenge for their many sacrifices. They were wound tight as springs on a garage door. They relished the chance to spar with Tim, who generously provided them with opportunities to successfully execute every scoring maneuver, take-downs, breakdowns, rides, reverses, and pinning, all within each two or three-minute period. In other words, Tim sucked.

Tim could have dedicated himself to getting better, but here again, there was the matter of pain. Pain that far exceeded anything he had experienced in track. Every wrestler must develop a tolerance for prolonged pain. They routinely became twisted and contorted into grotesque positions, while attempting to exert full-out effort. Winning required strength and agility, but more than anything else, you needed to block out the pain, maintain your wits and execute the moves that were specifically designed for each predicament. It was a mental state

Tim never mastered. However, after the first few weeks of excruciating training, he did acquire a very effective coping strategy – losing quickly.

Tim might have been able to endure the pain and the losing long enough to complete the season. He actually kind of liked wrestling. He got along well with his teammates and coaches. He valued their esprit de corps. It felt good getting into shape, relative to his wimpy baseline. It was also a source of comfort knowing that if he ever got into a scrape with some sadistic teenage psychopath, of which there were many around town, there would be a whole team of ass-kickers that would have his back. However, there was one element to wrestling he found intolerable. It was the thick, raw, toxic, god-awful, overpowering stench of the training room. The coaches kept the room at the temperature and humidity of a sauna, but it wasn't anything like hot yoga. This was fifteen to twenty high school boys exerting themselves to the breaking point over one or two hours. They were dripping with sweat after the first five minutes, stinging their eyes, streaking the squeaky rubber mats, producing a sweltering haze in the oxygen-deprived air, and stinking to high heaven. The wretched stench rivaled the putrid, plague-infested corpses that the Khan's Mongol Golden Horde catapulted over the walls of Caffa to spread the Black Death. It was a ridiculous, HAZMAT level of stink. A stink that slithered under the closed wrestling room doors, sending a foreboding warning to all those who approached. It was a stink so profound that when the doors opened only momentarily, it wafted into the main gym and down a nearby hallway to the choir room, sending sopranos and baritones into disgusted gagging fits. The garnish on this depraved environment was the frothy fragrance of their gym clothes. Few high school boys ever think to wash their gym clothes. This was particularly true for wrestlers. Afterall, why bother? Just walking into a wrestling room was like diving into a pool of pungent odors that permeated your pores and every type of fabric. For some guys, excelling in this poisonous climate was a source of pride. Tim found it to be an affront to his humanity.

Tim's wrestling career reached its zenith a few weeks before the end of the season. He had not yet won a match. He only qualified for two meets, just because the superior teammate in his weight class, Ronnie, had been sick once, then later injured. Prior to their meet with the defending state champions, the West High Warriors, Ronnie failed to make his weight class. He couldn't work out while recovering from his injury and he lapsed into a feeding frenzy of pizza, Coke and cinnamon rolls. He didn't have enough time to resume food deprivation and shed all of his excess pounds. The coach sounded despondent when a few hours before the meet he told Tim he would be representing the team in the 106-pound weight class.

The West High gymnasium was packed to the rafters with bloodthirsty West High Warrior fans and a respectable number of devoted, but fatalistic, Regis Royal faithful. Being in the lightest weight class, Tim's match was the first of the evening. He was sitting at the end of a row of metal folding chairs when Coach waved him over. The Coach remained sitting as Tim approached. Tim tried to muster some enthusiasm to offset his dread, "What's the plan Coach?"

Coach continued to look straight ahead and said flatly, "Try not to get hurt, Tim."

Tim's stomach was churning, and his head was spinning as he stood on the edge of the mat, waiting for the referee's signal to come forward and engage his opponent. Tim fidgeted with terror, literally girding his loins by pulling on his ill-fitting singlet. He prepared to do battle with Bob Wilson, a senior, two-time state champion. Bob looked at Tim from the opposite side of the mat with a cold, steely stare, pumping his fists in and out, jumping up and down, stretching his neck side-to-side. His physique was chiseled. His biceps and calves bulged. He looked like a leopard hungrily waiting to feast on a gazelle.

The ref waved them to the middle of the mat. The first period begins with the combatants standing. Bob and Tim bent forward, extended their arms, grabbed each other around the back of the neck with their right hand and grabbed each other's forearm with their left hand. Although their weights were similar, Bob was notably taller and longer. In almost all instances this would give Bob an advantage, more distance to guard against assaults and more leverage to execute maneuvers. Except at the very beginning, when both competitors usually attempt to dive underneath their opponent's embrace and grab their legs for a takedown. It's more difficult to get under a shorter guy, so the taller guy has to find another way to maneuver around the back. Tim knew that if he had any chance of scoring and avoid being totally dominated, he would have to make his best, most decisive move at the start of the first period.

When the ref blew his whistle, Tim immediately ducked under Bob's arms and launched himself towards Bob's legs. Bob countered by jumping back and wrapping his arms around Tim's torso. Tim was barely able to reach far enough to grab one of Bob's ankles with both of his hands. Prussian Field Marshal Helmuth von Moltke the Elder famously said, "No battle plan survives contact with the enemy." Tim's only strategy for victory disintegrated in less than four seconds. After securing his arms around Tim's waist, Bob began to pull himself upright. Tim lost his grip on Bob's ankle with one hand, but he was able to lurch upward just enough to grab Bob's knee. Tim's head and upper body were now twisted sideways, affording him a direct view of his teammates, their mouths open and heads in their hands. With a powerful pull, Bob was able to stand erect. The force snapped Tim's grip on both Bob's ankle and knee. He tried to break Bob's hold on him by swiveling 45 degrees, so he was now hanging upside down, looking back between Bob's legs. Bob tried to take control of Tim's upper body by jerking Tim upward, adjusting his arms one at a time from around Tim's hips to Tim's back, squeezing him and restricting his breathing. Tim responded by grabbing both of Bob's upper thighs. Tim's efforts had the unintended consequence of securing his face firmly in Bob's crotch, while Bob's chin rested on top of Tim's groin. It was a cruel moment for Bob and Tim to establish an equilibrium, neither one of them able to gain further advantage. They were thus adhered to each other as they jerked about for what seemed an eternity.

High school wrestling fans are used to seeing boys in absurd positions while intertwined with each other. Some of these body arrangements could resemble images from the Kama Sutra, and in another context, could be interpreted as obscene. The crowd did not react to the boys' humiliating predicament with laughter or derision, for which Tim was grateful. Nonetheless, Tim was mortified. His worst fears had been realized. A superior athlete had him in the most emasculating, ungodly grasp possible, in the center stage of a large arena, with a massive audience comprised of most everyone in the world who knew him and his family.

Ironically, it was Bob's superior strength, skill and experience that released Tim from his anguish and led to Bob's own demise. Bob's determination had been forged at the highest level of championship competition. He mentally constructed a path to victory. His plan was to, in one continuous motion, break Tim loose, throw him on his shoulder, drop to his knees, lower his shoulder, and throw Tim down with his shoulder blades pinned to the mat, thereby completing his coup de gras in short order. In a massive burst of energy, accompanied by a savage yell, Bob pulled up and back, yanking Tim's arms from Bob's legs and extracting Tim's head from Bob's groin. Tim's upper body spun out and up. The West Warrior faithful roared, envisioning imminent victory. What Bob didn't anticipate was Tim being lighter and weaker than his other opponents. Bob's excessive effort generated enough centrifugal force that at the apex of Tim's flight over his shoulder, Bob's hold loosened just enough for Tim to twist and slip through his arms. He slid down Bob's back as Bob's knees were descending. Tim landed directly on the back of Bob's right calf. At the moment of impact Tim's ear was planted against Bob's heel and he heard a sickly pop. It was the sound of Bob's Achilles tendon rupturing. What Tim couldn't hear was the simultaneous tear of Bob's anterior cruciate ligament. Bob fell forward. As Tim rolled off Bob's leg, Bob rolled on his back and grabbed his knee. He grimaced in agony. Tim was shocked to see Bob in such distress. Tim tried to stand, but when Bob kicked his other leg out it knocked Tim's foot from underneath him and he fell forward. Tim's full weight landed on Bob's chest. The ref dropped to one knee next to them and slapped the mat. Then he grabbed Tim's wrist and stood up with Tim's arm in the air, displaying the victor to the astonished fans.

The ref looked down at Bob and realized he was seriously hurt. The West coach and trainer rushed to Bob's side. The crowd was silently stunned. Tim stepped back, flushed with guilt. The crowd stood and applauded as Bob was carried off the mat. The Regis team restrained their congratulations of Tim out of respect for Bob's injuries, but he could see they were delighted as they poked and shoved him around. It turned out Tim's victory was one of only two all evening.

At practice the following Monday Tim was full of vim and vigor. His self-esteem and confidence soared. Perhaps it was because of the team's lopsided defeat against West that the coaches had cranked up the heat in the wrestling room. It was steamier than ever, and within a few minutes, everyone was wringing wet with sweat. After a series of exhausting drills, Tim and Ronnie were sent to work out against each other in the far corner of the training room.

"Nice win against Wilson, Tim." Those were the first words Ronnie had spoken to him since the match.

"Thanks Ronnie, I gave it 110%. I'm glad I was able score some points for the team. Bob was tough, but I think some of my moves surprised him." Now, Tim knew better to think his wrestling skills had anything to do with the victory. It's a testament to people's ability to delude themselves and give themselves undeserved credit that within moments after Bob was limply carried away, Tim began thinking he had been transformed into a legitimate, competitive athlete.

"Seriously Tim? You really think you had anything to do with beating Wilson? You fell on his leg for Christ's sake. It was an accident, a one in a million fluke. No way you could ever beat him again. No way you could ever beat me. You've had your last match of the season, Tim."

Tim wasn't ready to surrender his newfound identity as a stud and relinquish his hard-won pride. "Well, yeah Ronnie, there was some luck involved, but I wouldn't go so far to say I had nothing to do with it. We'll just have to see if I have another match."

Ronnie took a great deal of pride in being a varsity wrestler. He had been pent up for weeks rehabbing a pulled rib muscle. He felt fully recovered and he was not about to let a sophomore bench warmer deprive him of competing in the last two meets. He lowered his head and blasted into Tim. The top of Ronnie's head landed just below Tim's ribs, knocking the wind out of him. Ronnie lifted Tim up on his shoulder, then drove him down into the mat. Ronnie did a summersault behind Tim. Tim staggered to his feet briefly, then crumbled to his knees, gasping for breath. Ronnie turned around and wrapped his arm around Tim's neck in a choke hold, pulling him backwards. Tim still hadn't regained his breath. Bob twisted Tim's neck with his arm and rolled him over. The last thing Tim remembered is Ronnie lying perpendicular across his chest with one hand holding his left arm down, and a knee on his right arm. Tim's nose and mouth were tightly embedded in the center of Ronnie's armpit. He was being suffocated in an epicenter of the wrestling rooms' fatally foul fragrance.

Tim had probably only passed out for a few seconds, but the next sensation he remembered is gagging and hacking on smelling salts, with his head on the coach's knee. The coach was barking, "Tim, Tim,

Tim, are you with me Champ? You with me? It looks like you took a pretty good blow. Try to get to your feet and go over there and sit by the wall." He helped Tim up, put his hand on Tim's back and gave him a light shove toward the wall.

Tim slid his back down the padded wall and sat with his eyes closed and chin up, trying to steady his breathing. Ronnie walked over and stood by him. "Shit Tim, sorry to put you out like that. I've been feeling really pumped up and ready to start knocking heads again. I thought you could take it. "

"No problem, Ronnie," not opening his eyes. "I must still be a little wasted from the match on Saturday. It's fine."

After practice, Tim passed up a ride and walked home. He concluded it was time for his high school athletic career to end. As Jim McKay would say on ABC's Wide World of Sports, he had experienced the thrill of victory and the agony of defeat, both within three days. Ronnie's sudden reality check had focused Tim's mind. Having his face planted in Ronnie's odorous pit of doom was an experience he didn't need repeated.

Chapter 4
Call of the Wild

Tim no longer had wrestling practice after school, so he had more time to hang out with old friends and a broadening group of new associates. He started catching rides to and from school with Johnny Joe, who by then had matured into just being called Joe. Joe was on the tall side and a good-looking guy. He was well liked, but he didn't go out of his way to socialize. He was comfortable keeping his own company. He had maintained his quiet confidence from elementary school. He was a talented, can-do fella, with a little air of mystery about him. Joe was one of the first in his class to turn sixteen and for his birthday he was given a Goat, a black 1964 Pontiac GTO, with a 7.5-liter V8 engine, five on the floor stick shift and a hair trigger clutch. It was a premier muscle car. Joe's GTO cemented his status as a cool character. Joe was generous with his assets and his thoughts. He would let Tim attempt to tame his wild black steed in the K-mart parking lot after hours. Tim would sputter and lurch across the tarmac trying to harness the enormous horsepower underneath his feet, while Joe, seemly oblivious to Tim's struggles, calmly reflected on his latest discoveries in art, music, and literature.

Other than his wicked wheels, Joe's tastes were unconventional, at least by Regis High School standards. Rather than having photos of hot cars, hot girls or sports idols like Bart Starr and Wilt Chamberlain on his bedroom walls, Joe had just one large poster of a banana over his bed, just a single big yellow banana. It was a recently released Andy Warhol print. Warhol was getting a lot of media exposure, which was fitting, given the theme of his work reflected on mass media and consumer culture. However, Warhol's popularity usually didn't penetrate down to sixteen-year boys in the Midwest. The banana was in keeping with Joe's nature, subtly bold and quietly confrontational with midwestern sensibilities.

Tim considered himself to be a pretty astute music aficionado. He had an extensive and eclectic collection of albums, including Bob Dylan, The Byrds, Simon and Garfunkel, Donovan, Stevie Wonder, Ray Charles, The Lovin Spoonful, the Rolling Stones and, of course, every Beatles album. Joe took Tim in broader and more obscure directions. He introduced Tim to jazz and blues. They would sprawl out in Joe's bedroom and get lost listening to Thelonious Monk, Charlie Parker, Miles Davis, John Mayall and Muddy Waters. Joe loved rock music too, but he preferred more cutting-edge groups, with more exploratory sounds than the usual fare found on AM radio. His favorite band was The Velvet Underground, a New York group associated with Warhol. Joe was the first guy to buy Cream's debut album. Tim was exhilarated by every musical twist and turn Joe steered him towards. Nothing turned Tim on more than Jimi Hendrix's first release, *Are You Experienced?* After listening to the first song, "Purple Haze," Tim realized he was not experienced at all. Hendrix sounded like nothing before. It was psychedelic blues rock delivered with supercharged passion. It was wild, but totally under control. Hendrix was a musical genius with total mastery of his craft. Joe and Tim bought headphones just so they could listen to *Are You Experienced?* racing right and left through their skulls.

Joe's personal library was also distinctive. The most risqué book high school students read in those days was, *Catcher in the Rye.* It was set years earlier, but the storyline captured a similar adolescent sensibility that still resonated. The books Joe was into went well beyond J.D. Salinger, into worlds and life experiences most Regis students hadn't yet imagined. Jack Kerouac's *On the Road* and *The Dharma Bums* were some of his favorites. These stories ignited a romance with the road that lingered for the rest of Joe and Tim's lives. A wanderlust that would take them to places Kerouac hadn't even imagined. More profoundly, Kerouac created a vision for living and thinking that challenged their middle American values and lifestyles.

One frigid night in February 1967, Joe, Steve, Warren, and Tim were in the K-Mart parking lot shortly after the store closed, popping donuts on the icy, snow-packed black-top. The first two rules Midwesterners learn about icy winter driving are 1. Pump the brakes to slow down or stop, and 2. Turn into a skid, meaning in the same direction that the rear of the car is swerving. When you do the opposite on a slick surface, i.e., slam on the brakes and turn away from the skid, the vehicle will spin. The faster you go and the harder you brake, the more you spin, 180 degrees, 360 degrees or multiple 360s, AKA, donuts. Joe wasn't cavalier about the well-being of his GTO. He had plenty of room to maneuver and the edges of the parking lot were buffered by 10-15-foot-high mounds of plowed snow. He had become very adept at making up to three full donuts before sliding gently into the snowbank. After making a couple of runs, the boys saw headlights turning into the opposite end of the parking lot.

Warren was in the front seat and spotted them first. "Jesus, are those cops? Turn off your lights Joe or they might bust us."

Joe said, "I'm not sure if they're cops, but let's sit here until we know for sure."

The mystery sedan stopped in the far corner of the with its lights on and engine idling. It didn't appear to be cops unless it was an unmarked car.

Steve found Joe's paperback copy of *On the Road* in the back seat. "Have you read this, Joe? What's it about?"

"It's about travel and adventure and freedom. It's about what I want to do with my life. It's about what we all should do while we can. Think about it. Where would you want to go if you could go anywhere?"

Without hesitation Tim said, "That's a no-brainer, Colorado, then California. I'd be a ski bum in Vail, then I'd go to San Francisco for the summer to hang out in Haight-Ashbury."

Steve was also decisive, "I'd head to Chicago, live in one of those apartments overlooking Wrigley Field and watch the Cubs play every afternoon."

Warren dreamily imagined, "I'd make a beeline for Huntington Beach, California. I was built for the sun, surf and sand. I'd be hanging ten and playing guitar for my bikini-clad groupies." Warren had moved to town the previous summer. He grew up on Long Island, New York. His father's promotion with the railroad brought them to town. Warren's East Coast pedigree provided a much needed outside influence to Regis High School. Warren's smile could light up a room and his relaxed good humor immediately charmed his new classmates. Within weeks of arriving, he seemed like an old friend.

Warren asked, "Where do you want to go, Joe?"

"I'd head east and then just keep going. I'd spend some time in New York, in Greenwich Village. I'd go to The Blue Note to hear Miles Davis and The Bitter End to hear Dylan. I'd hang with Warhol and Lou Reed. Then I'd go to London, hang with the Beatles and the Stones, pick-up some threads on Carnaby Street. Then I'd go to Amsterdam, smoke some weed and learn to paint. Then I'd fly to Kathmandu, smoke hashish, drop some Sunshine Acid and learn to meditate."

It should be noted that, at that point, none of them had taken any mind-altering substances, beyond sneaking an occasional beer.

Tim asked, "Where the hell is Kathmandu, and would you really take LSD? Aren't you afraid of having a bad trip and freaking out?"

"Kathmandu is in Nepal, in the Himalaya Mountains, north of India. It's a very spiritual place. I'd hang out with a sadhu, a Hindu holy man. I'd learn to transcend my body, maybe even levitate. If you get really good at meditating, you can literally float above the earth. The acid would only be supplemental, to enhance the meditation experience and open additional regions of my mind. I wouldn't freak-out because I'd be in this beautiful, nurturing environment."

So, there it was, while the rest of the guys were dreaming of Chicago, Colorado and California, Joe had detailed plans for New York, London, Amsterdam and Kathmandu. They wanted to learn to ski and surf, but Joe wanted to learn to meditate and float above the earth.

The suspicious car backed up, then quickly accelerated forward, speeding directly towards the parked wanderers. Halfway across the parking lot the mystery mobile slammed on its brakes and spun in a circle once, then twice. Its front bumper slammed into a snow pile about ten feet to their left, knocking an avalanche of snow loose and scaring the holy shit out of them.

The driver's side window rolled down and Mike stuck his head out. "What's happening brothers? How'd you like my little pirouettes?"

It was then that they recognized Mike's 1960 Ford Fairlane.

Joe yelled, "What the hell do you think you're doing Mike? You could have killed us. I would have killed you if you'd hit the Goat."

"Hey, no problem man. I was totally under control. I gave you guys a pretty good rush though, didn't I?

"Yeah Joe, no problem," Warren chuckled. "You wanted an out-of-body experience and Mike almost gave you one."

Chapter 5
Rumblings

Tim kept up with current events more than most kids, as demonstrated by the magazine mosaic he started on his bedroom wall at the beginning of January, but he was just an observer of these events. He hadn't yet developed a framework to analyze what he was displaying or to form many convictions about what he was scrutinizing for hours on end. Joe didn't hand him a blueprint, but he did pass along some building blocks for Tim to construct his own world view.

Although Joe's family was affluent, his father owned a large commercial real-estate agency, he was the only person Tim knew who had developed an explicit working-class consciousness. Michael Harrington's *The Other America* made a big impact on Joe, and he discussed it at length with Tim. The notion that America's economic and political system was intentionally built to maintain the power and wealth of a privileged few was counter to everything Tim had previously been told. America was supposed to be the land of opportunity. The American dream was there for the taking by anyone who worked hard and took personal responsibility for their own destiny. Reading Harrington, Tim re-experienced an old disquiet. *Is this fair? Are whole neighborhoods or even regions of America languishing in poverty, because everyone who lives there is lazy and irresponsible? Could it be that where people are born, where they live, will likely determine their economic destiny? Are many Americans playing against a stacked deck?*

As a third grader, the injustice of having your place of birth determine whether your soul was saved or bound for limbo had opened a crack in Tim's faith. Now, he was trying to reconcile his unease with the economic injustices Harrington described with the Catholic ethos regarding poverty. The Franciscan sisters took a vow of poverty. They often spoke about the virtue of poverty and the dangers of materialism.

Catholic missions were dedicated to serving the poor. Tim questioned why the sisters weren't more upset by the political systems that oppressed people. He wondered why the sisters weren't all socialists. Then it dawned on him. The sisters thought the poor were blessed. They also thought the rich would be blessed, if they gave to the poor, particularly through Catholic organizations. If the poor will inherit the Earth, it means they will always be around. It's all part of God's plan. Poverty was made to sound so virtuous, and Tim bought it for a while, but his patience was running thin.

The civil rights movement had been prominent in American life for years. The Civil Rights Act passed in 1964 and the Voting Rights Act passed in 1965, but in 1967 segregation was still common in most parts of the country. Joe wanted to learn more about racism and the civil rights movement, so he read *Black Like Me* and *The Autobiography of Malcolm X*. He borrowed his father's hardcover copy of William Styron's *The Confessions of Nat Turner*, which deeply disturbed him. Tim's parents were supportive of the civil rights movement. They were appalled by stories about Jim Crow discrimination in the south and by television images of the brutal suppression of protesters in Mississippi and Alabama. They rarely talked about racism in their own town though.

One Saturday afternoon Joe and Tim were sprawled out in Tim's bedroom. They were listening to the Vanilla Fudge rendition of, "You Keep Me Hanging On," the Strawberry Alarm Clock's psychedelic rock, "Incense and Peppermints," and *The Doors*, "Light my Fire." Joe was looking at the photos on Tim's wall when he said matter-of-factly, "You know, Tim, someday this town is going to blow up and all hell is going to rain down."

Tim didn't have any idea what Joe was talking about. "What, what do mean, blow up? Why would it blow up? This place is so boring, sometimes I want to blow it up myself, but why would anyone else want to?"

"I'm telling you Waterloo is a powder keg. Someday soon the black people here are going to start fighting back like they are in Mississippi and Alabama."

Tim was shocked by the notion that anything like what was happening in the south would ever occur in his hometown. "Look, I know a lot of black people here don't have it easy, but it's nothing like the South!"

"Are you kidding me, Tim? Can you really be that naïve?" This was about the most disparaging remark Joe had ever said to Tim. It reflected how strongly he felt about racial issues and how long he had been stewing over them. "Waterloo is one of the most segregated places in the country outside of the South. Why do you think it is that there aren't any black people here on the west side?"

"I dunno, I haven't thought about it much. I suppose blacks choose to live in their own community, that they're more comfortable there."

"Listen to yourself, Tim. You're saying there aren't any black people in town who want to live on the west side, where generally housing values are better and most of the development is happening? Do you know what happened when that black assistant principle at Logan Junior High moved into a house on Irving Street? They had death threat calls every day and their house was vandalized all the time. The cops did nothing about it. They only lasted there three months. I heard a guy say to my dad once that if a real estate agent showed a house on the west side to a black family he would be run out of business. Even if they showed the house, most banks won't give mortgage loans to black families who want to live over here."

"Joe, I had no idea. I never heard about any of this. Is it really that bad?"

"It's been that bad from the beginning. Most of the black families in town were recruited to come here from Mississippi in the 1920's. The meat packing plant needed strike breakers to help them crush the union. The black workers were only paid half of what the white workers made, even after the strike ended. They were required to rent houses on the northeast side. This town has kept the Black community down ever since. The racism here isn't always as blatant as in the South, but it's just as real. Tensions have been building for years. It just takes a spark to ignite an explosion."

Tim didn't doubt what Joe was saying, but it just didn't jibe with his experience in their tranquil, unexciting little burg. "I don't know, Joe, I understand what you're saying, but I don't see things ever getting to the point of exploding." I don't think there would be any violence."

"There's already violence, Tim. You just don't see it or hear about it. The cops kick the shit out of blacks here all the time. Look, you don't have to take my word for it. Just ask Charlie."

Charlie Cummings was one of only seven black kids in their sophomore class of three hundred students. Regis was the only Catholic high school in town, and it drew students from parochial elementary schools all over the area. Regis tuition was very cheap in those days. Most of the faculty were priests and nuns, who received next to no wages for teaching. Regis could afford to offer very generous sliding scale tuition and lots of scholarships. Charlie's family wasn't poor. His father had a good paying union job as a welder at the John Deere tractor plant. He was also a vocal union steward. His mother was a public elementary school teacher. Charlie hung out with them regularly, but he was on the quiet side and he rarely revealed what he was thinking. He had a quick wit and he was fun to be around, but his parents kept him on a short leash and they made sure he prioritized his schoolwork.

Tim couldn't let what Joe was telling him just sit. He went downstairs to the kitchen telephone and called Charlie. "Hey Charlie, how you doing? Do you have a minute? I have a question."

"Yeah, what's going on? What's the question?"

"Has your family ever thought about living on the west side? Would you want to live over here?"

"What's this all about Tim? Why are you asking me this? Why are you hassling me about this shit?"

"I'll tell you in a minute, but can you just tell me. Would you want to live over here?"

"You're asking me the wrong question, Tim. It doesn't matter whether we want to live on the west side or not. What matters is that we can't. The question is why can't we? I would think you would know that."

"Jesus Charlie, that's fucked-up. Something has to be done about that shit."

Tim expected a quick affirmative response, but there was a long pause instead. "Charlie? Are you still there?"

Another pause followed. Then Charlie said softly, but with a level of tension in his voice Tim hadn't expected, "There's lots of things that have to change Tim, and they will, but this place is going to explode before it happens."

Chapter 6
Class Acts: 5th Period
Religion

Regis High School required one religion course each year. These were not survey classes in world religions. They were mostly about Catholic theology and morality. Tim liked religion class. They were taught by priests who tended to be scholarly, and they used a Socratic teaching method that kept the students engaged. This was very different from elementary school catechism classes, where the nuns injected kids with antiviral doctrine aimed at warding off temptation and inoculating them against the evils of the world. High school religion classes posed moral questions and debate was encouraged.

The Sophomore Religion curriculum included the closest thing resembling sex education that Regis offered. Consequently, the Sophomore Religion classes were segregated by gender. Although the boys would have been fascinated to hear the girls' thoughts on sexual matters, it's likely the girls would have been reticent to share their thoughts around the boys. The boys might not have been reluctant to speak, but they wouldn't have been as honest with the girls present. Everything they uttered would have been calculated to have some desired effect on the girls.

Tim's class was taught by Father Hogan. He was a big, burly man, with a crew cut and a deep voice with lots of vibrato. He had a radio announcer's voice. He was smart, witty and very affable. He had a master's degree in clinical counseling from DePaul University. He spoke with relaxed authority. The attribute the boys most admired about him was that he was a good listener and he treated them with respect. They trusted him.

Sexual instruction at Regis was more theology than biology. Father Hogan wanted the boys to know the basics about male and female sexual physiology, particularly related to menstruation and insemination, but significantly more time was spent discussing Catholic sexual morality, particularly masturbation, extramarital intercourse, and pregnancy. One day immediately after the bell rang at the start of class, Father Hogan walked briskly into the room, set his black attaché case on his desk, stepped up to the front row and said, "Gentlemen, I assume by now you all have had an intimate encounter with one or both of your hands. So, how has that been going for you?"

The boys knew what was coming. Previous classes had passed down all the subject matter they would be covering. They looked around at each other and sheepishly grinned. After a pregnant pause, Jeff Swanson was the first to raise his hand, "I've developed a close bond with my right hand. We do favors for each other. I try not to spend too much time with my right hand, or my left hand gets very jealous."

The class erupted in laughter, which relieved some the initial tension. Several other hands popped up. Steve said, "I call my right hand Ramona. It's not the most attractive hand, but it treats me very well."

Tim was still embarrassed by the whole subject, but as more guys chimed in, he became more relaxed.

Mark Olson could barely spew his contribution to the discussion out through his cackling. "I'm so fond of my left hand that I'm going to give it my class ring. We plan to stay together for the rest of my life!"

Another guy said, "I can't commit to just one hand. I'm young and there are so many hands out there to get to know."

Father Hogan had been quietly smiling, but he was ready to take control of the conversation. "Alright, alright gentlemen, it's heartwarming to hear how close you've become to your hands. But ask yourselves this, is your relationship with your hands more important to you than having a meaningful, loving, relationship with a girl? Are you prepared to spend the rest of your lives alone with your hands? Most importantly, are you willing to walk through life outside the grace of God? Because these are the consequences you need to be prepared to accept. Satisfying yourselves will diminish your ability to have a satisfying, healthy relationship with a girl. It will risk your ability to have a normal, lasting relationship with a wife. Satisfying yourselves is an abuse of God's gift of sexuality. It is a sin and God's grace will be further from reach. "

The class sat silent and motionless. Father Hogan had just dumped a ton of emotional ice water on them. It was enough to quell any thought of a hard-on. By this stage in their Catholic education, they were becoming desensitized to fiery condemnations and threats of eternal damnation. However, the bleak picture Father was describing of a lonely, loveless life was darkly ominous. About 75% of their idle time awake and 90% of their time dreaming was spent thinking about girls; how to have a relationship with them and how to have sex with them. If satisfying themselves further reduced the long odds of their having a sexual encounter with a girl, it would be a powerful disincentive. Tim was not the only one concerned.

Steve broke the silence, "I get it Father. I'm not willing to blow off my relationship with girls, no pun intended. I'm going to break up with Ramona."

Mark chimed in, a little less giddy this time. "Yeah, I'm not going to wear my class ring until I find a girl to give it to. Someone who will be more satisfying than either hand.

Mike joined in, "You got us Father, we're going to control ourselves until we get so horny we'll have to find a girl with nice hands, or something much better."

Mike's comment struck a nerve with Father and put him over the edge. "Enough gentlemen, we will have no disrespectful talk about girls in this class. Sexual relations outside the sanctity of marriage is a sin. It will damage you and the girl. It puts you both at grave risk. You risk dishonor, shame, disease, pregnancy, and it will be a stain on your souls."

Mike was taken aback by Father's indignation. It was something they had rarely heard. "I'm sorry Father. I didn't mean to be disrespectful. But I just turned sixteen and marriage is not anywhere on my radar yet. I'm not sure if what you're asking of us is realistic. "

"First of all, Michael, it's not a matter of me asking you anything. It's a matter of God's law, a matter of right and wrong and mortal sin. It's because God loves you and he knows the harm that can come to both boys and girls. Having sex outside the sacrament of marriage can alter your entire life. Michael, you said marriage is not on your radar, well then, are you ready to be a father? Are you ready tomorrow to accept that responsibility? Your decisions have consequences gentlemen. Your behavior has consequences, not just for yourselves, but for others as well."

Once again, Father sent chills through them. He prompted grave visions of life's possibilities that most of them had never seriously entertained. It was a sober reality check aimed at restraining powerful adolescent impulses. It was a strategy of fear that had kept adolescent sexual behavior somewhat in check throughout much of human history. However, human history had been altered only seven years earlier. In 1960, the US Food and Drug Administration had approved use of the first birth control pill explicitly intended for contraception purposes. It was the quintessential game changer. Sexual mores had already been shifting during the 1950s, illustrated by the publication of Playboy magazine, which quickly diverted boys' attention away from the lingerie section of the Sear's catalogue. Now, for the first time, there was a safe, effective, affordable, and accessible means of disconnecting sexual behavior from pregnancy.

Joe was the first one to ask out loud about this breach in the Church's moral firewall around sexuality. "I don't mean to be disrespectful Father, but doesn't the pill take pregnancy out of the sex equation?"

"I don't mind you asking about the pill Joe. In fact, we need to discuss it. Gentlemen, what would you assume if you knew a girl was taking the pill?"

Amid a few snickers, Craig Ward provided a predictable response, "I would assume that I should ask her out as soon as possible. I'd take her to the Colony Club for dinner and dancing. Then I'd forget to put enough gas in the car to get home."

"Exactly!" Father replied, "You would assume that she wanted to have sex, that she was planning to have sex. How long would it take for every other boy in this school to find out and assume the same thing?"

There was a chorus of replies, "About a week." "Less than a day." Mike went one better, "I already told everybody."

"So, the first point gentlemen, is that girls at Regis know this. That's one reason why they don't want to use birth control. The second point is that they need a prescription to get the pill and that requires their parent's permission. Regis parents aren't going to approve of them using birth control. Do you know why?"

Andy replied uncertainly, "Because they don't want their daughters' having sex?"

"Correct," Father replied, "And why don't they want their daughters' having sex?"

Most of the class replied, "Because, they don't want them to get pregnant."

Joe was mystified by the course of this logic and had to ask, "Wait Father, are you saying parents don't want their daughters' using the pill, because they don't want them to get pregnant?"

Father smiled at Joe and said with a very caring tone, "Joe, the only certain way to not get pregnant is to not have intercourse. If using the pill encourages sexual activity, the risk of pregnancy increases. Besides, there is a larger, more profound reason why parents don't want their daughters or sons having sex. What might that be gentlemen?"

In unison the class replied, "Because it's a sin."

"Correct!" Father said. "Again, sexual intercourse outside of the sacrament of marriage is a sin. Moreover, even within a marriage, sexual intercourse without the potential for procreation, without the potential for creating life, is a sin. Using birth control is a sin. Using the pill is a sin."

For the first time in this discussion, Tim raised his hand, "What about the rhythm method father? I heard Catholic couples can use the rhythm method to avoid having more babies"

Although Tim had heard about the rhythm method, he really wasn't sure exactly how it worked. The general idea was to abstain from sex around the time each month when a woman is most fertile. It sounded a bit complicated, and he understood it to be a far less reliable means of birth control.

"We'll talk about the rhythm method in much more detail later Tim, but you are correct. Natural birth control is not a sin, because it is based on natural biology and God's plan."

For the first time since the third grade, Tim once again found himself openly challenging a key tenet of Catholic faith. He couldn't help it. He was struck by the incongruity of what he had just heard, and he needed to get it resolved.

"Father, you've often said that sin is not just about what we do, but what we think and what we intend to do. If we intend to do a bad thing, it's just as wrong as if we did it. If the intent of using the rhythm method is to avoid pregnancy, then why is it not a sin too? The intention of using the rhythm method is the same as the intent of using the pill or any other kind of birth control."

"As I said, Tim, natural birth control is still following God's plan, all other means are artificial ways of getting around God's plan."

This natural versus artificial argument wasn't cutting it for Tim. "But Father, the intent is the same and the sin is the intent. It's just that the pill seems easier and more reliable. If natural birth control is OK, then why is the pill not OK?" Aren't most medicines artificial? I've never heard that using medicine is immoral because they're artificial."

Father Hogan paused for a few moments and gave Tim a troubled look, then he said, "The pill is not medicine Timothy. The differences are clear. If it is not clear to you, then you should pray for greater understanding and faith in Our Lord."

Tim had nowhere else to go with his query, except further from his fading spiritual shadow.

Chapter 7
Class Acts: 6th Period
English Literature

Tim's class following Religion was English Literature and the contrast could not have been starker. Miss Ballmer was the newest and youngest member of the Regis faculty. She was a 25-year-old graduate of Norte Dame who came to Regis at the beginning of the school year. She spent her first post-graduate year studying in London, then six months traveling around Europe on a Eurail Pass. She was a budding playwright, talented enough to be accepted into the prestigious University of Iowa Writers Workshop. For reasons unknown to Tim, she left that program after one term. The Regis administration was thrilled to hire her. They loved her Notre Dame pedigree and they needed help with their theater program. She was born and raised in the Chicago area, and she didn't have any previous connection to Waterloo, so it seemed a bit strange that she would be interested in teaching at Regis. Tim later learned that her boyfriend, Frank, was a volunteer with a new federal program, Volunteers in Service to America (VISTA). He was assigned to help with economic development on the northeast side, but much of what he was actually doing could be described as community organizing. Miss Ballmer's term of service teaching at Regis would coincide with Frank's VISTA commitment. The Regis administration didn't know anything about Frank, not because Miss Balmer hid it, they just didn't ask. Their enthusiasm for her would likely have been dampened had they known. Cohabitating with a boyfriend would have been a deal-killer.

From the moment Tim entered Miss Ballmer's English literature class it became the highlight of his day. It was like walking out of Regis High School and into a Paris salon, an exhilarating world of intellectual and emotional exploration. There was another aspect of Tim's experience in Miss Balmer's class that should not be minimized. She was radiantly beautiful, an angelic vision, a feast for his eyes. Her clear, melodious voice made him feel like he was being serenaded. She was roughly 5'5", slender, with shoulder length dark brown hair. She could have been mistaken as Audrey Hepburn's twin sister. She usually wore bright, fanciful dresses or skirts that barely met the Regis dress code length requirement. All the boys were quietly mesmerized every time she sat on the front of her desk with her legs crossed. As effective as Father Hogan's lessons were in subduing the boys' amorous urges, each time Tim walked into Miss Ballmer's class he fell desperately in love again and again. He routinely had to mentally resist becoming aroused. Fortunately, her lessons were so engaging, her enthusiasm for literature so infectious, that most of the time the students were completely engrossed in discussing whatever readings she assigned.

The standard sophomore English syllabus left Miss Ballmer enough flexibility to add works that reflected her own tastes and interests. After covering a couple of requisite Shakespeare plays, a Mark Twain novel, Arthur Miller's *The Crucible* and Tennessee Williams' *The Glass Menagerie*, there was time for one more assignment at the end of the term. She chose a play that never would have appeared on the Regis core curriculum, Edward Albee's, *Who's Afraid of Virginia Woolf?* It was an intense drama, laced with profanity, about a middle-age married couple playing mind games and verbally shredding each other during an evening at home with their guests, a young married couple they just met, who squirmed from embarrassment and horror at their host's viciousness.

The class had the weekend to read the play. Weekend assignments were always dicey propositions. Tim was certainly not the most conscientious student, but he always finished Miss Ballmer's assignments on time. He would do anything possible to make a good impression on her. On Monday, as usual, he made a point to get to her classroom as fast as possible before the bell rang. He cherished any opportunity to talk with her individually. As he sat down, he said, "Good afternoon, Miss Ballmer, how are you?"

She was standing at the windows, writing in her notebook. She looked up at him with a warm smile. She greeted everyone with a warm smile. "I'm fine Tim. How are you?"

"I'm good, good, real good." Tim wasn't sure where to go with this precious little conversation. The best he could come up with was, "Did you have a nice weekend? Did you go to the game?"

"What game was that, Tim?

"The Regis versus Dubuque High basketball game. It was pretty exciting. It went to double overtime, but we lost. What did you do?" It felt awkwardly familiar for Tim to ask her that, but he was desperate to expand his relationship with her beyond the classroom.

She hesitated for a moment, then she smiled again and said, "Actually, we went to Chicago to listen to music. It was a lot of fun."

Music was a subject Tim could run with, so he asked, "What music did you listen too?"

"I doubt it's anyone you would know Tim. We went to see Yusef Lateef at Joe's Jazz Showcase on State Street." The whole "We," portion of her response escaped him.

"That's incredible! I love Yusef Lateef! I'm a huge fan! I can't believe you heard him live! It would have been a blast to be there." Tim's reply was total bullshit. Joe had a Yusef Lateef album and Tim could barely recall hearing it. What he really loved though was the fantasy of going to Joe's Jazz Showcase on State Street with Miss Ballmer.

"Wow Tim, I'm surprised you know about Yusef. Not many kids your age listen to jazz."

"Oh, I love jazz, Thelonious Monk, Charlie Parker, Miles Davis. Maybe I can turn you on to some of my records sometime." Again, total bullshit. He didn't own any of those records. They were all Joe's. Tim worried that he sounded like he might be hitting on her. Something along the lines of, "Hey baby, do you want to come up to my apartment and see my etchings?"

Miss Ballmer cocked her head to the side and gave him what looked like a big sister smile, "That would be nice Tim. Feel free to bring them to class sometime."

By that time, the classroom had filled, and the bell rang a few seconds later. Miss Ballmer never had a problem getting the class to quiet down. With a few quick, light steps she bounced from the windows over to the front row of desks, "Well class, I hope you were able to finish the Albee play. What did you think of Martha and George? What do you think was going on?"

Sarah Kloss was shell shocked by the play. "Those were the most disgusting people I've ever heard! What kind of people talk to each other like that, not to mention their poor guests!"

Marcia Cook agreed, "They were so nasty it was actually scary. I fully expected one of them to kill the other."

Bill Bailey pronounced his diagnosis, "They were both psychos, certifiable looney toons. Although I have to admit, I thought their mental torture tricks were kind of entertaining." This comment provoked a number of gasps and groans.

Tim had to say something in order to demonstrate to Miss Ballmer that his head was in the game, "It was almost like Nick and Honey were caught in a trap set by George and Martha, like flies caught in a web."

Sarah said, "You know, the characters were so extreme, they hardly seemed real to me. It was more like an adult horror show."

Mike felt the need to counter Sarah, with his typical brand of cynicism, "I don't know, the whole thing just sounded like another day in the life to me, business as usual in the all-American family."

Miss Ballmer interjected, "Well not exactly the all-American family Mike, but it's also not a fantastical depiction of what can go wrong in a relationship."

Without raising his hand, Joe calmly, clearly, shared his assessment, all the while staring out the classroom window, "The fantasy is how we imagine ourselves and our lives. The nightmare is when reality forces us to abandon our fantasies, our illusions, the scripts about what a good life should look like. We look for other people to blame, other people to punish. We blame anyone other than ourselves, so we lay it all on the people we're closest to." The class quietly digested what Joe said, no one was quite sure how to respond.

Miss Ballmer took a moment as well. Then she smiled at Joe and said, "Well Joe, I think that might be about right sometimes."

Tim had to admit he was more than a little jealous of Joe's insightful analysis and Miss Ballmer's approving reaction. She looked around the class, "Let's all think about how we handle our disappointments, some big, some small, ones that come up routinely in our lives. Then think about how you might respond when that disappointment is about the entirety of your life. Imagine how you would feel, how you might behave."

Julie Blake was emphatic, "Well I certainly wouldn't act like either George or Martha."

Miss Ballmer shrugged and made a sideways, skeptical expression, "I hope not Julie, but how do you know? Anyway, I'm more interested in the sources of our disappointments in the first place? Maybe you can think about how that script Joe was talking about gets written?"

Who's' Afraid of Virginia Woolf had recently been made into a movie starring Elizabeth Taylor and Richard Burton. All that star power was generating a huge amount of buzz. Miss Ballmer made an audacious suggestion, "You know, *Who's Afraid of Virginia Woolf is* playing at the Paramount now. I plan to see it Thursday night. Would anyone like to join me?"

OK, so number one, teachers don't ask their students to go to movies with them. The exception was when Tim's 1st grade class, along with the entire school, went to see *The Ten Commandments*. Number two, this was an R rated movie, which means kids under 18 could not attend without being accompanied by an adult. Number three, this was Miss Ballmer, the one person in the entire world Tim was totally infatuated with. A pack of rabid wild dogs couldn't keep him from going!

Tim was surprised, but pleased, that only nine students accepted Miss Ballmer's invitation, five guys and four girls. Fifteen students opted out. Several of them were either turned off or traumatized by reading the play. Some parents refused to let their kids go. Tim thought the smaller group would give him an opportunity for a more intimate experience with Miss Ballmer and increase the odds of their having a meaningful conversation. He wanted to impress her in the same way Joe's critique of the play had in class. As it turned out, the conversation he had that evening would be nothing like the one he had imagined. It would shake his world and possibly change the trajectory of his life. However, it had nothing to do with the *Who's Afraid of Virginia Woolf* and it wasn't even with Miss Balmer.

The film blew Tim away. All four actors were brilliant. Taylor and Burton were joined by George Segal and Sandy Dennis, as the young dinner guests. Many movies struggle to capture the expanse and depth of a play, but great movies can actually enhance the power and intimacy of a story. Tim was riveted watching the characters of George, Martha, Nick and Honey come to life on the screen. The ferocity of their attacks on each other was more frightening than reading the play and it was unsettling to see the deconstruction of their typical middle class lives. Tim was anxious to process his reactions with Miss Ballmer. When she learned only a few students would be joining her, she invited them to her apartment after the movie for a discussion over pizza and Pepsi.

Joe gave Tim, Sandy Anderson and Julie Martin a ride to Miss Ballmer's place. Tim imagined she lived somewhere on the westside, close to Regis, in a comfortable, newer apartment building. Joe turned in the opposite direction when they left the Paramount Theater parking lot. Tim was confused, "Where are you headed Joe?"

He nonchalantly replied, "To Miss Ballmer's pad. She lives on Van Buren Street."

"You're kidding. Why would she live over there?" Van Buren St. was on the northeast side, in the African American community. The street had a notorious reputation as a rough area and not particularly safe for white folks to walk around in, particularly at night.

Joe explained, "Because of her boyfriend's work. He's a VISTA volunteer."

Sandy said from the backseat, "Didn't you know that, Tim? I've talked with Miss Ballmer several times about Frank and the work he does. He sounds really cool."

Tim felt like a complete idiot. Given his secret obsession with Miss Ballmer, he should have known she lived with a boyfriend. He figured that, being new to town, she wouldn't have had time to develop any serious relationships. It never occurred to him that she came here with a boyfriend. He masked his surprise, "She might have mentioned him to me, and I just spaced it out. We talk about a lot of other stuff." His embarrassment soon morphed into a wave of disappointment. The feeling could have festered and settled into a deep depression, but other developments provided the distraction he needed to avoid being heartsick for long.

It was an old, rundown, smoky gray colored stone apartment building. They lived on the third floor. The creaky staircase was lit by a single bare bulb. Miss Ballmer opened the door with a broad smile, "Hi guys, welcome to our little Shangri La. Make yourselves at home." The living room was sparse. There were two armless wooden chairs and one beanbag chair, which were occupied by the students who preceded them there. There were large pillows scattered around the floor, that was partially covered by a faded and tattered Persian rug. Three pizza boxes on the floor were open and the other students were already indulging. The only other furnishings were a couple of floor lamps and a five-tiered bookcase constructed of cinder blocks and barnwood. Tim quickly scanned the book titles, which were a blend of politics, literature and a few coffee-table sized art books. Across the room there was a large portal into a bedroom. The original French doors had been replaced by a bead curtain. On the other side of the curtain, Tim could see the outline of a guy who seemed to be packing a backpack. On the wall behind the bed there was a large black and white poster with Huey Newton, founder of the Black Panther Party, sitting in a large African style wicker chair holding a rifle in one hand and a spear in the other.

Miss Ballmer called to him, "Frank, come here please, I want to introduce you to some of my other students."

Frank parted the bead curtain and stepped over the pizza boxes to greet them. He was taller than Joe, with long dark scruffy hair and rugged good looks that Tim immediately resented. Tim estimated Frank to be in his mid-twenties. He was wearing faded, bell-bottom blue jeans and a red, lumberjack style buffalo plaid shirt that was unbuttoned. He had a tee-shirt on underneath with a photo of someone Tim recognized from the news. It was Abbie Hoffman, one of the media-loving activist founders of the Yippies. Under the photo it said, "Never trust a revolutionary who doesn't laugh." Frank approached them with his hand out, beaming a big friendly grin.

Miss Ballmer seemed genuinely delighted and proud to introduce them, "Frank, this is Sandy, Joe, Julie, and Tim, more of my literary travel companions." She turned to her young charges and said, "This is Frank, my partner in crime."

"How are you doing guys? I've been looking forward to meeting you all. Judy really loves your class." Judy - this was the first time Tim had heard anyone refer to Miss Ballmer by her first name. He envied the familiarity. "Sorry I couldn't join you all at the movie, but I had a lot to finish before leaving on a trip in the morning."

Sandy asked, "Where are you going Frank?"

"I'm going to Washington D.C., to the Vietnam war protest at the Pentagon. It's going to be the biggest demonstration so far. Tens of thousands of people are expected."

Joe said, "Man, I'd love to go with you. The vibe will be incredible."

Tim was still feeling a little disoriented, having just learned about Frank's existence and now seeing that he was apparently some sort of dashing political radical. He asked, "So, you're opposed to the war?"

Frank turned towards Tim and looked mildly surprised, "Why yes, Tim, I'm very much opposed to the war. What do you think about Vietnam?"

Now you would think Tim would have been ready with an answer for such a straightforward question, particularly given that he was such an avid news junky. The Vietnam war was one of the two most significant, controversial issues facing the country, civil rights being the other. Closer to home, Tim was going to turn sixteen in just a couple of months, only two years away from being draft eligible. How could he not have an opinion about a war that already involved hundreds of thousands of US troops and thousands of American lives? Joe and Tim talked about everything under the sun, but Vietnam rarely came up, except when Joe expressed dismay about how the war was going and how he didn't want to have anything to do with it. None of Tim's other friends had much to say about it either. At that point, in early 1967, most of the country didn't quite know what to think about the war, although there was a growing opposition movement, largely centered on college campuses. The war had been going on for several years, but the recent pace of US escalation hadn't given the country an opportunity to consider all the ramifications. Given the size of US forces and their overwhelming firepower, there was little doubt that a US victory would be inevitable. Of course, there was another factor driving popular opinion. The government was systematically lying about the war, as evidenced years later by the release of the Pentagon Papers and, much later, the memoirs by former leaders like Secretary of Defense, Robert McNamara. All that aside, there was another aspect to the war that personally reinforced its righteousness in Tim's thinking. Thinking that had not evolved much since the 6th grade. It was Vietnam's link to "The Chosen One."

Righteousness had triumphed, and God's will had been done, on November 8, 1960, when John Fitzgerald Kennedy (JFK) was elected President of the United States. JFK was the first Catholic president. Tim's parents were appalled by the blatant anti-Catholicism exhibited during the campaign. There were constant questions about whether the Pope would be running the country if Kennedy won. It reached a level that Kennedy felt compelled to give a nationally televised address about it. When JFK beat Nixon by an historically close margin, Tim's family was ecstatic. They couldn't have been prouder.

JFK was the total package. He was the perfect standard bearer as the first Catholic president. He was a strikingly handsome war hero and the youngest president ever. He had a beautiful, graceful, classy wife and two young, adorable children who were Hallmark greeting card cute. He was a smooth talker, with a quick wit. He was charming, persuasive and he inspired the nation. He had this strange Boston accent that Tim hadn't heard before that added to his mystique. The McIntyres thought JFK was as virtuous as any man could be, without being a priest. Tim adored him. He wanted to emulate him in every way possible.

Tim was a 5th grader in 1962, when on an October school day, he decided to walk home for lunch. He turned on the television while eating his tuna sandwich. A breaking news report came on NBC with Chet Huntley and David Brinkley. Program interruptions were rare events in those days, long before there was cable channels announcing breaking news continuously. They reported that JFK had announced a total naval blockade of Cuba. Kennedy gave an ultimatum that the blockade would remain until the Soviet Union's nuclear missiles were removed from the island. The consensus was that in the next few hours and days the world would either be saved from this nuclear threat or annihilated by it.

Tim threw down his sandwich and raced out the door. His classmates were playing flag football when he got to the school playground. He rushed onto the field waving his arms to stop the game. "Hey everybody, Kennedy is taking on the Ruskies. The US Navy has surrounded Cuba. There might be a nuclear war!"

Everyone stopped and looked around at each other. Then Johnny Joe said, "Jeepers Timmy, calm down. You need to get a grip kid. I'm sure they'll let us know if there's going to be a nuclear war."

Tim continued breathlessly, "But they are letting us know. I just heard Huntley and Brinkley warning us! This is it! This is what those drills have been preparing us for! We need to get ready! We need to go home, stock up on food and water and hunker down in our basements!" Just then the school bell rang, and the kids started filing back into the building. Tim threw up his hands in exasperation. He followed them inside, sat down in his desk and went brain dead as Sister distributed their math test.

The crisis continued for 35 more days. Then Khrushchev and Castro backed down and removed the missiles. Tim's hero, John F. Kennedy, had stared down the Soviet threat, saved the country and saved the world. Tim trusted him as much as the Pope. The guy was a saint.

One sublimely pleasant spring day in 1963, without a care in the world, Tim returned from lunch period and lazily plunked down at his desk in Sister Maria Del Rey's 6th grade class. He loved Sister Maria Del Rey. She was a calm, kind, gentle soul, with a hearty sense of humor. Every afternoon, she reserved time to read to her class the most enthralling stories, none of which were explicitly religious. Every student knew she believed in them, that they were all basically good kids, even if they messed up occasionally. Most importantly, Sister Maria believed they all could learn.

Sister brought the post-lunch ruckus back to order. "Well class, I've been looking forward to this afternoon for weeks. The St. Ignatius Rhetoric Competition is my favorite event of the year. I can't wait to hear your presentations. I know you will all do your best."

Tim was thunderstruck! His thoughts raced. *"Wait a minute, what's happening? Presentations? This afternoon? How can this be? I knew about the rhetoric competition for 6th, 7th and 8th graders. Sister told us to start thinking about our presentations weeks ago, but how could this be happening now? We certainly needed to be reminded!"* Of course, Sister had reminded the class, days earlier, when Tim had been excused in the afternoon for a dental appointment. You know that recurring dream everyone has about sitting in a class and being given a test you knew nothing about and were totally unprepared for? Well, that's exactly the reality Tim was facing, except the results of this failure would be immediately apparent to all.

The St. Ignatius Rhetoric Competition had three rounds. In the first round, students were required to present a five-minute persuasive argument on a topic of their choice in front of their own class. There were two classes at each grade level. The students in each class voted for their top five presentations. The second round happened immediately later that same afternoon. The finalists from each grade level would repeat their presentations in front of all the students in the school gymnasium. A panel of teachers then selected ten presenters to move on to the third and final round. This occurred back in the gymnasium the following evening, with both students and parents invited to attend.

Tim had nothing, no topic, no argument, no clue. Fortunately, the presentations were given in alphabetical order and his last name was midway down the list, so he could buy a little time. He was paralyzed with panic through the first five or six presentations. Then it occurred to him, "*What would JFK do?*" The president frequently held live televised press conferences. He would make a few opening remarks, rarely referring to notes, then he would take questions from reporters. He never seemed rattled or hesitant, regardless of how complex the topics or hostile the questions were. He would often make jokes. Some were self-deprecating and some were aimed at kidding the reporters. His jokes were disarming and seemed to charm the pants off everyone. So, "*What would Kennedy do?*"

Tim was barely tracking the presentations before him. Sally talked about why her family's furniture business was the best in town. Steve talked about why the Cubs were going to win the World Series. Mary Ann argued why the whole country needed to be on Daylight Savings Time. Almost everything in school was done in alphabetical order, so Tim knew the precise order of everyone in his class. Hearing them being called to the front was like the count-down to a NASA rocket launch. Eventually Sister said, "Timmy, you're up."

He took a deep breath, then rose and stood next to his desk for a moment. He slowly paced to the front of the room with his head bowed. When he turned to face the class, he was transformed. In a better than average imitation of a New England accent he began, "My fellow Americans, I want to welcome the St. Ignatius 6th grade class to the White House today. I just want to say that all of us in Washington D.C. are very proud of you. You are the smartest students in the country, and you have brilliant teachers. I know that you all will have wonderfully successful lives. Some of you might even have the opportunity to walk on the moon someday. You probably have lots of questions for me, so let's use the rest of our time to address them."

Tim didn't come up with the accent on the spot. He'd been mimicking Kennedy since before the election. JFK sounded so distinctive that Tim didn't find it difficult to replicate the vocal style. The president's mannerisms came easily as well, including how he jabbed the air with his finger for emphasis.

Everyone in the class loved it. Hands popped up all over the room. He called on Mary Ann, "Yes, young lady."

"Mr. President, can the government help St. Ignatius build a new school cafeteria? The one we have now is really old and the roof leaks sometimes. Also, the food sucks."

Tim had already thought of one answer he wanted to give and he was hoping to find a question he could use it for. "Young lady, ask not what your country can do for St. Ignatius, ask what St. Ignatius can do for your country." The class roared with delight.

Johnny Joe had his hand up, sporting a sly smile. Tim suspected Johnny Joe had thought of a zinger and he had to give him a chance to take a shot. "Yes, young man."

"What about Cuba and the Bay of Pigs? What was going on with that? Castro kicked our butts. It sounds like it was a big mess."

"Pigs? I'm the president. What in the world would I know about pigs? You good people are from Iowa. You know a lot more about pigs than I do. Please let me know when you all find out what was going on with those pigs."

For the first time that afternoon, Sister Maria Del Rey interjected herself into a presentation. She smiled at Tim and asked, "Mr. President, based on all your life experiences, what advice would you give to these St. Ignatius students?"

"I'm so glad you asked me that question Sister. I would strongly advise them to work hard, always get their homework done on time and always listen to their teachers. Most importantly, always eat your fish sticks, your delicious, wholesome New England cod fish sticks. Growing-up on Cape Cod, we would have fish sticks and chocolate milk every day for breakfast, lunch and dinner. It builds strong bodies and strong minds. I attribute a large part of my political success to eating fish sticks and chocolate milk."

Tim had been glancing at the classroom clock during his performance. When the second hand hit his five-minute mark, he quickly wrapped-up. "Thank you all for inviting me to your classroom today. I look forward to seeing some of you in Congress one day. Maybe you can get more done than the current group of clowns we have there."

Tim strutted back to his desk amid rousing applause, including Sister's enthusiastic clapping. When the votes were tallied, the students had put him in the top five. Tim was not pleased, *"Oh, my God! What have I done?"* His goal had been to survive the moment and to not be humiliated. He was relieved to have dodged all of their bullets and somehow come up with a few semi-coherent answers. But how could he possibly pull it off again?

An hour later, he was in the gymnasium, on a stage overlooking 200 students, most of them older than him. Half of the school's faculty were there, including the principal, the fearsome, humorless, Sister Joan. Her stare could burn a hole through your soul. One misstep in Tim's extemporaneous performance and she would roast him. Students from the other classes had heard about Tim's faux press conference. He assumed they would be ready to pepper him with questions aimed at tripping him up or embarrassing him. He was nearly paralyzed with fear.

The finalists from all three grades were blended alphabetically. The second-round presentations were more polished than the ones in his classroom. An 8th grade boy pitched a ban on nuclear weapons. A 6th grade girl made a case for the Second Vatican Council to approve saying the mass in English, rather than Latin. A 7th grade girl argued for banning pesticides, like DDT. They all sounded convincing to Tim.

By the time it was Tim's turn to present, he could see the audience was hungry for something more entertaining. He strode to the microphone at center stage, with his head down. He turned around with his arms held high and revealed his metamorphous. Tim was imbued with the unflappable panache of JFK, and he prepared to duel with his inquisitors. His opening remarks were like round one in the classroom. Then dozens of hands shot up. He fielded the questions in rapid fire.

Q: "Tell us more about how you saved those sailors on PT109?"

A: "It was a piece of cake. I'm a world class dog paddler. I swam them all to safety, three at a time. One on my back, one on each shoulder and I pulled one along in my teeth."

Q: "What's the best thing about being married to Jackie?"

A: "She makes the best grilled cheese sandwiches. All the ambassadors love them. "

Q: "When are we going to get a man on the moon? "

A: "As soon as we figure out how to get him back."

Q: "What do you think of Nixon?"

A: "He's a fine fellow and he would make a good mayor of Des Moines. I wish him all the luck."

Tim shot back a half dozen more answers, like a slugger in a batting cage, knocking each one out of the gym with his pithy answers. When his time had expired, he left the audience wanting more. Even Sister Joan's head was nodding in approval. Once again, he had sealed his own fate. The panel of teachers voted him through to the finals the following evening. The thought of it made him sick to his stomach. He was going to have to pull off his mad gambit yet again, this time in front of a couple of hundred adults, including his parents.

"You're going to do what?" Audrey was not quite getting her son's rhetorical schtick. She and Mac were pleased that he made it into the finals of something – anything, but their son's routine sounded uncomfortably unconventional.

Mac was starting to catch on. "So, this isn't a talent contest? It's a speech contest?"

"Yeah, that's right, these are supposed to be persuasive speeches. I'm persuading people that I'm JFK and that I know the answers to their questions. It's a different approach, but it seems to be working."

Audrey was still not impressed, "So, you're just making it up as you go? It sounds sloppy, and risky. I hope you don't end up making a fool of yourself."

Mac was more instructive, "I think you better study up for this Tim. You don't want to be caught spewing a bunch of malarkey."

Tim agreed, "Yeah, I'm going to do that."

But he actually hadn't thought about studying anything for the final round. He'd been getting by winging it so far and he wasn't sure if he could study for something so spontaneous and unpredictable. Mac was probably right though. This time he had a few hours to prepare, and the stakes would be much higher. He started by re-scanning the newspapers from the past 3 days. There were the usual news articles about the still early US military operations in Vietnam and the Viet Cong body counts. Then he remembered that his dad had a book about Vietnam that he hadn't yet read. It was written by a former American naval physician named Tom Dooley called, *Deliver Us from Evil.* Dooley spent several years in Southeast Asia during the 1950s and early 1960s. He was a fervent anti-communist and a devout Catholic. He was closely aligned with the current president of South Vietnam, Ngo Dinh Diem, who was also a Catholic. Tim later learned Dooley had worked for the CIA, but the book didn't mention that.

Tim didn't have time to thoroughly read the book, but he was able to browse it enough to catch the two primary themes. First, the Viet Minh guerilla fighters, then later the North Vietnamese communists and Viet Cong, were perpetrating atrocities on the democracy-loving South Vietnamese. Second, the United States had a moral obligation to save the South Vietnamese. It seemed like the same argument JFK was making about Vietnam, so it sounded about right to Tim.

Tim anticipated getting different, more serious questions from the parents at the finals. He determined it would be better to be less glib. Perhaps he might use the opportunity as a platform to share some of his own political opinions, as ill-formed as they were.

Tim was back on stage the following night, but this time he was wearing a sport coat and tie. All of the contestants had fine-tuned their performances and were bringing their A game. Marilyn spoke about the Second Vatican Council with even more passion. Rita Burns turned some heads by advocating for women priests. Tim could see the pastor of St. Ignatius parish, Father Mark's displeasure in the glare he threw at Sister Joan, who was trying to contain her smile. An 8th grader, Tommy Kilkenny, prosecuted the argument that a little known emerging English pop group that had not yet set foot in America, *The Beatles*, were the greatest musical geniuses since Beethoven and they were going to be bigger than Elvis.

Tim approached the microphone having already acquired JFK 's persona. After two rounds of performing presidential press conferences, he felt more comfortable in the role. He felt emboldened, even a bit grandiose. He modified his opening remarks and laid on an even thicker Boston accent, "My fellow American, I stand here as your president, prepared to lead this great nation in fulfillment of its destiny. I will be a beacon of freedom and democracy for the world. With all Americans working together, there is nothing we cannot achieve! Now I would be happy to take your questions." It worked. The parents were delighted and applauded vigorously.

The first question came from a mother Tim didn't recognize, "How do you like being president?"

Tim's answer reflected how he was actually feeling at that moment, rather than the JFK character he was playing. "I believe I was born for this job. Everything I've experienced in life has prepared me to be president. I welcome the challenges and I'm going to do the best possible job for all Americans." He was oozing hubris by this point.

The next question came from Johnny Joe's dad, "What are you going to do about my taxes?"

Tim was already aware of the first rule of politics, "Sir, I am committed to keeping your taxes as low as possible and squeezing every bit of value out of your hard-earned tax dollar. Unfortunately, in order to pay for your tax cut, I'll have to raise the taxes on everyone else here in this gymnasium."

He wasn't sure what the intent was behind the next question from a grim looking man in the back. "What do you think about Martin Luther King?"

Tim was certain how he wanted to answer, but he thought he should first lighten things up a bit. "I believe Dr. King is the fittest man in America, he hasn't stopped marching for years. But more importantly, racial discrimination is a stain on America and must be eliminated. Segregation in the South, and everywhere else, must be eliminated." He was expecting a wild round of applause, but there was only a smattering of tepid clapping.

There were a handful of other domestic questions about the Kennedys' home in Hyannis Port, the Kennedy kids and, of course, Jackie. Then came the final question from an anguished looking woman in the front row who acted like she was actually asking the President of the United States a question. "Mr. President, what are you going to do about Vietnam?"

At last, someone finally asked the question he was most prepared for. "It is the United States' obligation to stand with the people of South Vietnam and protect them from the horrors of the Viet Cong. As the world's greatest superpower, the United States must halt the advancement of godless communists, no matter where in the world they are. Thank you all for coming out this evening and God bless America."

The audience rose in a standing ovation, with the notable exception of the woman who asked the last question. Tim backed away from the microphone waving both of his raised hands. He thought that, if he had been old enough to run for president, he might be able to get elected. In lieu of being inaugurated, he did win the St. Ignatius Rhetoric Competition. It was the crowning achievement of all his years of parochial education.

Six months later, Tim was sitting in his 7th grade desk on a Friday afternoon. Sister Joan came on the intercom and announced in a somber tone, "Boys and girls, it has just been reported that President Kennedy has been shot in Dallas, Texas. Please bow your heads and pray for him." There was a collective gasp, followed by whimpers and shocked, confused glances around the room. Everyone put their heads down and prayed. A half hour later, Sister Joan came back into the classroom. She was visibly shaken and choked up, "I, I have to tell you that, that, President Kennedy has died." When the sobbing began to subside, she continued, "We will all proceed over to church in a few minutes for a mass, to pray for President Kennedy, his family and for our country."

The world stood still. Grief gripped the entire nation. Everyone was disorientated and the loss consumed everyone's thoughts. Tim was home alone that Sunday morning, while the rest of his family went to an earlier mass. He was watching the continuous television news coverage of the assassination, when he witnessed live, in real time, Jack Ruby shoot Lee Harvey Oswald dead. Tim was frozen. He felt numb.

During the ensuing four years, from 1963 to 1967, US troops in Vietnam increased from 16,300 to 485,600. US Casualties rose from 118 to 11,153. The escalation increased dramatically after Congress passed the Gulf of Tonkin Resolution in 1964. It was prompted by an alleged attack on two US destroyers by North Vietnamese patrol boats.

So now, in 1967, perhaps it was past time for Tim to revisit his thinking. "Really Tim, I'm interested in knowing what you think about Vietnam. The way the war is going, you could wind up there before long." Frank sounded concerned, not at all confrontational.

Everyone in Miss Ballmer's living room became silent and all eyes were on Tim, waiting for his reply. Miss Ballmer tried to come to Tim's rescue, "Come on Frank, don't put Tim on the spot. We're supposed to be talking about the movie, not geopolitics."

Tim couldn't wimp out in front of Miss Ballmer. "No, it's fine. I've been thinking about the war. It's just that it's complicated. There's a lot of angles to it, a lot of different perspectives."

Joe was relishing an opportunity to talk about the war, especially with someone like Frank, who seemed knowledgeable and committed to his beliefs. Here it was, 1967, and Frank was the first adult they had met who was vocally opposed to the war in Vietnam. Joe wanted to seize the opportunity. "I'd like to hear more about what you think, Frank. I doubt if any of us have heard someone with your perspective."

Sandy said, "Yes Frank, we want to hear more about why you're against the war. Sorry Miss Ballmer, but right now this seems more important than talking about the movie."

Miss Ballmer could see they all agreed with Joe and Sandy. "I'm fine with that. Are you up for expounding about the war Frank? I've never seen you pass up a chance to share your opinions."

Frank smiled and shrugged, "Well, the whole reason I'm going to D.C. is to try to change some minds. I might as well start here."

They all sat down on the floor pillows. It was obvious from the start that Frank had a lot of practice making his case and had honed his arguments. He opened with a follow-up question, "Tim, you said there were lots of different perspectives on the war. Tell me some reasons why you think we need to be fighting in Vietnam? We can discuss them one at a time."

It'd been four years since Tim's impassioned, crowd-pleasing speech to the St. Ignatius parents. The arguments supporting the war hadn't changed much. This time, however, Tim reiterated them with far less certainty. "OK, well, the first one I suppose is that the South Vietnamese should have the right to choose their own government and that they want to live in a democracy, not a communist state."

Frank leaned toward Tim and slowly nodded his head, "Democracy. Does South Vietnam have a democracy? I'm not sure they've had an honest election yet. Their last elected president, Diem, was murdered in a coup that our CIA ordered, or at least supported. Of course, he was so unpopular that Buddhist monks were setting themselves on fire to protest him. They've had three military coups in the past four years. I'm not sure we've done much to bring democracy to South Vietnam. I'm not sure we've done much to bring them a government most Vietnamese people even support."

Tim had to pause for a moment and absorb what Frank had just said. He knew South Vietnam had struggled to maintain political stability, but he didn't know the US government, our CIA, had been involved in overthrowing their government, or played a hand in Diem being murdered. That would have happened when JFK was still president. Diem was a Catholic for Christ's sake! "Wait a minute Frank, are you saying Kennedy ordered Diem to be killed? I just don't believe that could be true."

Sandy leaned back and shook her head, "I swear, Tim, sometimes you can be such a choir boy."

In a different context, that comment could be construed as a compliment, but Tim knew it wasn't. It meant that he was innocent and naïve. At that stage in his adolescent male awakening, it was an embarrassing slight.

Frank raised an eyebrow and said, "I don't know if JFK ordered Diem killed, but he certainly gave a green light to the coup knowing Diem would likely be killed. Kennedy wanted him out, regardless of whether some people might die. Look Tim, I can tell you're a good guy who wants to know the truth, but at some point, we all have to decide whether to believe what we want to believe or accept the facts as they are and what makes sense. I don't want you to just accept what I say. Keep your eyes open and keep looking for the truth. But let's move on. What's another reason for the US to be in Vietnam?"

Tim was increasingly uncomfortable taking the role of spokesperson for the war. "Well, this is not me saying this, but there's the domino theory. The argument goes something like, if we let communist expansion continue unchecked, we'll eventually be fighting them on the beaches of LA and Miami. Marx, Lenin, Mao and Stalin's faces will be on Mount Rushmore. We'll all be sent to work on collective farms or put in reeducation camps."

They all laughed at that notion, including Frank. Then he said, "So illiterate Vietnamese farmers, fishermen and villagers are willing to fight and die against the US, because they want to destroy Disneyland?

Tim, the Vietnamese have been fighting this war for 20 years, starting against French colonialism. It's fundamentally a war of national liberation. Yes, it's also a proxy war between world powers like the US, Russia and China, but that support enables them to fight, it's not why they fight. Besides, the communist world is not monolithic. There are enormous tensions between China and Russia. The North Vietnamese see China as a huge threat. Did you know Ho Chi Minh reached out to the US for an alliance before he turned to Russia for assistance?"

The students were all stunned. They hadn't heard anything about this. Was it true that the US could have stopped the war before getting involved?

Joe looked incredulous and really pissed off, "How do you know this, Frank? How could we all not know this?"

Frank turned to Joe and said flatly, "The evidence is there for anyone who wants to see it, Joe, documents and witnesses, both American and Vietnamese. Of course, you never heard about it. The powers that be are too invested in the US government's narrative. On the rare occasions when officials have been asked about it, they brush it off as something not to be taken seriously."

Frank turned back to Tim, "Is there anything else, Tim? Any other reasons why you should leave your home here in Iowa to fight and die in a Vietnamese rice paddy?"

The personal framing of the question was making Tim queasy. He paused a few seconds, then hesitantly said, "Well, they did attack us. I mean, the North Vietnamese did attack our navy."

It was Frank's turn to look incredulous, "Right, a couple of North Vietnamese patrol boats attacked two US destroyers, trying to blow them out of the water and provoke the largest military force on the planet to rain hell down on them. There were no US casualties, and no US ships were lost, yet they use this incident to justify sending tens of thousands more troops into harm's way. Does that even sound plausible, Tim? I don't know what actually happened, but everyone knew LBJ and McNamara had been itching for an excuse to escalate the war. Sometimes our government hides the truth and sometimes they just make shit up."

Miss Ballmer had enough of the conversation, "Well, I'm not lying when I say that I'm exhausted. I have to be at school early tomorrow and Frank has to go stop the war. Let's call it an evening. "

Tim was sincere when he said, "I appreciate you talking with us Frank. You've given me a lot to think about."

Joe said, "Yeah man, what you laid on us was really heavy."

Frank's expression turned grim, "Yes, it is very heavy, and a lot of people are being crushed. The war is so far removed from your high school lives here in Iowa, it's hard to relate to it. But I'm glad you're open to hearing some hard truths. I don't want you guys going to your senior prom one day, then a few months later becoming sausage in the Pentagon's Vietnam meat grinder. You need to enlighten yourselves now, then get ready to act. There's a revolution coming."

The subdued students left the apartment together and paused at the bottom of the stairs. Joe was visibly agitated. He started pacing back and forth, shaking his fist. "I knew this war was fucked-up and everything we've been hearing about it has been bullshit!"

Sandy was also upset. "I'm not sure what to believe. Frank seemed to know what he was talking about, and it made sense, but we just met him. I've never met anybody as radical as Frank. I mean really, he was talking about a revolution!"

Tim smirked a bit at that comment. "How many radicals are we going to meet here in Iowa, Sandy? It's considered a revolutionary act for guys to let their hair grow over their ears. The closest thing we've ever seen to a protest is a cafeteria food fight."

Joe was still worked up. "Seriously, I can't just stay quiet about this crap. We can't be lemmings going over a cliff, just because it's supposed to be un-American to criticize the war."

Joe drove Sandy and Tim home, while talking non-stop. "We've got to educate ourselves. We can't just rely on the information people in authority are feeding us. We can't rely on what we see and hear on television. I'm not letting this go."

A few weeks later, rumors spread that Frank had been beaten up and arrested in Washington, D.C. It was said he came back to Iowa briefly, but instead of returning to the VISTA program, he moved to Chicago and completely devoted himself to resisting the war. Miss Ballmer didn't talk to her students about any of this, but they could see she was troubled, melancholy and less enthused about teaching. She left Regis at the end of the school year. Bloody images of the war became a dominant theme on Tim's bedroom wall.

Chapter 8
Class Acts, 7th Period
Latin

There were three language options at Regis, French, Spanish and Latin. The first two had their own constituencies, but marketing was needed to fill the Latin classes. Beginning as freshman, students were regularly advised that Latin would be the most useful language if they wanted to pursue higher-level professions. The argument went that legal, medical, and other scientific terminologies were rooted in Latin, so it would be easier to study these disciplines if you knew the root meanings. Also, Latin was the original Romance language, so if you mastered Latin, you could more easily pick up the others. Students who had been altar boys thought they had a jump start on Latin, given they had already memorized the mass liturgy in Latin. The pitch was surprisingly effective. There were two sections of Sophomore Latin, one in the morning, taught by a young priest named Father Otto. The other was the last period of the day, taught by an elderly nun named Sister Rita.

Latin class required concentration and memorization, so it was painful to study it in the late afternoon. The morning section always filled first. Tim's typical lackadaisical approach to registration landed him in the 7th period section. Sister Rita had a remedy for students' lagging energy, diminished attention spans and wandering minds. She was old-school. She ran her class like a drill sergeant, with a ruler in one hand tapping out recitations on the students' desks as she patrolled the aisles. One of her more charming instructional techniques was to hang in the back of the room, barking English words and phrases for them to recite back to her in Latin. When she noticed someone gazing out the window or heads nodding down fighting an urge to nap, she would sneak up from behind and give them a full-throttled open-handed whack on the back of the head. Her students had years of conditioning to this type of pedagogical approach. They thought Sister Rita's assaults were more amusing than abusive.

One winter afternoon Sister Rita cut her instructions short for an announcement. *"Alumni, opus tuum, quia magni momenti operam denuntiatio*! I am very proud to announce that our own Senior Latin scholar, Ted Kemp, has been elected National Student President of the Junior Classical League, the largest Latin and Greek education organization in the country. This is a tremendous honor for Ted and for Regis High School. The Junior Classical League's next annual assembly will be in July at the University of Arizona in Tucson. We want Regis to be strongly represented at the assembly and give Ted our full support. It will be a wonderfully enriching experience for everyone who attends. It will be an opportunity to interact with other young scholars from all over the country. We will need at least 25 students to make a group trip viable. I urge you all to talk with your parents and let me know as soon as possible if you can participate."

The students' initial reaction to Sister's proposal was a collective yawn. What could be more boring than a Latin convention? Why would they ever want to interrupt their precious summer vacation for a week-long Latin meeting? Then an influential junior, John Poole, had a revelation. John was Warren's older brother. He was just as affable as Warren, but more audacious and ambitious. He was also a visionary. John sat himself down at Tim and his chums' table in the cafeteria the following day, "OK, guys, you all need to talk to your parents about going on this Latin trip. It's going to be a blast."

Mike just about spit out his juice, "You can't be serious! How could a Latin assembly be a blast? I can't think of anything I would be less interested in doing, especially during the summer."

John was insistent, "Believe me, you don't want to pass this up. Father Otto came over to our house to talk with my dad about getting a group discount on train tickets. He showed dad his photo album from the assembly last year in Nashville. There were 2,000 kids there, the majority of whom were girls, and I mean some really sharp looking girls! Oh, and get this, there was a toga party. A real live, girls wrapped in sheets, Greek and Roman toga party! You don't need much imagination to realize the possibilities. Father Otto wants to make this a grand tour

64

of the Southwest. Think about it, a two-week road trip with a huge gang of Regis Revelers! At this point, they only have four or five chaperones lined up. It would be one big rolling party!"

Tim was impressed, "You know, John, I want you around if I ever need to sell a clunker car. I can't believe it, but you've actually got me interested."

Mike agreed, "I was sold when I heard toga party."

Joe bought into John's vision, but he wasn't eligible. "Crap, this is the first time I wish I was taking Latin instead of French."

John offered a solution, "You can still find a way to go, Joe. Just tell Father Otto that you're in Sister Rita's class and tell Sister Rita you're in Father Otto's class. Hell, you could probably tell Sister Rita you're in her class and she wouldn't know any better."

Joe wasn't into deceptions. Besides, his dad wanted him to help fix up some of his rental properties over the summer.

The concept of a raucous Regis Royals road trip caught fire. Within a couple of weeks, 150 students had signed up. Sister Rita was overjoyed by the enthusiastic response. Father Otto was pleased that there were more participants to cover the costs, but he was also anxious, because despite the huge response from students, only one additional adult had volunteered to chaperone. Other than Sister Rita and Father Otto, there were John and Warren's parents, along with Mary Walsh's mom, who was known to be very laid back. The thirty to one adult to student ratio seemed about right to the students and it became a central part of John's marketing pitch. The guys were pleased that John's salesmanship was just as effective with the girls as it had been with them. Whatever lines he was laying on them, the final enrollment was more than half girls.

Tim's parents were mystified that he would be interested in attending a Latin convention. His mom was suspicious of his motives, "Where did this newfound love of Latin come from Timmy?"

"Jeez mom, I'm not going because I love Latin. I just think it would be interesting to meet kids from around the country, most of them are probably honor students. Besides, you know how much I love the Southwest and Dad can never take time off work long enough to go that far on vacations. I turn sixteen in a few weeks, and this would be a great way to mark the occasion."

"Well, it does sound more wholesome than some of the other things you might spend your time doing this summer. It's reassuring to know Father Otto and Sister Rita will be chaperones. You can go, as long as you pay for it yourself."

Chapter 9
Tucumcari to Tucson

So, it came to pass that in late July 1967, one hundred and fifty-two Regis students and five overwhelmed adults boarded one of the last remaining passenger trains in the Midwest. They rode the Rock Island Railroad all afternoon and all night, through Des Moines and Kansas City, to the end of the line in Tucumcari, New Mexico. A swarm of Regis Royals occupied three full train cars. Spirits were high and the mood was festive, but they were all relatively well-behaved. After they arrived in Tucumcari the following morning, they boarded three chartered Trailways buses for what was planned to be a two-day journey to Tucson. Despite the large number of paid participants, it was still a bare-bones trip. There were no arrangements for travel accommodations, other than sleeping on the train and buses. While in Tucson, they would be staying in the University of Arizona dormitories.

The first stop on their grand tour of the Southwest was the Carlsbad Caverns National Park, about a five-hour drive from Tucumcari. They were dazzled by the caverns and spent several hours marveling at the stalactites and stalagmites. The pace of the day was relaxed and they leisurely re-boarded the buses, anticipating the night drive to Albuquerque. As they pulled away from the parking lot, one of the buses began having clutch problems. The driver was having difficulty getting the bus into second and third gear. The bus's maximum speed would not exceed 35 mph. It had to be repaired, and Albuquerque was too far across a remote stretch of desert for the work to be done there. The closest option was El Paso, Texas.

The drive to El Paso was a slow grind. They limped into the Trailways bus barn around 10:30 PM. Mr. Poole and Father Otto talked with the mechanics, while Mrs. Poole and Mrs. Walsh made rounds with the students. Sister Rita napped in her bus seat. When the men returned, the adults huddled. After they broke from their deliberations, they beckoned the students off the buses and gathered them around. The adults looked tired and forlorn.

Father Otto was their spokesperson, "OK, Royals, we appreciate your patience. We have a bit of a dilemma here, but we also have a plan. The night crew can begin working on the bus, but the repairs won't be completed until tomorrow morning. There isn't room in the other two buses for everybody at once, so we need to be creative. Half of you can return to the buses and get a few hours of sleep. The others will have to keep yourselves occupied until it's your turn to sleep. Now turn around and look across the street. That bridge you see there will take you over to Ciudad Juarez, Mexico. There's plenty to do and see over there. The manager here tells me the stores and restaurants are open all night, so you can pick-up some souvenirs and snacks. It's 11:00 PM now. I want everyone who chooses to go to Juarez to be back here by 3:00 AM sharp– understood? Now, who wants to be in the first group to sleep?"

The students looked at one another in bewilderment. Did they just hear Father Otto say that they could cross the border into Juarez Mexico, unchaperoned, in the middle of the night? Are Mr. and Mrs. Poole really OK with this? Sister Rita was still asleep on the bus. Tim looked over at Warren's parents and Mrs. Walsh. Their faces were stamped with defeat.

John was the first to speak up, "I'm not at all tired, Father. I wouldn't mind doing some shopping in Juarez."

Most of the other guys quickly followed suit, nodding and raising their hands saying, "Yeah, we're not tired either." They didn't have anything specifically in mind for going to Juarez, but they had a pretty good hunch that there were possibilities for adventure there not readily available in Iowa. Most of the girls figured out what was up and wanted nothing to do with it. They chose to sleep. Everyone milled around for a few minutes, then informally broke up into smaller groups. John organized a group of ten, thinking it would be the ideal size for both safety and celebration. Their band of merrymakers included John in the lead; Sam, Jack and Sarah were 11th grade friends of John; Warren, Mike, Jim, Sandy, Julie and Tim were the sophomore contingent. Sandy and Julie were among Tim's closest friends.

It turned out the bridge Father Otto directed them over was not the main one leading to the bustling tourist district. They walked across the dimly lit span with more than a little trepidation. The border guards on both the US and Mexico sides barely gave them any notice and they didn't even ask to see the kids' identifications. They dropped down into a dark and quiet barrio. John acted as though he knew where to go, but he didn't have a clue. The others followed him around random corners leading into dark and dirty alleyways. The few people they passed seemed either indifferent or hostile to their presence.

Warren was the first to challenge his brother's sense of direction. "John, this isn't getting us anywhere. Let's go back to the bridge and start over."

The girls were way more emphatic. Sarah said, "John, get us the hell out of here!"

Julie also raised her voice, "This is not good, John! We need to stop dinking around and get out of here!"

John was reluctant to retreat. "Hey, I got this. Can't you hear all the activity somewhere over there?" No one could hear a thing.

Just then, two happy-go-lucky guys looking about their same age approached them out of nowhere, "Hola amigos, do you know where you're going? You know this is not a good place for you to be. There's a lot of very bad things that can happen to you here. We can help you."

John welcomed their offer, "Yeah, that would be great. We're looking for entertainment. Do you know where we can find some music, some bars? "

One of their rescuers smiled and said, "Oh sure, no problem, but can you give us a little help as well, say $10?"

The Royals were taken aback by how quickly the friendly gesture had become a business transaction; however, they were eager for help. John tried bargaining, "We can't give you $10, but how about $3?"

"Oh amigo, for $3 we can point you to a way out of here, but that would not be enough to find you a bar."

"OK then," John said," We can give you $5. Take us to a bar with good music."

The two entrepreneurs laughed and told the young lost souls to follow them. The Royals needed their guides' help more than they had initially realized. They had wandered deep into the barrio and a long way from any tourist haunts. After fifteen minutes of twists and turns, they emerged onto a bright and bustling avenue, filled with shops, taquerias, dive bars and nightclubs. The stores' merchandise and restaurant tables spilled out onto the sidewalk. The street was filled with pedestrians, many of whom were gringos.

Their guides stopped in front of a closed hardware store. Off to the side of the entrance, there was a wide winding colorfully tiled staircase, with a wrought iron handrail. There were several traditional Mexican style dresses hanging from the railing. The high ceiling second floor windows were open and there were multi-colored lights flashing inside. They could hear familiar music coming from above. It was a band playing the top of the pop hit "Louie Louie," by the Kingsmen, with a Spanish accent.

Their guides were enthusiastic, "Come on amigos, you'll have a really good time in here."

John paused and looked up, "This seems like a fun place. You guys go on up. There's something I want to pick up quick. I'll join you in a few minutes."

The girls' instincts told them the place would not be much fun for them. They exchanged skeptical glances and Sarah said, "I don't think so, boys. We want to do some shopping. We're going with John."

Sandy grabbed Tim's arm and pulled him aside, "Tim, I've got a bad feeling about this place. I seriously don't think you should go up there."

He brushed off her concern, "Come on Sandy, they're playing, 'Louie Louie' for Christ's sake. How rough can it be?"

John and the girls walked off. The girls threw several worried glances back at the guys, like a farewell scene in a tragic movie.

The six intrepid boys and their two guides slowly ascended the staircase. They rounded a corner at the top of the stairs and confronted a very hulky, heavily tattooed Mexican man, with a shaved head and a killer's stare, sitting on a stool. Their guides greeted him, "Buenos noches Ismael, como estas?" The doorman said nothing. The boys walked by him, trying to avoid eye contact.

They entered a dark, cavernous room. The only illumination were some dim lights behind the bar, red and blue spotlights around the stage and a revolving disco ball hanging from the ceiling that transformed a spotlight beam into twirling stars on the black walls. The quintet on stage were still playing "Louie Louie," for at least the third time in a row. There were fifteen to twenty people in the room, only about ten percent of its capacity. Oddly, almost all of the patrons were young women. The two guides led them to a table in the middle of the room. They just started to sit down when two waitresses approached. The guys were relieved to hear them speak English, "Bienvenidas boys, what can we get you?"

Mike didn't hesitate, "I'll have a margarita!"

The other boys were more tempered and ordered beers. Immediately after the waitresses returned with their drinks, the boys were surrounded by the young women from the bar. None of the girls spoke much English and what they did know seemed to come from a limited script. A very pretty girl, with long dark hair and a short tight skirt leaned against their table and directly faced Tim, "Hola bebe, Quieres algo de compañia?"

Tim didn't understand her, but it sounded like she was asking if they wanted company. The best he could come up with was, "No hablo español."

Jim suggested, "Hey Tim, try laying some Latin on her."

He gave it a try, "Ita, quaeso sedens." She had no idea what Tim said, so he went back to English and gestured, "Yes, please sit."

She smiled, turned around, sat down on Tim's lap, put her hand on his leg and giggled, "¿Podrías comprarnos unas cervezas por favor?" Tim shot a befuddled look at Jim, hoping he could pick up what she was saying, but Jim was thoroughly engrossed with another young lady sitting on his lap, with both her arms around his neck. When Tim turned back to the girl on his lap she said, "Beers, please buy us beers."

The waitresses returned with the first round of drinks. Each boy had a girl parked on top of him and they all requested beers. Jack yelled out to the waitresses, "Beers for the girls please!" Mike had just taken a sip from his first drink when he said, "And another margarita for me, por favor."

In spite of the language barriers, everyone was having a really good time. The girls obviously found the young Norte Americanos oh so charming, oh so attractive, witty, and amusing. They must have, the way they fawned over them, stroking their fingers through the boys' hair, rubbing their thighs, and laughing at everything they said. The girls pulled all the boys up on the dance floor, where they convulsed to the best tune in the band's repertoire, an extended Spanish version of, "Gimme Some Lovin'", by the Spencer Davis Group.

After three rounds of "Gimme Some Lovin'", the band took a break. The dancers returned to their table, winded and sweaty. Mike tripped on a chair leg. He fell against the edge of the table, cutting his chin and spilling his fourth margarita, which he had kept in his hand the entire time he was dancing. Jim caught him before he hit the floor. "Whoa there party boy," Jim said, "I think you've hit both your face and your limit of margaritas for tonight buddy." Jim grabbed a napkin and pressed it against Mike's chin to stop the bleeding.

Tim noticed that their two guides had left. Then he looked at his watch and said, "I think we better get going. It will take us a while to find our way back." Then he looked toward the bar and said, "Can we have our check please." No one at the bar acted like they heard him, so his new girlfriend yelled, "Trae a los chicos su cuenta!" She then turned to the other girls and said, "Vamos al baño." The boys barely noticed when the girls all drifted off.

A minute later, the waitress came over, handed Jack the check and strolled back to the bar. Jack admired the waitress as she walked off before he looked down at the bill and yelped, "What! What the hell is this? This can't be right! This says we owe $700 US dollars! We only had a few beers. Even with Mike's margaritas, we shouldn't owe more than $80 or $90!"

Jim called back to the waitress, "Senorita, por favor, there's been a mistake."

The waitress ignored Jim and stayed standing next to the bar. Instead, the man mountain they had passed by the door stood up from his stool, walked over to their table, and parked himself directly face-to-face with Jack. At the same time, a smaller, but muscular man who had been sitting at the far end of the bar the entire time, got up and walked over beside Jack. He had black, slicked-back hair, and a long scar on the side of his chin. He wore a half unbuttoned, shiny deep purple silk shirt. He spoke in very clear English, "What's the problem my friends?"

Jack stammered, "There's been a mistake on our bill. It says we owe $700, but we only had a few beers, so it can't be that much."

Tim looked over towards the bar and saw three other criminal type men coming through a back door. They stopped several feet short of the boys' table and stared at them menacingly.

The purple Romeo took the bill from Jack and looked it over. "There's no mistake here friends. You've been charged for sixteen beers and four margaritas."

Warren spoke up, "Right, that shouldn't add up to more than $80."

The violently violet villain holding the bill suddenly straightened up and spoke more sternly, "What kind of a place do you think this is boys? Do you think this is a dive bar? This is a private club. There's an entrance fee and an entertainment fee. Didn't you see the charges posted by the front door? Didn't you enjoy the entertainment? We saw you dancing to the music. Didn't you enjoy the girls?"

Jack's voice became higher and even more shaky, "Sure, we had a good time, but we just..."

"You just fucking what?" The purple pirate interrupted and started to rage, "You just wanted to fucking skip out on your bill? You just wanted to fucking cheat us! Who the fuck do you little shits think you are?"

Warren tried to calm the situation, "Look, we don't want any..."

Magenta man interrupted again, "What the fuck don't you want? You don't want to fucking pay what you owe? You want to fuck us over?"

The band meandered back on stage and began to play "La Bamba." The six boys were frozen in terror. Tim nervously glanced towards the front entrance and saw John walk into the room. John stopped abruptly a few feet inside the door. John could see that a nasty situation was rapidly escalating. Tim's relief at seeing John join their ranks was shattered when John suddenly whisked around and bolted back through the entrance.

"What the hell!" Tim thought, *"How can that damn coward abandon us like that? Especially his own brother! That's not like John."*

Their purple persecutor became more threatening, "OK you fucking little pricks, give us what you owe, or we'll take everything you've got ourselves and then take you all apart piece by piece."

Tim had never experienced this kind of fear and he struggled to formulate a coherent thought. He wanted to summon some courage, but his mind went blank. Then an image popped into his head. A recollection from the only kind of physical combat he had previously experienced. He thought, *"What would Ronnie do?"*

Tim was certain any attempt to extract themelves from this dangerous drama would require an element of surprise. He clasped his hands together as if praying and then bent his knees into a crouch. He began trembling and wailing, "Please, please senors, don't hurt us! We don't want to cheat you! We'll give you whatever you want! We'll give you whatever we have! Just please, please don't hurt us, please!"

Tim's companions looked at him with their mouths open, confused, and embarrassed. The bald behemoth and the purple pimp looked down at Tim and sneered. Then from his crouched position, with his face down, Tim sprang towards the middle of the shiny silk shirt directly in front of him. He plowed the top of his head into the bottom of the lilac lout's sternum, driving him back into the table behind him. Tim rolled to the side and turned around to see his tormentor sitting on the floor, gasping for breath, and holding the back of his head where it had hit the table. Tim threw himself at him from behind and hooked his arm around the thug's throat pulling him backwards. Tim shouted at his companions like a crazed banshee, "Fuck these assholes! Knock their fucking heads off!"

Jack and Warren jumped on the tattooed giant. Sam and Jim planted their feet, braced their legs, and clenched their fists, preparing to defend themselves against the onslaught of the three men charging at them. Unfortunately, Mike was too debilitated to be useful. His heart was in it, but he was in a tequila stupor, spinning around, wildly swinging his arms. The band pumped up the volume on, *La Bamba*, as the melee spread across the room.

Tim was sitting on the floor, pulling back on the neck of his opponent, with his legs wrapped around his opponent's torso, when he saw John race back into the room, followed by three stout, uniformed American soldiers. The tallest GI, the one with stripes on his shirtsleeve, shouted, "Hey motherfuckers, get the fuck off those kids!"

Everyone stopped momentarily and looked at the soldiers. The three guys who had been pummeling Sam and Jim halted and then moved towards the four saviors. The burley bald doorman threw off Warren and Jack. He reached into his pocket and pulled out a long, thin,

74

shiny black knife handle with a white mother-of-pearl inlayed dragon on the side. He pressed a button on the top side of the handle and a six-inch blade whipped out from the other side. He took a few steps towards the soldiers. John picked up a chair and threw it at the hand that was holding the switchblade. The knife flew out of the bouncer's grasp and slid across the floor. The muscular, Mexican-American looking soldier dashed to pick it up. The other two soldiers grabbed beer bottles off a nearby table. They held the long necks of the bottles, smashed them against the metal edge of the table and threatened their attackers with the bottles' jagged broken bottoms. The four assailants ceased their advance. The plum-colored punk Tim had in a choke hold stopped resisting, so Tim let up on his grip slightly. The band stopped playing and the room went silent. The only noise was Mike, still flailing about, bumping into tables and chairs, slobbering, "I'm going to kick the shit out of all of you motherfuckers."

The lanky sergeant grinned and slowly, softly said in a twangy cowboy accent, "Well fellas, it looks like y'all are having a real good time here. I hate to cut your evening short, but I'm thinking y'all might want to just mosey on out of here now."

Tim released his chokehold on his now hapless foe, who was light-headed from asphyxiation. Tim got back on his feet, and with his compadres, staggered over next to John and the soldiers. They all started backing towards the entrance. Jim stopped suddenly, stretched out his arms and said, "Wait guys, we almost forgot to give these fine folks what we owe them." He grabbed a wallet from his back pocket and pulled out a $10 bill, walked over to the nearest table and laid it down. The other four boys did the same. Warren took a wallet out of Mike's pants and laid down a $10 bill. None of the bar bullies made a move, but they stared daggers at the gringos as they backed out of the club.

Warren put Mike's arm around his shoulders and helped him stumble down the winding stairs to the sidewalk. They gathered at the bottom of the steps. They were all still panting and shaking from their intense adrenalin rush. Jack turned to John, "How the hell did you manage to round up the cavalry so fast?"

John had his hands on his knees, still trying to catch his breath, "It wasn't a problem. Fort Bliss is in El Paso. There're soldiers all over the place." He pointed down the street, and sure enough, they could see many other men in uniforms scattered among the crowd.

The boys profusely thanked Sergeant Nelson, Corporal Gonzales and Corporal Wentz and vigorously shook their hands until the soldiers felt compelled to pull away. Sam said in a hyperventilating laugh, "Man you really saved our asses. I don't think we could have gotten out of there alive without you."

Corporal Gonzales chuckled, "It looked like you kids were holding your own, but I suggest you not go into any more places like that until you're a little older." The three soldiers then bid them adieu, turned, and nonchalantly sauntered down the sidewalk.

As the young conquistadors headed down the street, Jack started yelling, "What the hell were you thinking back there Tim! You could have gotten us killed! What if that bald-headed beast had pulled out that switchblade on us right after we jumped on him! We could have been cut to pieces!"

Sam agreed, "Yeah, Tim, we still had a chance to talk our way out of it. Besides, it's just money. A stunt like that wasn't worth the risk."

Tim wasn't feeling at all remorseful. Truth be told, he was elated. He was the smallest guy in the group and the only one who was able to gain dominance over his opponent. Jim and Sam had welts on the side of their faces. Jack had a napkin stuffed into his bloody nose. Regardless, Tim felt obliged to express some regret. "I don't know what came over me guys. I thought for sure they were going to waste us, so I lost it." Then another thought hit him. "By the way, John, why didn't you come up to the club with us in the first place? What was it you wanted to pick up? And where did the girls go?"

John replied, "The girls weren't really interested in shopping. I escorted them to the main border bridge. After they crossed over, they took a taxi back to the bus barn." Then John flashed a devilish smile and flickered his eyebrows up and down, "After the girls left, I was able to find what I was looking for. It's something for all of us." He reached into the pocket of his jeans and pulled out a rolled-up plastic baggy filled with brownish-green shredded leaves. "A whole lid of Mexican weed, compadres! Pure Acapulco Gold. I got a great deal."

Jim was shocked, "Shit, John, put that away! You're going to get us all busted. I don't want to rot in a Mexican jail! What's a lid anyway?"

John laughed knowingly and put the baggy back in his pocket. "A lid is an ounce. You don't need to freak out, Jimbo. Nobody in

Mexico gives a shit about pot. We're not going to smoke any of it over here anyway. We've had enough excitement for tonight."

They crossed the main border bridge without any officials stopping them on either side. They managed to walk back to the bus barn by 2:50 AM. Sleepy students were hanging out by the buses, some staggering in and out of the buses to swap seats. It turns out they were not the only ones to take advantage of the lax age limits in Juarez. A handful of other guys seemed a little worse for the wear, particularly the ones who indulged in tequila. One Junior, Bill Welch, was behind the bus garage puking his guts out. Jack, Sam and Jim were able to slip into the back of the bus unnoticed, before Father Otto and Mr. Poole returned from checking on the mechanics. The boys continued to lay low for the next couple of days until their wounds were less apparent. Mike sobered up enough to get into the bus without drawing much attention. Remarkably, all of the students who crossed the border made it back before Father Otto's deadline. The adults gave no indication of being aware that some students had returned totally strung out.

The crippled bus clutch was replaced, and the Royal Rabble were on their way out of El Paso by 8:30 AM. The passengers in all three buses were extremely subdued. Some kids looked semi-comatose. The Regis Royals' road trip rolled on across the New Mexico desert.

They arrived in Albuquerque around noon. Their destination was the Sandia Peak Tramway. Father Otto thought spending the afternoon hiking the trails at the top of the tram, on the gentler east side of the mountain, would provide a cool respite from the desert's blast furnace heat. Then they would continue driving overnight to Tucson.

The Royals started coming alive as they entered the tramway parking lot. They were anxious to stretch their legs. They grew excited looking up at the majestic reddish massif in front of them. Iowans who dwell in an undulating sea of corn and soybean fields are awestruck by mountains. For them, approaching a mountain range was like Dorothy gazing upon the Emerald City or Moses looking down on the Promised Land. The prospect of a lazy afternoon walking alpine paths seemed like the perfect antidote for the hangovers from their Juarez misadventures.

The throng of Royals filled several tram cars, so they arrived at the top sequentially in groups of 15-20. The 4,000-foot ascent took about 15 minutes. Warren, Julie, Sandy, Jim, and Tim were on the second tram car. Warren started organizing their excursion before they disembarked. "We should get far from the maddening crowd up here. We've been crammed together like sardines for the last three days. Let's explore the untamed realms of this mountain."

As soon as the tram doors opened the five mountaineers scampered away from the others, skipping the visitors center and snack bar. They headed past the Crest Trail sign and soon came to a sign saying, "La Luz Trail." They could see it winding down the cliffs they had just soared over. Warren spotted a rock outcropping about a half mile south of the trail. "Hey, that looks like it would be a cool place to hang out. The views would be spectacular, and we'd have the whole place to ourselves."

The bushwhack from the trail to the rock overlook seemed treacherous, but manageable, so they agreed to give it a go. They descended the steep La Luz trail, rounding five long switchbacks. They left the trail when it appeared they were at about the same level as their destination. They traversed a steep slope for a few hundred yards, then crossed a narrow meadow that took them to the base of the rocks they wanted to settle in. They scrambled up and over to the west side of the outcropping. The view was indeed breathtaking. Their hearts raced when they looked down the sheer drop-off below. After a few minutes, they became acclimated to the precarious setting, and they relaxed a bit.

Warren let out a big sigh and said, "Well, gang, I think it's time we all get a little higher."

Sandy was puzzled, "What do mean? We just got here. I don't want to go back up yet. I thought you wanted to hang out here."

"I do, but that doesn't mean we can't get a little higher." Warren pulled out a plastic baggy from his jeans. "John split his stash with me. I'm going to roll up a joint. We can all take a few hits if you want."

Julie and Sandy didn't know about John's score in Juarez and they were thrown for a loop. Julie said, "What the hell is that? Is that marijuana?

Sandy asked, "Where did John get that? Was it in Juarez?"

Warren grinned, "Yeah, he said it's pure Acapulco Gold. It's good shit."

Tim was quite sure none of them had ever smoked marijuana before, including Warren. He doubted any of them had ever been in the presence of marijuana. Not that they hadn't been curious about it. There had been an enormous buzz about pot for the past year. It was becoming a defining feature of the burgeoning counterculture. The primary barrier to them satisfying their curiosity was that they didn't have a clue where to find marijuana in Waterloo.

Given Jim's reaction to seeing the dope in Juarez, Tim was surprised that Jim was the first to say, "OK, there's no time like the present. Let's do it." Jim had gone through quite a metamorphosis from his pudgy days in the third grade. They both went out for track as freshmen, but Jim stuck with it. Jim started the year at the back of the pack, but he quickly began losing weight, which motivated him to continue getting into better shape. He became more competitive as the season progressed. He started winning races during his sophomore year. Jim had always been an outgoing talker, but his new trimmer, athletic physique spurred him on to success in other endeavors, like theater and being the lead singer in a rock combo called "The Sharks."

They all agreed to take a few puffs of pot, so Warren took out a packet of Zig-Zag rolling papers that John had also purchased in Juarez. Sandy asked, "Do you know what you're doing Warren?"

"Not really, but I saw it done once on a news report about the increasing marijuana menace. It's done like those cowboys in movies roll their cigarettes. It's not that complicated."

It turns out, it was that complicated. Warren struggled to stuff the grass into the paper and roll the joint, while sitting on a rock ledge, balancing the plastic baggy and papers between his knees. He made a mess of it on his first three tries, spilling reefer out the sides of the paper and onto his lap. On each attempt, the whole project would disintegrate between his fingers.

Julie became exasperated, "For crying out loud, Warren, give it to me."

Warren fumbled the joint fixings over to Julie. On her first attempt she was able to come up with a reasonably sound, but loose and asymmetrical, doobie. She licked it and handed it back to Warren. He lit it, took a long deep hit, held it four or five seconds, then coughed the smoke out spasmodically for the next minute. When Warren regained his composure, he held the joint out towards Tim and said, "Wow, that was a rush! Here, give it a try."

Part of Tim was extremely reluctant to cross the threshold of getting genuinely stoned for the first time in his life. He didn't know what to expect and he worried that he might not be able to handle it. But the allure of experiencing an altered consciousness overcame his reticence. He was entering an age with a strong sense of becoming, without any sense of what to become. He thought it would be reasonable to explore different ways of being, on a route to becoming something. He plucked the joint from Warren and took a long drag. He held it for one second before the smoke exploded in his lungs. He erupted into a hacking fit and quickly passed the joint to Julie while he was still recovering.

Julie, and then Sandy, took more cautious hits, but they still coughed out the smoke. Jim took the joint from Sandy. After observing the others' techniques and struggles, he tried a different approach. Instead of one big long drag, he inhaled it in three short bursts. Consequently, he was able to hold it in for five or six seconds, then he exhaled slowly without coughing. They looked at each other approvingly and then adopted Jim's method for their second and third rounds passing the joint.

They sat there on their rock roost for a couple of minutes, gazing out over Albuquerque, without saying a word, waiting to see what would happen next. The sunlight passed through and around scattered clouds. Slowly swirling colors, shades and shadows moved along the Rio Grande River below and the vastness beyond. Gradually, the landscape and colors became brighter, sharper, almost crystalline.

Jim's head was cocked to the side, with his mouth slightly open. He appeared to be in a trance. Then he said, "Everything seems really, really different out there."

Sandy nodded, "Yeah, it does seem different."

Warren said, "I wonder if it's really different or if it only seems different."

Tim chuckled, "It only seems to seem different."

Julie laughed and said, "That seems to seem about right to me."

They all roared with laughter and Jim said, "It only seems to seem to seem about right."

Tim was busting a gut and said, "Nothing seems like it seems."

Sandy snorted, "Yes, and that seems to seem all wrong!"

Warren raised both of his arms and pronounced, "It seems that we're all stoned."

Everything they said after that struck them as hilarious. They reflected on the previous 48 hours of the Regis road show and all the different characters in their troupe. Everything and everybody were uproariously funny. Tim thought he had never laughed so hard. As the revelry continued, Tim had another thought that was becoming clearer and irresistible. He and Julie had been friends for so many years that he had taken their relationship for granted. Sitting on that ledge, sharing that spectacular view, laughing together, experiencing new sensations together, he realized that he didn't just like Julie, he was attracted to her. She was pretty, clever, daring and a lot of fun to be with. They were soulmates. He guessed that she felt the same way about him. He had an overwhelming urge to embrace her and kiss her. He was restrained by the thought of the intense ribbing he would get from their friends. He also didn't want to knock them both over the precipice that was only a few feet away. He resolved that at the first opportunity to be alone with Julie he would confess his true feelings for her.

None of them had any idea how much time had gone by, when Sandy looked at her watch and said, "Oh man, we need to get going. We're supposed to be back at the bus in a half hour."

Warren had an idea, "We can save a lot of time by skipping those switchbacks. If we head straight up from here, I think we'll hit the top of the La Luz trail close to where it joins the Crest Trail."

They agreed it was a brilliant strategy. Unfortunately, they were all totally wrong. It was the consequence of their inexperience navigating mountains, coupled with their hazy euphoria. Warren had seriously miscalculated the course of the trail. The switchbacks he planned to shortcut led farther to the north, where it intersected the Crest Trail.

They climbed down from the rocks and crossed back over the meadow. The slope above the meadow quickly became steeper as they picked their way around boulders and shrubs. They came to the bottom of a long rock face. They could see a route up and over the rocks that had some hand and foot holds. The pitch of the slope above the rocks seemed to level off a bit. Warren started to climb first, followed by Sandy and Julie. Tim motioned to Jim to go next, but Jim hesitated. He turned to Tim and said, "I'm not sure I can do this."

Tim was baffled, "What do you mean you can't do this? You have to."

"I don't know what's come over me, Tim. I started to freak out as soon as I saw this sheer cliff. I was feeling a little dizzy at times back there on the ledge, but it was manageable while I was sitting down. Now I feel paralyzed. I don't know if I can move. I've had some problems with vertigo when I get on ladders, but nothing like this."

"Look Jim, we don't have time to backtrack to the trail and we're not going to leave you here. It's perfectly safe, just go slow and don't look down."

Julie yelled down, "What's going on?"

Tim responded, "No problem, we're coming."

Jim reached up, grabbed two rock handles and raised one leg up to a foothold. He paused there and looked back down at Tim with wide, watery eyes. He didn't say anything. Tim thought Jim might throw up.

Tim took a step up, getting close to Jim's ear, and whispered, "You can do this Jim."

Jim painstakingly alternated between hand and foot holds until he had climbed about ten feet, then he froze. Tim was a few feet below him and called up, "How are you doing, man?"

Jim's voice was trembling, "My head wants to keep going, but I can't convince my arms and legs to move."

Tim thought for a moment, then calmly said, "You won't have to Jim. We'll move them for you. Just close your eyes and let us do it for you."

Tim hollered to the others, "Hey guys, Jim isn't feeling well, and he needs some help. Can you come down and give us a hand?"

Julie reversed her climbing sequence and descended until she was close enough to Jim for her to reach his hands, which were latched tight to two rocks above his head. Sandy followed and positioned herself parallel to Julie on the other side of Jim. Warren asked if they needed him, but there wasn't enough room for anyone else.

Tim told Jim, "Just keep your eyes closed. We'll position your hands and feet where they need to go. Julie, Sandy, grab Jim's wrists. I'm going to boost him up to the next foothold, then you pull him up to the next handholds. Tell him exactly where you're going to put each hand." Tim put his left hand under Jim's heel and his shoulder on the bottom of Jim's butt. After Tim secured his stance, he called out, "OK, now on the count of three - one, two, three." With the aid of the girls pulling, Tim pushed up on Jim's butt and attempted to guide Jim's foot up to next place it could be anchored. Jim's heel slipped out of Tim's hand and sprung back into Tim's chin. The foot knocked Tim away from the rock wall and left him dangling by his right hand. Jim instinctively started to kick his leg in an attempt to find a foothold. He inadvertently kicked Tim in the face. Tim shook off the blow and swung back to grab Jim's ankle. Jim was able to raise his leg to the next foothold. He opened his eyes momentarily and was able raise his other foot on his own to get locked into a new position. They continued this routine up another ten feet or more.

They were getting exhausted, but there was only another four or five feet remaining to reach the ledge above. Jim was breathing rapidly and said, "You need to give me a couple of minutes guys."

Julie got close to Jim, put her hand on his chin and turned his face towards hers. "Jim, look at me." Then she closed her eyes and gave him a long hard kiss. Jim's eyes popped wide open. Julie kept her face close to Jim and said, "Listen, I've been wanting to tell you this since the trip started.   I think you're wonderful. You're a really cool guy and I love how you sing on stage. When we get to that ledge up there, I'm going to give you a big hug and kiss you like a you're a rock star."

They were all surprised, but Tim was also crestfallen. He wanted to let go of Jim's foot and hurl himself off the cliff. Instead, he heard Julie call, "OK, everybody, one last push on the count of three… one, two three!" This time, Jim didn't hardly need their help. He thrust himself high enough for Warren to reach down, clutch Jim's wrist and pull him up over the top of the ledge. Sandy climbed up next, followed by Julie and then Tim. They gave each other hugs, but Tim only feigned a hug with Julie. She then turned to Jim, put her arms around his neck and gave him another passionate smooch.

Sandy and Warren whooped. Warren said, "Jesus guys, get a room."

Jim smiled and blushed, "Thanks guys, that was really embarrassing. It shouldn't have been such a big deal for me to climb up here, but it wasn't something I could control. The pot made me really dizzy and I couldn't move."

The remaining slope to the top of the ridge was steep, but walkable. By the time they reached the top, they were sweaty and dusty. They were also way overdue to be back at the bus. Father Otto and Mr. Poole were waiting for them at the top of the tram. They were relieved to see the missing trekkers, but not happy. Mr. Poole sounded exasperated, "Where in the world were you kids"?

Jim quickly answered, "We got off on the wrong trail in the woods and lost track of where the tram was. We ended up going way too far south."

When they got back down to the buses, everyone was pissed off at them. They were over an hour late. The parking lot was radiating blistering waves of heat. The drivers didn't want to keep the buses idling for fear the engines might overheat, so everyone had been sweltering without air-conditioning. The five offenders had to absorb the hostility of the raging Royals. They sat down quietly and looked contrite. The atmosphere in the bus melted away any lingering high they might have had from the weed. The sun set two hours after they left Albuquerque. They rolled on into the desert night towards Tucson. Tim nodded in and out of sleep. He felt wasted and demoralized. Once again, he had experienced a thrilling emotional high, followed by a crushing defeat and dejection. This time, in only a matter of minutes.

Chapter 10
Wise Man from the West

Tucson glistened in the early morning desert sunlight. The Royals slowly roused from their slumped, contorted slumber. The buses turned onto University Boulevard and crept down the long, manicured, deep green lawn of the University of Arizona Main Mall, lined with towering palm trees. They slowly spilled out of the buses and began to orient themselves to the beautiful, expansive academic oasis. The Regis delegation registered for the JCL convention at the Student Union Memorial Center. There they learned that they had, by far, the largest contingent of any school in the country. Prior to their arrival, there had been a growing buzz about Regis being an emerging hotbed of Latin revival and that they were champions of classical scholarship.

Their questionable academic profile aside, the Royals would be more accurately described as the most disheveled and hygienically challenged students on campus. No other group had traveled overland so far. They'd been crated together for four days, often in hot, steamy conditions. They were in desperate need of showers. The girls and boys were guided to their separate dormitories. Before the trip began, Jim and Tim had briefly discussed rooming together, but when Tim got off the bus, he approached Warren about sharing a room, and he agreed. Tim wasn't angry or resentful with Jim. He just didn't want to be around him if he started to reflect on what happened with Julie. The thought of it was too much of a bummer.

The rooms were spartan and sterile, but Tim was excited to be housed in a university dormitory. It offered him a tantalizing preview into the college lifestyle he hoped to experience in a couple of years. After settling into their own rooms, the boys started mingling in each other's rooms, plotting how they were going to optimize their time on campus. Small groups ventured out to get the lay of the land. The rest of the day was laid back. They thumbed through the JCL Convention materials and scanned local radio stations. They cleaned up for the welcoming ceremony that evening. The keynote address would feature their own Regis Royal favorite son, President Ted. They scrubbed off the grime from the road, combed their hair, drawing a sharp straight part on the side, donned white short-sleeve dress shirts, black slacks, and clip-on ties. They were as clean-cut as young men could be.

Dinner was on their own in the Student Union cafeteria. Warren, Jim, Steve, and Tim ambled into the bustling dining room and surveyed the scene. They were delighted to see a wide assortment of quality food offerings. There was no comparison with the breaded fish sticks and pizza bread entrees in the Regis cafeteria. Pizza and spaghetti were considered exotic ethnic foods in Iowa. Tim's family would occasionally dine on the wild side and stretch their culinary boundaries with canned chow mien vegetables served over canned dried noodles. The UA serving line had entire sections of authentic Asian and Mexican cuisines, most of which Tim had never tasted before. The boys maximized their food trays' potential with stacks of tacos, burritos, and enchiladas. To test their virility, they grabbed packets of extra hot sauce. They commandeered a table next to the dining room windows. They gazed outside and observed the high school conventioneers streaming in and out of the Student Union. John's prediction had been correct. There seemed to be significantly more girls than boys. Everyone was smartly attired. The girls were either wearing summer dresses or skirts. The boys wore dress shirts and ties, some even had bow ties. Tim was reminded of telling his mother there would be lots of honor students here.

One boy caught their attention, although at first, they weren't sure if he was a boy. He was slender, with fine features, and he had long wavy brown hair that tumbled down to his shoulders. He was wearing the standard white short-sleeve shirt and dark slacks, but he added his own flare. His tie exploded with vibrantly colored flowers and over it hung a silver necklace with a large silver peace symbol medallion. The outside bottom of his pant legs had been split about 10 inches high, triangles of paisley print fabric had been sewn in to create wide flamboyant bellbottoms. At Regis, it was considered rebellious for boys to have hair that came over the top their ears. Except for rock bands on television, they had never seen hair so long on a boy.   They overheard snarky comments coming from four guys at the next table. One strapping lad said, "Hey look, we have ourselves a real live hippie."

Another thoughtful young scholar said, "Yeah, but is that a hippie guy or a hippie chick"?

When the long-haired wonder entered the dining room, the blokes at the next table started to whistle and taunt, "Hey there good looking." "How you doing honey?"

The boy casually walked by them, oblivious to their jeering. He acted as though he had heard it all before and it just rolled off his back. He went through the serving line and sat down at a table by himself. A minute later, two very good-looking girls, one with long blonde hair and the other with dark curly hair, joined him. The three of them were very friendly and animated. The girls were clearly, unabashedly attracted to him.

Jim said, "He looks like a musician or maybe some kind of artist."

Warren said, "Whatever he is, he seems to be a babe magnet."

Tim surmised it was the rock-star effect, which provoked a tinge of resentment, stemming from the Jim and Julie incident. The fellow intrigued Tim, and he was determined to learn more about this long-haired lover boy.

Student President Ted Kemp's keynote address did himself and the Regis Royals proud. He looked the part of a nerdy high school Latin student, rail-thin, horn-rimmed glasses and a bit awkward, but he exhibited a sarcastic wit that was unexpected and entertaining. "Good evening patricians, plebeians and centurions. It's both exhilarating and disturbing to see you all amassed here together, co-mingling as it were, for the 40th annual assembly of the Junior Classical League. By the end of the week, you will all be sorted into your proper social classes, as deemed by the gods. Over the next few days, the weak among you will be culled during the academic competitions and athletic games, banished to your dormitory cells to ponder your bleak futures. The rest of us will bask in the rarefied air of victory. Otherwise known as the Student Union terrace dining room.

"Some might ask, what would hundreds of teenagers be doing at a Greek and Latin convention? Seriously, what the heck are we doing here? We should all ask ourselves, what the heck am I doing here? *Quod ego sum facis hic?* Let me hear you ask, *Quod ego sum facis hic? Quod ego sum facis hic?*" Ted repeated the Latin question until the crowd picked up the chant. Ted raised his hands to ask for quiet before he continued, "Some would say we're here because of our love of Latin and Greek, and our devotion to keeping these ancient languages alive. Some would say it's because we value classical cultures and philosophy. But I say the answer is found in the immortal words of Socrates and Seneca. We are all here because, '*Quod erit amet.*' It will be fun! Let me hear you say it, *Quod erit amet, Quod erit amet, Quod erit amet!*' The students quickly picked-up the cheer. "*Quod erit amet,*" became the mantra for the rest of the convention. They said it as a greeting and a goodbye. They said it whenever they discussed what to do next. Warren and Tim even said it before they went to sleep. It became their guiding principle, their north star.

Back in the dorm room, Jim, Mike Warren, and Tim lamented Joe's absence. Tim was sure Joe would be urging them to optimize their experience, "Man, Joe would be loving all of this. If he were here, we wouldn't be moping around in this room. We'd be somewhere out there, exploring everything Arizona has to offer."

Jim agreed. "Yeah, Joe would be sneaking us into the clubs downtown at night and leading us up Mount Lemon during the day."

The thought of Joe's wanderlust was inspiring Warren, "Man, the palm trees around here have me thinking about California. I'm 90% of the way from Iowa to Surf City. I can almost taste the salt air. I've got to find a way to get myself on a surfboard."

Tim's impatience became a call to action, "Come on people! Joe doesn't need to be here for us to figure out how to have a good time. Warren, you don't have to be in California to surf."

Warren shot Tim a look that said he was talking nonsense, "What the hell are you talking about Tim?"

Tim jumped down from the top bunk and opened the door to the hallway. "Come here guys. What do you see?" The hallway was long, empty and quiet. It was after 11:00 p.m. and most everyone else on their floor had crashed.

Warren and Jim leaned out of the door and looked down the hallway. Tim leaned out behind them and whispered, "Use your imaginations compadres. I see a long run of blue and white frothy breakers crashing down that hallway. I see the three of us rocketing in front of them on our boards, dancing on the curls and hanging ten with our toes. *'Quod erit amet' guys.*"

Tim walked to the sink, picked up the empty metal waste basket underneath it and started filling it with water. Jim and Warren looked at Tim bewildered. Tim took the waste basket into the hallway and threw the water down on the hall's shiny linoleum floor. The water quickly spread the width of the hallway and reached almost to the end by the elevators. Tim walked back to the sink and filled the basket again. This time, he turned the other way and again threw the water down the hallway. He went back into their room and got his bottle of shampoo. He walked the length of the hall squirting shampoo back and forth along the floor. He turned to Warren and Jim, raised his arms, and said exuberantly, "Surf's up!"

They took off their shirts, pants, shoes, and socks. They splashed their way down to the end of the hall by the elevators. One by one, they took a short running start and then glided down the slick hallway floor, bending their knees, mimicking surfboard riders. With each successive run they became more daring, crouching lower, spinning, pirouetting, and sometimes falling on their butts. As they became more raucous, dorm room doors started to pop open. Guys from other rooms joined in, flying down the sudsy linoleum surf, shooting the hallway pipeline. Some of the older guys had been playing poker in John and Sam's room at the other end of the hall. They had stumbled on a clear channel radio station out of San Diego that was featuring the Beach Boys. They brought their transistor radio into the hall, which provided the perfect soundtrack for the faux beach party. They slid along and sang along to, "Good Vibrations," "Help Me Rhonda," "Barbara Ann," "Surfer Girl" and "Surfin' USA."

The revelry continued to escalate. Several booster shots of water were thrown down the hallway. Soapy bubbles floated through the air. As their voices became louder, the volume on the radio was turned up, which prompted them to further ramp up their own volume. They were so totally absorbed in the joy of the moment that they totally lost track of their circumstances and surroundings. They were in a foreign dormitory, on a foreign campus, in a foreign state.

Mike tried to raise his game. He raced down the hall in his underwear, with his shirt off, and threw himself on the floor, belly flopping with his arms outstretched in front of him. When he slowly slid to a stop at the end of the hallway, the stairway exit door opened and Father Otto stepped in front of him. Mike looked up, flashed a grimacing smile, and said, "Good evening, Father."

Father Otto raised his gaze from Mike's chagrin grin to the frozen figures down the hall. Most of the guys quickly retreated to their rooms and slammed their doors, leaving a half dozen captives stranded in Father's disapproving gaze. They didn't move as Father sloshed his way down the hallway. He halted a few feet from them, raised his arms out to the side with his palms outstretched, and in a surprisingly controlled tone said, "Come here boys." As they gathered around him, he put a hand on Tim's shoulder. Mike meekly joined them in his soaked underwear. Father put his other hand on Mike's shoulder.

Father looked each one of them in their eyes and began speaking, lowly and slowly, "I was in my room, sitting by the window, enjoying the freshness of the dry desert air and the fragrances of the campus foliage. Imagine my bewilderment when I felt a drop of rain on my forehead. There was no indication of showers in the night sky. I looked up at the ceiling the moment a second drop landed on my eyelid. I stood up and followed a line of water running across the ceiling from the middle of the transom. I assumed this was the result of a leaky pipe and I wanted to investigate further before calling Campus Facilities. Now I see that the culprit is not a pipe. Instead, I find the source of the problem is some young men that I had mistakenly trusted. The source of the problem is that those young men lacked respect for their hosts, respect for their own school's reputation, and lacked respect for themselves. Now round up all the others. Then go to your rooms, grab all the towels you can find and clean up your mess. I'll speak with the university in the morning to see what the extent of your restitution should be."

Father Otto calmly turned around and walked back down the hallway, slightly slipping a few times along the way. After he passed through the exit door, Tim said flatly, "*Quod erit amet.*"

Mike turned to him and said, "Shut the fuck up, Tim."

The following morning, Tim attended his first JCL competitive event, Greco-Roman wrestling. These were not serious competitions. They were designed to encourage student interactions and build camaraderie among the attendees. Twelve JCL scholars signed up for

90

wrestling, eight boys and four girls. Jim was the only other Regis student in the group. Tim was surprised to see that the long-haired man of mystery from the cafeteria had registered for the same session. Adding to the intrigue, two of the jocks who had taunted him were also there. Everyone's attire was teenage civilian, t-shirts, shorts, and sandals. The event was officiated by a jovial middle-aged JCL instructor, Mr. Growder. He wore a pin-striped toga and a baseball cap.

"Welcome ladies and gentlemen to the first session of the JCL Classical Games of 1967. Here you will engage one another in spirited competition, with honor and good cheer. May the goddess Nike inspire your performances, so that you can be crowned with the laurel wreath of victory. The young ladies will be competing in the grass circle to my right and the young men will compete in the grass circle behind me. The boys will be divided into two size groups, which I will determine. Let's first introduce ourselves. Please share your first name and where you are from."

The competitors learned that the burley blonde bullies, George and Chuck, were from Youngstown Ohio. The teenage Jesus figure, Josh, lived in El Cerrito, California. The four girls were all friends from the same school in Appleton, Wisconsin. They signed-up for the Greco-Roman event as a lark.

There was no question which size group Tim would be assigned to. Jim barely made the cut to the bigger group, that included the loudmouth jocks. When Mr. Growder told the slender hippie to join the smaller unit, he protested, "Excuse me sir, but I'd prefer to be in the bigger group."

"Suit yourself young man. I just want everyone to have a good time."

The jocks were puzzled by the hippie's request. Josh calmly stepped over to the biggie batch of gladiators. Tim detected a slight smirk on Josh's face as he positioned himself right next to Chuck, the larger of the two loudmouths.

Mr. Growder explained the rules. The matches would be abbreviated, just one three-minute period. Greco-Roman rules only allow holds above the waist, so Tim couldn't use any of his favorite leg takedown maneuvers. He was matched with Kevin, a scrawny kid from Brookline Massachusetts, who was about a dime taller and a nickel lighter than Tim. Kevin was lighthearted about the event. He confessed that he had no competitive wrestling experience. He had never even seen a wrestling match. He had assumed the other young classical scholars were equally inexperienced. Tim hadn't lost all of the muscle mass from his stint on the wrestling team, so despite being limited to upper body holds, he was able to quickly dispatch Kevin by getting behind him and throwing him to the grass. Kevin seemed to get a kick out of being thrown around. He giggled his way out of the circle. Tim appreciated Kevin's sense of humor, but it made the win less satisfying. Although Jim was not a wrestler, he was from Iowa, so he knew enough to efficiently defeat his bigger, but out-of-shape opponent, Larry from Chattanooga.

They progressed through the matches, which were filled with lots of joking around and laughter. The two girl matchups were surprisingly fierce, especially given they were supposed to be friends. The girls seemed to relish the opportunity to mix it up. The last match was the marquee event of the morning, Josh versus Chuck. Chuck was clearly anxious for a chance to dominate the wispy figure who had foolishly asked to challenge him. He bobbed up and down waiting for the start. In contrast, Josh looked nonchalant, even serene, standing still, with his arms crossed, maintaining the same slight smile.

Mr. Growder blew his whistle and Chuck immediately attacked. When he lunged, Josh nimbly stepped to the side and Chuck stumbled past him. Chuck turned and took another shot, but Josh again jumped to the side. Chuck was becoming flustered. He spread out his arms on the third assault, ready to grab Josh if he tried leaping to either side. This time Josh stood still. Instead of jumping away, he grabbed Chuck's right wrist and forearm with both of his hands. He turned backwards, bent over, stuck his hip into Chuck's abdomen and pulled him over his shoulder, throwing him to the ground. Chuck landed on the grass with a thud. He sat up, looking stunned for a moment and then flashed anger. He jumped back on his feet. He charged at Josh again. This time Josh grabbed Chuck's left wrist with both hands, spun under his arm, twisting it, while making a windmill motion, flipping Chuck into a somersault, and planting Chuck's back harshly on the ground. Chuck took a little longer to sit up, then he unsteadily stood up. The spectators could see the embarrassment and fury in Chuck's ruby-red cheeks. He no longer wanted to defeat Josh, he wanted to pulverize him.

Mr. Growler looked concerned that the match was becoming too serious, but he wasn't quite sure what to do. Josh turned to him and asked, "Excuse me sir, how much time do we have left?

Mr. Growler looked at his stopwatch, "Ahhh... you still have two minutes, but we could call it a draw now."

Josh turned to Chuck and said, "What do you say Chuck? Shall we call it a day?

Without saying a word, Chuck made one last charge. Josh again stood still, but this time he made a move that looked vaguely familiar to Tim. He took a wide stance and bent forward. When Chuck made contact, Josh wrapped his arms around Chuck's torso and dug his shoulder into Chuck's abdomen. The force of Chuck's charge hitting Josh's shoulder, bent Chuck backwards. He fell on his back with Josh on top of him. He was immediately pinned to the ground. Mr. Growler quickly took Josh's wrist, raised it up and declared Josh the winner. "Splendidly done gentlemen. Congratulations to all of you for competing with such strong hearts and good humor. Now on to your next session." He then handed out plastic laurel head crowns to all of the victors.

Jim and Tim walked away with Josh. They looked back and saw George giving Chuck a hard time about his humiliating defeat.

Tim was baffled by what just happened, "What was that you were doing back there?"

Josh nonchalantly replied, "The first two throws were Judo moves. The last one was more Jiu-Jitsu."

Tim was only vaguely familiar with Judo and Karate, having only seen them demonstrated a few times on TV. The whole martial arts scene had not yet taken hold in most of America. Tim had no idea what Jiu-Jitsu was. Regardless, Jim and Tim were enormously impressed.

Josh asked, "What sessions are you guys going to next?"

Jim said, "We're both signed up for some races over at the stadium, but we're not that into it. What about you?"

"I'm registered for the Latin Jeopardy contest at the Memorial Union, but I'm not really into that either. Would you like to get stoned instead, then get some lunch?"

Jim and Tim looked at each other wide-eyed. Then Tim said, "Well sure, but where can we go to get stoned?"

Josh shrugged, "I think we can just walk along and keep our distance from everybody else. I have a joint already rolled on me."

They sauntered down the middle of the University's long front lawn, passing a joint between them, blissfully oblivious to Arizona's draconian penalties for possession of marijuana. They crossed Campbell Avenue and entered a pleasant, shady residential neighborhood. It felt liberating and exhilarating to escape the campus. Then again, it might have just been that they were getting more than a little loaded.

Tim was anxious to know more about this hip figure who so casually suggested getting high at 10:30 in the morning. "So, Josh, where exactly is El Cerrito, California?"

After exhaling a long hit off the joint he replied, "It's in the East Bay, north of Berkeley."

Jim was impressed, "East Bay, you mean San Francisco Bay? You live in San Francisco?"

Josh was amused by the need for clarification and the apparent mystique San Francisco held for them, "Yeah, the San Francisco Bay area, but I don't go to the city much."

Tim asked the obvious follow-up question, "So, Josh, how's the 'Summer of Love' going?"

The 1967 pronouncement of "The Summer of Love" was a clarion call that rang out from San Francisco's Haight-Ashbury neighborhood, the epicenter of hippiedom in the America. The idea was to generate a critical mass of good karma to hyper-energize the counterculture movement, including support for the civil rights movement, the anti-war movement, free-love and chemically induced altered consciousness. Thousands of young people from all over the country were descending on Haight-Asbury. This extended "Happening" even had its own theme song, "If You're Going to San Francisco," by Scott McKenzie. It had a powerful, romantic appeal for Midwestern teens, but for them it seemed hopelessly distant and unobtainable.

Josh's response was not as enthusiastic as Tim expected, "To be honest, I'm not that into the whole "Flower Power" scene. The Haight has become a freak show. It's hard for me to take it too seriously. I mean, I turn 18 in February, as in draft eligible. I'm going to graduate next spring. I'll likely head to college and get a student deferment for now, but the war is getting too close and too real for me to act that… well, light-hearted. The music scene this summer has been incredible though. I was in Monterey a few weeks ago."

Jim and Tim stopped dead in their tracks. They were getting high with an eyewitness to the Monterey Pop Festival! Jim was unabashedly in awe, "Are you kidding? You were really at Monterey Pop? Who did you see there?"

Josh had experienced first-hand the highest concentration of 60's rock icons that had yet to be assembled. It was the precursor to Woodstock, on a much more intimate scale. This time Josh answered with his own unabashed amazement. "It was far out man. I heard everybody. The emotional intensity of Janis Joplin gave me chills. *The Dead* were playing in their own beautiful zone. Ravi Shankar elevated the entire scene. *The Who* literally destroyed their instruments during their finale. But there was nobody, nobody, like Hendrix. Listening to him was like dropping Sunshine LSD, and I swear, I hadn't taken or smoked anything beforehand. It was like a religious experience when he set his guitar on fire! If you ever get a chance to see any of these people, do whatever it takes."

"Oh man," Jim moaned, "That sounds so cool. I would have given my right frontal lobe to be there."

The importance of music in their lives went way beyond something they just enjoyed. It was their sustenance. They used music to color their world. It shaped their attitudes and their moods. The types of music they listened to were not just a matter of taste, it defined them. It wasn't just the genre of music they preferred; it was where they found it. Although top 40 radio in the 1960's was filled with brilliantly creative music, including an endless string of Beatles hits, the gateway to the counterculture's soundtrack was underground radio. Their musical lifeline in the Midwest was the 50,000-watt, clear signal channel, KAAY in Little Rock. Specifically, Clyde Clifford's late-night show, *Beaker Street,* was their gateway to alternative sounds. The show was eclectic, but primarily featured "Acid Rock." You could also hear the early gestations of "Progressive Rock." *Beaker Street* is where many Midwest youth were introduced to Hendrix, Cream, The Grateful Dead, Led Zeppelin, Pink Floyd, The Mothers of Invention and The Moody Blues. *Beaker Street* was the only place they could listen to long cuts and extended portions of whole albums. The only other place to discover the best new tunes was through their own underground word-of-mouth network. Tim's access was primarily through Joe. For Josh to be able to hear these rock legends live was beyond anything they could have dreamed.

But there was something about Josh that seemed incongruous to Jim. "So how did you go from the Monterey Pop Festival and Jimi Hendrix to a Latin convention in Tucson?"

Josh shrugged, "My girlfriend is really into JCL. She's the student president of the California chapter. She and her girlfriend convinced me to come. I'd never been to Arizona, so what the hell. Besides, I kind of like Latin. There's something kind of mystical about it."

Mystical, that was a spin on Latin Tim hadn't considered. Josh was becoming more intriguing with each hit off the joint. Tim was also pleased to learn that the two girls who joined Josh in the cafeteria were likely his girlfriend and her friend from home. It was less irritating than thinking he was attracting random girls from the available pool attending JCL. The three of them were forming a quick bond. They had already passed through two friendship filters, marijuana, and music.

Decades later, there would be widespread angst about America's fractured cultural landscape, the shredded social fabric, and tribal politics. It's sometimes forgotten how deeply bitter and dangerous those divides were in the 1960s. Youth culture was also tribal. There were tastes and behaviors that not only reflected one's own personality, but they also determined what tribe you belonged to. A teen's attitude about marijuana was one of those determinants. Smoking grass was not just about getting stoned. It was a statement. It was a rejection of all the crap that had been foisted on young people about marijuana, going back to the 1936 movie, *Reefer Madness*. Getting stoned was an act of defiance. An assertion to make up your own mind about what's safe, what's healthy, what's acceptable? It went hand-in-glove with opposing the war and supporting civil rights. It was subversive. Smoking pot was done with friends, by passing a joint or a pipe between friends. It was a shared risk, a shared act of rebellion. Smoking pot together was like taking an oath. Once you found out someone smoked grass, you knew you were in the same tribe. Tim had taken his first hit of pot only days earlier, but his desire to try it began months earlier. His identification with the counterculture had been growing for the past year. When Jim and Tim shared that joint with Josh, Tim felt like they had become blood brothers.

Later that afternoon, Jim and Tim introduced Josh to Warren and Mike. They were also impressed with Josh's California credentials. Mike liked Josh's pedigree, "El Cerrito, I love the sound of California towns."

Josh translated, "It means 'The Hill.' My neighborhood sits up high, overlooking the bay and the city."

Mike continued, "Yeah, but El Cerrito sounds so cool, like the name of a convertible sportscar cruising along the Pacific Coast Highway, or like the burrito special I just ate that was topped with loads guacamole and sour cream."

Josh got a kick out of Mike. "There's nothing I love more than hitting the road in my El Cerrito, pulling up at the drive-in and ordering me an El Cerrito Grande special."

Warren had a different focus, "So which one of the girls sitting with you in the cafeteria yesterday is not your girlfriend?"

Josh smiled and replied, "Kayla is the one with the dark frizzy hair. She's great, but pretty intense. The tall blonde is my girlfriend, Rebecca. I'll introduce you to them."

For the next four days they all became thick as thieves. They mostly blew-off the rest of the JCL program, with the exception of Rebecca, who was committed to her role as the California chapter president. The boys would make strategic appearances at the plenary sessions, ensuring they were observed by Father Otto and Sister Rita. Then they'd bolt for hours at a time. Josh took on the role Tim imagined Joe would have taken, coming up with ideas for excursions around Tucson. Sometimes Julie and Sandy would join them. They explored the shops along 6th Avenue. They spent a couple of hours at the Tucson Art Museum. One morning they broke up into pairs and hitchhiked to Bear Canyon, at the base of the Catalina Mountains.

Hitchhiking was a more common and acceptable mode of transportation for young people in the 1960s. It was a practice used to get around town or around the country, even going coast-to-coast. On some popular routes, there would be lines of hitchhikers waiting their turn for a ride or to be randomly selected by a driver. A few years later, Tim's parents would drive him to the edge of town and drop him off on the side of the highway, where he would hitchhike back to college. Over the years, Tim would hitch from the Midwest to Colorado, to California and up the west coast. All kinds of drivers would give him rides, middle-aged salesmen in suits, grandfatherly types, truckers, a few shady characters, and even young moms with kids in the back. Mostly though, he got rides from other young people, many of whom had hitched themselves. Hitching started to wane during the following decade, following several high-profile murders.

Warren invited Kayla to hitch with him to Bear Canyon. Jim and Mike paired up and Tim went with Josh. They found Bear Canyon on a map in the phone book's Yellow Pages, and they memorized the route. The three pairs arrived at the trailhead parking lot within 15 minutes of each other, which was remarkable, given it took each pair three or four rides to get there. They hiked the canyon trail up to Seven Falls. It was magnificent. It was 11:00 on a Wednesday morning and they had the whole place to themselves. They climbed the falls and splashed around in the pools at each level. They sat down in the highest pool, smoked some pot, laughed until it hurt, and marveled at the desert landscape.

Tim thought about how fleeting their time together would be and he felt an urgent need to know more about Josh and Kayla. Warren was clearly infatuated with Kayla. Tim also thought she was interesting and cute. She reminded him of Janis Ian, a young folk-pop star who had a recent hit called "*Society's Child.*" Tim asked her, "So Kayla, how did you and Josh become friends?"

Kayla chuckled, "We didn't really become friends, we were practically born friends. Our parents have been friends since they were kids. Since we've been toddlers, I've been the one to give Josh a kick in the ass once in a while, to get him out of his own head. I'm the one who introduced Josh to Rebecca. I'm the one who got him a job this past year. His parents wanted to kiss me for that."

Julie asked, "Tell us about your family, Josh. What does your dad do?"

"My dad's a theology professor at the Pacific School of Religion. My mom's a pediatrician."

That revelation excited Julie, "Wow, your mom's a doctor! That's wonderful!

Kayla said, "Yeah, she's been my pediatrician my whole life."

Sandy asked, "So what religion does your dad teach?"

Josh shrugged, "Christianity mostly, but he teaches about all the major world religions. He specializes in the Reformation though. My mom's actually Jewish, so we're all very ecumenical."

Once again, Josh had scrambled Tim's thinking. First, his dad studies and teaches religion, but he doesn't identify with a particular religion, except maybe being a generic Christian. Second, his mother is Jewish. In Tim's world, a mixed marriage is a Catholic married to a Protestant. A Christian father and a Jewish mother would be an exotic marital mash-up. Third, Josh's mom was a doctor! Tim had never heard of such a thing! None of the mothers he knew had jobs outside of their homes, let alone being a doctor.

Jim asked, "So what religion are you, Josh?"

Josh pondered the question for a few seconds, then he said, "I'm not sure what the right label would be, but probably the closest description of what I believe would make me a pagan."

Tim masked his shock and thought, "*A pagan! Did someone in the third grade fail to make their pagan baby payments and baby Josh got away?*" Josh was the first person Tim had ever met who identified as being a pagan. Tim never thought he would ever actually meet a pagan. So much for his image of pagans being headhunters with bones stuck through their noses.

Warren asked, "So what does it mean for you to be a pagan?"

Josh leaned back against a rock and looked at his feet as he moved his legs in and out across the water, making small swirls on the water's surface. "I guess it means that if there is a God in the universe, then the universe is where I look for God. I believe that to understand God, I need to understand the stars and the galaxies. To understand God, I need to understand cells, and molecules and atoms. Of course, I'll never completely understand any of it, but I can marvel at it all. I can seek to understand it. I can seek the truth about it. Maybe that's another definition of what I am. I'm a seeker. Contemplating the mysteries of the universe is how I pray. Nature is where I experience spirituality."

"Well now," Mike said, "That's some pretty heavy cosmic shit you're laying on us, Josh."

Josh softly giggled and raised his gaze. He scanned the waterfalls and the canyon below. The others joined him, silently absorbing their beautiful surroundings; the clear cascading stream; the terracotta canyon walls dressed in Saguaro cacti, Yucca and Desert Broom; the brilliant blue sky accented with cotton ball clouds. It dawned on Tim for the first time that none of them had a camera. He would never have any photographs of this place, of these people, of this day, of this entire trip. They would only be left with the images in their minds. Tim was fine with that.

The following evening after dinner, the tribe, including Rebecca, Julie, and Sandy, set out for Tumamoc Hill. They wanted to watch the sunset from the Steward Observatory overlooking the city. A city bus got them most of the way there. It didn't take long to trek to the top. They found an isolated spot a short distance off the trail, with a 180-degree view looking north across the valley to the Catalina mountains. They didn't have any pot with them on this, their final flight from campus. Josh's meager stash had been exhausted and Warren acquiesced to John's demand for him to return the remainder of his allotment. They didn't miss the herb though. As the sun descended to their left, a spectrum of warm colors flowed east along the clouds. The day's last light sharpened the hues and contrasts on everything below and edged a halo along the top of the mountains' dark silhouette. Lights from the city began to emerge, spreading across the valley like a grounded Milky Way. It was like sitting in the middle of a Maxfield Parrish painting. They were mesmerized.

Jim turned to his California comrades and asked, "What are you guys going to do when you get back home?"

Rebecca answered, "My parents and I are going to tour some college campuses on the East Coast. Then we'll come back and take a look at some options in California."

The notion of touring the country to look at colleges was something that never would have occurred to Tim, and it struck him as extravagant. He had to ask though, "So you're not considering any colleges in the middle of the country?"

Rebecca shrugged and said, "No offense, but it never occurred to me. I'm embarrassed to admit it, but everything between California and the east coast is a big black box to me. That's why meeting you guys has been so great. You've taught me about an alien place I knew nothing about."

100

Mike laughed, "Have no fear Earthlings, we aliens come as friends. We only want to trade our corn in exchange for learning your bizarre West Coast ways."

Kayla wasn't amused by Mike. She said, "Rebecca's an academic superstar. She's a Type A workaholic who excels in everything she tries. Colleges are beating down her door to recruit her. On the other hand, Josh and I are on our way to being blacklisted by most reputable universities."

That surprised Tim, "You're kidding? I assumed you were both star students."

"Oh, our grades aren't the problem," Josh said, "but our high school transcripts might not hold up well against the FBI's shit list. Remember that job Kayla said she got me? It's working for *The Berkeley Barb*. Kayla works there too. I do illustrations and Kayla works in circulation. She wants to become a photographer there.

Sandy asked, "What's *The Berkeley Barb*?"

"It's a newspaper," Kayla explained. "It's distributed around the country, but I'm not surprised you haven't heard of it. It's an underground paper, sort of the west coast version of *The Village Voice*, but more radical. You can't find it most places. *The Barb* reports stories most news media won't cover. It's fighting for civil rights, for worker rights and to the stop the war. That's why the government would love to shut it down. We just assume we're all under FBI surveillance. I wanted to work there as a way to support the anti-war movement. The pay's crap, but we've both learned a lot."

Josh added, "They also run a lot of stories about music and culture. They have some far-out cartoonists too, like R. Crum's 'Keep on Truckin' strip. Man, that guy has to be tripping when he comes up with his ideas. Think of the *Berkeley Barb* as *Mad Magazine* grown up, dropping acid and becoming a revolutionary. I think you guys would like it. If you want, Kayla can get you free subscriptions."

Kayla went on, "We plan to start our own underground school paper this fall. The El Cerrito High School student newspaper is called the Gaucho Gazette. We're going to call our paper the Gonzo Gazette."

Julie asked, "What does Gonzo mean?"

Josh said, "Gonzo means a lot of things, daring, unconventional, a bit bonkers and badass. I like to think it means telling stories some people don't want known. We're prepared to let the chips fall where they may. We want to open some eyes at El Cerrito High. We'll show the faculty and administration what's really on students' minds and we'll let the students know how they can open their minds. We'll do most of our own reporting and writing, but *The Barb* said we can also reprint their stories about the war and corruption. I expect the shit will hit the fan every time an issue of the *Gonzo Gazette* come out."

Kayla jumped up and raised her fist, "At least now we'll be the ones throwing their shit back at them, rather than just eating their shit!"

Rebecca sighed, "I'm just afraid you guys will be the ones in deep shit."

Kayla looked down at all of us sitting. She spoke like a lovely little Lenin. "There comes a time when we all have to decide who we are? Are we just going to be witnesses to injustice or are we going to take responsibility for doing something about it? Are we going to be pawns of corporate interests or are we going to reject their exploitation? Are we going to be victims of the military machine or are we going to shut down the war? Morality and immorality aren't just about what we do, it's also about what we fail to do."

So, there it was, Tim's Tucson takeaway. Who he was, who he would become, what kind of life he would have, would be the sum of all the things he doesn't do, as much as what he does. Reflecting on those photos in his bedroom would amount to a life of illusions, if he doesn't engage with the world those photos portray. Each day he'll be presented with choices shaped by forces outside of his control. From there, he will have to own his life, by intention or by default. Some choices will lead him down short paths, some circular routes, and some will require course corrections. Some will be the beginnings of lifelong journeys, like stumbling into 7th period Latin or deciding to take a walk with Josh.

They expected memories would be made at the toga party on their last night at the JCL National Assembly. The scene that greeted them in the Student Union ballroom certainly left a lasting impression. Consistent with their modus operandi, the boys arrived late, and the festivities were well underway. The expansive ballroom was adorned with the trappings of the Roman Forum, including carboard columns, cardboard statues, and banners with the Roman eagle standard placed all around the perimeter. The real head-snapper was the couple of thousand students and adults decked-out in colorful tunics and shawls. Many of the students took creative liberties with their toga designs. Some togas bore school logos and mascots. Some were autographed by friends, like in a yearbook. Some of the guys looked like Roman senators, but they updated their haute couture with ties and baseball caps. Others were gladiators, with shields and swords. Apparently, gladiator helmets were in short supply, so some of the guys made do with football helmets.

It was the girls who stole the show. There's nothing more fetching than teenage girls wrapped in sheets. Some of their togas were long gowns slit on the side. Some were as short as tennis skirts. This was, after all, the era of the miniskirt. They all had colorful ropes or bejeweled belts around their waists.

Tim's mom had given it her best shot, but his toga was a bit drab, so he livened it up with a tie-dyed shawl. It was his first attempt at tie-dye, and it was pretty much a mess, but he was proud of how distinctive it looked. Jim and Tim topped off their outfits with their laurel victory crowns.

The band also wore togas, with shawls printed like sheet music. In a departure from the Roman Forum theme, the music rocked! They were playing the Young Rascals hit "Good Lovin" when Jim and Tim walked in. Teen dances often start slow, and it takes a while to get folks out on the dance floor. The unique nature of this event gave everyone a sense of urgency to get the party rolling. The floor was already packed with frenzied dancers.

Warren wasted no time and dashed away to find Kayla. Jim wandered off. Tim assumed he was looking for Julie. Mike was already roving the dance floor looking for unattached girls. Tim felt an urgent need to find a dance partner and he started to look for Sandy. Then it hit him that there were hundreds of girls there that he hadn't met yet, and he would never have another chance to meet. The room was flush with possibilities that emboldened him. He quickly recalled what the guys referred to as "The ART," (Ask Rejection Theory). Some core ART assumptions were: 1. Girls at dances are with other girls about 90% of the time. 2. Any guy can find a girl to dance with at least 10% of the time. 3. The more groups of girls you ask to dance, the quicker you'll find the one in ten that will accept. 4. Being rejected by a group of girls counts the same as being rejected by one girl. The ART also entailed several asking tactics. One tactic Tim had tried, with mixed results, was called, "The PH Factor," (Proxy Hunk Factor). The steps were as follows: 1. Find a tall, handsome male model type guy. 2. Approach a girl or group of girls and tell them your friend, the tall stud, let's call him Bobby, would like to dance with them, but Bobby is really shy. If they agree to dance with Tim, Bobby would be willing to cut in. 3. Once on the dance floor, try to make a quick impression, before the girl asks about Bobby. If necessary, confess the ruse, hope she's a good sport and she's having a good enough time to keep dancing.

The frenetic dancing, the pulsating rock and roll, and the toga attire, infused Tim with a sense of abandon. He didn't feel the need to use the PH Factor, but he stuck with the ART principles. He was confident that turning on his charm and his own brand of sex appeal would be enough to land him a dance partner, which was delusional. He approached three attractive girls standing close to the dance floor with the swagger of a young Caesar. "Good evening, ladies. My name is Timothy, son of Mac, from the northern hinterlands. I've come to plead for your assistance. You three maidens look so lovely, so elegant, so chic, that I can't determine which one of you to dance with. Besides, I don't want to be responsible for disrupting your tantalizing trio. I would be most honored if we could all dance together. _Quod erit amet._ It will be fun!" They looked at each other and laughed. Before they had a chance to respond, Tim took the hand of the girl on his right and the hand of the girl on his left. He looked directly at the girl in the middle and said, "Come hither, for the music beckons us."

The band started playing, "Gimme Some Lovin." It was a standard for every band that year and the Tucson group's cover was even more rousing than the Juarez band's version. Tim fancied himself to be a good hoofer. Although he now disdained much of the pop music on Dick Clark's "American Bandstand" television show, he enjoyed watching the kids dance and he practiced some of their more creative moves. He high-stepped and weaved between his three anonymous dance partners, keeping them entertained with his choreography. He gave each girl fleeting individual attention, throwing in some classic swing and jitterbug moves, taking their hands and twirling them around. The band transitioned to playing Van Morrison's "Brown Eyed Girl," which gave Tim an opportunity to gesture his infatuation with each of the young Roman goddesses.

The ante for Tim's trifecta gambit was upped when the band's female lead started singing Lulu's "To Sir with Love," a slow dance. This was when girls would often cut off their dancing dalliance with a strange guy. To avoid all three girls running off, Tim put his arm around the waist of the closest girl, pulled her closer, put her hand against his heart and began to sway to the music. She rested her head on his shoulder. The other two girls shrugged and walked off. A few moments later Tim's partner turned her head and softly spoke into his ear, "I like your style Timothy, son of Mac, from the hinterlands." Then she rested her head back on his shoulder.

Tim immediately fell in love. His heart was racing. He closed his eyes and held her a bit tighter. He hoped she wouldn't notice when he began to get excited. John Poole's voice popped into his head, *"A toga party. Think of the possibilities!"*

As they slowly swayed in a circle, Tim opened his eyes and saw Julie standing directly in front of him, directly behind his new Juliet. Julie stared at Tim inquisitively. Then, she tapped on his partner's shoulder. The still nameless girl stopped dancing and turned around. Julie said, "Excuse me, but I'd like to dance with my boyfriend now."

The girl didn't make a fuss. She looked back at Tim and smiled, "See ya, Timothy of the hinterlands."

"To Sir with Love," was still playing. Julie took Tim's hand, put her other arm around his waist and started taking the lead dancing. "Who the hell is Timothy of the Netherlands and what line of crap were you feeding that girl?"

"It's Timothy, son of Mac, from the hinterlands. I have no idea who she is, but that line of crap was working really well, thank you very much. Speaking of crap, what was that about wanting to dance with your boyfriend?"

Julie snickered, "That line of crap worked pretty well too, thank you very much."

When the song finished, Tim suggested they take a break, "Let's get some air." They walked outside onto the ballroom's fourth floor terrace. It was a beautiful desert night. A cool light breeze was blowing through the palms. They rested against the terrace railing.

So, I thought you'd be dancing with Jim."

Julie looked bewildered. "Why would you think that?"

"Well, you certainly appeared enamored with him on Sandia Peak. You as much as declared your love for him."

Julie was offended, "I did no such thing! I did what I could to get him off that cliff. I got his attention. I tried to boost his confidence and I gave him something to look forward to at the top. Look, I like Jim a lot. He's a good friend, like you, but I don't love him."

Tim's spirits soared! His feelings for Julie were reignited by the prospect of a second chance with her. He didn't want to let another opportunity to capture her affection slip away. He climbed over the terrace railing and stood on the ledge facing her.

"Are you crazy Tim? Get your ass back over here!"

"Please Julie, I need your help to climb off this ledge. One kiss will lure me back before I plummet to my death!"

Julie laughed and gave him a peck on the lips.

"Seriously Julie, do you think my life is that cheap?" But it was enough to get him to climb back over the railing and ask her less dramatically, "Do you think I could be more than just a friend like Jim?"

Julie put her head down. "I don't know what to think anymore Tim. I don't know what to feel these days. This is the time in our lives when the whole world should be opening up for us, but it seems to be crashing down, spinning out of control. The whole way we were raised and taught to understand the world seems like a massive fraud."

Tim needed to bring the conversation back to the here and now. "I'm confused about what's going on in the world too, Julie, but what about us?"

"You're a dear friend Tim, and maybe more, but I don't know if I can feel that close to anyone right now. That kind of clarity escapes me."

"Ok, so I can work with that. Let's be unclear. Let me possibly be your boyfriend."

Julie lifted her head. Her eyes were sad, but she smiled at Tim. "Let's possibly go back inside and dance the night away."

Julie left Tim where everything else in his life stood, in a tangle of uncertain emotions and an uncertain future. It was a fitting place to be at sixteen, in 1967. His uncertainty would only escalate in the coming year when all hell would break loose.

Chapter 11
The LIME JUICE

Regis High School students had an identity. It was outwardly manifested by their garb. Girls were required to wear the classic parochial school uniform; black patent leather shoes; blue, grey, and green plaid skirts, scrupulously extending down below the knees; white blouses and navy-blue blazers, with the Regis coat of arms patch on their breast pockets. Boys didn't have uniforms, but they did have a strict dress code, slacks (no jeans) and dress shirts with a collar. Inwardly, Regis students believed their education provided them a degree of moral certitude that was unavailable to public school students. They considered themselves the good guys. During Tim's first two years at Regis, he took pride and comfort in his Regis identity. Even if he didn't know what direction his life was headed, Regis would provide him the moral armor to protect him from evil and a moral compass to steer him along a virtuous path.

As Tim began his Junior year at Regis, his outward persona remained much the same, although he kept his shaggy hair at the limits of the Regis coiffure code. However, his self-identity and *weltanschauung* were drifting away from the Royals' ethos. He wasn't rebelling or rejecting Regis per se. He wasn't angry or resentful. It was more like a long-standing relationship that had run its course. *"Really Regis, it's not you, it's me. We're just going in different directions. There are lots of other nice Royals out there for you. We can be friends, but let's give each other some space for now."*

At the outset of the year, Tim decided to forego participation in any Regis extracurriculars, so he could pursue cold hard cash. His family had limited financial resources and they expected him to earn his own spending money. More importantly, if he chose to attend college, it would have to be on his own dime. Having turned sixteen the past spring, he was now employable. He landed a job at the FoodValu supermarket, stocking shelves, sacking groceries, and carrying them out to customers' cars. After returning from Tucson, Tim started working full-time for the rest of the summer. Once school resumed, he chose to continue working as many hours as possible, from 4:00 PM to 10:00 PM, three or four days a week, and one eight-hour shift on the weekends. Once a week, he would work from 5:00 AM to 7:00 AM unloading semi-trucks. He loved it all, the money, the sense of independence and the camaraderie with his co-workers. His schoolwork suffered, though. He'd get home from work at 10:00 PM and his mom would have a frozen Swanson's turkey dinner ready for him. He'd retire to his room to finish homework, but he usually couldn't last more than a half hour before collapsing in bed.

Tim's estrangement from school wasn't unique. There was a segment of the student body that felt similarly divorced from the core culture at Regis. Their attitude about Regis was summed up by their sarcastic mantra, IGAS, i.e., "I Give a Shit." They injected IGAS into their conversations about all sorts of issues they confronted, most often those related to school.

Some of these wayward souls still pursued academic interests or extracurricular activities in sports, theater, and music, but by and large, they turned their sights outward. Jim lost interest in track. He continued to participate in a few theater projects, but his primary attention was focused on music. Warren rekindled an earlier interest in playing bass and Mike's casual interest in the drums morphed into devotion when he realized how much natural talent he had. Jim decided *The Sharks* needed to be reinvigorated, so he brought Warren and Mike into the band. The reconstituted *Sharks* rapidly grew in popularity. Their musical prowess steadily improved, with the band more committed to practicing. Much of their success could be attributed to their growing stage presence. Jim was becoming more confident as a lead singer, creating his own interpretations of popular songs, performing covers of obscure songs, and performing a few songs he had written. Warren's bass playing was expressive, and Pat, the band's original lead guitar player from East High School, was the best around. Surprisingly, it was Mike who put the biggest stamp on *The Sharks'* image. Mike's role model was Keith Moon, the maniacal drummer for *The Who*. Mike strove to match Moon's fanatical fills. He assaulted the drums with genuine zest. He had a symbiotic relationship with the audience. His energy was boosted by the crowd's approving response to his antics.

On a late fall evening, *The Sharks* were playing the "Saturday Nighter" teen dance at the YMCA. The dance was affectionally known as the "Saturday Fighter," because of the frequent rumbles that broke out in and outside the hall, usually involving rivals from different high schools. The band had recently mastered The Who's, "I Can See For Miles", an explosive high-octane tune that revved up both the band and the audience. It was the last song of their first set. That night, the band was so pleased by their performance and the crowd's reaction, that they circled back through it a second time, becoming more and more animated. They landed the finale of their rousing rendition right on beat. But Mike wasn't ready to expel the adrenaline the song had generated. He immediately started-up again, wailing wildly on the drums. The band looked on, bobbing up and down in delight. After about a minute-long extemporaneous drum solo, Mike leaped up from his stool, kicked his hi-hat cymbals over with one leg, kicked the bass drum over with his other foot, then proceeded to throw his tom tom drums and snare drum off the front of the stage. Jim was fortunate to step aside in the nick of time to dodge a drum that whizzed by his head. The already exuberant crowd went wild. Modeling Mike's aggression, guys started shoving each other around and, within seconds, a full-scale brawl erupted. Someone in the crowd picked up the snare drum and threw it back up on stage, hitting Mike in the nose.

Tim was observing the mayhem with some amusement while standing with Steve and Sandy against a wall on the side of the dance floor. Out of nowhere, a kid Tim didn't know was tossed into him, spilling Tim's Pepsi. After Tim pushed him away, the kid turned around and reflexively slugged him in the stomach. Tim doubled over and groaned. When he looked up, the stranger scrapper was winding up to punch him in the face. A hand grabbed Tim's assailant's arm and spun him sideways. It was Tim's former teammate, Ronnie. He had a big grin, as though he was relishing the opportunity to intervene. Ronnie didn't say anything. He just laid a fierce uppercut into the unfortunate kid's jaw, lifting him off his feet. The kid fell back, but he didn't fall to the floor. He just staggered away into the tightly packed turbulence.

Tim tried to sound matter of fact as he winced and coughed, "Hey Ronnie, it's good to see you. How you been?"

Ronnie looked very pleased with himself. "Hey Tim, I'm doing good. Well, take it easy." He then plunged back into the maelstrom.

Sandy grabbed Tim's wrist and raised his arm, "Another triumph for Timothy, Son of Mac, from the hinterlands."

Tim was mortified. "Jeez Sandy, what else did Julie tell you?"

"Just that you know how to shift your natural charm into overdrive when you want to. You could have used a little more charm on that guy."

"Hey, I was just standing here trying to stay above the fray. It was Ronnie's charm that saved this gorgeous face. I could use a little more of Ronnie's charm."

Steve laughed, "Using Ronnie's charm would have probably put you in the hospital."

The Sharks retreated to calmer waters stage left. Mike held his hand over his bloody nose. Several cops raced into the hall to break things up and a large part of the crowd fled the scene, down the stairs and into the street. The YMCA Assistant Manager, a large, heavy-set middle-aged man, waded into the melee and separated several of the combatants. When the battling ceased, he turned around and shot a look that could kill at the band. He panted heavily as he walked up the stage steps and straight into Mike's face. "If you ever try another stunt like that again, the only place you'll every play again is your garage" Then he turned, walked back down the stage steps and resumed herding kids out. The dance was shut down.

Joe was never that involved in Regis related activities and during his sophomore year he was feeling increasingly alienated from school. His political interests were becoming more earnest. He spent a lot of time over the summer working alone, doing maintenance at his father's properties. He read voraciously about the history of worker's rights and the labor movement, America's "Gilded Age," the Robber Barons and political corruption, post-civil war racial politics and ongoing racial discrimination. He was infuriated that virtually none of what he read had been mentioned in any of his history classes. After Frank's revelations about the roots of US intervention in Vietnam, Joe delved into books about post-WWII US foreign policy in Southeast Asia, Central America, the Middle East, and Africa. He was amazed that all of this information was readily available from books and magazines in his town's little Carnegie library. When he found a reference that was not available on the library shelves, he would ask for it to be ordered - and they would get it! Most of these books weren't written by politicians or political pundits. They weren't partisan. They were scholarly treatises and just, well, history. They weren't based on opinions, speculation, or conspiracy theories. They cited documents and first-hand accounts - witnesses to history. Joe was enraged that all of this had been hidden from him, hidden from most Americans.

Joe was finding it harder to contain his convictions. It could be difficult to get him to talk about other subjects, but he didn't need prompting to talk about politics. The guys were hanging around Steve's basement on a Friday evening, listening to music. Jim put on a Buffalo Springfield album, and he started to softly sing along to "For What It's Worth," *"There's something happening here. What it is ain't exactly clear."*

Joe snickered cynically, "It's clear there's not much happening around here."

Steve feigned being insulted, "What do you mean, here in the basement? This is a very happening place, full of happening people!" Steve's basement had become their unofficial headquarters. His folks pretty much gave them free reign down there. It was not uncommon for six to ten guys to spend the night there, sometimes even the whole weekend. The boys thought Steve's mom was a sweetheart. She would occasionally bring them sandwiches and snacks. They all thought Steve was a great guy too. He was a lot of fun, a pleasure to hang with. He had good instincts about peoples' character.

Warren chimed in, "It's always happening wherever I am. I'm a happening guy!"

Steve concurred, "That's right Warren. Wherever you are is where you happen to be."

Joe remained serious, "No, I mean this place, Waterloo, Iowa, and most everyone at Regis. They're oblivious to what's going on in the world, or if they do know, they act like it has nothing to do with them. They're all caught up with themselves and all the trivial bullshit that clutters up their lives."

"Yeah," Warren replied, "How dare they think about their own lives so much."

"Shit Warren, you know what I'm talking about."

They could count on Charlie to bring some blunt reality to the conversation. "I don't see us doing anything much different to change anything. Are we shaking anybody out of their complacency? Hell no, we're not. We're not even changing ourselves. I'm no different. The only things I've changed in my life are my socks and my underwear."

Although in many respects Charlie was feeling disconnected from Regis, he continued to be an academic star. He was determined not to let his GPA or his class standing slip. He dedicated himself to getting a full scholarship at the most prestigious university possible. But increasingly, Charlie was looking outside of the classroom for his education. He and Joe regularly exchanged books. Charlie gave Joe James Baldwin's books and Joe gave Charlie Michael Harrington's books.

Charlie's cousin, Toni, was also in their class and she was hanging out with them that day. She was studious like Charlie, but less obsessive-compulsive about it. She was confident, not shy about saying what was on her mind, and she could be bitingly sarcastic. Some people, particularly some adults, would label her as "having an attitude." For this crowd, flipping shit effectively was an attribute they highly admired. Toni smirked, "Maybe, Charlie, you can work on changing your socks more often, then you can work on changing the world. While you're at it, maybe you can change that shirt once in a while. What is this, day four?"

Joe was on a roll. "Hey man, I'm not talking about changing the world. I just want to lay some reality on people. Starting with the people at Regis. Like what they're doing in that *Berkeley Barber* paper Tim has been getting. There's some heavy shit in there man!"

About a month after Tim returned home from Tucson, he received a rolled-up package in the mail, wrapped in plain brown paper. It was postmarked from Berkeley, California. There was a note from Josh inside. "Hey man, feed your head with this. All you need is love, Josh." Tim's mom was curious what it was. He told her it was a student newspaper from one of the guys he met in Tucson. She was satisfied with that.

"It's the *Berkeley Barb,* not Barber, Joe. I wish I had more copies to spread around. Obviously, there's no way the city library would carry it, let alone the Regis library. They'd probably report me to the FBI just for even asking."

Joe persisted, "No kidding Tim, but that's more reason why we should be doing the same thing, spreading the real news, spreading the real truth. The truth people need to hear."

Tim couldn't imagine, "What do you mean, Joe? Are you saying we should put out a paper like the *Berkeley Barb?*"

"No, but maybe we could do something like the *Gonzo Gazette.*"

Rolled-up in the middle of the *Berkeley Barb* was the first edition of the *Gonzo Gazette.* It was a very simple, short format, 4-page tabloid. On the right side of the masthead was a photo of El Cerrito High School, overlain with a peace symbol. The headline story was an attention grabber, "Gaucho Boys Prepare to Die." The story was a series of interviews with El Cerrito Senior boys, some intending to enlist in the military after graduation, some anticipating being drafted and some planning to find ways to dodge the draft. The thrust of the story was that they were all at risk of dying for a useless, immoral cause based on lies and a misplaced notion of patriotism. The inside headline was equally sensational, and Tim thought it was far more dangerous for Josh and Kayla to print, "School Board Slum Lord!" It exposed an El Cerrito school board member who owned a large number of dilapidated apartment buildings in the area. The apartments had an extensive history of tenant complaints and recorded building code violations.

Tim still couldn't see it, "Joe, we wouldn't last 15 minutes at Regis if we tried printing anything like the *Gonzo Gazette!*"

"You're probably right man, but wouldn't it be a beautiful way to go out?"

The thought of them putting out a newspaper got Al and Dean's craniums cooking. Both of them were good athletes and they played on the Regis basketball team, but their sensibilities were less like jocks and more like hippies. In part, this was rooted in them both coming from the Eastside of town. The dominant Regis culture was more bourgeois and Westside oriented. They were both natural rebels, with a heavy dose of smart-ass. They also had lots of street smarts.

Al was a pugilistic, gruff, feisty fellow, who was more bark than bite. His husky voice and sneers belied his age. Al worked part-time at the National Cigar Store, where there was a not-so- secret illegal bookie operation in the back. His gambling prowess enabled him to parlay his meager resources into a substantial stash of cash. His first thought was predictable, "Hey, we could publish an abbreviated version of the Racing Forum and run our own book!"

The idea met with Joe's scorn. "That's great, Al, then we could be expelled, busted and sent to prison all in one fell swoop."

Dean covered his personal expenses by selling magazine subscriptions door-to-door. His witty pitches not only got him through a lot of front doors, he would often be invited to join his prospects for meals. Dean also thought a paper might have entrepreneurial possibilities, "I could sell advertisements for businesses that cater to students, like Pizza Hut."

It was Tim's turn to be cynical. "What businesses in this town would advertise in an underground newspaper? They'd take one look at it and think we were a bunch of bomb-throwing Bolsheviks."

Rick had a humorous disdain for convention and authority. He wanted to reprint *The Barb's* cartoons, which were filled with wicked political and social commentary. Randy was a lighthearted guy who was popular with the ladies. He thought jokes would help sell the paper. "Tim, you said Josh told you *The Barb* was *Mad Magazine* grown up. How about a paper that's a teenage *Mad Magazine*? It should be raw, raunchy, and immature. Let's dare to be stupid."

That sentiment resonated with Mary Whitman. She was a natural cut-up. The gang loved her dry delivery of one-liners, often self-deprecating. "Yeah, I can take the lead on that. I excel at stupid and juvenile," she said without cracking a smile. "I could do an advice column, like *Dear Abby,* except we could call it, *Dear Abbie Hoffman.*"

Julie had a lot on her mind that she wanted to share. "I'm with Joe. I want to shake people up. I'd like to write an opinion column. I'd call it, *The Bold Bitch.* I would use it to fight for women's rights. For example, why is it the only athletic opportunities girls have at Regis are golf, tennis, and cheerleading?"

Larry O'Malley was the quintessential, good humored, laid-back hippie type, albeit with hair short enough to comply with Regis regulations. He was tall, lanky and in a perpetual slouch, whether sitting, standing or walking. Although he didn't bring a lot of energy to their endeavors, he was always game for anything. "Man, a newspaper would be far out. We could use it to spread the good word about culture, music, art and shit."

Sandy loved that idea. She had an artistic sensibility, and her creations were inspired by the psychedelic posters from the Fillmore West in San Francisco, album covers like Cream's *Disraeli Gears*, and artists like Peter Max, Milton Glaser and Mati Klarwein. "Larry's right, we can blow peoples' minds with all kinds of far out graphics. We could portray the world in a kaleidoscope of designs and colors." Sandy was adorable, caring and good hearted. She assumed a motherly role early in life. Her mother died of cancer a few years earlier and her father was in frail health. Her nurturing nature spilled over to her friends.

They had lots of ideas. They had lots of enthusiasm. But they had very short attention spans. They didn't lose interest, they just lost track. Their musing about putting out an underground paper was only one of several meandering conversations that day. Something as bold and complex as publishing a newspaper would require sustained focus, and they had too many competing issues and interests. They were at an age and in a time when new revelations were coming at them fast and furious. They were being bombarded with new concepts, new phenomena, new experiences. The most valued conversations introduced new insights or new possibilities on a boundless range of topics. Their most shocking revelations were called, "Mind-Fucks."

"Did you know that the universe is expanding? They've calculated backwards to figure out that everything in the universe originated from a big bang about 14 billion years ago, when all the matter in the universe was condensed into the size of a period! I mean, bend your brain around that!"

"There are these Hindu gurus that have mastered transcendental meditation so well that their bodies can actually levitate!"

Their obsession with music and musicians intensified with a steady stream of new bands, with new sounds, emerging from cities all over the country, all over the world. There were The Jefferson Airplane, The Grateful Dead, Big Brother and the Holding Company, Quicksilver Messenger Service and the Steve Miller Band from San Francisco; The Buffalo Springfield, The Byrds, The Turtles, The Doors and The Mothers of Invention from Los Angeles; The Rascals, The Lovin' Spoonful and Velvet Underground out of New York and New Jersey.

However, the most creative musical frontiers continued to emanate from the UK; Cream, Pink Floyd, Jethro Tull, The Moody Blues, King Crimson, Yes, Donovan and the spunky Irishman, Van Morrison. Even well-established British bands continued to evolve. The Beatles released *Sergeant Pepper's*, followed by *Magical Mystery Tour*. The Stones followed suit with their own psychedelic album, *Their Satanic Majesties Request,* and The Who released their first concept album, *The Who Sellout*. The Regis rejects could barely keep up with them all and they competed for who would be first to discover the next new sound.

The boys craved personal information about these musicians, who were becoming legends, rock gods. There was a dearth of information sources. Aside from the megastars, most of these bands didn't get much mainstream media attention. Some of the hottest bands were almost completely absent from television and radio. There was an early rock magazine called Cheetah, that featured stories on young new artists like Jackson Brown. Rolling Stone magazine started publishing in November and the boys leaped at each new edition that appeared on the newsstand at The National Cigar Store, the only place in town that carried it. The information void was filled with rumors and speculation about the likes of Eric Clapton, Ginger Baker, Frank Zappa, Keith Moon, Mick Jagger, Jerry Garcia and Grace Slick. A couple of years later, the underground buzz culminated in the quintessential rock conspiracy theory, that Paul McCartney was secretly dead. Larry completely bought into it, "Seriously, you can hear it on side four of the *White Album*, on the song *Revolution #9*, play it backwards on the part where they repeat 'number nine' over and over. I swear, you can hear John say, 'Turn me on dead man!' Then go back and listen to the end of *Strawberry Fields* on *Magical Mystery Tour*. You can hear John say, 'I buried Paul!' Paul might have died a couple of years ago!" It's amazing how much traction this absurd story got. It was an indication of how mysterious and obsessive rock mythology had become, as well as kids' appetite for new revelations that would "Blow their minds."

The rapid-fire stream of consciousness conversations in Steve's basement were also influenced by their fascination with chemically induced altered states of consciousness. They continued to be frustrated by their inability to score marijuana. Their experience with pot in Tucson whetted their appetites for more euphoric fits of frivolity. Alas, their

116

limited circle of contacts had limited reach to find a limited number of dealers in their area. So, they fell back on the mother's milk of adolescent asinine behavior – beer. They had several pipelines to score some brew, one of which was via Tim. The young assistant manager at the FoodValu, Jeff West, was more than happy to fill Tim's orders for Schlitz, Old Milwaukee and PBR, for a slight, "Risk management," mark-up. Jeff was fired a few months later. He thought he could disappear from the store for hours at a time, like the manager. He found out his rank did not afford him the same privileges. Jeff was replaced by Ken, an even younger assistant manager, who was still in high school and not willing to jeopardize his position by selling Tim beer. This development required Tim and his buddies to hone their skills at making fake driver's licenses, which was a lot easier in those days, because licenses did not have photos and the official color was the same as pool chalk. Their acquisition of addictive habits included cigarettes. By the end of the year, almost all of them were solidly hooked on nicotine.

As much as they enjoyed the adventure of consuming beer illicitly, it felt too mainstream, too mundane, too bourgeois for their emerging counter-culture identity. The predictable course of a beer buzz from silly, to sloppy, to snoozy, didn't satisfy their interest in diverse mental, physical and spiritual experiences. They tried ramping-up the alcohol level with Colt 45 and other malt liquors, but that only amplified and accelerated the typical beer trajectory. In the absence of weed, or hallucinogenic substances, like LSD, mescaline, or psilocybin mushrooms, they had to get creative. They experimented with off-the-shelf pathways to nirvana. Larry O'Malley was their principal researcher. Larry convinced them that morning glory seeds could produce a psychedelic experience similar to LSD, so they purchased more than a dozen packets of seeds. Following Larry's instructions, they washed and soaked them. Then they each ate two packets. The seeds did have a potent effect alright, primarily nausea.

A few weeks after the Fall semester started, Joe picked up Tim for school, then Warren, then Larry. When Larry slipped into the back seat with Warren, he broke out a bottle of what appeared to be cough syrup. "Brace yourselves brothers, we are about to go day tripping on the magic bus."

Warren chuckled, "What are you doing with that Larry? Do you want cough syrup on your breath, so you can feign being sick?"

"Gentlemen, I assume you've all experienced the medicinal benefits of Romilar CF cough syrup. I also assume you and your mothers have always been meticulous about taking it in the prescribed dose of two tablespoons every four to six hours. Have you ever wondered how such a small quantity of medicine can pack such a huge punch and be so effective in squashing your coughs? Would you be interested in knowing what puts the magic in this elixir?"

Joe said, "OK Doctor O'Malley, you have our attention. Please continue."

"As you can see here on the label, the two active ingredients in Romilar CF are dextromethorphan and codeine. That dextro shit is a hallucinogenic and codeine is a narcotic! In other words, this is great shit man! Two tablespoons will knock your cough out, but if you drink a whole bottle, you'll be knocked for a loop for hours! "

Tim was appalled by the idea. "You can't be serious, Larry. You want the three of us to drink that whole bottle of Romilar! We'll probably puke it all up."

"No Tim, I'm saying we should each drink a whole bottle. Here, I've got two more."

Tim threw his hands up in exasperation. "Are you fucking kidding me! What is this, a suicide pact?

Joe was guarded about the idea as well. "Where did you hear about this, Larry?"

"The most reliable of sources. Howie Campbell is a total Romilar freak. He swears by it." Howie Campbell was a well-known wild man at West High School. He cemented his reputation by doing acrobatic flips off the highest cliffs at the local rock quarry.

"Well, why didn't you just say so," Tim said sarcastically. "If Howie says it's cool, then sign me up."

"Seriously guys, if we want to expand our horizons, we have to be willing to walk to the edge sometimes. I mean, if we want to make an omelet, we have to break some eggs."

Tim was beside himself. "What the fuck are you talking about, Larry?

Joe said, "That's a really bad metaphor in this case, Larry."

Warren, on the other hand, was ready to have his brain scrambled. "What the hell, let's do it. I don't have much going on in my classes today. This might be the most worthwhile experience I'll have all day."

Usually, Tim could rely on Joe to be the voice of reason in these situations. But much to Tim's surprise and chagrin, by the time they pulled into the school parking lot, Joe seemed to be coming around to Larry's overdosing proposal, "I could use a new perspective on Regis. Maybe this will improve my attitude about the place."

Tim was now the lone holdout, and resistance to peer pressure wasn't usually his strong suit. "Crap, I suppose all three of you guys expect me to go along with this."

Larry held up two surrendering hands in front of himself, "Hey man, it's totally up to you. If you'd rather slog through the Tuesday doldrums while we explore an alternative universe, that's your oh so predictable decision. I will in no way think the less of you. You won't be any more of a boring little chicken shit than you already are. After all, that's one of your most endearing attributes and why I think of you so fondly. I mean that sincerely."

"That's a beautiful sentiment Larry, much appreciated. You're such a dear." Tim turned around, reached into the back seat, and took the bottle of Romliar out of Larry's hand. He plopped back in his seat, twisted the cap off, grimaced, held his nose, tilted his head back and proceeded to gulp down the entire bottle. The nasty taste made him shiver. Then he said, "You guys are assholes."

Larry handed Warren and Joe their bottles and the three of them chug-a-lugged in unison. "Well boys, Larry proclaimed, nothing ventured, nothing gained!"

Joe and Tim had 1st period home room in the cafeteria study hall. Mr. Nussle was the faculty study hall monitor. Right after the 1st period bell rang, he announced that the students would be electing their home room representative to the student council. It was a slapdash process. It rarely generated much interest. Mr. Nussle called for nominations. "OK kids, who would like to participate in student government. It's a good opportunity to grow your leadership skills and it will enhance your resumes." His enticement was followed by dead silence. He waited a minute, then said, "Come on people, this is your chance to have some say in things around here."

Dean smiled and raised his hand. "I'll throw my hat into the ring Mr. Nussle." Tim knew Dean well enough to know he had no real interest in student government. Tim assumed Dean was nominating himself as a lark, or maybe as a chance to further hone his bullshitting skills.

After Dean nominated himself, the thought popped into Tim's head that maybe he should run. Tim had his own jaded motive. He wasn't particularly interested in what was happening at Regis, but he often speculated about his political potential, spurred on by his 6th grade rhetoric success at the podium. Without any further thought, he raised his hand. "Mr. Nussle, I'd like to give it a try."

"Thanks for stepping forward gentlemen. Dean and Tim will now have two minutes each to tell you all why they would be your best choice to represent you. Dean, you can go first."

As Tim expected, Dean was brilliant. He confidently strode to the front of the cafeteria and faced the students with an expression of upmost sincerity. He began by speaking softly, "My fellow Royals, we have suffered in silence for too long. We have bent under the yoke of oppression for too long. We have yielded to tyranny for too long." Dean gradually raised his voice. "It's past time to take our student government back from the cabal of corrupt power brokers that have stolen our voices! It's past time for the student council to have representatives who will speak for you, the huddled masses; for you, the downtrodden; for you, the exploited proletariat. It's past time for a student council that speaks for you, the lowly front-line students, toiling away, day-in and day-out, in the educational trenches. I would be honored to be that voice, your voice. Someone who will raise your voices up to the heavens and bring down the student council's walls. Can I hear a hallelujah?"

The cafeteria responded, "Hallelujah!"

Dean never cracked a smile as he walked back to his table, but he did have a bounce in his step, and he nodded in recognition of the students' applause. Mr. Nussle was amused. "That was quite inspiring Dean. I only wish that I could vote in this election. Tim, I'm sorry you have to follow that."

Tim slowly rose from his table and paced to the front of the cafeteria. As he turned to face the room, it dawned on him that 45 minutes earlier he had consumed an 8-ounce hallucinogenic cocktail. It crossed his mind that he might need to be concerned. However, that brief moment of anxiety quickly receded. Rather than feeling panicked, Tim felt strangely exhilarated. Then he realized, he felt more than exhilarated. He felt great! He was pumped. He was going to own that room! He spread his arms high and wide. Then he called out like a town crier, "Brothers and Sisters, let us give thanks to our colleague, Dean. We should applaud his selfless pledge to fight on our behalf. But I fear Dean has a dark vision for Regis. He only sees turmoil and conflict ahead of us. He wants to lead us into a quagmire of recriminations."

Tim felt another surge of energy and elation. "I have a different vision for Regis. I see all of us, students, faculty and staff as one force for good. I see us joining together, arm in arm, in peace, love and harmony! I see a Regis awash in light and color. I hear Regis filled with laughter and song, not anger and sorrow. I hear music. I hear that sweet, sweet rock and roll music!"

At this point, Tim started to feel a bit light-headed, but his thoughts were still coming in hot. "So, what's it going to be Royals? When the bell rings and you go out into those hallways, what are you going to tell your friends? Are you going to tell them that you've succumbed to despair, that you've chosen to go down Dean's dark road to destruction? Will you tell them that you've embraced his dystopian vision? I don't think so. I think you're going to tell them that you voted for a brighter future, that you're going to follow Tim towards the light. You're not going to walk down that hallway hearing a funeral dirge ringing in your head. You're going to hear Wilson Picket singing, "Land of 1000 Dances." Tim didn't recall having memorized the lyrics, but the words flowed forth from him, while his hands clapped, and his hips swayed.

> "One-two-three uh, one-two-three, Ow, uh, alright, uh!
> Got to know how to pony, like Bony Maronie.
> Mashed potato, do the alligator.
> Put your hands on your hips, yeah.
> Let your backbone slip.
> Do the Watusi, like my little Lucy. Hey!"

Mr. Nussle tried to break him off, "Tim, your time is up, thank you." It was to no avail. Joe leaped to his feet. He was glassy-eyed and had the biggest smile Tim had ever seen on him. Joe began singing, *"Uh, na-na-na-na-nana-na-na-na-na-na-na-na-na, Na-na-na-na,* I need somebody to help me say it one time!"

Then Dean stood up and the three of them continued to sing, *"Na-na-na na-na na-na-na-na-na-na-na-na. Na-na-na-na, woow!"*

Other students joined in, *"Na-na-na-na-na na-na-na-na-na-na-na-na."*

"Tim, everyone, please return to your seat," Mr. Nussle implored.

Dean was more effective restoring order. "Royals, Royals, please, please be seated. I have an important announcement." The singing subsided, partially because nobody could remember the rest of the lyrics. "As much as I relish the opportunity to serve you, I'm withdrawing from the race and casting my vote for Tim McIntyre. I say, let the light shine in with Tim."

It was a simple hand tally and Tim won unanimously. The problem was he had already lost all of his enthusiasm for student government. Moreover, he was now beginning to feel sick to his stomach. By the time the bell rang at the end of the first period, he was close to losing his cookies. He steadied himself against the hallway wall as he teetered towards the student health office. There wasn't anyone there when he arrived, so he sat down on a padded bench, leaned back, and closed his eyes. The room started swirling.

A few moments later, Joe wobbled in and sat down beside Tim. He sounded shaky, "I have to get the hell out of here Tim, before I totally lose it."

A minute later, Larry and Warren joined them. Larry had it together more than the others. "Man, Howie wasn't bull-shitting. This is a trip. Problem is, I can't function in class anywhere close to normal. We're going to get busted if we don't bolt."

Just then, the school nurse, Sister Monica, entered the office. "What seems to be the matter boys?"

Warren became their spokesperson, "I think we're all getting the stomach flu Sister, or maybe it's food poisoning."

Sister squinted and said, "I have to say boys, this looks more than a little suspicious."

122

Their credibility was bolstered when Tim suddenly lurched forward and stumbled into the health office bathroom, where he proceeded to puke profusely.

Sister quickly wrote four passes for them to go home.

There were no official repercussions from this episode, but it did provoke rumors that filtered through the student body and the faculty. The boys were generally tight-lipped about it, but they did share their chemistry experiment experience with their small cadre of counter culturists, so who knows how the story might have spread from there. Speculation centered on what substances they had consumed. Many students and faculty were convinced it was LSD, the most notorious hallucinogenic. Regardless, from that morning on, the four boys were marked men.

The wayward sons' reputations were further eroded a week later, after an incident in Mr. Wagner's American History class. Wayne Wagner was the highest-ranking layman on the faculty, Assistant Dean of Boys. He was also an assistant football coach and a certifiable dick. He was tall and broad, with a short blonde crew-cut and a perpetual smirk. He also had a very pronounced waddle when he walked, that resembled a duck. Charlie, Joe, and Tim registered for American History when Father McLaughlin was listed as the instructor. Father Mac was highly respected, a bona fide scholar, a riveting lecturer, and a good soul. On the first day of class, the students were shocked to learn that Father McLaughlin had taken a sudden leave-of-absence and Mr. "Lame Wayne" Wagner had replaced him. The students anticipated the semester would be filled with Wagner rambling off topic about himself, using lame football analogies, to make lame points about the way his lame version of the world is supposed to work. Charlie, Joe, and Tim thought they would need to endure Wagner. They weren't intending to confront him.

They were studying the Civil War. Their textbook focused on military strategies, battlefield tactics and casualties, more than the social, political, and economic dynamics surrounding the war. Slavery was identified as an issue, but racism was largely left alone. The textbook devoted less than six pages to Reconstruction, and pretty much summarized it as an unmitigated disaster. Wagner felt a need to share his own commentary about it. "Reconstruction was an ongoing insult and assault on the people of the South. Grant's treatment of the South after the war was a crime, masked as a policy. Corruption ran amok. It took decades for the South to recover its dignity. The bitterness has lasted to this day."

Charlie had a personal interest in the Civil War. He had read extensively about it long before taking the class. "Excuse me Mr. Wagner, but I think there were also some pretty cool things that happened during Reconstruction."

Wayne flashed his notorious smirk at Charlie, "So, what cool things might those be Charlie?"

"Well, public school systems were started throughout the South, where there hadn't been hardly any before. Manufacturing increased, where there hadn't been much before the war. But the main thing was that almost four million slaves were freed and they were given the right to vote. Black people were elected to all kinds of offices, even to Congress. I think those things were pretty cool."

Wayne was becoming visibly irritated. "Most of those elections were shams Charlie. Corrupt carpetbaggers manipulated the negro vote, either for themselves or for uneducated negro candidates they put up for office, negro men the northerners could control. It was a travesty. Grant didn't have a clue what was going on. He was a drunkard."

That comment triggered Joe. "You mean Ulysses S. Grant? The guy who led the Union Army to victory and saved the United States? You mean that Grant?"

You could hear Wagner's frustration in his voice. "Success on the battlefield doesn't necessarily translate into politics and effective governance, as your textbook explains."

Now it was Charlie who was exasperated. "But the textbook doesn't explain much of anything! It doesn't explain how Andrew Johnson was a former slave-owner who vetoed laws that gave rights to black people. It doesn't explain how Grant supported civil rights and sent troops to protect blacks from being massacred. It doesn't explain how the US Justice Department was established in order to fight the Klu Klux Klan. It doesn't explain how President Hayes sold out southern blacks in a backroom deal that he withdrew troops from the South, turning his back on atrocities against blacks and allowing the establishment of Jim Crow laws."

Wayne wasn't smirking anymore. His jaw was set tight and his eyes were filled with barely controlled anger. "Look boys, you're responsible for learning what's in the textbook. Anything else you choose to read and believe is up to you, but you're not going to bring it into this classroom. There're many versions of history out there, some of them downright radical. In here, we stick with the textbook."

Tim couldn't help himself. He turned his head towards the window and said, "Heaven forbid we should bring some knowledge into this classroom."

Wagner slammed his hand down on his desk, "Mind your tone young man. That's enough gentlemen. This discussion is over!" Wayne turned his back to the class and began writing their assignment on the blackboard. His rage was transmitted through the screeching chalk. The boys knew Wayne would be itching to retaliate. He found an opportunity the following week.

On "Wednesday Study Nights," Regis opened its doors for students to study together, use the school's resources and consult with teachers in their classrooms. Tim was in serious need of help. It was December, and his heavy work schedule at the FoodValu had been too much for him to keep up with schoolwork. It was the end-of-semester crunch time, and he was facing failures or incompletes in several classes. He couldn't possibly catch up during his 1st period study hall. He asked for his work schedule to be changed, so he could have Wednesday evenings off.

Joe picked up Tim in the GTO. Tim wasn't surprised to see Charlie and Toni with Joe, because they rarely missed a Wednesday Study Night. Tim was surprised to see Mike. "Well, dig this, the prince of rock and roll has decided to get an education!"

"Hey man, I'm getting a real-world education every day, but I have to kick ass at school for the next three weeks or my folks will kick my ass. The Sharks have been practicing and playing gigs so much on the weekends lately that I haven't gotten anything else done."

An early winter snowfall coated the Regis parking lot. The snow muffled the sounds outside and brightened the frosty evening. As they plodded through the snow towards the school's back entrance, they could see a tall, hunched figure standing next to a pillar, smoking a cigarette. When they got closer, they realized it was Mr. Wagner. They were disconcerted to see his signature smirk appear when he recognized them. "What have we here? Do you kids still think you can learn something in school?"

Charlie stayed respectful. "Yes, Mr. Wagner, we all have quite a bit of work to get done."

"I'm sure you and Toni would get a lot done Charlie, but I doubt these other three intend to do much schoolwork. As a matter of fact, their brains are probably too doped up to get much of anything done.

Joe was not in the mood. "What the hell is that supposed to mean?"

"From what I've heard Joe, you boys have been so busy getting high on drugs, that you can't even make it through a class period. Heck, I wouldn't be surprised if you were all high right now."

Mike was incensed. "That's crazy, of course we're not high. We just want to do some homework."

Wayne threw his cigarette down on the sidewalk and stomped it out, then he jabbed his finger at them. "I might not have enough evidence to report anything specific to your parents yet, but I'm going to be watching you boys like a hawk, and I'm damn sure you aren't coming into this school tonight to disrupt these other students. The Regis Study Night is no place for druggies."

That set Tim off. "Wait a minute Mr. Wagner. I took off work to come here tonight. You don't have the right to keep us out of school."

Tim's challenge only further inflamed Wagner. "You need to wake up Tim. I not only have the right, I have the responsibility to protect the student body from bad influences, most especially drug influences. Charlie and Toni, I've never had any trouble from either of you, but seeing you here with these characters has me concerned. I'm not sure what you all have been up to tonight, but I'm not taking the chance of letting any of you in. If I see any of you inside this building tonight, you'll have to serve detention for the next week - understood?"

Tim could feel Mike about ready to explode, so he put his hand on Mike's shoulder. They all stayed quiet. Wayne shot them a parting smirk, turned around and walked back into the building. The rejects trudged back to Joe's GTO, stood around and tried to compose themselves.

Mike was the first to speak, "Lame Wayne, what an epic asshole."

Joe was equally enraged. "I can't believe it. There he was, actually standing in the schoolhouse door to keep us out. He looked like a caricature of George Wallace in a standoff with Martin Luther King!"

The analogy was too much for Toni. "Now don't go comparing yourself to Martin Luther King. We're not exactly freedom fighters. This isn't exactly Selma, and Wayne didn't sic his dogs on us. Besides, it was only a matter of time before you guys got nailed for drinking that cough syrup shit."

As Toni spoke, she started to write Lame Wayne in the snow, with the toe of her shoe. Then she drew two duck webbed footprints next to it. Without a word, they all started to write Lame Wayne and draw more duck footprints in the snow, each version getting bigger. After they completed a dozen or so iterations, they stood back and laughed at their handiwork. Then Mike raced to the hill behind the parking lot. He bounded up 40 feet to the top of the hill, sat down on his butt and slide down, then to the side, making a neat L-shaped depression in the snow. They all got the idea and raced to the top. They took turns sitting down, sliding, and writing the next letter. When they finished, they stood at the bottom of the hill and admired their creation, a very large and legible LAME WAYNE, paired with two giant duck footprints about 30 feet high and 100 feet long. It was cathartic. They got back into the GTO and didn't give it another thought.

They should have all gone home and done their homework, but they were pretty worked up, so they headed over to headquarters, Steve's basement. Most of the gang were there. Everyone got riled up when hearing that Lame Wayne refused to let their compatriots enter the school building.

Julie went off, "Who the hell does that shithead think he is? Well, I'll tell you what he is. He's a little Hitler! From now on, instead of saying, 'Good morning Mr. Wagner,' I'm going to just say, 'Sieg Heil!'"

Rick fumed, "Who the hell does he think we are, his peons?"

As per usual, Charlie was more measured and introspective. "So, who do we think we are? We're not really druggies? We're certainly not revolutionaries. Maybe we're all just fuck-ups."

Joe was defiant, "Whoever we are, I'm not going to let Lame Wayne define us."

Toni was down with that, "OK, so let's define ourselves. Who are we? Who do we want to be? What do we call ourselves?"

True to form, Mary took a sideways stab at an answer. "I think you're all world class wise-asses, so I suggest we call ourselves something equally sarcastic and wise-ass. How about "Juniors United in Catholic Education?"

Steve roared, "I love it! It's cynical as hell, but that's too much of a mouthful. What's the acronym? Hey, we'd be The JUICE!"

Warren embraced it. "Yeah man, The JUICE. That sounds cool. It's got pazazz."

Sandy thought about it some more. "It's missing something. What kind of juice, apple juice, orange juice? Those all seem pretty boring. We need to be something colorful, something more unusual. How about the lime juice?"

Julie wasn't satisfied, "Yeah, but what would the LIME stand for? It needs to be something far out, something subversive."

The question was tailor made for Larry's cosmic consciousness. "Let's see, how about Lovers; yeah, Lovers of; Lovers of International; Lovers of International Mind Expansion! That's it, LIME!"

That was it! The LIME JUICE perfectly represented where they were at that moment on the space-time continuum, somewhere between the cosmic and the ecclesiastic, between Aquarius and Augustus. It was the moniker they needed to navigate the remainder of their adolescence. The LIME JUICE moniker gave them what all teens yearn for, a most proper identity.

The following morning, Joe was giving Tim a ride to school. It was a bright, clear, frigid December dawn. They were about a mile and half away from school where they could see Regis on the high ground in the distance. The sun was glistening brilliantly off the snow on the hillside behind the school. There it was, as clear as the top row of letters on an optometrist's eye chart, "LAME WAYNE," in shimmering geoglyphic lettering and those huge duck feet turned outwards. The boys knew immediately that they were going to be crucified.

Tim sat in first period home room study hall, listening to Sister Ruth say the daily prayer over the intercom. After the prayer, Sister Ruth announced, "Would the following students please report to the Administration Office; Joseph Snyder, Michael Russel, Timothy McIntyre, Charles Cummings and Toni Cummings."

By the time Joe and Tim reached the waiting area outside of the principal's office, the others were already there, sitting on a long bench. Mike stood up and gathered the suspects around him. He addressed them in a low whisper, "Listen up, when we get in there, nobody else say a word. I've got this."

Joe wasn't so sure, "What do have in mind Mike?"

Toni wasn't the type to let someone else be her spokesperson, let alone a wild card like Mike. "Yeah, what kind of crazy idea do you have up your sleeve?"

"I mean it," Mike said forcefully, "Just let me handle this. It's going to be fine."

Father Parker opened his office door and summoned them. They filed in and lined up in front of his desk. Tim was surprised not to see Mr. Wagner in the room. Father Parker was a somewhat mysterious figure at Regis. He'd been the principal for many years, but he kept a low profile. He was a stern, lurking presence around the building. His public persona was emotionally contained, but he had a reputation for being mercurial during tense private encounters. The defendants didn't know what to expect, but they feared the worst.

The office was adorned with Catholic and secular icons, a large crucifix (every room at Regis had a crucifix), an autographed photograph of Pope Paul VI, a photo of Father with Congressman H.R. Gross, framed diplomas, and a bookshelf filled with community awards. The place oozed both sacred and temporal authority. Father Parker spoke from his desk chair, while the accused continued to stand. "Gentlemen and lady, the public display in back of the school that greeted me this morning is one of the most disrespectful acts I have ever witnessed, but before I say anything more, I need to hear what you have to say for yourselves."

Mike quickly spoke-up, "Father, it's true that the five us were together last night when we went to Study Night. It's true that we had an argument with Mr. Wagner, when he refused to let us enter the school. It's true that we were mad and thought Mr. Wagner was being really unfair. But these four people had nothing to do with what happened after that. They all went home with Joe. I was the only one who stayed and wrote LAME WAYNE in the snow. I was the only one who drew those duck feet."

The four others shot glances at each other, but kept their mouths shut. They were quietly shocked by what Mike was doing, falling on his sword for them. It didn't feel right.

Father tilted his head and scanned their expressions. "I'm not quite sure what to make of this. You four, is Mike telling the truth?"

Tim was the first to silently nod his head in the affirmative. Joe, Charlie, and Toni quickly followed. Tim felt like a total shit. They all did.

"Alright then, I'll have to go with what you've told me, Michael. You'll report to detention for the next two weeks. You are banned from all extracurricular activities for the next month. Now go down to the maintenance garage, get a shovel and push broom. Then go out there and erase everything you've written. You are all dismissed. Oh, and Michael, I want you to go to Mr. Wagner before the end of the day and apologize."

When they reached the hallway, Joe swung around and grabbed Mike by his shoulder. "What the hell were you doing back there, Mike? You shouldn't have taken the heat for all of us. We didn't ask you to do that. You really put us in a bind."

"I know I didn't have to do it, and I didn't intend to put you in a bind. But last night we said we were going to define ourselves as the LIME JUICE, right. So, what does that mean? To me it means two things. One, that we're united in getting each other through this parochial place. That we need to have each other's backs. Two, we each have to find our own way to transcend all this crap. When I saw Lame Wayne written on the hill this morning, I knew I was responsible for starting it. I decided that no matter what discipline they handed-out, I could handle it. I could rise above it. I could transcend it. We're the LIME JUICE, damn it. We're all just liv'in, lov'in and learn'in." Besides, IGAS, right?

Tim ran into Mike after school and asked him if he had apologized to Wagner. Mike shrugged and said, "Yeah, I went straight to Wagner's office after Father laid it on me. I knocked, walked in and told him I was sorry for writing his name in the snow. He just stared bullets at me and told me to go back to class. I could hear in his tone a thirst for vengeance"

Chapter 12
The Chronicle

Donny Stevens was Tim's cousin on his father's side, the protestant side of the family. He was two years older than Tim and he had graduated from West High School the previous Spring. Donny was a handsome, solidly built kid who played multiple sports. He was also a solidly good egg. He was the kind of guy people liked to hang with. Tim lost touch with Donny when he hit high school, so he was in the dark about why Donny and two friends decided to enlist in the Marine Corps immediately after graduation. Donny completed basic training over the summer, and he was in Vietnam by the end of August. During the Vietnam War, the Marines had the highest casualty rate of any branch of service. They comprised 2.7 percent of total US forces, but they had 25 percent of all the casualties.

Donny's brother Daren was Tim's age. They'd been in Boy Scouts together and they would still hang out occasionally. Donny began writing Daren and his parents from the time he started basic training and Daren would read the letters to Tim. The first few correspondences reflected Donny's gung-ho attitude, although he acknowledged that it was the hardest physical and mental challenge he had ever experienced. *"I thought I was in pretty good shape before, but I had no idea what being combat fit meant. They're turning us into incredible hard asses, if they don't break us first. I guess what doesn't kill us will make us stronger."*

After Donny arrived in Vietnam, he began writing Daren separately from his parents. The letters to his parents remained largely upbeat. The tone and content of his messages to Daren were more candid and personally revealing. *"This place is fucking crazy Daren. We're all jumpy as hell. We never know from one moment to the next where we're going or what exactly we're going to be doing. I was just told they're going to make me a side gunner on a Huey. I've got to be honest with you Daren, it scares the shit out of me.*

I've never liked heights and now I'm going to be hanging out the side of a helicopter. I suppose I'll get used to it."

Donny wrote Daren four more letters, each one describing harrowing experiences and Donny's darkening mood. *"We made two runs yesterday, shuttling Marines in and out of a hot LZ. My hands were too shaky to write this until today. We took heavy fire going in and out. We had some gruesome casualties on board. Some of them didn't make it. I'm worried that maybe I'm not going to make it. I love all you guys, Daren. Please keep writing and praying for me. It means a lot."*

Donny's next correspondence was full of rage, the kind Daren had never seen in Donny before. *"I hate this fucking place. I hate these fucking people. There's no way to know who's going to thank you and who's going to kill you, although a lot more people have tried to kill us than have thanked us. What the fuck, Donny, we're here fighting and dying for their freedom!"* There were five more pages with tales of terror, lust for vengeance and pangs of remorse. *"I don't recognize myself here. I hate what I'm becoming."*

A letter arrived right before Christmas that revealed a new and disturbing turn. *"I swear Daren, I don't know what I'd do if I couldn't get high. If the VC don't kill us, the boredom in between action will. We can't just sit around waiting for the next horror show. Fortunately, I can easily get anything I want, and I've tried about everything you can imagine. I've actually had some pretty good times with my brothers on base. I'm pretty much stoned most of the time. Please, please, please don't say a word about this to mom and dad. Don't hang onto any of these letters Daren. Get rid of them as soon as you read them!"*

Joe and Tim were up in Joe's bedroom listening to an album by a new group called Iron Butterfly. Their song, "In-A-Gadda-Da-Vida", was an unusual sounding psychedelic rock tune that was getting quite a lot of radio play. The heavily distorted guitar and low, dark vocals were putting them in an edgy mood. Tim had brought over the most recent weekly issues of *The Berkeley Barb* and the December issue of *The Gonzo Gazette*. They agreed that *The Barb* was losing its way. It was becoming more self-absorbed with its own radical identity, espousing the most extreme views possible, accented with violent illustrations. It was infatuated with the French student protest movement and it reprinted articles by their French counterparts. Surprisingly, the underground high school paper, *The Gonzo Gazette*, seemed more mature and well-written than *The Barb*. *The Gonzo* had substantive stories told in ways that high school students could relate to.

One story Kayla wrote titled, "Fatal Futility," really struck a nerve with Joe. It was an obituary for a recent El Cerrito High graduate who had been killed in Vietnam. Kayla interviewed several of his former classmates, who described him and their lives together before graduation. Kayla didn't have the details about his death, but she did find some information about the skirmish he was killed in. It was a search and destroy action through a cluster of villages east of the port city of Hue. The area had supposedly been cleared of Viet Cong fighters several times in the past, each time resulting in a sizeable official VC body count. The point of Kayla's story was the futility of US strategy in Vietnam and the tragic loss of young lives for such an ignoble cause. The story agitated Joe, "Shit, Tim, this kid could be us in a year or two.

"That kid could be my cousin Donny at any moment. He's a Marine in Nam right now. He's been writing his brother since August. The war is fucking up his head bad." This was the first time Tim had mentioned Donny's letters to anyone, and he instantly regretted saying anything about it, even to a close friend like Joe.

"Damn it, Tim, that's exactly what people need to know about. That's exactly what kids at Regis need to know about. It's stories like the one Kayla wrote that move people, that bring the war home, that make the war real, that can change minds about the war. I bet the story in the El Cerrito newspaper was nothing like the one Kayla wrote. It probably whitewashed the real story about how and why he died. It probably described it as just some noble, 'ultimate sacrifice, an act of patriotism.' Your cousin's story needs to be told. We need to rally the LIME JUICE and get that damn newspaper together. We need to stop fucking around.

"Hold on Joe, we can't write a story about Donny. Those letters are private. He even told Daren to destroy them after he read them. Besides, it would kill his parents to see what was in those letters, especially if they were made public."

"We wouldn't have to say the letters were from Donny. We could mask his identity. Look, let's not make any decisions about this yet. Maybe we won't even do that story, but we should still put a paper out that tells the truth, the truth people can't find anywhere else."

"OK Joe, I'm down with that, although I don't know the first thing about how to put together a newspaper– do you?"

"Hell no, but I've been thinking about it. Julie's sister, Monica, has a job in the University of Iowa print shop. She might be able to help us. Monica's cool. She's been involved with organizing campus protests in Iowa City. Julie told me Monica's even had some contacts with the SDS, you know, Students for a Democratic Society."

"I know what the SDS is Joe. I also know the FBI is freaked out about them. Their involved with some pretty radical shit. We need to be careful."

"Fuck the FBI! Hell, Tim, we're talking about putting out a newspaper, not blowing up a fucking building."

The following day, Joe and Julie called Monica in Iowa City. Amazingly, Monica loved their plan to put out an underground paper and she was happy to help. "I hope you shake the shit out of those assholes up there."

Monica suggested they come down to Iowa City to meet with her and her friends to talk about how the process might work. Tim had Sunday off at the FoodValu, so they decided to head down after he got off work Saturday afternoon. Recalling what Tim heard from Rebecca in Tucson, he told his folks they were going to Iowa City for a campus tour. His mom wasn't enthused about the University of Iowa. She preferred Tim attend a Catholic college, but she knew he couldn't afford it. So, on a bitterly cold January afternoon, Joe, Julie, Sandy, and Tim sputtered down to the University of Iowa with Jim in his recently acquired used Volkswagen minibus. It was a frigid trip. The VW's feeble defrost fan could barely maintain a clear view through the windshield. They were fired up, though. The University of Iowa campus had become a hotbed of activism. Every emerging radical organization in the country had taken some root there. They were excited about experiencing one of the most thriving counterculture communities in the Midwest.

They parked the VW bus on Clinton Street in downtown Iowa City. Monica's apartment was up a long narrow staircase, in a 19th century commercial building, above The Deadwood Tavern.

As they approached the top of the stairs, they were enveloped in the pungent smell of incense. From behind Julie's apartment door, they could hear the Moody Blues playing inside. "Nights in White Satin" was echoing hauntingly through the hallway. They had to knock three times before Monica answered. As soon as the door opened, marijuana smoke rolled out of the room behind her. She was wearing a flannel shirt and bell-bottom jeans adorned with white bleach stains. Her long brown hair looked like it hadn't been combed in several days. Tim thought she looked super cool. She yipped and gave Julie a big hug, then she hugged each one of them. Entering the apartment was like walking into Xanadu. There were colorful tapestries hanging from the ceilings, political and rock concert posters all over the walls, beaded curtains in the doorways, blue, red and purple lights overhead. There were four other people in the living room, two guys and two girls, seated on floor pillows, surrounding a large hookah pipe. After they were all seated, Monica introduced her companions. James looked like an older Josh, with black shoulder-length hair. Alan had ginger hair, permed into a huge white-man's Afro. Jody had the Joan Baez look going on. Denise wore black glasses and looked like Marion-the-Librarian from *The Music Man*. Tim thought she was beautiful.

Monica set the scene for the evening. "I tell you what, let's talk about your newspaper and the revolution tomorrow. Tonight's going to be really special. I wasn't sure if this would work out when we talked on the phone, but we have a surprise for you. She turned to Jody and held out her hand. Jody placed a manila envelope in Monica's palm. Monica opened it and took out what looked to be a stack of tickets. "Guys, the Jefferson Airplane are playing at the Iowa Fieldhouse tonight. It's going to be incredibly far out and we're all going!"

The young pilgrims almost leaped out of their seats. Julie yelled, "How the hell did you get all those tickets!"

Monica matter-of-factly replied, "We work in the print shop - remember. We can print anything."

Warren was skeptical. "You mean these are counterfeit? Are you sure they're going to work, that we won't get busted?"

Monica took another ticket out of her pocket and held it out in her other hand. "This is a legit ticket that I bought. Can you tell the difference? Look, there's no reserve seating at this concert. There's no seating at all on the main floor, just standing room. The whole place is general admission. It's almost like they want people to make their own tickets."

Monica looked side-to-side at her companions, with a sneaky smile, then she looked back at the juniors. "There's one other thing. I wasn't sure if this was a good idea for you kids, but I couldn't let you go to a Jefferson Airplane concert unaided." She set the tickets down and held out her hand again. James handed her a plastic baggy filled with some kind of brown, chunky, slimy goo. "We're going to take a journey down the rabbit hole tonight children. Magic mushrooms will take us there."

Tim asked warily, "Whoa, magic mushrooms, do you mean psilocybin mushrooms?

Monica was reassuring, "Of course, I don't want you to try them if you don't want to. There's a right way and a wrong way to do shrooms. Everyone who decides to take them has to be a family for the rest of the night. We need to stick together and take care of each other. If we eat them before we leave the apartment, they'll start to come-on sometime after we get to the concert. Then we'll have to stay together in one place. Nobody goes anywhere alone, not even to the bathroom. After the concert, we'll come straight back here and chill out for the rest of the night."

Straight up, Tim was scared. Tripping on magic mushrooms was a whole higher level of distortion than overdosing on cough syrup. It would be in mind-bending category like taking LSD. However, he'd been curious about what it would be like to have a genuine psychedelic experience, and a Jefferson Airplane concert seemed designed to be such an occasion. Denise came back from the kitchen with a large bowl of plain yogurt. Monica mixed-in the mushrooms and then dished out the disgusting concoction evenly into smaller bowls. She handed each of them a bowl and said, "Bon appetit!"

They hit the street about fifteen minutes later. Everyone around seemed to be streaming towards the Iowa Fieldhouse. It was bitterly cold and windy, but people were in high spirits. By the time they crossed the Burlington Street bridge over the Iowa River and were marching up the hill to the Fieldhouse, the stream of people had turned into a wide river of humanity. They filed past the ticket-takers without a hitch. Most people raced to the main floor to get positioned as close to the stage as possible. Monica thought it best for them to carve out their own space on the upper deck. It was a good call. They were able to get seats on either side of the aisle in the first two rows by the railing, looking directly at the stage. They got settled in for the ride.

The scene below was unlike anything Tim had ever seen. The entire main level was packed with thousands of young people. Most of them were sitting on the floor, like they were at a picnic. The loudspeakers on stage were playing some Grateful Dead jam. Clouds of tobacco, marijuana and hashish smoke billowed up from all over the arena. Tim was stunned by how brazen it was. There were a few cops standing near the doorways, but they seemed unconcerned with the illicit drug use. Balloons and beachballs were being tossed in the air and bounced all around the crowd. Frisbees were flying everywhere. Lots of people were blowing bubbles into the air. The atmosphere was pure joy.

The opening act was a local band called The Mother Blues. As the lights were lowered, Tim sensed a tingling running down his arms and legs. He attributed it to the excitement of anticipation, but he wondered if the mushrooms might be kicking in. The band played some outstanding original rhythm and blues numbers. At the conclusion of their third song, all the stage lights went dark. Then the band started to play a slow, dreamy, jazzy instrumental. As the tune progressed, a white cloud started to rise up from behind the stage and float into the audience. The fog crept across the floor until it reached the back of the arena, then it rose towards the upper deck. Suddenly, two white and two blue spotlights flipped on from behind the stage. The shadows of the band members were projected into the fog. The shadows danced all around Tim. At that moment, a rush ran through his body. He realized that he was tripping for real, or more accurately, for unreal.

The lights came up after the Mother Blues left the stage. Tim and his fellow mind travelers looked at each other with stunned expressions, then they exploded in laughter. Tim looked around the arena and discovered it had been transformed. The people below sparkled. There were rainbows around every source of light. When he swung his head from side to side, the images in his sight would streak side to side. He had heard about this phenomenon. They called it "seeing trails." He played around with the effect, whisking his head around to maximize the long contrails that objects were leaving behind. When he stopped and fixed his gaze, objects would shrink, then grow, then pulsate. Sounds fluctuated from crisp to muffled. His vision fluctuated between sharply focused to fuzzy. The vast interior of the Fieldhouse throbbed and warbled.

Tim felt energized and jittery, as if an electrical current was running through his body. His feet were tapping manically, and his fingers were fidgeting. The most profound impact was in his mind. He was no longer sure where he was, how he got there, or why he was there. He recognized the people around him, but he was no longer sure if he really knew them. He didn't feel anxious about all of this uncertainty. He interpreted it to mean that everything had been recreated, reborn. He was intrigued that his previous assumptions about the reality around him were now up for grabs. He was discovering a new way to experience existence. He marveled at the novelty and hilarity of it all, until the lights dimmed again.

The Jefferson Airplane made their entrance in the dark and began playing exotic, melodic rock riffs. Colorful psychedelic patterns emerged on a giant screen behind the stage. The light show became brighter and the patterns more frenetic as the music became quicker and louder. A spotlight shot down on Grace Slick. Her deep, dramatic, strident, confrontational voice erupted,

> *"When the truth is found to be lies,*
> *and all the joy within you dies,*
> *don't you want somebody to love?*
> *Don't you need somebody to love?*
> *Wouldn't you love somebody to love?*
> *You better find somebody to love."*

Tim felt like she was speaking directly to him. *"Yes Grace, yes of course, I do need someone to love. We both do. I'm searching, just like you!"* He felt an overwhelming need to be close to her, to make eye contact with her. Without any of his companions noticing, he slipped off and walked up the stairs to the upper concourse. He found his way down a broad iron stairway and on to the main floor. The crowd had surged toward the stage, coagulating into a massive, throbbing organism. He would not be deterred from his mission to have an intimate encounter with Grace. He snaked his way under arms and through slight gaps between swaying hips, until he was pressed flat against the stage. Grace Slick was directly above him. She was captivating. The throngs in front of her were mesmerized. Jorma Kaukornen's psychedelic blues guitar riffs soared

138

above and around the melodies. Jack Casady's bass provided a rhythmic anchor that allowed the audience to drift freely through the band's long jams. Moments became minutes, which became lost measures of time.

The Airplanes' performance reached a crescendo, then suddenly ended. The band exited and waited for the deafening audience adulation to exhaust itself, before they returned to the stage for the obligatory encore. It had to be the quintessential San Francisco psychedelic anthem, "White Rabbit."

"One pill makes you larger, and one pill makes you small.
And the ones that mother gives you
won't do anything at all...."

Tim's magic mushroom moment had merged with the song. He and Grace had gone down the rabbit hole together. She ordained his condition when she proclaimed, *"Feed your head. Feed your head. Feed your head!"*

The fieldhouse lights popped on, momentarily blinding him. The band took several bows and waved their way off stage. Tim had no idea what to do, where he should go, or how he would get anywhere. A feeling of high anxiety and paranoia overwhelmed him. The crowd began to suck him backwards. He turned away from the stage and allowed himself to be pushed along with the hippie horde. Eventually, the crowd squirted out through the fieldhouse doors into the starry, piercing cold night. Wherever they were going, Tim worried that he was getting farther away from where he needed to be. The surroundings became darker and more expansive. It seemed as if he had left the city, that he was wandering in a vast wasteland. He sensed the contours of a valley. Yes, he was walking through a valley. Some of the people around him started to slip and slide. He focused downward and saw there was nothing but ice and snow beneath him. Then he looked up over his right shoulder and saw a distant structure stretching across the valley. There were lights and movement on top of it. It was a bridge! He realized that he was not in a valley. He was walking on the frozen surface of the Iowa River. The riverbank he had descended was a hundred yards behind him. The opposite bank was roughly fifty yards in front. At the moment of this realization, everyone around him froze in place. They all heard it, a slow low crunching, cracking sound. Panic rose inside Tim's chest.

People started to yell and shriek. Everybody gingerly began to move forward, slowly gaining traction on the ice, until they could quickly shuffle. Tim could see and feel the ice cracking under him, creating spider web patterns with each step. He heard some footfalls breaking through the ice, creating small splashes. His left foot slipped backwards on his final lurch towards the shore. He fell forward, face first into the brushy bank. He was the last person to reach safety. The climb up the riverbank was steep and slippery, but there were enough branches to grab that allowed him to pull his way up to the street. He still had no idea where he was or which way he should go, so he melded with the people coming across the bridge. The swarm led him back downtown, where he could see lights flashing around a sign for The Deadwood Tavern.

Tim walked to the top of the stairs and stood outside of Monica's apartment door. He was trembling. His eyes were glazed with tears. He wanted to rejoin his friends, but he was afraid that he wouldn't be able to function in their presence, or in anyone's presence. He didn't think he could put together a coherent sentence. The apartment door, the hallway walls and ceiling, were all moving, breathing. Waves of colors were radiating from the light fixture overhead. He sat down on the hallway floor, crossed his legs, put his head in his hands and tried to compose himself, to find himself. *"Would this ever end? Would he ever get his mind back?"*

Minutes passed, or maybe it was hours. The door at the bottom of the stairs opened. Monica, Julie and the entire troop clogged the doorway. Monica yelled up the stairs, "Tim, where the hell have you been! We've been looking everywhere for you! You scared the shit out of us!"

Tim tried to focus down the stairs. His vision was blurred through his tears. "I got lost. I'm really sorry," were the only words he could formulate.

Monica let Tim into the apartment, where they each adjourned to a comfortable nesting spot, their individual sanctuaries. No one said much. Tim could see that everyone was struggling for words. Everyone was absorbed in their own thoughts, in their own journey. Alan put a Miles Davis album on the stereo. They replayed the record until dawn, until everyone arrived at sleep.

They slept until early afternoon. Denise, Monica, and Alan made a big batch of scrambled eggs and a stack of toast. Then they got down to business over coffee and brunch. Monica had already thought it through. "A small, four-page tabloid format would be quick and easy. I'm going to give you some page mockup templates to take back home. Type up your stories, cut them up and lay them out with your photos and graphics on the dummy pages. I won't have time to do any editing, so whatever you put together is what gets printed. Denise, Jody and I will do the linotype setting. James and Alan will take it from there. We won't be able to run more than five hundred copies."

Joe asked, "So what do you think this is going to cost?"

Monica shrugged, "Don't know yet. It depends on what we can get away with off the clock at work. We won't charge you for our work. It's another way for us to support the cause. There might be some expenses for materials."

Julie spoke for them all. "This is unbelievable! We can't thank you all enough. If there's anything we can do for you guys, please let us know."

Jody leaned in and looked earnestly at each one of them. "What you can do for us is be very careful and look out for each other. You know there's going to be major blowback from what you're doing. If you say what needs to be said, it's inevitable. Just be careful!"

A few days later, on the first afternoon Tim wasn't scheduled to work at the FoodValu, they got together after school in Steve's basement for the first meeting of *The Lime Juice Chronicle* publishing team. Their first item of business was determining how they were going to do business. They needed to decide how they would make decisions. They shunned having a leadership hierarchy and opted to work as a collective. There would be no top-down dictates. Larry proposed a consensus model for making decisions, but they looked around the room and thought that was setting the bar too high. Although they had a lot in common, the LIME JUICE encompassed a wide range of personalities, temperaments, ideas, and opinions. A majority rules rule would be much more realistic.

Once that was settled, they agreed everyone would volunteer for their own roles and responsibilities. Joe, Charlie, Toni, and Tim would primarily write political stories. Julie wanted to write stories about women's issues. Jim, Warren and Larry wanted to write about music, movies and the arts. Sandy wanted to be the artistic director. Mary would be the photographer and write an alternative style advice column. Rick and Steve wanted to pick out cartoons and write humorous columns. Steve and Al would search for interesting sports stories, but they were cautioned not to write in a way that would associate the paper exclusively with Regis. Dean wanted to see if he could sell advertisements, assuming anyone would want to be associated with an underground newspaper in the middle of corn country.

Steve asked, "I wonder what Mike wants to do?"

Joe asked, "Where the hell is Mike anyway?"

Jim answered, "Mike has detention again this week. Wagner has been on the prowl for him ever since his confession. He found a chance to pounce Friday afternoon. Mike was running late for his Music class and Wagner caught him alone in the hallway. He accused Mike of trying to skip school, which is nuts, because Music is his favorite class. It really pisses me off. Wagner's clearly out to get Mike. It also screws up our band practice."

Tim shook his head and said, "This is not good. Wagner doesn't let go of grudges and Mike isn't one to sit still for being persecuted. Mike said he could transcend anything they threw at him, but Mike is going to reach a breaking point."

"We all have our breaking points," Julie warned, "Remember what Jody said about being careful and taking care of one another? I think we need some way to mask our identities when The Chronicle comes out. I think we need to use pen names when we write our stories. Above all, none of us should tell anyone who's behind this."

Mary already had her pen name. "I said I wanted my column to be *Dear Abbie Hoffman,* but I think I'll make it *Dear Abigail Hoffman.* You can just call me Abby though."

Julie had been thinking about it too. "I've refined my brand. I'm going to be Badass Babs. You can just call me Babs."

Joe wanted his pen name to be Coyote, as in, Wile E. Coyote. Warren picked up on the cartoon theme and decided to be Road Runner. Toni wanted to be Natasha, from The Adventures of Rocky and Bullwinkle show, so Charlie went with Boris. Steve then became Rocky and Rick became Bullwinkle. Larry would be Marvin, as in the Looney Tunes Marvin the Martian. Al was Bugs, as in Bunny. Jim would be Mr.

Peabody and Tim would be Sherman. Sandy was Tweety Bird. Dean didn't need a pen name, but they thought he should still have an alias, so he became Yosemite Sam.

The Lime Juice Chronicle had been gestating for months. It was time for them to go into labor and bring it to life.

Chapter 13
Tet

Any illusions Americans had about the war in Vietnam being well in hand and coming to an end anytime soon were shattered in early 1968. On January 31st, during the Tet lunar New Year festival, when hostilities usually waned, the North Vietnamese army and Viet Cong guerillas launched coordinated attacks on American and the Army of the Republic of Vietnam (ARVN) forces throughout South Vietnam. It began with a full-throttled assault on the Keh Sanh combat base. Two divisions of North Vietnamese army regulars and Viet Cong laid siege to the base, defended by two regiments of US forces. The two biggest shockers came shortly later when the northern city of Hue was overrun. Many residents of Hue were massacred. Then, for the first time, attacks occurred within the South Vietnamese capital of Saigon, including an assault inside the US embassy compound. Front line reports were broadcast nightly by the three major national television networks. The war was coming directly into the American public's living rooms. They saw reporters hunkered down with Marines in Hue, pinned behind piles of rubble. They saw soldiers at Khe Sanh scrambling for cover in sandbag bunkers, as mortar fire rained down on them. Correspondents filmed from the doors of Huey helicopters as they came under intense fire while trying to pull casualties out of hot landing zones. They saw Vietnamese civilians screaming in terror as bombs went off in the streets of Saigon. Every American was unnerved by the same images invading their domestic lives, every evening, week after week.

American forces eventually gained the upper hand, but American confidence had been badly shaken. After the legendary CBS anchorman Walter Cronkite stopped buying what the pentagon had been selling, even Tim's parents started to express misgivings about the war. However, the thought of the United States losing a war to a small, poor country like Vietnam was unimaginable to them. Tim's dad's thinking reflected that of many from his WWII generation, "The stakes are too high for us to simply walk away, Tim. Something needs to change though. Whatever we've been doing, it clearly isn't working."

The LIME JUICE were also rattled by the intensity of the Tet offensive violence, and they were further enraged by the continuing upbeat assessments by military leaders. The war was feeling closer to home as students were getting closer to draft age. They felt a heightened sense of urgency to help stop the carnage. Turning public opinion against the war was a matter of life-or-death, possibly even their own. They gave themselves a deadline to publish the first issue of *The Lime Juice Chronicle* by February 21st.

Coyote, AKA Joe, would write the paper's front-page introduction, stating unabashedly that their mission was to, "*Print the truth others would not dare.*" Natasha (Toni), would write the first editorial, titled, "The Truth about Tet," saying the offensive exposed the US lie about the war being winnable. Roadrunner and Mr. Peabody (Jim and Warren), titled their music review column, "*The Lime Juice Fresh Squeeze,*" with the tag line, "*Hearing the best of what's fresh.*" They wrote glowing reviews of the Beatles album, *Magical Mystery Tour* and the Otis Redding album, *The Dock of the Bay.* Dear Abigail Hoffman (Mary) didn't have any letters to respond to yet, so she and Badass Babs (Julie) wrote some unsolicited advice on how girls should stop taking Home Economics classes. Al and Steve worked on an insightful piece about how athletics at West and East high schools reflected the broader racial tensions in the community. It would soon prove to be prophetic. You could have knocked Tim over with a feather when Marvin (Larry) announced he wanted to write a book review. The book hadn't even been published yet, but Larry had read some advanced excerpts from Tom Wolf's, *The Electric Kool Aid Acid Test.* The subject matter resonated with Larry, but they told him it would have to wait for a later issue. Rocky and Bullwinkle (Randy and Rick) selected their favorite cartoons from the Berkeley Barb, The New Yorker and Playboy. They weren't concerned about copyrights. It was highly unlikely anyone would see or care about a high school underground newspaper in the backwaters of the Midwest. If they did, well, good luck suing them. Sandy came up with a trippy *Lime Juice Chronicle* masthead, with green lettering in Chicago Tribune font. Two limes on a branch and a slice of lime above the masthead showered the lettering with lime drops. The tag line below read, "All the News That's Fit to Squeeze."

The feature article would be a reprint of the "Fatal Futility" story from the Gonzo Gazette. Josh and Kayla were more than happy to have their piece read by a wider audience. Although it wasn't a local story, *The Chronicle* needed something that would personalize the war. Joe repeatedly asked Tim to get Daren to share Donny's letters and to make them the featured story. Tim finally agreed to ask Daren about it, but he wouldn't put any pressure on Daren, and they would have to assure him that the letters would remain anonymous. As Tim expected, Daren was horrified by the suggestion to have the letters printed. He was planning to destroy them, as Donny had directed. Daren also feared his parents might find them. The idea was dropped, and *The Chronicle* moved forward with Kayla's story.

To their astonishment, Yosemite Sam (Dean) had managed to secure a handful of advertisers and distributors. Two record stores and the National Cigar Store agreed to run ads and to sell *The Lime Juice Chronicle* on their premises. Dean also found four students who would sell the papers at each of the area public schools. They decided early on that distributing the paper at Regis needed to be done clandestinely, by someone not associated with any of them.

The notion of turning a profit was debated. Joe wanted the price set low, to maximize readership. Toni wanted to earn enough to support local civil rights campaigns. Jim thought the proceeds should pay for a LIME JUICE collection of new albums. Al thought they should make a trifecta wager with the Cigar Store's bookie operation and parlay their meager earnings into a small fortune. They decided the printed price would be $0.50, just enough to cover any costs they might incur along the way.

They were surprised and disappointed when Mike told them he couldn't take an active role with *The Chronicle*. Mike was on thin ice at Regis, and he couldn't afford any more missteps. Wagner continued to hound him, sending him to detention twice more, once for smoking in the school parking lot and once for playing drums in the band room without permission, when he was supposed to be in study hall. Mike was even more upset when he heard Wagner had been bad-mouthing him to the rest of the faculty. He thought all of his teachers would sour on him. He felt depressed and demoralized – destined to fail. His grades continued to slide. Wagner notified his parents that any further disciplinary problems would result in a suspension. They promptly clipped Mike's wings, grounding him from everything except band practices and performances, which they would drive him to and from.

The LIME JUICE tried their best to be supportive, but Mike still struggled to see the light at the end of his ordeal. He became more withdrawn. "I'm in exile, guys. I'm worried it might be a life sentence. If I disappear someday, write a nice obituary for me in *The Chronicle*. Let everyone know that I loved the LIME JUICE and that Wayne Wagner can go fuck himself."

By February 17th, they had everything written, designed, and laid out on the mock-up boards. They would deliver them to Monica in Iowa City the following day. They gathered in Steve's basement to celebrate and admire their work. As they congratulated each other and raised their Pepsi cans to toast their muses, Josh, and Kayla, they heard the phone ring upstairs. A few moments later, Steve's mom yelled down, "Tim, your mom is on the phone. She needs to talk with you."

Tim jogged up the stairs and took the call from the phone on the kitchen wall. His mom sounded more upset than Tim had ever heard. "Oh, Lord, Timmy, Daren just called. Donny's been killed! A Marine chaplain just left their house. I just can't believe it! Bill and Arlene are devastated. Donny was such a sweet boy. Your father and I are heading over there now. Daren said he wants to talk with you. You need to call him right away."

Tim called immediately. Daren picked up on the first ring. Tim hadn't formulated what he would say, "Jesus, Daren, I'm so..."

Daren cut him off, "Tim, where are you? I can pick you up. We can go over to Byrnes Park to talk."

Daren said he wanted to talk, but when Tim got in his car, Tim was the only one who spoke. "Shit, Daren, of course I knew it was possible Donny could get killed, but I still can't believe it's happened. It's totally fucked-up."

Daren silently stared straight ahead. He squeezed the steering wheel with his left hand, while pounding his right palm against his thigh and wiping tears from his cheeks. Five minutes later, Tim brushed snow off the top of a picnic table and sat down. Daren was too agitated to sit. He paced back and forth in front of Tim, still choking back tears. Tim quietly gave him time. Donny sat on the picnic table next to him. He rested his elbows on his knees, squeezed his hands together and stared down at the ground. Tim asked, "What did the chaplain say? What happened?"

Daren didn't look up. He breathed deeply to calm down, then he softly replied, "The chaplain said Donny was shot while loading wounded marines onto his helicopter. You know, Tim, that kind of made me feel better, knowing he was doing something he would be proud of. I know it's stupid, but I was also glad to know he was shot while he was on the ground, knowing how much he was scared of heights."

Daren turned his head twice to glance at Tim, then he pulled an envelope out of his coat pocket and handed it to him. "I got this two days ago."

Tim's hands trembled slightly as he pulled a letter out of the envelope, unfolded it, and softly read out loud.

> *"Dear Daren, I really appreciate all your letters. I love hearing about what's going on back home. Sorry I haven't written in a while. To be honest, it's hard knowing what to say. I don't want to write about what's been going on here. It's too messed-up and I try not to think about it. I just want to think about what I need to do to survive, like putting one foot in front of the other, until I can walk out of here. There's one thing I do want to say Daren, no matter what, do not come here! Don't let yourself be sent here. Do whatever it takes to not come here. Tell your friends not to come here. I've thought a lot about why the hell I ever enlisted. I didn't know a damn thing about this place or about this war. I just thought it would be a cool thing to do. You know, serve my country bullshit. I wanted to test myself and do something I could be proud of, maybe even be a hero. But I'm not proud about being here Daren. I'm only proud of my brother Marines and how we try to take care of each other. Everything else is bullshit. So, don't even think about coming here Daren. Promise me you won't. I'll be home before you graduate, and I'll sit on you if I have to.*
>
> *I love you bother,*
> *Donny*

148

They sat silently for a few moments, then Daren said, "Donny wanted me to destroy his letters. That's what I planned to do, but I haven't. Now Donny's gone, and his last message to me was to not go to Vietnam, to tell my friends not to go to Vietnam. People need to hear what Donny was saying, Tim. You can have the letters to write your story, but you need to promise me three things. One, Donny needs to stay anonymous. Two, you won't say anything about the drugs. Three, you'll let me read the story before it's printed – understand?

"Of course, Daren, I promise. I don't want anything to blow back on you or hurt your parents. You're doing the right thing. You're doing what Donny would want you to do."

Joe was horrified to hear about Donny's death, but he couldn't mask his excitement about printing Donny's letters. "I think Donny's letters will have a big impact Tim. I mean Kayla's' story was great, but Donny's story will hit home much harder. We can bump "Fatal Futility" to our next edition."

"It won't be Donny's story, Joe. Remember, I promised he would stay anonymous. We have to be very careful, so he can't be identified."

"Oh, I know, I know, Tim. We'll be careful, but we need to be clear that Daren was a local kid, one of our kids. We also need to get this done fast. I don't want to move our deadline back."

Over the next two days, Joe, Toni, and Tim poured over the letters. They tried to piece them together in a way that best told his story and conveyed his message. On February 19th, they fit the final draft into the revised layout boards. The whole LIME JUICE team stood around the table and read it one more time. They felt like Donny was speaking to them from the grave, even though he hadn't yet come home to be buried.

They wanted the headline to grab the readers' attention, *"Fallen Marine's Final Message Home."* They used a common soldier's pseudonym, so readers could feel a personal connection.

"Joe's not coming home, but his message for us has. Joe was a son of our town, one of our finest. He went to Vietnam to serve his country. He thought it was the right thing to do. Joe sacrificed his life for his comrades during the Tet Offensive. Before he was killed, he wrote letters

to his brother that described the reality of this far away war. His final letter before his death had a stark message for his brother, and all of us.

Joe believed in the war when he enlisted, during his basic training and in the first few days following his arrival in Vietnam. "I'm fired-up about being here and putting my training to use. It feels good to be part of something bigger than myself, defending this small country against communism and protecting our country."

It wasn't long before Joe began to question how the war was being conducted. "We're going to different places trying to find the V.C., but we rarely do. They always seem to be a step ahead of us. When we do make contact, they fight like hell and then evaporate. Then they come back as soon as we're gone."

Joe was the kind of kid who got along with everyone. He genuinely wanted to help the people of South Vietnam, but he started to question how the Vietnamese really felt about US military forces. "I thought we'd be greeted as liberators or saviors. When I go to Saigon on leave, the people are very friendly, but it's totally different in the countryside. They seem afraid of us. They don't trust us, and we don't trust them."

Before long, the mistrust grew into resentment and hatred. "I feel rage whenever I see them. These are the people who are killing and maiming my buddies, the people who want to kill and maim me. They just stop and stare at us, but when we aren't looking, they either become V.C. or they're helping the V.C."

Sometimes the rage turns to revenge and violence. "We've done some bad things to these people, things I can't share, things I'm not proud of. I'm afraid of who I'm becoming."

Just days before he was killed, Joe wrote his final letter home. He didn't want to talk about the war. He only wanted to send an urgent message to his brother and his friends. It was a message for all of us. "There's one thing I do want to say, no matter what, do not come here! Don't let yourself be sent here. Do whatever it takes to not come here. Tell your friends not to come here. I've thought a lot about why the hell I enlisted. I didn't know a damn thing about this place or about the war. I just thought it would be a cool thing to do. You know, serve my country bullshit. I wanted to test myself and do something I could be proud of, maybe even be a hero. But I'm not proud about being here. I'm only *proud of my brother marines and how we try to take care of each other. Everything else is bullshit. So, don't even think about coming here."*

If you no longer trust what our government is saying about the war in Vietnam; if you aren't sure about what the media is reporting about the war; if you don't trust those at home who are protesting the war, then just listen to Joe."

The story needed to be short and to the point. After all, it was only a four-page tabloid, so space was limited. Besides, they couldn't add too many details that might compromise Donny's identity. The LIME JUICE were pleased with the story and thought it packed a powerful punch, but Tim was racked with doubt. *Did it convey what a great guy Donny was? Did it honor his sacrifice enough? Was it true to what Donny wanted us to say? Did it reveal too much, so people would know this was Donny?* Most of all, Tim was worried about what Daren would think.

They met at the Pizza Hut. "How you doing Daren? How are your folks?"

"Donny's body is supposed to arrive home in a few days. I'm anxious for him to come home, but it scares me too. Donny's death hasn't been totally real yet. When we see him, see his body, well..." Daren turned his head and stared out the window. He clinched his hands in front of his mouth and fought back tears. Then he faced Tim, lowered his hands to the table and said, "Show me what you've got." When he finished reading, he handed the draft back to Tim and said, "You did a good job Tim. A few days ago, I would've worried about people knowing this story was about Donny, but right now, I just don't give a flying fuck."

The atmosphere in Monica's Iowa City apartment had taken a somber and sober turn. The Tet offensive had ignited calls for more aggressive opposition to the war. The winter had chilled protest activity on campus, but planning was underway for confrontational mass demonstrations at the first sign of Spring. Some radicals were arguing for more violent action, like firebombing the Armory building on campus and the ROTC office. Monica and Alan strongly objected to violence against people or property. For them, it was all about winning hearts and minds. They were in a heated exchange with James about this when the LIME JUICE arrived. Monica answered the door. After she let them in, she immediately returned to arguing with James, "This nonsense about bombings and sticking it to the pigs is idiotic. Sure, we need to be provocative, and in their faces, but not violent. It's like what Martin Luther King says, peaceful protest is not passive, but violence will just turn the public off. We'll become what we're resisting. Besides, the cops and National Guard are much better at violence than we are. It won't work. We'll lose."

Mike had wanted to come to Iowa City with Joe, Julie, and Tim. He still needed to keep his distance from *The Chronicle*, but he thought getting out of town would be a relief from the stress he was feeling at school. Mike hadn't met Monica and her friends, so Tim was taken aback when Mike was the first to wade into the debate. "So, if you don't think violence will work, Monica, what type of confrontations do you have in mind? What do you think will tip the scales against the war?"

"Nothing we do here in Iowa City is going to tip the scales against the war, Mike, but we can be one of a thousand cuts that cripples their ability to carry out the war. Mass mobilization requires organization and every day we're getting more organized, more coordinated around the country. Some of the strategies we've been learning come from an activist in Chicago, Saul Alinsky. He wrote a book years ago called, *Reveille for Radicals.* He's got a new one in the works now. He's come up with these brilliant ways for people to use their collective power to gum up the works of huge organizations and bring them to their knees."

That prompted James to crack, "So, you think we can stop the war with pranks? Maybe we can grind the war to a halt by putting sugar in the gas tanks of their jeeps and helicopters? Maybe we can break the back of the military by wrapping the Pentagon in toilet paper."

Monica laughed, "Actually, those are tactics I can see Jerry Rubin and Abbey Hoffman using. I'm not a big fan, but the Yippies are right about one thing, it helps to have a sense of humor and to make people smile. We're going to try some direct action tomorrow at the Joint Military Enlistment Office. It'll be fun and really piss them off. We have several dozen students lined up to go in and ask about enlisting. We're going to overwhelm them. Anyone seriously interested in enlisting won't be able to get near the place. You're all welcome to come along."

Mike started to reply, "Sure, but what...."

152

Monica interrupted, "What am I thinking? I'm so sorry. You guys came down here to talk about *The Chronicle,* and we've been rattling on and on about the revolution."

Joe piped in, "Well, *The Chronicle* is about the revolution too, so no problem. We have the first issue put together. We're super excited about it, particularly the feature story."

Julie pulled the layout boards out of the portfolio bag. Joe handed a typed copy of Donny's story to Monica. She leaned back in her beanbag chair. When she saw the headline, her eyes widened. After she finished reading, she looked up and said, "This is incredible! Is this for real? How did you get this?"

Joe started to answer, "Hell yes it's for real. He's..."

Tim stopped Joe from saying anything more. "Yes, it's real, every word of it. We know who wrote those letters. We've seen them, but we can't say who the letters are from. Joe's not his real name. We promised to keep his name strictly confidential. The only thing we can say is that he was a local guy, a kid from Iowa."

Monica handed the story to James. By the time he finished reading, he was clinching the paper tightly and rapidly tapping his foot. "This is powerful shit, people. This story can't be confined to a few hundred copies of *The Lime Juice Chronicle.* It might be more meaningful locally, given he's an Iowa kid, but the message would resonate anywhere in the country. Look, there's an informal network of underground papers, sort of an underground wire service. This story should go out to all of them. What do you say?"

Tim appreciated Julie saying, "It's up to Tim. He's the one who got the story."

All eyes were on Tim as he mulled it over. He remembered what Daren told him, that he didn't give a shit anymore if people found out it was Donny. "Hell yes, you can send it out to those other newspapers. This is the guy's dying message. If it causes one other kid to rethink going to Nam, it'll be worth it. It's what he would want."

The following day, on a quiet, chilly Sunday morning, one thousand copies of *The Lime Juice Chronicle* flew off the University of Iowa presses. That same day, Monica, James, and Alan mailed copies of the *Fallen Marine's Final Message Home* story to editors at twenty underground newspapers, including the *Village Voice* and the *Berkeley*

Barb. Tim personally mailed a copy to Josh and Kayla, inviting them to reprint Donny's story in *The Gonzo Gazette*.

They were excited to get back home and start distributing the inaugural edition of *The Chronicle*, but Mike wanted to stay until Monday, so he could take part in jamming up the Joint Military Enlistment Office. He would come up with some excuse to tell his parents, and they could tell the school. Perhaps he would use Tim's line about going on a campus tour. His parents would love that. Mike said he would hitchhike home. Monica said she would keep an eye on Mike. She smiled and reassured them there would not be any serious trouble. "It's going to be all about peace, love and having a little fun."

As soon as they got back home Sunday evening, they delivered *The Chronicle* to their distributors at the three public high schools. Their distribution methods at Regis had to be more discreet. They arrived at school early Monday morning and placed stacks of *The Chronicle* on the sink counters in each of the girls' and boys' bathrooms. The faculty rarely entered the student bathrooms, and the custodians usually didn't go there until after school. They started to see a smattering of students with the paper during first period. The number of students reading it grew between each class period. By the time Julie and Tim sat down together during their lunch period, they could see *The Chronicle* all over the cafeteria. Their ears were tuned into the buzz in the dining hall. "What is this?" "Where did these come from?" Who's did this?" Who the hell are Coyote and Badass Babs?" Of course, The LIME JUICE stayed mum. They swore on a stack of Bob Dylan albums that they wouldn't say anything about who was behind *The Chronicle*.

As the afternoon progressed, they heard more students sharing their opinions about what they'd read. Some reactions were pretty hostile. "It's just a bunch of hippie crap." "Badass Babs sounds like a badass bitch." "I don't understand why Babs and Abigail are so upset about Home Economics? I mean, how can Home Economics make anybody mad?" "Yeah, and Natasha's story about Vietnam sounds like she's a communist." "These assholes are freaks. Their brains are fried from drugs." "How did this crap get into our school?" "I didn't think Regis had these kinds of people." "Who said they're from Regis? I bet they're from West High."

154

But there were lots of positive comments too. "That Coyote character kicks ass and he's not taking prisoners! I can't wait to see what he writes next." "I loved Abigail and Babs! I mean, how come only girls are taking Home Ec. and Typing? For that matter, why am I taking Home Ec. and Typing?" "I think Roadrunner and Mr. Peabody's album reviews were cool. I never heard of those bands." By the end of the day, the bulk of the conversations focused on *A Fallen Marine's Final Message Home.* "Do think that story about Joe is real, that the letters are real?" "It was so sad. It's really upsetting." "Do you really think Joe is from around here?" I haven't heard about anybody from Regis being killed in Vietnam yet." "Who could it really be?" Of course, there were cynics. "No way is that story real. It's just a bunch of made-up anti-war bullshit. No real Marine would write that crap."

Tim wanted to linger around after school to hear more reactions and to get a sense of whether anyone knew who was responsible for *The Chronicle*, but he had to run to work. After his shift, he headed to the LIME JUICE nerve center - Steve's basement. Tim was relieved to see Mike was there and he was surprised to also see Monica's friend Alan. They had just arrived from Iowa City. They were both still pretty hyped up. Mike was sitting on the overstuffed sofa, rapidly taking hits from a Pepsi bottle. Alan was quietly pacing around the room. Charlie wanted a full account. "Settle down, Mike. Start from the beginning and take your time."

"Fuck man, the way it went down, it was really intense! Things got way out of hand, fast, but honestly, it was a blast. Monica didn't have much of a plan. It started out pretty light-hearted. Alan and I were the first people at the enlistment center. There was only one Navy dude there. We strutted in with big smiles on our faces saying we wanted to enlist in the Marines. He asked me how old I was. I told him I was turning 18 in April."

Charlie said, "And he bought that?"

"Hell yes, he bought it. It's true. I do turn 18 in April, I'm a year older than most of you guys. My parents held me back a year before I started first grade. It was my mom's idea. She thought it would give me an edge. Anyway, we sat down and started to fill out these forms. I just made shit up. I signed my name. Jack Mehoff."

Mike picked up the pace, becoming more agitated as his story progressed. He looked like he was on the verge of hyperventilating. "A few minutes later, four more guys showed up saying they wanted to enlist. The Navy guy told them they would have to wait and to take a seat. Then James comes in with five more guys saying they wanted enlistment forms. The Navy guy started to get suspicious. He told them they would have to come back another time, to call and make an appointment. Monica advised us not to get into any hostile confrontations. If we ran into any resistance from the recruiters, we should back off and let the next group come in and bog them down. But Monica's directions were more than what James could handle. He insisted that he needed to enlist right then and there. The recruiter then realized we were all bullshitting him. He got into James' face and yelled at him to get out, for all of us to get out. That set James off. He shoved the Navy guy away and called him a baby killing pig. While they were going at it, another recruiter, an army guy, came in from the back room. He stopped at the desk I was sitting at and called the cops. Then he walked right past me and joined the Navy guy in shoving everyone towards the door.

"For a second, I thought about jumping the recruiters from behind, but I knew that kind of thing wasn't part of the plan and how strongly Monica felt about avoiding violence. I decided to cut out the back, but on my way, I passed an office filled with file cabinets. I walked in and saw a basket on the desk. It was filled with a stack of completed enlistment forms. It hit me that these were guys signing up to go to war and that I might be able to stop them. I grabbed the forms and stuffed them into my jacket. Then I walked out. I passed another office that was being remodeled. There were a couple of white paint cans on the floor that had been opened. I grabbed them and walked back to the first office, opened each file drawer one-by-one and dumped the two cans of paint into each one. It was so cool man, paint oozing down from drawer to drawer and flowing across the floor. It was a royal mess.

"I bolted for the door, but when I got into the hallway, a cop yelled at me to stop. As soon as I looked around, I saw James jump on his back, then another cop pulled James off. The first cop came after me. I shot through the back door into a parking lot. The cop was only a few steps behind me. He chased me around the lot, swinging his club in the air, screaming that he was going to kick the shit out of me. He was yelling, calling me a cowardly little prick." Mike started laughing

156

hysterically. "The cop had a problem though. He was built like the Pillsbury doughboy. He couldn't touch me. I was running circles around him, laughing, and telling him he should go to Nam to work off a few pounds, but I tried to stay polite. I kept calling him sir and flashing him the peace sign. He finally stopped chasing me and went back inside. I went around the front of the building. There must have been fifty or sixty students there, shouting at about twenty cops. The cops had full riot gear on. I could see them dragging James out the front door, with his hands cuffed behind his back. He was putting up a good fight, but they got him into a patrol car and drove off. Alan came up beside me, took my arm and pulled me away. It was a trip man. It blew my mind."

Tim looked over at Alan and asked him, "What happened then?"

"They fired tear gas canisters over the crowd and everyone took off in all directions. I could see it coming, so Mike and I got far enough away that it didn't bother us. It was a real shit show though. Monica organized a group to go bail out James. She asked me to give Mike a ride home. She feels bad that he got caught up in this."

Over the next few weeks, the controversy at Regis about *The Lime Juice Chronicle* died down. The wall of silence held, and the LIME JUICE were confident the paper wouldn't be linked to them. Two weeks later, they started to talk about putting out a second issue.

Tim swung by his house after school, before heading to work. The mail was sitting on the kitchen table. He recognized the two packages wrapped in brown paper. The smaller one would be *The Gonzo Gazette*, the other one would be *The Berkeley Barb*. He took them up to his room and opened *The Gazette* first. There was a note from Kayla and Josh paperclipped to the front page. "Congratulations on your *Fallen Marine* scoop. The whole country will be hearing about it soon."

The story about Donny's letters home was on the front page of the *Gonzo Gazette*. There were no edits or additions. It was just as they had written in *The Chronicle*. Then Tim opened *The Barb*, and there it was, the front-page headline, "*Dead Marine Says Get the Fuck Out of Vietnam*." He was pissed that they had distorted the quote and he quickly read the story to see if they had made any other changes – they hadn't. Tim relaxed when he remembered *The Barb* wasn't sold anywhere in town and it was very unlikely anyone would ever see it. However, Kayla and Josh said the whole country would see the story. *How could that be?*

You put all the underground papers in the country together and the readership would probably only add up to the population of one small town – right?

When Tim got back home after work, his mom said Al wanted him to call. "Hey, Al, what's happening?"

"Jesus, Tim, get ready for this. I went to the National Cigar Store after school. I was scanning the magazine rack and saw they're now carrying *The Village Voice,* and there it was, on the damn cover, 'Iowa Marine's Final Message Home.' I picked it up and found the whole story, just like we wrote it. I freaked out! This is way cool man. Do you know how many people read the *Village Voice?*"

"No, Al, I actually don't know how many people read the *Village Voice.*"

"I have no idea either, but it must be a lot. I mean, if the National Cigar Store sells it here in the middle of Iowa, it must be sold at a shitload of other places. It's so cool man. *The Chronicle* is going to have a much bigger impact than we ever thought possible."

"You've got that right, Al. I never imagined."

How could Tim have imagined? The story had been written for a high school underground newspaper, for Christ's sake. They didn't even use their real names and they used an alias for Donny's name. There's no way any of these other papers could verify whether the story was legit. Tim assumed Kayla and Josh vouched for its authenticity with *The Barb,* but what about the others? He could only conclude that they believed it, because they wanted to believe it, because it supported what they thought about the war. Tim was thrilled to think lots of people might see Donny's story and that it might make some people rethink the war, but greater notoriety brought greater risks. As the story's exposure grew, so did Tim's anxiety about being exposed. He took some solace knowing that other more mainstream news organizations wouldn't run a story that couldn't be verified. It only took another week for him to learn how wrong he had been.

Not long after Tim first learned to read, he started reading the morning Des Moines Register every day. He was first drawn to the comics, particularly the bright colored funny pages in the Sunday edition. He progressed to the sports pages, where he followed his adopted teams and heroes, like the Twins and Harmon Killebrew; the Vikings and Fran Tarkenton; and all the Iowa Hawkeye teams. Along the way, he'd spot some hard news stories of interest, about wars, disasters, crimes, and politics. As his interests broadened and his reading prowess improved, he was drawn to editorials and opinion pieces by national columnists, like David Broder. He was a devoted fan of the Register's Donald Kaul and his column, Over the Coffee. The Des Moines Register was Tim's paper of record, his window on the world, his trusted broker of truth. It was therefore profoundly consequential, when a few days later, while crunching on his Grape Nuts and taking his first wake-up sip of coffee, Tim unfolded the Des Moines Register and read the front page below the fold headline, *"Iowa Marine's Letters Home: Questions Grow."*

Tim's eyes froze on the headline, reluctant to move on to read the story. He momentarily tried to disassociate what he was seeing from Donny, from Daren and from himself, thinking this must be about another Marine, and someone else's letters. The delusion was fleeting, and he braced himself for a crush of accountability.

> *"In recent days, a story has been circulating around the country in the alternative press about an Iowa Marine killed during the Tet offensive. The Marine had purportedly written letters home about his disillusionment with the war and warning others to avoid Vietnam. The Register has been trying to identify the deceased Marine and verify the existence of the letters. Pentagon records determined that four Marines from Iowa have been killed in Vietnam since the end of January. The Register has reached out to the families of these casualties. All four have said the letters cited in the stories were not written by their sons. Three of the families stated that the letters cited in the stories were inconsistent with the communications they have received from their sons.*
>
> *"The Register has contacted The Village Voice editor, Ron Samuelson, who said they had not independently verified the story's source, but they had been assured by The Berkeley Barb that the Marine's identity was known and the accuracy of the letter's content. The Berkeley Barb has not responded to our inquiries about the story."*

Tim set the paper down and pondered his next move. He desperately wanted to talk with Daren, but he didn't want to call his house, fearing Arlene might pick up. He decided it would be best to keep his head down and carry on, go to school, go to work, go home, repeat.

That evening after work he went straight home, walked into the den, and sat down on the sofa next to his mom. She was watching the local Channel 7 Eyewitness News. The news anchor wrapped up the commodity futures report, then said, "Our next story concerns the growing controversy over letters purportedly written by an Iowa Marine, who was recently killed in Vietnam, letters that were critical of the war. The Des Moines Register is reporting that the source of the letters could not be verified. However, the Eyewitness News team has spoken with the Marine's family, who live here in Waterloo. Bev Swanson is with the family now and has this report."

Tim's mom turned to him with a confused expression, then she turned back to the TV. The next shot was in a very familiar looking living room. "Craig, I'm here with Bill and Arlene Reed and their son Daren. The Reed's eldest son, Donny, was tragically killed in Vietnam in February. Folks, we're so sorry for your loss. Can you tell us about Donny?"

Bill responded, "Donny was a fine young man, our pride and joy. He loved his family and he loved his country. He died trying to save his fellow Maines."

"I understand you spoke with the Des Moines Register recently and told them the letters being cited in newspapers around the country were not written by Donny. Is that right?"

Arlene answered, "When the Register called us and read us those quotes from the letters, they weren't anything like what Donny had written to Bill and me, but after the call, we learned from our son Daren that Donny had sent him the letters quoted in the newspapers. It was hard for us to believe, but Daren showed us the letters."

"So, Daren, tell us about the letters Donny sent you."

"Donny joined the Marine's because he wanted to defend his country and help the people of Vietnam. He wasn't there long before he saw that things were different from what he expected, different from what he had been told. He thought the way we've been fighting the war was turning the Vietnamese people against us. The way things were going, he didn't think we could win and that a lot more people were going to die for no good reason. The main thing he wanted to tell me was to not go to Vietnam, no matter what."

Bill broke in. "We're very proud of our son. We were shocked to read what he wrote to Daren, but we're glad he told Daren what he truly felt. Donny loved Daren and wanted to protect him. We don't want to lose our other son. We don't want any more sons to be killed."

"And Daren, why did you decide to share the letters with newspapers like the *Village Voice* and the *Berkeley Barb*?"

"I didn't talk to any of those people. The only person I talked to about the letters was my cousin Tim McIntyre. I told him he could write a story about it for his high school paper. He wrote a good story about Donny, but I asked him not to use his real name. I also said he could share the story with other newspapers."

"Thank you again folks, we're so sorry about your loss and the ultimate sacrifice your son has made for our country. For Channel 7 Eyewitness News, this is Bev Swanson reporting."

Tim's mom rose from the sofa, switched off the TV, turned around and stood in front of him. "What in the name of God is this about, Timmy? You wrote a story about Donny for a high school newspaper! What high school newspaper, and why were you talking to radical papers like the *Village Voice*? Start talking to me Timmy."

Tim took a deep breath. There was only one path forward. "Yeah mom, everything Daren said is true. But more importantly, everything that Donny wrote about Vietnam is true, and both Daren and I thought it was important for people to know about it. Donny's dead, mom – dead, and he shouldn't be, he didn't need to be. I wrote the story because Donny wanted people to know the truth about the war and he didn't want others to die."

"So, what's this high school newspaper Daren talked about?"

"It's called *The Chronicle, The Lime Juice Chronicle*. We started it to write stories we couldn't find anywhere else, like the story about Donny."

"Show me, Timmy."

Tim went to his room and brought back the first edition of *The Chronicle*. He handed it to his mom. She sat back down on the sofa and perused it for a minute. He quietly sat down next to her, waiting for her verdict.

"It breaks my heart to hear Donny sound so sad and afraid. I know all wars are terrible, but I don't know what to think about this war anymore. I do know that this story will make a lot of people very upset, including some families who've lost their sons in Vietnam. This newspaper of yours Timmy is not going to be good for you. It looks and sounds like one of those hippie papers. It looks radical and people will think you're a radical. You have to stop this, Timmy. "

"I don't know mom. I just don't know what's going to happen."

The next morning, Tim slipped into a side door at school and entered the cafeteria right as the first period bell rang. He took a seat at a table with Joe and Dean. They looked at each other like deer in the headlights. Dean was the first to speak, in a distraught whisper. "Jesus, the fucking Des Moines Register, Eyewitness News! I can't believe your cousin would rat you out like that Tim. Have any reporters contacted you, Tim?"

"Daren didn't rat me out. He was in a tough spot. He knew his parents would learn about the letters sometime. Besides, how could he deny the truth about what Donny wrote?"

Joe agreed, "It had to go down this way. As soon as *The Register* questioned the letter's existence, someone had to step up and tell the truth. Better it was Daren than one of us having to answer those questions. "

Mr. Nussle was determined to keep a lid on conversations that morning. "You need to stop the chatter boys, or you'll have to sit separately."

When the first period ended, Tim made a beeline through the hall to his 2nd period geometry class. He tried to sit inconspicuously at a desk in the back row. As soon as he was seated, Mr. Bartels, who was standing behind his desk looking down at a note he was holding, called to him, "Tim, would you come up here please." Mr. Bartels continued to look down as Tim slowly rose and walked up to the front of his desk. He looked up at Tim sympathetically. "Tim, Father Parker would like to see you in his office."

Tim looked at him blankly for a few seconds before replying, "OK." Tim continued to stand still in front of Mr. Bartel's desk.

Then Mr. Bartels said, "Now, Tim."

"Oh, OK." Tim walked out of the classroom and down the hall in a trance-like state. He could hear The Doors playing their funeral dirge in his head,

162

This is the end, beautiful friend.
This is the end, my only friend, the end.
Of our elaborate plans, the end.
Of everything that stands, the end.
No safety or surprise, the end.
I'll never look into your eyes again.

Tim entered the administration office, where Mrs. Frost sat behind the counter. She looked at him and silently pointed towards Father Parker's open door. As he entered, he could see Father behind his heavy Mahogany desk. Mr. Wagner was standing to the left, glaring at him with steely cold contempt. Wagner's teeth were clinched tight, and his jaw set as if he had just bitten through a ball bearing. There was no one else in the room.

Father pointed to the straight back pine chair directly in front of his desk, "Take a seat, Timothy."

Father Parker took a moment to quietly look Tim in the eyes, then he glanced over at Wagner to get his assessment of Tim before continuing. "You've stirred up quite a hornets nest Timothy. My phone has been ringing off the hook. Parents want to know about you, about your Marine story, about your newspaper. They want to know if Regis condones what you've written, if Regis approves of your newspaper, and if not, what will we do about it?" While Father was speaking, he opened a desk drawer, pulled out a half dozen copies of *The Chronicle* and set them on top of his desk.

Wagner burst in, "And the answers to those parents are no, we don't condone it. No, we don't approve of it, and yes, we're going to do something about it. We going to come down on you like a ton of bricks!"

Father raised his hand, "Before we get to all that, Timothy, we need to know who you've been working with on your newspaper? Who's this Coyote? Who are Boris, Natasha and Mr. Peabody? Who's Roadrunner and who's this Badass Babs?"

Wagner jumped in again, "I bet that Mike Russell is one of them. He's a cowardly little loser and he has no business being a student here at Regis."

Father raised his hand again, keeping his eyes on Tim, without even glancing at Wayne. "Timothy?"

"Mike had nothing to do with *The Chronicle* – nothing. As for the others, you don't know them. You might think you know them, but you don't. Just like you don't know me." Tim didn't plan to be defiant. Hell, he didn't even think he was capable of it. It was the demand for him to betray his friends that triggered his anger, particularly after Wagner accused and insulted Mike. Tim was still inspired by Mike's martyrdom over the Lame Wayne incident.

Wagner slammed the palm of his hand on Father Parker's desk. "How dare you talk to Father like that, you sniffling, insolent, degenerate freak."

"Mr. Wagner, please. Timothy, you see the kind of emotions you've generated. This newspaper of yours is not something Regis can tolerate. It says here that it will print things others won't. To me, that says you'll print things that shouldn't be printed, things that are inappropriate to print, perhaps even indecent to print."

Wagner couldn't contain himself. He jabbed his finger down on top of the stack of newspapers. "This trash is un-American. It undermines our country in a time of war. It betrays our troops. If you were slightly older, I'd call the draft board right now and tell them to pack you off to Vietnam."

This time it was Tim that shot Wagner a contemptuous look. "All we want to do is tell the truth and write about the things students really care about. If you really cared about students, you'd want to know what we're thinking."

Father raised his voice and said sternly, "This is not a discussion, Timothy. There will be no more editions of *The Lime Juice Chronicle*, or you will no longer be a student at Regis. You've already overstepped the boundaries of acceptable behavior and violated the Regis student conduct code by tarnishing the school's reputation. For that you will have to serve two weeks of detention and you're banned from any Regis extracurricular activities for the rest of the year, including the student council and Spring Prom. Am I being clear Timothy?"

"Yes Father, I understand."

"Good, you're dismissed. You can return to class now." Tim was almost out the door when Father called at him, "Oh, and Timothy, what does this Lime Juice title mean?"

Tim stopped. He continued to face the doorway. He turned his head slightly sideways and replied, "It stands for Juniors United in Catholic Education, Father. The Lime is just something that tastes sour."

The next morning, *The Des Moines Register* did a follow-up story about the Iowa Marine, with an update that he had been identified as Donny Reed, a graduate of West High School. It was brief. It didn't refer directly to anything in Donny's letters. It ended by noting that Donny was the 171st Iowan killed in the Vietnam War. Many more would follow.

Chapter 14
Moondance

The tempest surrounding *The Chronicle* only lasted about as long as Tim's sentence to detention. He heard a shitload of feedback during the first few days. Some folks thought the paper was really cool. They liked the look, the content, and the audacity to pull it off. Some people were most impressed by all the notoriety the *Fallen Marine* story had gotten. They wanted to know who the others were that put the newspaper together. Tim refused to crack, knowing the fate that would befall them.

Tim expected most of the hostility he encountered. The majority of Americans still supported the war. The justification frequently being, "My country right or wrong," or "America, love it or leave it." The Regis student body's sentiments were similarly divided. The taunts he heard in the hallways included, "Commie asshole," "Hippie prick," "Fucking freak," and "Degenerate druggie." He was less prepared for the level of violence with which he was threatened. Being told he would have the shit kicked out of him was fairly run of the mill stuff. It was the death threats that were most unnerving. "The penalty for treason is death." "You'll never know when it's coming, when someone comes from behind and slits your throat." "They should do to you what the Green Berets do to the V.C., cut off your balls and stuff them down your throat."

Castration aside, it was the indifference Tim found most disappointing and discouraging. Most students could give a rat's ass about *The Chronicle* or Donny's letters, or for that matter, anything political. Here it was, the spring of 1968, the country was at war, racial tensions were boiling over everywhere, a culture war was dividing generations, it was the middle of a heated presidential campaign, but most Regis students seemed oblivious to it all. Perhaps oblivious is too harsh a judgement. Underneath, Tim knew most students had some thoughts about what was going on in the world, but that's not how it felt at the time. The hottest topic around Regis was who was asking who to the prom? Granted, his exclusion from the prom made it particularly irrelevant, but he wasn't sure he'd be interested in it anyway. He didn't have a girlfriend. He was interested in lots of girls, yes, oh my yes, but always the ones who weren't interested in him. If he was honest with himself, he'd have to admit that the absence of romance in his life likely contributed to the fervor of his political passions. How many revolutions have been stoked by the fires of love spurned?

Tim's refuge from the turbulence crashing through the halls of Regis were the placid aisles of the FoodValu supermarket. His simple, straightforward duties at work soothed his soul. The Zen-like routine of "Pulling the shelves," moving row after row of cans, boxes, bottles, and jars forward into neat, flushed lines, bringing order to the jumbled stacks created by shoppers, served as an alternative to the lack of order or sense of control in the rest of his life. If only Mr. Bartels's geometry problems could be as easily solved as the spatial puzzles posed while trying to optimize the capacity of a grocery sack. If only all his interactions at school were as satisfying as carrying out bags of groceries for grateful customers.

Perhaps it was because of his lowly status on the FoodValu organizational chart that Tim didn't sense any significant tensions among his co-workers. It was a remarkably congenial bunch, particularly given the fascinating array of characters among the full-timers. Chuck was the store manager with decades of experience. He had his role down to a degree that he didn't feel a need to be around the store more than twenty-five percent of the time. Chuck had many, somewhat mysterious, outside interests, so he deferred much of the day-to-day store supervision to his two assistant managers, Arnie and Ken.

Arnie was another seasoned grocery veteran, close to retirement. He was hands-on with every type of task in the store. He particularly enjoyed carrying out bags for customers, chatting with them about any topic under the sun. He liked sharing sage advice with the younger employees, most of whom were part-time and still in high school. "Love whatever you do and take pride in doing it." "Don't sweat the small stuff." "Trust is hard won and easily lost." "It's a people business. Everything starts and ends with people."

Ken was only a year older than Tim. He was working almost full-time during his Senior year at Regis. He'd been accepted into Marquette, and he planned to go to law school. Ken knew he was too young to give much sage advice, but he modeled lots of admirable behaviors and he did share his outlook on life. "I figure, if I want to succeed in the future, I should start succeeding now." In their own different ways, both Arnie and Ken made you want to do a good job.

Lyle and Hilda ran the meat department. Lyle looked like the quintessential butcher, round and stout, with a neck as wide as his skull, forearms bulging from his sleeves and a bushy mustache. He had a rough and colorful past, filled with stories he loved to share, like his time in the Navy, stationed in the Philippines. He loved to play the scoundrel, chasing Hilda around the meat department trying to spank her bottom. It would be totally unacceptable workplace behavior in later years, but both Hilda and Tim thought it was hysterical. Hilda would then grab a meat cleaver, turn around and chase Lyle. Lyle had his own brand of sage advice, "If they don't like it, fuck'em," and, "The more things change, the more they stay fucked up." Lyle would occasionally talk about organizing the workers to join a union. He'd been a member of the United Meat Packers years earlier. Tim asked him what he was unhappy about at work. Lyle said there wasn't anything in particular, he just thought it was the right thing to do, and he would love sticking it to the suits at FoodValu.

Hilda was a large German woman with a thick accent, who married an American G.I. she met in the desolation following World War II. She said he saved her from starvation and abuse by other occupying soldiers. Given her past, she was remarkably light-hearted. "We always need to find time for a little fun, my sweet schnecken."

Carl managed the bakery. He was a quiet, soft-spoken fellow and somewhat of an enigma. It was the nature of his craft that his workday started at 3:00 AM and he would usually be gone by the time Tim's after-school shift began. Periodically, Tim would come in before school and clean the bakery before Carl left work. Carl seemed genuinely interested in Tim, what he was up to, what he liked to do, and what he thought about things. "How's school going?" "What are you reading?" "What kind of music have you been listening too?" "What are your plans after graduating?" "Do you go to church?" Carl didn't feel a need to share advice, but he occasionally let Tim know what he thought. "The things I heard in church never made much sense to me. I figure it's more important to just do the right thing."

Doug was the official manager of the produce department, but from what Tim could observe, Deanna really ran things. There were no women managers at FoodValu. That's the way it was most places. Deanna was wonderful and she reminded Tim of the moms he saw on TV shows. She was smart, funny, and kind. Tim trusted her. He would occasionally share his innermost secrets with Deanna. He told her his worries about the future. Should he go to college? His fear of getting drafted and going to Vietnam. His frustrations with girls. On the latter topic, she was an authoritative advisor. "Sweetheart, when you ask a girl on a date, you're not testing yourself, you're testing her. Does she have any potential for you? Regardless of what she says, it's not a judgment on either one of you. If she says yes, then fine, you move on to the next test. If she says no, then fine, neither of you will waste any more time. You dodged a bullet. Learn from it and move on."

Tim's bond with his FoodValu family was further cemented when some of his LIME JUICE co-conspirators were hired. Steve and Randy joined him stocking, sacking, and carrying out groceries. Sandy was a checker. She quickly mastered the cash register, her fingers flying smoothly over the keyboard like a virtuoso. Before long, all three of them easily assimilated into the FoodValu zeitgeist, calmly going about whatever needed to be done.

As Tim became more marginalized at Regis, his focus shifted towards work. He wondered if he belonged at work more than at school, whether the FoodValu was his best path forward, rather than high school, rather than college. Then he thought about the draft and his options, student deferment, defiance, or death. A student deferment was the default for cowards, so it was his obvious choice. Tim felt all his prospects were on a downward trajectory, along with his self-esteem. His face couldn't hide these funky feelings. His gloomy demeanor was apparent to everyone. His mom, bless her heart, was ever the realist. "I'd say being down in the dumps is the appropriate response under the circumstances. I'd be more concerned if you *weren't* taking the situation seriously." His dad was a bit more encouraging. "This will pass Tim. Just take your medicine and keep your nose clean. Things will start looking up again." Deanna gave him the best kick in the ass with a message he reflected on many times since: "I could tell you to cheer up, Tim, but it wouldn't make a damn bit of difference. Only you can decide how long you want to feel shitty and be down on yourself. Let me know when you decide to feel better."

The Monday evening shift tended to be slow with less demand for sacking and carryout. Tim was restocking the dairy cooler at the back of the store when he heard Janet, a checker, call on the intercom, "Carryout please." He headed directly to the front of the store, but he didn't see any shoppers at the checkout. Janet smiled at him and said, "Steve took care of it, Tim." He returned to the dairy cooler. A couple of minutes later, he heard Sandy call on the intercom, "Clean-up in aisle four please." He went to the back room and fetched a mop and bucket cart. He pushed it over to aisle four, but there wasn't anything broken or spilled. He went to the front of the store and asked Sandy what the problem was. She replied, "Oh, Steve took care of it." Tim returned to the dairy cooler wondering how Steve could have cleaned up the mess so fast and where did he get the other mop cart? He no sooner started to stock the milk again when he heard Hilda on the intercom, "Meat department assistance please." He walked, suspiciously, to the other side of the store. He stepped behind the meat counter and through the swinging doors to the meat department, but nobody was there. He looked for Hilda in the meat cooler and then in the breakroom. She was nowhere to be found. Back at the dairy cooler, he heard Janet call again on the intercom, "Price check please." He hesitated to respond, but after a few moments he headed to the front. Predictably by now, Janet said, "Never mind Tim. Steve's taken care of it."

Totally exasperated, Tim replied, "What the hell's going on, Janet?"

She shrugged and said, "Sorry, Tim, Steve's just more on the ball than you are today."

Sandy poked more fun from the next register, "You need to up your game, Tim."

Normally, Tim would enjoy some good-natured shit-flinging, but he was in no mood. He grumbled and sulked his way back to the dairy cooler. He halted in front of the cooler's glass doors and found the milk shelves he had just stocked were empty. The store was closing soon and there weren't many shoppers around, so it didn't make sense for the milk to be gone so quickly. Then Ken came on the intercom, "Carryout please." Tim hesitated longer this time, but then reluctantly responded. When he got to the checkout counters there was nobody around. He looked out into the parking lot and didn't see any cars. He walked to the entrance and the automatic doors were locked. It was a minute past closing. Then he heard Steve on the intercom, "Tim to the back please." Tim was genuinely pissed. He marched to the back, through the storeroom's swinging metal doors. Steve was sitting on a stool, his back against the wall, laughing, holding the intercom mic in his hand. "Carryout please, Tim. Price check please, Tim. Cleanup in aisle four please, Tim." Following behind Tim, through the swinging doors, came Janet, Sandy, Hilda, and Ken. They gathered around him and erupted, "April Fools!"

Tim closed his eyes, tilted his head back, let out a big sigh and thought, *"Of course, it's April 1st!"* He had sleep-walked through the day, unaware of the date or the occasion. He uncharacteristically struggled to be good-humored about the prank. His co-workers weren't about to let him get away with it. They jostled his hair and shook him by the shoulders. Hilda poked her elbow in his ribs. "Brighten-up my sweet schnecken. We want to see that smile of yours again." Sandy said, "Yeah, we know you've been having a rough time at school and all. We just wanted to cheer you up."

Ken had a big shit-eating grin and said, "Look on the bright side, Tim. With school going to hell you can always spend the rest of your life working at FoodValu. I'm sure they'd love to have you."

"Thanks, Ken, that's a beautiful thought, but the rest of my life could be pretty short if I get drafted."

Sandy said, "I don't see you getting drafted, Tim. I do see you living in Canada maybe, or the south of France. Then she added, "Did you take your mom's car to work? Can you give me lift home?"

"Sorry, Sandy, Joe gave me a ride to work. I'm going to walk home."

Steve offered, "I can give you guys a lift."

Tim was in a solitary mood. "Thanks, Steve, but it's a nice night. I think I'll walk.

He was surprised when Sandy said, "Yeah, it is a nice night. I think I'll walk with you."

The Iowa spring was too young for the trees and shrubs to begin budding, but the night was mild enough to bear promise of colors to come. Tim's house was a little more than a mile from the store and Sandy lived only a few blocks from him. Their route took them through Memorial Park, spanning a hillside that overlooked their neighborhood and the cornfields beyond. The full moon was bright enough to cast shadows and illuminate the view. They stopped at the playground on top of the downward slope. It was equipped with the standard array of play devices they'd grown up with, none of which can be found on playgrounds today, having been deemed to be deadly instruments of childhood destruction. There was a twelve-foot-long seesaw and a tall metal-framed swing set, with sling seats suspended by chains that could propel kids fifteen feet into the air, where they could either "parachute" into a freefall with an uncertain outcome or kids could attempt the mythical 360-degree full rotation. There was a tall metal slide, with open sides, an iron jungle gym and monkey bars, and most murderously of all, the ubiquitous merry-go-round. It was a steel plated disk topped with steel handrails, capable of generating enough centrifugal force to fling the heaviest child off or provoke projectile puking, or both. Kids loved those merry-go-rounds.

Tim and Sandy sat down on the edge of the merry-go-round and slowly pushed it side to side with their feet as they gazed out on the magical moonlit landscape. Sandy gave Tim a nudge. "Seriously Tim, why so glum lately? Seems like it's more than just being in hot water at school."

"Yeah, I suppose it is. I suspect it's because my life is in shambles, that I'm failing in just about every aspect of my existence, except for sacking and carrying out groceries. I'm a superstar in those departments."

"What the hell are you talking about, Tim?"

"I actually thought *The Chronicle* and the story about Donny might make a difference, that Donny's death might mean something, that my life might mean something. But I don't think it mattered at all. It just got people stirred up for a few days, then everything went back to busines as usual."

"Jesus Tim, I guess you're right. You must be a failure. You're a sixteen-year-old kid in the middle of Iowa and you haven't managed to stop the Vietnam War yet. It must be time for you to throw in the towel."

"I'll be seventeen next week, and like Joe said, we're not looking to change the world. We just want to change a few minds."

"Well, how do you know you didn't change some minds? Look, Tim, the important thing is you did what you thought was right. You acted on what you believed in. You should feel good about that."

"But that's the other thing, Sandy, I'm not sure what I believe in. I mean, after eleven years of parochial education, I'm failing at being a Catholic, too. I just don't buy into it anymore. But that doesn't mean I know what else to believe in because I don't. Which could mean that I'm damned to burn in the flames of hell for all of eternity."

"Oh, come on, Tim, sometimes you do love being melodramatic."

"Love! Yes, you're right. I love to love lots of things! But love is another thing I'm failing at. I mean, where's the love, Sandy? When I do muster the courage to tell a girl how I feel, I get a pat on the head and an 'Oh, that's nice,' sympathetic look. You know what happened with Julie and me last summer. It wasn't even that Julie was hot for someone else, she just had no interest in me."

"OK, Tim, I shouldn't do this, but I'm going to tell you something and you have to promise me you won't ever repeat it to anyone."

"What? What is it, Sandy? You know you can trust me."

"I mean it, Tim! I'll stomp on your balls if you repeat a word about this."

"OK, I get it. What is it?"

"There is someone else, Tim. Julie is… hot, for someone else."

"But who could that be? She said she didn't love Jim and I don't think she's been dating anyone else."

Sandy turned, looked at Tim for a few seconds and took a deep breath. "It's Mary, Tim. Julie loves Mary, and Mary loves Julie."

"What do mean, love? You mean like they're really close friends who love each other?"

"No, Tim, I mean love-love, as in romantically in love. This is all pretty new. They've had these feeling for a long time, but they only told each other a couple of months ago. They both told me about it just a few weeks ago. Now damn it, Tim. Remember you promised not to tell a soul! Can you imagine what would happen if this got out around school?"

"I know, of course, I would never tell anyone. I wouldn't even know what to say." That was true. Tim didn't even have a word in his vocabulary for girls who loved each other romantically. The concept was not even in his imagination. Father Hogan had said some things about homosexuality in religion class, but it was always in the context of men, Sodom and Gomorrah and eternal damnation. "Jesus, Sandy, I had no idea."

"Of course, you didn't, neither did I, but there it is. It's kind of sweet really."

"I suppose it is. I mean, I like them both a lot. But man, their life at Regis would be hell if people found out."

"Are you kidding? They wouldn't have a life at Regis if people found out."

"Well, I'm glad you told me, Sandy. It helps me understand a little better what happened between Julie and me. Although, it doesn't answer the question of why I can't get a girl to like me seriously."

Sandy shot Tim a totally exasperated look, then she swung her left arm around and wacked him with her hand on the back of his head. "So, what am I, chopped liver?"

"Christ Sister Rita, what did I do?" When Tim turned to look at Sandy, he was struck with another epiphany, like the one he had about Julie on the side of Sandia Peak, only this time he hadn't smoked pot. He wasn't high. He wasn't altered in any way. His mind was as clear as the lens on a telescope peering at the rings of Saturn. He was looking at Sandy, his dear friend Sandy, his pretty, smart, talented, funny, strong, trustworthy, shit-slinging friend Sandy. The person he spent more time with at school and at work than anyone else. This is Sandy, the friend he could always count on. This is Sandy, who he thinks just said she likes him, seriously likes him. This is Sandy, wonderful wise Sandy.

Tim put his right arm around her shoulders and his left hand on her thigh. He slowly leaned toward her and kissed her, only his eyes were closed, and he missed her mouth badly, landing his lips on her ear lobe. Sandy placed her hands on his cheeks, pulled him in alignment with her eyes, leaned in and gave him a long, passionate kiss right smack on the lips. They held each other tight as they slowly fell backwards onto the

174

merry-go-round, their momentum pushing it slowly clockwise. Their hearts took a giant leap and landed on the moon that night, fourteen months before Neil Armstrong landed there and took one giant step for mankind.

Chapter 15
Burn Baby Burn

The passion play that is high school life can be totally absorbing. Students obsess about their looks, their identities, their relationships, their place in the social order and their futures. The membrane that surrounds their world can be impenetrable to outside influences and events. Until that is, those outside events become their world.

For the three days after Sandy and Tim revealed their affections for each other, they were blissfully, demonstrably, insufferably infatuated with each other. They spent every possible moment together. They shot mushy looks at each other while side by side or from across the room. They looked for opportunities to, not so discretely, steal a kiss. It was a nauseating display for some. Joe thought it was sickeningly sweet, "Look, I know you two have a thing going on, but could you tone down the lovebird routine a bit."

Julie thought it was sweet, but in good way. "You two look so great together. I've never seen either one of you this happy."

Jim found it disconcerting, because it was so out of character for both of them. "Where did this paperback romance shit come from? It's like you've both been put under a spell by some witch's potion. I hope you snap out of it."

Friday night would be the first chance for Sandy and Tim to go out on anything resembling a date. The Sharks were playing at the Electric Park Ballroom, the largest and nicest teen dance venue in the area. The Electric Park would occasionally book some pretty big bands and this was the first chance for The Sharks to play there. It was their biggest gig yet. The LIME JUICE were hyped with anticipation.

Sandy and Tim were both working after school at the FoofValu on Thursday night. It was April 4th. The store was busy, and Tim was working up front with Sandy, sacking and carrying out groceries. At about 7:30 PM, Tim took a couple of bags out to the parking lot for a woman and her young daughter. There was a car parked right next to hers. There was a man in the driver's seat with the window rolled down. The engine was turned off, but the radio was on, and he had the volume turned up. As Tim was loading the groceries into the back seat, he could hear what sounded like some breaking news on the man's car radio. Tim asked him what was going on. He replied gravely, "Martin Luther King has been shot in Memphis. I think he might be dead. "

The woman Tim was helping put her hands over her mouth and gasped, "Oh no, that's horrible! How could anybody do something like that, to kill such a wonderful, peaceful man!"

The man in the car replied, "I'm afraid there are a lot of people who would do it. It's a tragedy for the country. With King gone, things are only going to get uglier."

Tim walked back into the store and whispered the news to Sandy. When she winced and choked back tears, the woman customer she was checking out asked her what was wrong. Sandy told her Martin Luther King had been killed. The woman didn't say anything. She just raised her eyebrows, made a mild, "hummph." Her expression seemed to say, *"That's interesting."*

Sandy slammed the cash register drawer shut, handed the woman her receipt and walked off towards the breakroom. Tim called after her, then he followed her to the back. When he got to the break room, she was standing with her arms folded, wiping tears from her cheeks. She turned toward Tim, kicked the chair next to her and said, "Why is hate always winning and why doesn't anyone seem to care?"

"Hate doesn't always win, Sandy. King himself said the arc of the moral universe is long, but it bends towards justice."

Oh, for heaven's sake, Tim, three days ago you were all doom and gloom. Martin Luther King gets murdered and now you're being Pollyanna about it."

I'm not trying to be Pollyanna, Sandy, I'm really upset about King too, but I'm just trying to be reassuring, like you were for me."

"OK, but sometimes when I'm angry and upset, I don't need reassurance, I just need someone to vent to." Credit Sandy for sharing one of the most useful bits of interpersonal wisdom Tim would ever hear.

As the news spread around the store, reactions ranged from shock, to dismay, to indifference. The tepid reaction by some reflected the store's location and customer base. This particular FoodValu was located on the far west side of town. Although Waterloo had a large black community, there were still no black families on the west side and FoodValu rarely had black customers. There weren't any black employees either. Dr. King was a huge national figure and his assassination shocked most white folks, but the news was not personally, emotionally, viscerally traumatic for most of them. There was a different reaction on the east side.

By the time Tim got home from work and turned on the 10:00 news, there was a report from a candlelight vigil in a downtown park. There had also been some outbursts of rage and vandalism on the east side, but news of the assassination unfolded too late in the day to fully take hold. Everyone knew there would be far stronger reactions to come. As Joe had foretold and Charlie had confirmed, racial tensions in town were a powder keg ready to be ignited. Martin Luther King's murder was more than a spark, it was a like bomb going off in the middle of a munitions depot.

Tim and Sandy were still looking forward to the Electric Park on Friday night. They hoped the dance might provide some respite from the unsettling cloud of uncertainty hanging over the day. The huge morning headlines about King's assassination was followed by reports of riots breaking out in cities across the country. There were angry local voices quoted in the paper and predictions of serious trouble in the coming hours and days.

Soon after the Ballroom doors opened, Charlie, Sandy, and Tim were helping the Sharks set up their equipment on stage. Tim was surprised to see Charlie there. He thought Charlie might decide to go to a NAACP demonstration downtown. Charlie said he wanted to support the local NAACP and voice his anger about King's murder, but he and his parents heard other groups were planning violence, so he agreed to stay away. He was worried about Toni though. She was going to the demonstration with her two older brothers.

People slowly trickled into the ballroom as the sound system played top 40 songs. The Sharks weren't expecting a big crowd because they were just a small-time high school band. They were happy to see the three tiers of tables and booths lining the dance floor filling up. There were lots of Regis kids there, but they also recognized people they knew from the three public high schools. The band was excited about playing for a big audience; however, Tim was uneasy, knowing that this blend of esteemed academic institutions representing all areas of town could be volatile. He might have just been projecting his own generalized anxiety, but behind all the fun-loving banter going on, he sensed an underlying tension in the crowd.

The Shark's opening set included a string of rousing rock and roll numbers, including their crowd pleasing covers of "Gimme Some Lov'in," "I Can See for Miles," and "Born to be Wild." The dance floor was packed, which is always a positive metric for a band. During the first break, Sandy and Tim went up to the stage to let the band know how great they sounded. Joe and Charlie joined them. Joe said, "Hey guys, I agree you're killing it, but how about starting your next set by saying something to recognize the moment we're in, something dedicated to Martin Luther King?"

Charlie added, "Yeah guys, it seems like something needs to be said or done. We shouldn't pretend nothing has happened."

Jim looked down, thought for a few seconds, then nodded in agreement. "You're right, how about I get things started, then the band can join me. I think we have the right number for this." Then he turned and huddled with his bandmates.

Jim got on stage alone with his acoustic guitar. "Hey everybody, before we get back to the party, we'd like to play a couple of songs to remind us of the awful tragedy last night. Then he started singing Bob Dylan's, "The Times They Are Changing." It was a beautiful rendition and most of the audience really got into it, but Tim could hear a few people grumbling. One thuggish-looking greaser snarked, "What is this, a fucking folk festival hootenanny?" Jim remained poised throughout the song though.

The rest of the band joined Jim on stage and began playing a song that Tim absolutely loved, but he'd never heard The Sharks play before: Simon and Garfunkel's, *Sound of Silence.* They were nailing it. Jim and Warren's harmonies were spot on. Mike even added some baritone on the chorus, while keeping the perfect pace with his brush sticks. Then, while ending the third verse with, "But my words, like silent raindrops fell, and echoed in the wells of silence," someone yelled, "Cut the crap! We want to dance!"

The Sharks responded by ramping up the volume on the last verse,

> *"And the people bowed and prayed,*
> *to the neon god they made,*
> *and the sign flashed out its warning,*
> *in the words that it was forming,*
> *and the sign said,*
> *'The words of the prophets are written on the subway walls,*
> *and tenement halls,'*
> *and whispered in the sound of silence."*

One beat after The Sharks hit the last note, Jim grabbed the microphone and said, "And now everyone, I ask that we all bow our heads for a few moments of silence in memory of Dr. Martin Luther King, a man of peace, who sacrificed his life for freedom and justice."

The ballroom complied with Jim's request and stood still for a few moments, until the silence was broken by a young man's sardonic voice coming from the middle of the dance floor, "One less commie nigger!"

Charlie was standing just left of the stage with his friend and neighbor Eddie Frazer, an eighteen-year-old black Senior at East High School. They both bolted in the direction of the hateful cry like they were shot from a cannon. There was a gaggle of six guys laughing and smirking about fifteen feet in front of the stage. Charlie and Eddie blindsided them, throwing all their fury at them, landing fists to their heads, then tackling two of them to the ground, where they unleashed another flurry of punches. A pack of white guys leaped on Eddie and Charlie. Four black guys who were way in the back by the leather booths, charged through the crowd to rescue Eddie and Charlie. The mayhem spread out in all directions from the epicenter, until the entire dance floor was engulfed in the brawl. Fighting even broke out between groups sitting in the booths. Most of the crowd didn't want to have anything to do with the fighting and they fled for the exists. Some people were gawkers who stood around for the entertainment. Some were street

180

fighters who were always looking for opportunities to test their skills. But there were also those who were consumed by hate and rage, intent on inflicting as much injury on their enemies as possible, without regard for their own peril.

Sandy and Tim were standing stunned backstage. They totally lost sight of Charlie. Then Joe ran up to Tim, grabbed his arm and pulled him forward, yelling "Let's go!" They jumped off the front of the stage, along with the rest of The Sharks. Their mission was not to fight, it was to pull Charlie out of harm's way. They were immediately swallowed up in the pandemonium. It was like one of those bar room brawl scenes you see in movie westerns. Thankfully, they were in the middle of a dance floor, so there weren't any tables or chairs to smash over people, although some guys were using soda bottles and cans as weapons.

They spotted Charlie on the floor, trying to shield himself from kicks by two guys standing above him. Eddie had managed to get back on his feet. He, another black kid, and two white allies were fending off a half dozen white brawlers. Tim and Joe shoved the guys away from Charlie, pulled him to his feet, then tried to push their way back towards the stage. They didn't quite make it.

A time warp often occurs in these types of situations, so Tim didn't have a good read on how long it took the cops to descend on them. He knew the Electric Park always had a handful of security guards at teen dances, most of whom were uniformed off-duty city cops. Security would have called in more on-duty cops, but most of them were tied up at the demonstrations downtown. The cops aggressively pulled people off each other, throwing lots of punches themselves to get the job done. As the combatants were separated, they sorted themselves out, with the cops in the middle of the opposing sides. The aftermath was a bloody mess, with lots of bloody noses, guys spitting from bloody mouths, bloody cuts on heads, eyes swelling shut. Despite the fact that Charlie had never been in a fight before (he avoided them like the plague) he escaped with only minor damage, a contusion on his left cheek and a few sore ribs.

The cops scanned the crowd, then briefly consulted with each other. Suddenly, they all moved towards Charlie and Eddie. They grabbed them, another black kid Tim didn't know, and a white friend of Eddie's from East High. They handcuffed the four of them and pulled them toward the front doors. Charlie looked back at his mates, confused and scared. Eddie resisted arrest with every fiber in his body He struggled not be handcuffed. He tried breaking free while being dragged off the dance floor. The security guards responded by repeatedly slugging him in the stomach and punching him in the face. Eddie screamed obscenities at them continuously until they got him in the back of a patrol car. The four detainees were driven away in the back of two police cars.

The LIME JUICE followed the arrests all the way to the parking lot. As soon as the police cars drove off, they raced back inside and bounded down the broad carpeted stairs to the ballroom basement, where there were restrooms, a cloak room, and a row of eight pay phones along the wall. There was a line behind every phone. Everyone was calling to get rides home. The LIME JUICE split up into separate lines. They needed to contact Charlie's parents. Joe got to a phone first. "Hi Mrs. Cummings, this is Charlie's friend Joe. I'm really sorry to bother you, but there's been a huge fight over here at the Electric Park. No, no, he's fine. He's just a little banged-up. He's going to be OK. The problem ma'am is that Charlie's been arrested, and the police have taken him downtown to jail. I think you and Mr. Cumming should go there right away. We're heading there too."

The city hall, county courthouse, police station and jail were all just a few blocks from the park where the NAACP was holding its demonstration. There were city cops, county deputies and law officers from surrounding towns everywhere. There was lots of shouting through bullhorns and chanting, but Tim didn't see any signs of violence. Mr. and Mrs. Cummings arrived at the police station before them. Mr. Cummings was already engaged with the front desk officer, asking questions about how he could get Charlie released. He was employing all of his union negotiation skills. Whatever it was, it worked. After about 45 minutes, Charlie emerged from a heavy metal door with a buzz from an electronic lock. He hugged his mom and shook his father's hand. He turned to his comrades and asked, "Did you explain to them what happened?"

Before they could answer, Mr. Cumming said, "I don't want to hear it from them Charlie. I want to hear from you when we get home. Let's get out of here." They quickly left.

Mr. Frazer was not as effective negotiating for Eddie's release. He remained calm until it became clear they were not letting Eddie out that night. They said it was because of his age and that he had a prior arrest for fighting two years earlier. Mr. Frazer's pleas and persuasions devolved into shouts and demands. He went ballistic when the other two boys were released to their families. Two cops walked up on either side of Mr. Frazer and said he would be arrested if he didn't calm down and leave. He left, but he didn't calm down. The cops then turned and glared at Tim, Sandy, Joe, Warren, and Jim, who leapt up from the bench and got out of there as fast as possible.

Tim drove Sandy home in his mom's car. They were both rattled. Sandy said, "I genuinely thought someone was going to get killed back there at the ballroom. It's a miracle there wasn't somebody who needed to be taken away in an ambulance."

Tim had a different concern. "I can't believe they arrested Charlie and Eddie and not those guys from West High."

"Well, they did start it, Tim."

"No, they didn't! Those guys started it when they shouted, 'Commie Nigger.' Charlie and Eddie had every right to shut them up."

They didn't say much else until Tim pulled up in front of Sandy's house. He turned off the car and turned to her, "I'm really sorry the night didn't turn out the way we wanted. We didn't even get a chance to dance."

Sandy wiped a tear from her face and said sadly, "Yeah, I'm sorry too." Then she leaned over and kissed him on the cheek. She slid out the passenger door. Before closing it, she said, "I'm glad you're alright Tim. I'll see you tomorrow."

Tim's parents were still up when he got home. The battle of the Electric Park Ballroom had been on the 10:00 news. They were frantic to know if he was all right. He gave them an abbreviated account, including that Charlie had been unfairly singled out for arrest. They all went to bed wanting to put the night behind them. It took Tim a while to fall asleep, replaying everything in his mind. It was after 1:00 AM before the adrenalin finally wore down and he was able to fall asleep.

Sandy and Tim had eight-hour shifts scheduled on Saturday. They were both physically and mentally exhausted from the prior night's drama. They didn't talk much through the morning, but as the day advanced, they fell into their usual FoodValu groove, making light banter with their co-workers and customers. There was a slow spell up front after lunch, so Tim went back to restock some shelves. He was working in the cereal aisle when Joe found him. Joe walked straight up to Tim's face without saying anything. He stopped and stood there silently for a moment. He was trembling with anger. Then he blurted out, "Eddie's dead!"

"What the fuck Joe? How could Eddie be dead? He wasn't hurt that bad!"

"The cops said he hung himself in his cell. It's total bullshit. I don't know Eddie, and I don't know what happened, but I do know there's no way that guy would have hanged himself. The kid was a fighter. He wasn't depressed about being in jail. He was furious."

"How did you find out about this Joe?"

"I heard it on the car radio about half an hour ago. I went home and tried to call Charlie, but nobody answered. Then I came straight here."

When the word spread about Eddie's death, the damn broke. A large angry crowd gathered outside the city hall and police department. Cops in riot gear lined up in front of all the doors. Leaders from the Black community shouted through bullhorns, demanding to meet with the mayor and chief of police. Some nondescript city spokesperson from the mayor's office came out and read a statement saying city officials would meet with them on Monday. That caused the crowd to erupt. Bottles and rocks started flying towards the police. The cops reacted by moving into the crowd, wildly swinging billy clubs. The crowd dispersed into side streets. The sun was setting. It would be a long, dangerous night.

The fires began soon after sunset. Some were started in dumpsters, behind businesses on the northeast side. It was in the Black business district, but most of the businesses were owned by Whites. Rocks were thrown through glass doors and windows. Many stores were looted. Molotov cocktails were thrown at passing cars. The police were overwhelmed. They might have been able to contain one large mob, with the assistance they got from other law enforcement departments around the area, but there wasn't just one large mob, there were dozens of smaller roving groups, racing from site-to-site with the intent of setting as many fires and creating as much havoc as possible. Around 11:00 PM, several fires were ignited at the Sweeny lumber yard. The company was a regional wholesale distributor of all sorts of wood products. It encompassed three square blocks next to the railroad yard. The railroad complex included several large oil and gasoline tanks. The small fires merged and soon engulfed the entire lumber yard. The flames threatened the surrounding neighborhoods. Every firefighting resource in the region was called in. All they could do was watch the lumber yard burn and try to prevent the fire from spreading to nearby businesses and homes. Several homes were lost to the flames. At 12:30 AM, the fire hit an oil tank in the railroad yard. The explosion shook the ground a half mile away. Gunfire rang out throughout the night.

On Sunday morning, the Governor declared a state of emergency. An 8:00 PM citywide curfew was enacted, and the Iowa National Guard was called in. As the day progressed, guardsmen took up positions throughout the downtown and on the northeast side. Their presence was particularly heavy around government buildings. Demonstrations were banned indefinitely, until the state of emergency was lifted.

On Monday, the Waterloo mayor and police chief succumbed to political pressure and met with Black community leaders, but there were no agreements, except that they would meet again later in the week. There was no agreement on the primary demand, an independent investigation into Eddie's death. The ban on demonstrations moved the center of activism to East High School. Black students defied authorities by holding an unauthorized rally in the gymnasium. They drafted a list of four demands that they presented to the principal and the school district superintendent. The list included an investigation into Eddie's death, approval to form a Black Student Union, a commitment to hire additional Black faculty and to add a Black History course to the curriculum. The principal and superintendent refused to agree to any of the demands saying they would not bow to coercion.

The local and state news media covered the riots extensively. There was some national coverage as well, but it was overshadowed by much larger riots in over a hundred cities across the country. The local newspaper, *The Waterloo Courier*, ran page after page of stories with photos of the riots, the property damage and guardsmen patrolling the streets. They wrote about the unrest at East High and the meetings between city officials and Black community leaders, but there was very little information reported about what happened to Eddie.

Tim looked for Charlie as soon as he got to school Monday morning. He checked in Charlie's homeroom before and after 1st period, but Charlie wasn't there. As he headed to his 2nd period class, he saw Charlie and his parents coming out of the Administration office. "Hi Charlie. Good morning Mr. and Mrs. Cummings. How are you doing, Charlie?"

They cast a glum look at each other, then looked at Tim. Charlie gave the verdict. "We just met with Father Parker and Mr. Wagner. They said I'm suspended for the next five days, because of my arrest. They're going to review my case again next week."

"Oh man, I'm really sorry, Charlie, but I'll tell you what my dad said when I got in trouble. He said I would get past my problems. I just needed to learn from them and move on, move forward."

Mrs. Cummings sighed and said, "Charlie told us how you and his other friends pulled him away from the fight. We appreciate that, Tim. I'm sure you'll understand why Charlie, and all of us, need to pull back for a while and reflect on everything that's happened."

"I understand, Mrs. Cummings. I'll see you next week, Charlie."

Tim started to walk away, but Charlie put his hand on Tim's shoulder and stopped him. Tim turned around and Charlie said, "Eddie was next to me in the back seat of that cop car. He was pissed, but he was also pumped up. He felt great about taking on those assholes at the ballroom. He didn't care that we'd been arrested. Tim, Eddie wasn't depressed. He didn't kill himself. Someone killed him."

The county coroner released Eddie's autopsy report on Wednesday. Well, it wasn't really a report. It was a summary. It wasn't even a summary. It was a conclusion, a one sentence conclusion, *"The observational autopsy of Mr. Edward Frazer finds the cause of death to be asphyxiation, resulting from a self-inflicted strangulation by hanging."* That was it. No other details. It said, "observational autopsy," meaning they only looked at Eddie, so no lab work, no toxicology, no imaging, no surgical examination. They didn't even list details of what was observed. It was issued as a press release, so there wasn't even a press conference with opportunities for questions.

186

Of course, the Black community would have none of it. Despite the ban on assemblies and the Iowa National Guard presence, a large crowd gathered in front of the barricades outside the city hall and police department. Using bullhorns, leaders demanded release of the full autopsy report and again called for an independent investigation. The mayor and police chief probably thought the troops would protect them, so they didn't need to respond. This time, they didn't even agree to a meeting. You would think the stonewalling would make the news media go apoplectic and demand more information, but not much was said beyond comments about the report's brevity. The problem was that Eddie was not their primary story. The riots were the bigger news and made for better copy. In the national context, the riots were about Martin Luther King, not Eddie.

Charlie called Tim Thursday night after he got off work at the FoodValu. Charlie was agitated and talked rapidly, "Hey, Tim, listen, Toni and I talked with Joe. We all agreed that we need to put out another edition of *The Chronicle*. We need to tell Eddie's story and let people know what they're not hearing. Before you say anything, we know you can't be part of this. There won't be any bylines from Sherman. Father Parker and Lame Wayne would have you Shanghaied off to Vietnam if they thought you defied them by putting out another issue.

"Shit Charlie, it won't matter what I tell them. They'll think I was part of it anyway or that I know who was and they'll try to force me to give them names. Why don't you just go tell your story to *The Waterloo Courier*?"

"I tried! I called them earlier today and nobody wanted to talk with me. I don't think they want to print anything that might fan the flames. Most people who read *The Courier* want the demonstrations to go away. They don't want to read something that might keep the protests going."

"Well how about *The Des Moines Register* then? They aren't concerned about stirring up controversy. That's their bread and butter. Riots sell papers."

"Have you seen *The Register* this week? They're covering demonstrations all over the state, particularly the riots in Des Moines. No Tim, not on your life. This is our story, *The Chronicle's* story. Nobody can tell it better than us. I don't trust anyone else to tell it."

"Oh hell, I suppose you're right, Charlie. I guess I better resign myself to spending the rest of my days stuffing grocery sacks at FoodValu."

"Quit your bellyaching, Tim. You're on the fast track to success. If you play your cards right, you might be able to make weekend assistant manager in a few years. You're on the fast track to success, my man."

By Saturday morning, *The Chronicle's* newsroom, AKA Steve's basement, was firing on all cylinders, organizing their second, and likely last edition. They agreed that the entire issue should be devoted to Eddie Frazer and race relations in their town. Charlie took the lead in writing the headline story about Eddie. It would be a first-person account of what went down at the Electric Park Ballroom, the arrests and what Eddie said to Charlie in the back seat of the police car. Charlie also wanted to include details about Eddie's life, his close relationship with his two little sisters; that he loved music and playing football. Although Eddie didn't like school, he loved to read, particularly science fiction. He had a knack for fixing cars, worked long hours at a gas station and he wanted to be a mechanic. Charlie asked Eddie's parents for photos of him as a little boy and in his East High football uniform.

Toni wrote a story about the protests at East High, the reasons behind the students' demands, and why so many Black students weren't graduating. Al interviewed Black players on the East High football team. He grew up with many of them and he thought they'd trust him enough to talk. They'd been traumatized by Eddie's death, full of anger and fearful of what might happen to them if they got picked up by the cops. Al also interviewed the East High Athletic Director. For the past two years, there had been escalating tensions, including violence, between players and fans at games with West High School. He told Al the relationship between the schools had deteriorated so badly that the school district might decide to hold the game that fall at an undisclosed location, out of town, with no fans, which is exactly what happened.

Toni suggested that Julie and Mary interview Mrs. Madeline Williams and her husband, Rev. Fredrick Williams. Both were long-time community leaders and Madeline was the current spokesperson for the NAACP. Toni thought they should write a personal profile of the couple as a way to portray the broader history of the local Black community. The Williamses were happy to oblige, so these two young, white, middle-class girls from the west side, with yellow note pads in their laps, sat for hours in the living room of the two local civil rights icons, trying to capture their personal story and introduce them to the whole community.

Madeline spent her early years living in a four-room cabin on a tenant farm near Meridian, Mississippi, with her father, mother, grandmother and six siblings. Throughout her childhood she experienced the day-to-day oppression and indignities of the Jim Crow South. There were some good times, some loving times and some peaceful times, but the threat of calamity or violence always loomed nearby. There were no opportunities in Meridian for Madeline to have a meaningful education beyond elementary school, so in 1939 her mother sent her to live with her sister and brother-in-law in Chicago. She graduated from high school in 1943 and took a job as a waitress in a diner. A year later, she went to night school to learn bookkeeping. It was good timing for finding work because many young men had gone off to war.

One night after her accounting class, another student, a young white man, asked to talk with her over a cup of coffee. Madeline later learned the young man was an FBI agent. He spent the next few weeks trying to convince her to become a paid undercover informant after she became a certified bookkeeper. The Bureau had another informant who could get Madeline a job working at an Italian restaurant with an off-track betting parlor in the basement that was run by Chicago's Italian mob, known as "The Outfit." This was the same organization Al Capone had led before he was sent to prison in 1931. The Outfit was now run by a boss named Paul Ricca. After the Bureau's success prosecuting Capone on tax fraud charges, they were eager to examine any and all of The Outfit's financial records. The Outfit paid Madeline very well and the Bureau also paid her. After a year of being an informant, she could afford to pursue her dream, a college diploma.

Julie and Mary were riveted by Madeline's story. They were frozen in their chairs, eyes glued to this woman whose life was unlike any they had ever encountered. They hadn't taken a single note. Madeline paused and said, "Girls, do you think you can remember all of this."

They snapped out of their trance and Mary replied, "Ah, ah, yes, that was Paul Ricca. Is that with two c's?"

"Yes, dear, with two c's, but I think I'm taking you down a rabbit hole, so I'll cut the next part short. I worked for The Outfit for a little more than a year. Everyone was very nice to me, but I heard and saw some things that no young woman should. The work was pretty standard, except I was required to keep three sets of books, one for the restaurant, one for the betting parlor and one that blended the two, so they could deposit the gambling profits as if they came from the restaurant. Once the bureau was able to tie the bank accounts back to Mr. Ricca, well, as they say, it was time for me to get out of Dodge. I took my savings and enrolled at the University of Northern Iowa and got my business degree in accounting. It was there that I met Reverend Williams. I sang in the church choir and Reverend Williams was our conductor. It was there, because of him, that I became politically engaged. It wasn't long before we were engaged. The Reverend was the first love of my life, and he might be my last. Like I keep telling him, I'll just have to wait to see whether someone finer comes along."

The Reverend William's life was equally compelling. He was raised by his grandmother in the Roxbury neighborhood of Boston. She died from congestive heart failure when he was fifteen. The State of Massachusetts sent him to live in a state-run facility, but after ten months, he ran away back to Roxbury. He lived on friends' couches for a year until, at the age of seventeen, he enlisted in the Army. It was 1941, and documentation of age was not taken very seriously. He landed in France four days after D-Day and fought in the Battle of the Bulge, where he lost two toes to frostbite.

Mary and Julie again ceased taking notes. Julie asked, "Excuse me, Reverend, but did you have to shoot people? Did you have to kill anyone?"

"My dear, sometimes the answers we are most interested in require questions that shouldn't be asked. I will just say that death was our close companion and there were times when I thought my survival was unlikely. They say there are no atheists in fox holes. I don't believe that's true. My own faith was shattered by the horrors around me. However, I vowed that if I survived, I would devote my life to helping make the world more beautiful, more peaceful, more loving, and more

190

just. It was after the war that I decided my two best avenues to keep that vow were through the church and music."

Fredrick Williams used the G.I. Bill to pay his way through Boston University, where in 1951 he received a baccalaureate degree in music. He felt called to enroll at the Chicago Theological Seminary, because of its history of social activism, beginning with its founding mission to abolish slavery. The school was fully committed to the civil rights movement, and it embraced Martin Luther King's strategy of non-violent resistance. Reverend Williams received a Master of Divinity Degree in 1953. He became an associate pastor and choir conductor at a church close to the University of Northern Iowa. It wasn't long before he fell head over heels for Madeline. He proposed four months later and they were married three months after that.

"Maddy was the first love of my life and she'll definitely be my last. She'd beat me to death otherwise."

A few months after their wedding, Reverend Williams became the pastor at the local African Methodist Episcopal Church. From the outset, the Reverend and Mrs. Williams nurtured personal relationships with civil rights leaders around the country, including Ralph Abernathy, Roy Wilkins, and Martin Luther King. They led local efforts to address housing discrimination and discriminatory practices by the police.

Reverend Williams leaned forward towards Julie and Mary, folded his hands and rested his arms on his knees. "Eddie's death has shaken us all badly and we're determined to see that justice is done. It's wonderful that you two young ladies want to tell Eddie's story and our story, but you both need to be very careful. There are dark forces at work here, some we can see and some that are hidden. We'll be praying for you."

There's no way *The Lime Juice Chronicle's* four-page format could do any of their four feature stories justice, and they knew their obscure little underground paper had a very limited ability to grab the public's attention, but they were even more committed to getting their second edition printed than the first. This one was even more personal, even closer to home. It was about their own town, their owns friends and neighbors and what kind of a community they were going to be. Writing the stories felt like they were cleansing their souls. However, for Tim's part, he did next to nothing, no writing, no editing, next to no discussing.

Charlie meant it when he said the LIME JUICE didn't expect Tim to be involved, because they knew he was already in the crosshairs at Regis. But that wasn't the primary reason Tim was so disengaged. He didn't feel the least bit qualified or competent to work on these stories. He didn't feel he had the right to be involved. He was still embarrassed that he'd been so blind for so long to the ugly reality of racism and discrimination in his own hometown. It was time for him to step back and just listen.

It took two weeks to pull all four stories together. Each article linked back to two things, the need for an independent investigation of Eddie's death and adoption of the students' demands at East High. By the time they were ready to go to press, the rioting had ended, and the National Guard had been withdrawn. Tensions were still extremely high, though. Students at East High were still pressing their demands, and the Williamses were still leading efforts to get an outside investigation into Eddie's death by the State Attorney General.

Tim rode along with Joe, Toni, and Charlie to take the layout boards to Monica in Iowa City. Their mood was dark, and their conversations were filled with gallows humor. Charlie was particularly fatalistic about his situation. In several respects, he was much more vulnerable than Tim. He was still suspended from Regis, and a final decision on disciplinary action hadn't been made. Charlie wasn't writing the story about Eddie under a pen name, it was a first-person account of what happened at the Electric Park, so the story could be easily linked to him anyway. He told his parents that he was writing the story. They advised him not to do it, but they knew a mandate from them wouldn't stop him. "I told them I could either channel my anger through writing or by throwing rocks and Molotov cocktails." Charlie was clear-eyed about his prospects at Regis. "I'm going to miss you guys. I've enjoyed being at the top of the intellectual heap at Regis and having you all as my pawns to play with. It's going to be much more challenging at East. I'll have to actually start doing some work to stay on top of their grading curve."

Toni responded with her trademark sunny outlook. "Charlie, if you go to East High, you'll be so low on the pecking order that your skull will look like a damn golf ball. Don't worry though, I'll be there to protect you. If Regis expels you, it'll only take them a nanosecond to boot me too.

This brought out Joe's sarcastic sense of humor, "You guys might get kicked out of Regis, but if my dad finds out about this, I'll be kicked out of my family. He had two properties burned in the riots. I expect you all to take my name to your graves. When they threaten to nail you to a cross or drown you in holy water if you don't tell them who Wiley Coyote is, I expect you to be loyal and not give up your fearless leader."

Toni thought that was rich, "Leader? Fearless? The only place Wiley Coyote can lead us is off a cliff. On second thought, you're driving, so forget I said that."

Joe accelerated slightly and snickered, "I guess you're right Toni. I'm not the leader of this fiasco. It wasn't my idea to print another issue of *The Chronicle*. In fact, I should explain to Father Parker that I did everything I could to stop you and Charlie."

The conversation was freaking Tim out. "Jesus, you guys are really bumming me out! Remember how psyched we were about putting out *The Chronicle's* first edition. How about we drop this doomsday shit and try to recapture the magic."

Toni had the most appropriate response, "Fuck off, Tim."

Tim assumed Iowa City had experienced a similar degree of upheaval following MLK's assassination, but Monica told Joe on the phone the reaction there had been sad, but subdued. There had also been a lull in anti-war demonstrations on campus, since President Lyndon Johnson's March 31st bombshell announcement that he wouldn't run for re-election. There were now three anti-war candidates running for the Democratic nomination: Senator Eugene McCarthy, Senator George McGovern and Senator Robert F. Kennedy. A lot of students were turning their energy and passion towards the presidential campaign.

When they arrived at Monica's apartment, she greeted them warmly, then quickly turned her attention back to a heated exchange going on in the kitchen. The debate mirrored the fratricide happening among leftist activists around the country. Psychotherapists might describe it as triangulation. There was certainly a lot of pathology involved. It was another example of how civil wars are often the most vicious disputes.

193

The high schoolers parked themselves in the living room, having no interest in joining the argument. As Monica walked back into the kitchen she yelled, "What did you say?"

Tim could see Alan leaning against the counter. He stood up straight when Monica approached him and repeated, "Pretty boy Bobby is a pretender to the throne. He's an opportunist who only entered the race after McCarthy bitch-slapped LBJ in New Hampshire. McCarthy is the only one with the balls to win the election and has the guts to end the war."

Jody put her hands on her head in exasperation, "Oh my god, Alan, you can't seriously think Clean Gene can win the nomination, let alone the general election. He's got the charisma of a mortician! All the Republicans need to do is run ads of McCarthy meeting with Che Guevara in 64' and label him a communist. His campaign will go up in smoke like a puff from that damn pipe of his, and the war will continue to rage."

"Ok, so he's not a charismatic political bullshitter. He's actually a poet and he's got genuine convictions. Those things can inspire people too. You saw the hordes of young volunteers who worked their asses off for him in New Hampshire. Look, he might not be the Hollywood idol, prince of Camelot type you and Monica are so enamored with, but he's the real deal."

That really set Monica off, "Fuck you, Alan! How dare you imply we prefer Kennedy because of his looks. That's disrespectful bullshit! Jody and I are realists. McCarthy can't win and Kennedy can - period, full stop."

James had been holding back while sitting at the kitchen table, nursing a beer, with a cynical smirk. "You are all having the wrong argument. You're playing the same bourgeois game. The war machine owns both political parties. Change will only come with a real revolution and the revolution will come when we bring the war home to America."

Monica reasserted her position, "OK, OK comrade, we know you're the only true radical around here. You know what I think about violence as a strategy and all your other SDS crap. It turns people off and scares them right into the arms of the law-and-order Republicans."

James maintained his aloof tone. "I really don't give a shit if the Democrats lose. It was the Democrats who started this war, the brother of your boy, Bobby. If the Democrats lose, it will just hasten the day when the real revolution begins."

Alan shook his head in disbelief, "Oh man, James, you know what they call it when you lose? Losing. You know what they call people who lose? Losers."

Toni lost patience with the discussion. It was all irrelevant to anything she was concerned about at that moment. "Excuse me, Monica, while you all are talking about the election and the revolution, there's fires burning and black people dying right now back home. We really need to talk with you about *The Chronicle*. We need to show you what we've put together."

That brought talk in the kitchen to an abrupt halt. The kitchen cabinet crowd joined the kids in the living room. Monica sat down on the floor next to Charlie. He took the layout templates out of the portfolio bag and laid them down on the floor in front of her. Jody knelt next to Monica, while Alan stood behind her and looked down over her shoulder. After reading the front-page feature story about Eddie, the three of them looked up at the kids. Alan slapped his hand on his forehead and exclaimed, "Man, oh man, how the hell do you guys keep coming up with this stuff? This is explosive shit! Charlie, were you really in the cop car with that kid Eddie?"

"That's right, I was the last friendly face he saw. That kid was murdered, and most people don't seem to give a shit. People need to know the truth. I need to tell people the truth. We need your help to tell people the truth. So how about we cut the political science, presidential campaign bullshit, the people's revolution bullshit, and just start telling people the damn truth?"

Monica reached over and put her hand on Charlie's knee. "Of course, we're going to help, Charlie. Waterloo is my hometown too. But how far are you prepared to push this thing? This issue of *The Chronicle* needs to have a much bigger circulation than the first one. I mean like thousands more, and the backlash is likely going to be much fiercer."

Joe had been uncharacteristically quiet until then, "We're going to push this as far as it takes to get justice done. This is our hill to die on."

Tim kept quiet. There was a lump in his throat, and he thought he was going to throw up.

Chapter 16
Schism and Blues

Sensing imminent calamity, there was no need for Tim to run away and join the circus. No need for him to book passage on a freighter to Panama. No need to hide out in a smokey Casablanca nightclub. He could simply disappear into his own head. He could get lost in the twenty centimeters between his left and right tympanic membranes. Step one, don stereo headphones. Step two, stack albums on the spindle. Step three, place the stylus on a groove. Step four, lie down and close his eyes. He listens to the Moody Blues - anxiety stops chasing him. He listens to The Beatles – he gets lost in their dreams. He listens to Dylan – his worries become another verse. He listens to Simon and Garfunkel - his sorrows become poetry. He hums along to the Lovin' Spoonful – he can skip through his troubles. He listens to Hendrix - reality bends to his imagination. He listens to Otis Redding - his blues become badges. He listens to The Doors – the darkness becomes illusion. He listens to Michael Bloomfield - he exists only in the moment, only the now. He listens to Van Morrison - he dances with Sandy under the moonlight. He listens to The Stones – he's ready to kick ass.

Monica and company pushed their paper pilfering capability to the limit and printed five thousand copies of *The Lime Juice Chronicle* vol. 2. Joe, Julie, and Tim picked them up two days later and distribution began on April 20th. They stacked the copies of their tabloid on top of *The Courier* and *The Register* news stands all over town. They stealthily spread copies around drugstore magazine racks. They even went to church vestibules and put copies on top of the Sunday bulletins. They gave hundreds of copies to each of their distributors at East and West High Schools.

On Sunday evening, they convened in Steve's basement to ponder their final moves. They would again mail copies to Josh and

Kayla, *The Barb,* and *The Village Voice.* The big question was what they would do at Regis? Sandy proposed a simple solution. "You know, we don't have to play with fire and distribute *The Chronicle* at Regis. There's plenty of other places to put it. It's not like the people at Regis are going to make a big difference."

Charlie vehemently shook his head no, "We can't let Regis off the hook. They need to know what *The Chronicle* has to say and own what they're going to do about it. Regis is our school, and we can't let ourselves off the hook by not making sure Regis knows the truth.

Toni was also adamant, "I want Regis to see *The Chronicle* more than anywhere else. I want people to know who we are. I want people to know who to talk with if they're interested in learning more. I want the people who don't like it to say so to my face, so I can tell them to stick it up their ass."

Joe, Jim, Mary, Julie, Warren, Rick, Dean, Steve, Al and Larry all voiced agreement that they should distribute *The Chronicle* at Regis. Mike, being Mike, took it a step further and suggested he be the one to spread it around school, because he wasn't involved with the first edition. Larry, being Larry, proclaimed exuberantly, "We're going to blow their minds."

Warren sighed, "We certainly will, and then they're going to blow our minds."

Sandy said sheepishly, "Well, I guess we now know who looks like a jerk."

Toni put her arm around Sandy, "I guess we now know who the only sane one is."

Tim put his hand on Sandy's shoulder and handed her a copy of *The Chronicle.* "You can redeem yourself by delivering this to Father Parker tomorrow."

The LIME JUICE arrived at school a half an hour early. They each had about a hundred copies of *The Chronicle.* They put a copy on every desk in their homerooms and the surrounding classrooms. They laid a copy on each teacher's desk. They stuck copies on every bulletin board they could find. This was not a covert operation. There was nothing subtle about it. They all wore stick-on name tags with their *Chronicle* volume 1 pen names. Then they took their seats and waited. If anyone asked them about *The Chronicle*, they would tell them to read it first and then ask them questions. If any teachers objected to *The*

Chronicle, they would ask them to read it first. If anyone was sent to the Administration office, they would wait outside in the hallway to see who else joined them. Anyone still in class by the end of the first period would go to the Administration office to see who was there. If anyone had to see Father Parker, they would all go together. They speculated on how long it would take for them all to be dismissed from class and how long it would be before they would be dismissed from school. Charlie and Jim thought there might be a handful of students who would angrily confront them. They all pledged not to retaliate violently. They didn't want another scene like the Electric Park.

Funny thing, the initial reaction was not what they expected. As students and teachers meandered into class, they picked-up *The Chronicle* and quietly read it. The LIME JUICE were the only ones not reading it. Some students glanced at them and their name tags. Some looks were inquisitive. Some looks were concerned. Some students looked irritated. A few teachers asked them if *The Chronicle* was theirs. There were no angry confrontations. None of them were dismissed from class and sent to the Administration office. The first period bell rang, classes began, instructions proceeded as usual and then class ended with the bell.

A few students wanted to talk with them after class, but they raced to convene as planned in the hallway outside the Administration office. They exchanged reports. It was puzzling that *The Chronicle* hadn't generated more excitement. They were relieved that their heads hadn't yet rolled, but they were disappointed that people didn't seem more worked up. Their intent was to provoke outrage that would spur action, but *The Chronicle* generated about as much excitement as a pop quiz. They started to disperse down the hall towards their 2nd period classes. Tim was about fifteen feet from the front office when they heard a thunderous shout, like a sequence of mortar shells exploding around them, "Mr. McIntyre, Mr. Snyder, Mr. Russell, Mr. Cumming, Miss Cumming, Miss Whitman, I need you all to follow me - now!" It was Wayne Wagner. He stood with his hands on his hips. His brow was furrowed and his cheeks were flushed. He radiated a red-hot stew of rage and contempt. He seemed genuinely, viscerally, personally pained.

They looked at each other with their eyes wide and thought, *"OK, here it is, here we go."*

Sandy said to Tim, "We're coming with you," and all of the LIME JUICE started to move towards Wagner.

Wagner barked, "Stop right there! The rest of you get moving to your classes. I'll let you know if we need to deal with anyone else later."

Joe turned to the temporarily reprieved and moved his hands up and down in a calming fashion, "It's cool guys. You should get to class."

Wagner continued to stand in the hall as the six offenders filed by him through the door into the Administration office, then he fell into step behind them as they entered Father Parker's office. Father was standing next to his bookcase talking with two other men who had their backs to them. As the young muckrakers lined up in front of Father's desk, the two other men turned around. Tim recognized them immediately. The Waterloo mayor and police chief had been all over the local nightly news since the rioting began.

It would be disrespectful and insulting to say that these two men resembled stereotypes of their titles to the point of looking cartoonish. But indeed, the two men appeared to be stereotypes of their titles to the point of looking cartoonish. Mayor Fred Rollins had the proportions of a bowling ball. His short, wide neck and rolling chin gave the impression that his round head sat directly on his shoulders. His shoulders and arms sloped around and down towards his hips at the same pitch as the curve from his chest to his bulging belly, which was cinched by a belt with a buckle that faced the ground. He wore an oversized black suit, with baggy pants that covered all but the toes of his black wingtip shoes. He was crowned with a black fedora, that for decades had been standard attire for American men, but was now out of fashion. Fred's bulbous nose and puffy cheeks had a red tinge that hinted at his years of happy hours at the Elks Club bar. He sported a sharply cropped salt and pepper mustache that he likely intended to project dignity and gravitas, but it reminded Tim of Captain Kangaroo.

Chief William Bradford's head was shaped like a chiseled block of granite, stone-faced, with a long square jaw. He had a five o-clock shadow, even though it was 9:45 AM. His dark navy blue, brass buttoned uniform was pressed and stiff, like a coat of armor around his heart. He wore the black brim of his cap tilted low on his forehead, partially obscuring his eyes, but not obscuring his contempt.

Mayor Rollins placed his hands on his hips, taking a disciplinarian's stance, but Tim had to fight back a giggle, because he thought the mayor looked like he was about to do the hokey pokey. Rollins puffed out his chest, lowered his chin and tried to sound stern, "Do you kids have any idea what you're doing? This town was in flames a couple of weeks ago and it appears that you want to reignite the inferno." He held up a copy of *The Chronicle*, then slammed it down on Father Parker's desk. "This irresponsible rubbish of yours is playing with fire and it must stop!"

Chief Bradford took three steps forward and stopped directly in front of Charlie, with his arms folded. "Son, are you trying to tell people my officers killed that Frazer boy?"

Charlie stayed calm, "No sir, but it doesn't make sense that Eddie would kill himself. People think there needs to be a proper investigation."

The Chief pushed his face into Charlie, "Son, are you calling the police liars?"

Charlie took a few seconds to weigh his response, but his eyes never shifted away from the Chief's glare. "No sir, but it doesn't make sense for the police to be the only ones to investigate what the police did or didn't do. People have to trust the process."

The Chief threw his shoulders back. "You're telling me people don't trust the police?"

"I'm saying black people don't trust the police. It just doesn't make sense…"

Wayne Wagner interrupted, "It seems not much makes sense to you kids. Maybe that's because none of you have much sense."

Mayor Rollins pointed his finger at them. "I'm not sure what laws you kids might have broken by strewing this slanderous trash around town, but I'm going to talk with the County Attorney to see what charges can be filed."

The Chief warned, "Consider yourselves on notice. You've all become threats to public safety and we're going to be keeping a very close eye on the bunch of you." He turned to Father Parker, "In the meantime, Father, we're going to leave this situation in your hands."

Without another word spoken in the room, the mayor and chief marched towards the office door, leaving their immediate fates to Father

Parker and Lame Wayne. The Chief paused at the door and turned around. He growled, "What the hell is this Lime Juice crap supposed to mean anyway."

Tim continued to stand with his back towards the Chief and bellowed, "The Leftist International Media Enterprise! We're going global chief." Then he paused, trembling with anger, and softly added, "The JUICE is the truth that needs to be squeezed out of this town."

The Chief huffed as he walked out, "Just as I suspected, a bunch of commie punks."

Father sat down in his desk chair and tapped his fingers on top of his desk pad. "Charles, you've been suspended since your arrest two weeks ago. Now, with this latest incident, I regret that I must notify your parents of your permanent expulsion from Regis. Timothy, I couldn't have been clearer about not tolerating another publication of this newspaper of yours. I'll be notifying your parents that you too are expelled. Michael, my goodness Michael, is there any trouble you can't avoid? You're also expelled. Joseph, Toni, and Mary, I've not needed to discipline you three before. Therefore, you'll be suspended for the next two weeks and on probation for the rest of the academic year. Charlie, Mike, and Timothy, you'll need to talk with Mrs. Franklin out front about arranging to come in after hours to take your final exams. Now you're all dismissed."

Sure, Tim was bummed out about being expelled. For his entire childhood he had looked forward to going to high school at Regis. Although he'd been alienated from the mainstream for the past year, he'd been at Regis for three years and he felt at home there. It felt like he was being kicked out of his family. Yes, he'd miss being around his friends at school, especially Sandy. Sure, he was concerned about the impact of being expelled might have on his future. But none of that was his primary worry. He was most afraid of how this would hurt his parents. They had sacrificed a lot for Beth and him to attend Regis. The tuition was a significant extra expense on their modest income but giving them a solid Catholic education had been their priority. He knew they would be disappointed and worry he was heading down the wrong path. The thought of his life turning into a train wreck and he becoming a bum was unsettling enough; the thought of his folks having a son whose life was a train wreck and turning into a bum was intolerable.

Joe gave Tim a ride home. Tim hoped he could talk to his mom before Father Parker called her. He rushed into the house and called out, "Hi, mom."

He was relieved to hear her call back from upstairs, "What's going on Timmy? How come you're home from school so early?"

He slowly climbed the stairs and entered his parent's bedroom. His mom was changing the sheets. She could see something was not right. "OK, Timmy, what's wrong?"

He walked over to her and sat down on the bed. His mom sat down next to him. He held a rolled-up copy of *The Chronicle* 2nd edition in his right hand, and he laid it on her lap. She looked down, unrolled it and sighed. "Oh God, Timmy, not again. How could you do this again. I told you it would only bring you trouble. What happened at school? What did they say?"

"Father Parker expelled me, mom. He expelled Charlie and Mike, too. The others have been suspended."

Audrey jumped up, "Expelled! You're telling me that my son has been expelled from Regis High School? Oh my God, Timmy, how could you have done this?"

"Jeez mom, I didn't expel myself. Father Parker expelled me."

"You best not smart-talk me Timmy. It's the same kind of thing that's gotten you expelled. This is going to devastate your father."

"I'm not trying to smart-talk you, mom, and I'm really, really sorry. I didn't want to do anything that would hurt you and dad."

"Well, Timmy, that's exactly what you've done. Now what are you going to do?"

"Father Parker said we can take our final exams in a few weeks. I'll have to enroll at West High for my senior year. In the meantime, I can pick up extra hours at the FoodValu."

"You need to go to your room right now, Timmy. I'm so mad at you I could just spit."

Tim stood up and made his way out. He stopped at the bedroom door and said, "When you feel up to it, mom, I think you should read *The Chronicle*. I think it's important."

"What's in this paper is not important to me, Timmy. You're what's important to me."

Father Parker called about a half hour later. Tim's mom had not yet read *The Chronicle*, but she apologized profusely on Tim's behalf and offered assurances that nothing like it would ever happen again, if only Tim could come back to Regis for his senior year. Father told her he had to regretfully refuse. He said it would jeopardize the school's standing in the community if Tim continued to be enrolled at Regis.

Tim's mom waited for Mac to get home from work before telling him. The three of them sat down at the kitchen table as soon as Mac walked in. It was agony waiting for his dad's response. Mac took his time, shaking his head back and forth, then after a few deep breaths he said, "Good grief, Tim, you've managed to screw things up pretty bad. You're a seventeen-year-old kid. Why did you think you could take on the world like this? It's a big, tough world out there, Tim, and it will crush you if you're not careful. What if you're not able to graduate next year? You'll be 18 then and draft eligible. I'd say the military might do you some good, but not while this damn war is going on. You'd better do some serious thinking about your future."

Tim looked up at him and said, "Well, I guess that's one thing that's kind of encouraging."

Mac was puzzled, "What do you mean by that?"

"That you still think I might have a future."

His mom weighed back in, "It will be a few weeks until you can take your finals. You need to work as many hours as you can. Otherwise, you're staying home, you're grounded, understand?"

"I understand," then Tim stood up and repeated, "I really think you both should read *The Chronicle*. You might not like it, but at least you'll know why we did this."

There hadn't been any stories about Eddie in the local news for weeks. Local newspapers and television stations seemed to reflect the desire of public officials to move on from anything related to the riots. So, Tim was surprised and gratified when two days after they distributed *The Chronicle* around town, he spotted a story in the Regional section *of Des Moines Register* headlined, *"Questions Persist about Youth's Death."* The story lifted several quotes directly from what Charlie wrote for *The Chronicle*, citing the source as "a local newsletter." Then, when the afternoon edition of *The Courier* arrived at the FoodValu, Tim found another story about Eddie, on the front page, below the fold. This time, the story included an interview with Charlie, done the previous day. It was all Tim could do to keep from running up and down the aisles screaming, "In your face, motherfuckers!" His first thought was, *"Man, this will really put the heat back on the police and city hall."* His second thought was, *"Man, this will really put the heat back on us."*

Sandy had just arrived at work, coming directly from school. Tim caught her clocking-in back in the break room. He showed her *The Courier* story and asked what people were saying at Regis?

"The LIME JUICE are totally freaked out. Nobody thought people would be expelled or suspended for putting out another issue. It's not like there was anything obscene in it. It was so weird not having you at school today, Tim. I just wanted to cry."

Tim gave her a hug and asked, "Has anyone talked with Mike? I haven't been able to get hold of him."

"Yeah, Joe talked to him last night. Get this, Mike said he was going to volunteer with the Bobby Kennedy campaign! He said he was scared shitless about being drafted. Then I remembered that Mike has already turned eighteen and he's no longer in school. He'll have no shield against the draft if he doesn't get into West. Anyway, he thinks Bobby is the only one who'll be able to stop the war, so he signed up to help. I don't know, I never thought of Mike as a political campaign kind of guy. He's more of a Yippie street protester type."

Tim laughed, "Hey, maybe getting expelled will be the springboard for Mike's political career. I can see the headline now, 'Senator Michael Russell leads national campaign to legalize marijuana.' His official theme song would be Dylan's *Rainy Day Woman*." Then Sandy and Tim howled and sang together, "Everybody must get stoned."

When Tim got home from work, he went to the refrigerator to get a Swanson's frozen turkey dinner. Audrey called him to come into the den with her and Mac. Tim sat down next to his mom on the couch. His dad got up from his easy chair and walked over to turn off the *Dean Martin Show* on the television. He sat back down, folded his hands on his lap, nodded a few times and said, "Tim, your mother and I read your newspaper. We were surprised to see that, apparently you didn't write any of the stories, at least we didn't see your name or pen name. Be that as it may, your mother called Mrs. Cumming this afternoon. They agreed we should try to meet with Father Parker together on Friday to see if we can straighten this situation out. She tried to call Mr. and Mrs. Russell, but Mike said they were in Florida, celebrating their anniversary. I don't think they even know yet about Mike being expelled."

Tim didn't want to cry, but there he was again, fighting back tears. He wasn't sure exactly what they were saying, but it sounded like something he hadn't heard or felt since being expelled – hope. "So, what did you think about *The Chronicle*, about the stories?"

Mac looked over at Audrey, and she replied, "We think Father Parker has some explaining to do."

Fridays hold a special place in Catholic liturgy. Jesus was crucified and died for our sins on a Friday. First Fridays are designated to atone for these sins and to recognize devotion to the Sacred Heart of Jesus, symbolized by a heart wrapped in thorns, as in love demonstrated through suffering and sacrifice. Their meeting with Father Parker was scheduled on the first Friday of May. Tim couldn't help wondering if meeting on a first Friday would improve their odds for being forgiven, or reinforce the need for them to be punished, to do penance? What could Tim say or do to be saved? It wasn't a matter of confession. Tim had already done that. It was about remorse, but Tim felt no remorse in his heart. Mrs. McIntyre wanted the meeting immediately, but she was told Father's schedule couldn't accommodate them any earlier. Tim wondered what significance this might hold for him. Was the delay meant to accent the seriousness of his sins prior to offering him salvation, or to convey the hopelessness of his fall from grace and his inevitable damnation? What could anyone possibly say that might reverse his banishment? Whatever it was, his mother wouldn't give him any hints about what was on her mind. She would only say, "We'll just have to see."

Mrs. McIntyre and Mrs. Cummings would act as counsels for the condemned. Mothers were typically the liaisons between families and schools. Fathers were not expected to be distracted from their work obligations to attend to such matters. The mothers used the delay to confer with each other. Mrs. McIntyre would send Tim out of the room whenever the mothers spoke on the telephone. Charlie told Tim their moms were talking while Tim was at work. Charlie was also clueless about what the moms were up to. When Mike's mother returned from Florida, she was brought into the deliberations.

The meeting was scheduled for 11:00 AM. The three banished students and their mothers arrived at 10:45. Father's door remained closed until he emerged at 11:17. He didn't appear pleased to see them and he greeted them flatly with, "Please come in and have a seat." Wayne Wagner stood silently in his usual corner, to the left behind Father's desk, his back straight, his arms folded, contempt oozing from his eyes. Mrs. Cumming stopped beside her chair. She remained there, standing long enough to return Wagner's leer before sitting down.

Father sat down at his desk, leaned back, with his hands folded on his lap. "I want you to know that I understand your deep concern for your sons and how the decision to expel them from Regis must cause you great distress. However, I must be clear from the outset that this decision cannot be reversed. The publication your boys distributed around town and around this school has caused Regis significant harm and tarnished our standing in the community. More importantly, it threatened public safety at a time of great peril."

Mike started to respond, "Listen, Father, you need to understand," then Mrs. Russel put her hand on his shoulder and Mike stopped in mid-sentence.

Mrs. McIntyre jumped in. "Excuse me Father, but have you actually read *The Chronicle*? I mean fully read it. If you have, please explain to us specifically what you read that you believe harms Regis and threatens public safety?"

Father was visibly taken aback, shaken, and annoyed by being challenged so directly, "For heaven's sake, Mrs. McIntyre, the boys all but accused the police of killing that boy in jail! Our community has been racked by violence over such accusations."

Tim's mother pulled a copy of *The Chronicle* out of her purse. "With all due respect, Father, please show me where it's alleged that the police killed Eddie Frazer?"

Father took the newspaper from Mrs. McIntyre, but he didn't even unfold it. "Mrs. McIntyre, it's implied throughout the story that the Frazer boy didn't commit suicide, so what is the reader left to conclude? The paper is filled with grievances that stoke anger."

Mrs. Cummings had listened long enough. "Father, again, with all due respect, this little newspaper is not what's fueling the anger that's engulfed our community. It's years, decades, of injustice. It's officials

206

like the mayor and police chief refusing to listen to reasonable demands for an impartial investigation into the tragic death of a young man. These students have written stories that are about so much more than anger. They're also filled with love. The story about Eddie takes a name in a headline and makes him a human being, someone whose life had value. It describes a young man who few in this community knew, but those who did know him, loved him dearly. The story that profiles Reverend and Mrs. Williams should have been written years ago. They're both important leaders in our community whom lots of people in this town don't even know. They've had remarkable lives, filled with love, devotion and courage. I'm grateful that someone finally took the time to write about them. The two stories about the students at East High School are about more than their grievances. They're about young people who care deeply about their future and about justice. I for one am proud of them."

That last line triggered Insane Wayne. He'd been leaning nonchalantly against the window frame when he suddenly straightened up, unfolded his arms, and placed them on his hips. He spoke through clenched teeth, "Proud! You're telling us you're proud of those rioters, those arsonists, those criminals? These boys of yours are nothing but rabble-rousers. They've caused nothing but trouble all year and they should have been expelled long ago."

That set off Mrs. Cummings. She leaped from her chair, slammed her hand on Father's desk and pointed her other hand at Wagner. "Father, I want this man out of your office now! We have important business to attend to and it can't get done with him here."

Father raised both his hands, "Please, everyone, let's all calm down. Mr. Wagner needs to remain here, but please Wayne, let me speak on behalf of Regis." Mrs. Cumming sat down, and Father continued, "As I stated at the beginning, it's not possible to change my decision. I'm under enormous pressure to get control of this situation. The whole town has been traumatized by recent events and Regis cannot be responsible for any further violence and destruction."

Mrs. Cummings took a deep breath and then calmly said, "Father, I know you care deeply about Regis and its reputation. I understand you've been pressured by the mayor and the chief. You have a great deal weighing on you and I hate adding to your burdens, but you need to know this, the pressure you feel now will pale in comparison to what will be coming your way if these three boys are not reinstated. What they've written should be praised, not punished. What will happen to the reputation of Regis when the community learns your students have been persecuted for seeking justice? What will the bishop think when he hears Regis has bowed to political pressure and aligned itself with forces of discrimination and brutality? What will the people of this state, this nation, think when they see on television demonstrators marching in front of Regis day after day, demanding that these boys be treated fairly? What will they think when they hear the families of these boys giving press conferences, side-by-side with representatives from the NAACP, calling for Regis to explain why it's expelling young people for advocating equal rights under the law? I promise you, Father, if these boys are not allowed to return to school here, fair-minded people in this country will come to think of Regis in the same vein as the Ku Klux Klan, and Mr. Wagner here will be viewed as Iowa's equivalent to Sheriff Bull Conner down there in Alabama. I doubt that's the reputation you want to protect."

Wagner again started to fly into a tizzy, "Now see here lady...," but Father Parker cut him off again. "Mr. Wagner, would you please excuse us and wait outside."

Wayne's face was so red, Tim thought he might have a stroke. He stood there trembling for several seconds before complying with Father's directive. When the door closed behind Wagner, it was Mrs. McIntyre's turn to reveal what Father Parker was up against. "Father, the time we were given to wait for this meeting gave us an opportunity to measure support for our sons. Mrs. Cummings met with the Reverend and Mrs. Williams. You might not be aware that they have close personal relationships with civil rights leaders and organizations all over the country. We've been assured that they're prepared to amplify the cause of our boys. Mrs. Cummings also spoke with the Black students at East High. You can expect to see them marching outside your window Monday afternoon. I suspect there will be more than a handful of Regis students who will join them. I'm sure it will attract a great deal of media attention."

Father Parker looked white as a sheet. "This is outrageous, ladies! I can't believe you would resort to such tactics!"

Audrey continued, "Oh that's not all. I'm sure you know that none of our families are very well-to-do and we haven't been major donors to Regis, but Mrs. Russell and I have both served on the planning committee for the annual Catholic School Golf Tournament for the past five years. I believe that's your most important fundraiser of the year, isn't it Father? Well, I've spoken with the other members of the committee. All but two of them are prepared to resign if your decision isn't reversed. The tournament is scheduled for June 28th. I suppose it could still go on, but I doubt it would be very successful, particularly if we use the occasion to continue protesting the unwarranted actions taken against these boys."

Mrs. Russell spoke for the first time, "Of course, Father, we'd rather not have to do any of these things. It doesn't have to be this way. Some people like the Mayor and Police Chief might be upset by the stories in *The Chronicle*, but there are a lot of good people who would applaud what the kids have written, and they'll think their punishment is unjustified."

Mrs. Cumming brought their argument home with a cup of sugar. "We believe you're one of those good people, Father. We know you want to do the right thing. Please read the stories again Father. Read them with an open mind and an open heart. I believe the right decision will become clear then."

At that moment, it didn't matter anymore to Tim what Father Parker decided. He was so proud of his mom, of all three moms, that he felt they had already won. He felt so much love for them that he knew it would carry him through wherever he ended up.

Everyone sat quietly while Father Parker looked down at his folded hands. After a long meditative pause, he nodded a few times, raised his head, and scanned the six souls sitting in front of him. "Alright ladies, I'll read the paper again and then I'll pray. I'll make my final decision by tomorrow morning."

Tim would like to think it was the power of their prose that moved Father Parker, rather than the threat of a prolonged public relations nightmare and a loss of donors. He would never find out for sure. At 10:00 AM Saturday morning, Mrs. McIntyre received a call from Miss Barns, Father Parker's secretary. The boys' expulsions would be converted to suspensions for the final weeks of the academic year. As previously ruled, they would be required to complete their homework assignments and take their final exams after school hours. They could return to Regis in the fall, to complete their Senior year and graduate.

Audrey hung up and immediately called Mac at work. They spoke briefly. She told him the verdict and said goodbye. She then walked to the kitchen table, sat down and quietly started to weep. Tim had been listening from the kitchen doorway. He sat down at the table, put his arm around her and told her he loved her. She rested her head on his shoulder and said, "Please, Timmy, please, never put your father and me through anything like this again."

The remainder of the school year was weird, but kind of nice. Sandy picked up Tim's homework every day and brought it to the FoodValu. He spent a lot more time on the readings and doing his homework than when he was attending classes. He was banned from school activities, and he made an agreement with his parents that he wouldn't be going to dances or parties until he finished his suspension. He worked almost full time and he saved a lot of money.

Now that Mike could remain enrolled at Regis while under suspension, his panic about being drafted was relieved. This didn't diminish his sense of urgency to stop the war and his enthusiasm for Bobby Kennedy's presidential campaign. He continued to volunteer after school and on weekends. He threw himself into the nitty-gritty of campaign groundwork, phone calling, preparing mailings, helping to put together events. He became close with the other volunteers, particularly Sarah, who was a senior at West High School. His friends thought it was cool to see Mike so immersed and committed to doing something as important and positive as working for a presidential campaign.

Charlie was determined to not let his grade point average drop. He continued to devote lots of energy to schoolwork, but not having to attend classes freed up a lot of time. He got a job on the groundskeeping crew at the Gates Park golf course, and he continued to advocate for an independent investigation into Eddie's death. He participated in vigils outside of the jail. He wrote letters to the editors at *The Des Moines Register* and *The Waterloo Courier*. He wrote and called the offices of State officials and the US Justice Department.

By the middle of May, public pressure continued to mount, so the Governor ordered the Iowa State Police to conduct an external review of Eddie's death. In the meantime, due to all the controversy associated with Eddie's case, the County Attorney decided to drop the assault charge against Charlie. The ISP review wrapped up in less than two weeks. Their report confirmed that Eddie had died by hanging, but they said it could not be determined whether or not it was a suicide. No additional actions were taken. Eddie's family lost hope. The Black community continued to seethe.

Chapter 17
You Say You Want a Revolution

On the morning of Thursday, June 6th, a few days after summer vacation began, Tim woke up at 4:30 AM to go unload a semi-truck at the FoodValu. He took his mom's car to work. He usually switched her car radio to a rock channel because she always had it set to the local NBC affiliated news radio station. At that hour, the channel would broadcast the farm crop and stock reports. When he turned the radio on, he was surprised to hear what sounded like a live national news report. The reporter's voice was somber. He was at a hospital in Los Angeles. Someone important had been shot and died. Then the reporter repeated the headline – Bobby Kennedy was dead. Tim had gone to bed after listening to the evening news. Robert F. Kennedy was the projected winner of the California Democratic Party primary, a victory that would likely propel him to be the Democratic Party nominee for president. Tim remembered thinking how thrilled Mike would be. Now, Tim's first thought was how devastating RFK's assassination would be for the country. His second thought was how devastating RFK's assassination would be for Mike. He wouldn't have to wait long to find out.

Tim got back home from unloading the truck at 7:30 AM and hollered good morning to his mom. She answered from the den. "Oh Timmy, have you heard? Bobby Kennedy has been shot. It's just horrible."

Tim went to the den and sat next to her on the couch, where she was watching the continuous news coverage of yet another assassination. Her eyes were glued to the TV. She held a cigarette frozen to her mouth. A tear rolled down her cheek. "Why do they want to kill all of our heroes?" Then she put her hand on Tim's knee and turned to him. "You don't need to be a hero, Timmy. You just need to be good."

Tim laid his hand on top of hers. "No need to worry about that one mom. There's not much risk of me ever being a hero."

Then she patted Tim's knee and said, "Oh, by the way, Mike called a few minutes ago. Of course, he's very upset. I was so proud of all the hard work he'd been doing for Bobby. You should call him back right away."

Tim got up and called Mike. Mike wasn't so much sad, as he was pissed. "This is such bullshit man. I should have known they'd never let someone like Kennedy get elected."

"What are you talking about Mike? Who are 'they'? The news reports are saying it was some disgruntled Palestinian who shot Kennedy."

"Come on Tim, you don't buy all that crap, do you? Just like it was some disgruntled communist who killed JFK."

"Hey Mike, how about I get hold of Joe and we go over to the park and toss the Frisbee around for a while?"

The Frisbee had become their favorite pastime, their therapy. It put them in a Zen zone, good for body and soul. The Frisbee had largely replaced playing catch with a baseball or throwing around a football. It involved more creativity and they spent hours practicing new ways to toss and catch it. Sometimes they threw it around on the grass and sometimes on pavement, where they could skip it to each other. Mike, Joe, and Tim spread out in a triangle on the Byrnes Park parking lot. Some of their tosses had wide, high, boomerang trajectories and others were thrown like rockets aimed straight at each other, so they could catch it behind their backs, behind their heads or between their legs. Acrobatic catches were particularly impressive after skipping the disc off the ground.

Mike's throws were angry, zipping directly at Tim and Joe's heads. "I'm telling you, man, I've had it with playing politics, playing it straight. Violence only understands violence."

Joe grabbed Mike's toss and held the Frisbee on his hip. "What the fuck are you talking about Mike? Are you going to turn into a revolutionary? You're going to start blowing shit up?"

Tim piled on, "Hey Mike, maybe in five or six years you'll be able to grow a beard and look like the Norte Americano version of Che Guevara."

"Look, I'm just saying, working within the system to stop this war is doomed to failure, because the system is rigged. I was never cut out for the Democratic Party anyway. I'm better suited for the Youth International Party. I feel a kindred spirit with the Yippies."

Joe pitched the Frisbee in a high arch back to Mike. "By better suited for the Yippies, do you mean you're going to start wearing a loin cloth and a headband?"

"Abbie Hoffman and Jerry Rubin don't wear loin cloths. They're serious pranksters. They know how to get people's attention, shake things up and maybe get something done."

Mike threw another rocket towards Tim. Tim jumped, spun around, caught it behind his back and replied, "Yeah, they're brilliant at getting publicity for themselves, but I don't see them getting much else done."

Tim skipped the Frisbee over to Joe, who threw it nonchalantly over to Mike and said, "I talked with Monica down in Iowa City. James is now the head of the Students for a Democratic Society chapter there. He said Tom Hayden is going to be speaking in Iowa City in a couple of weeks. He's on a national tour to organize protests at the Democratic convention in Chicago. How about we go down there and listen to what he has to say?"

Joe's suggestion was Mike's ticket out of Funkville, "Man, I'm always up for going to Iowa City. We can score some weed there."

Two weeks later, Joe, Charlie, Julie, Mary, Sandy and Tim rode to Iowa City with Mike and his new girlfriend, Sarah, crammed into Sarah's 1963 Volkswagen minibus. They swung by Monica's apartment first. She and Denise were preparing to go meet Alan, who was downstairs at the Deadwood Tavern playing pinball. Tim was struck by their upbeat demeanor, given the downer mood of the country following the King and Kennedy assassinations. The anti-war movement was becoming more strident and militant. There were ominous signs of a massive confrontations with the authorities in Chicago. Tim expected Monica would be in dour spirits. Instead, she seemed ebullient, greeting them with warm hugs and saying, "I'm so glad you guys could come down! Iowa City is where it's at today! James has done a fantastic job organizing Tom Hayden's visit. It's generating so much positive energy!

214

Both the University and the City denied us permits for the rally, but James has a friend who rents a farmhouse out by Lake McBride. We have thirty acres to do whatever we want. It's much better than having it in town, as long as we can get the press to cover it. You can follow us out there."

As their VW bus puttered north out of Iowa City, they joined a stream of cars heading to the rally. When they neared the lake, the caravan turned down a long gravel lane, snaked around back of an old farmhouse between a barn and outbuildings onto a dirt track through a pasture surrounded by corn fields. There was a makeshift stage at the far end of the pasture. A handful of hippies directed traffic over the rough terrain into long parking rows. They piled out of the minibus and heard a band tuning up, doing a sound check on stage. As they neared the stage, the band members came into focus. Tim came to an abrupt stop, putting one hand on Sandy's shoulder and his other arm in front of Julie. "Oh my God! It's The Mother Blues! I haven't heard them since the Jefferson Airplane concert. Just the thought of listening to them might be enough to trigger a flashback. I might start tripping out again."

The notion of Tim tripping out was enough to trigger a flashback for Julie, who was totally freaked out when he disappeared at the Airplane concert. "Are you shitting me, Tim? We're going to have to sit on you all afternoon. I'm not going to go looking for you if you flip out and go running buck-naked into those corn fields."

They carefully scouted for remnants of cow manure piles, then they threw a blanket down on the long, pillowy grass. The crowd filled in behind them and eventually reached all the way back to the parked cars. Tim estimated there were a couple of thousand people assembled. Tom Hayden was a big draw. He was an emerging political rock star of the left. Hayden cut his political teeth in the civil rights movement, and he earned a lot of credibility as a Freedom Rider in Mississippi, working to register Black voters and getting the shit kicked out of him in the process. He rose to a leadership position within the SDS as it turned its attention to stopping the Vietnam War. Now, all the anti-war efforts around the country were focused on the Democratic National Convention in Chicago at the end of August.

They settled in on their blanket as the Mother Blues played a long jam version of the blues classic, "Green Onion." They were feeling good, having fun, more fun than Joe thought was suitable. "Man, the vibe here doesn't seem right. It feels more like a rock concert than a political rally. We're supposed to be organizing protests, not partying.

Four freaks occupied a blanket next to them. The hippies were in full regalia, the hair, the headbands, the tie-dye, the bleach-stained bell-bottom jeans, and the herb. A cloud of pot smoke enveloped them. The dude sitting closest to Joe overheard his comment about the wrong vibe. He turned to Joe and handed him a huge joint. "Here you go man, the revolution starts in our minds."

Joe held his hand up and declined. "I mean, seriously man, how the hell are we going to stop the war if we're all stoned."

The hippie smiled and said, "Shit man, the only way we're going to stop the war is to get stoned. I don't think we'll be able to face down the cops otherwise. If I'm high, I'll just giggle when I look at them all dolled-up in their fucking riot gear."

James took the stage to thank The Mother Blues and introduce Tom Hayden. James hadn't cut his hair since Tim last saw him. He hadn't cut his hair since Tim first met him. He probably hadn't cut his hair since he started at the University. Shoulder length hair was still a radical look in 1968, at least in the Midwest. James usually exuded a quiet intensity, but that day he was on fire. "Brothers and sisters, welcome to this beautiful new day in our struggle for peace and justice! As we look up at this blue summer sky, we must remind ourselves of the hellfire being rained down from the skies above Vietnam! As we lay back on this soft grass in this peaceful pasture, we must remember those who are dying in the rice paddies of Vietnam. As we listen to the soulful sound of The Mother Blues, we must use it as a clarion call to follow our hearts and together resist this unjust war, to stop this horror show, to fight back against the war machine! Look around you. We're the new army of peace and love. Our growing numbers will blow the military's mind. This is our movement. This is our time. Brothers and sisters, please help me welcome to Iowa, a warrior for civil rights, a man on the front lines fighting to end the carnage in Southeast Asia, the national representative of SDS, Mr. Thomas Hayden."

The crowd stood up and greeted Hayden with a rousing round of whoops, whistles, and applause. Tim turned to Sandy and said, "Jeez, that intro from James, I haven't heard that much fire and brimstone since the last time I watched Oral Roberts on TV. I guess rallying protesters is not much different than bible thumping to save souls."

Sandy had a similar reaction. "He did seem a bit self-possessed."

Joe approved of James' rhetorical approach. "James gets it. He understands that politics and religion have similar objectives, like practicing medicine and witchcraft. You have to first get people to believe, to have hope. I guess some people feel they need to get high first, but what they really need is to be inspired first. At least James reminded people we aren't here to party."

Tom Hayden didn't look or sound like a charismatic leader. Earnest? For sure. Committed? Absolutely. He had the look of a scruffy graduate student. He wasn't a natural public speaker. His strength of conviction moved him to stand in front of crowds. What he lacked in eloquence though, he made up for with clarity. "Each and every one of you who came to this farm today must commit yourselves to showing up in Chicago on August 26th! The National Mobilization Committee to End the War includes representatives from every ant-war organization in the country. Our massive presence will send an overwhelming message to the Democrats and to the nation that we will not tolerate the continuation of this war! The time is now! If you don't show up now, the killing will continue and some of you here today could be among the body count. You can show up in Chicago, or show up later in a body bag."

Charlie: "I really didn't need to hear that last line."
Sandy: "That sounded a little harsh."
Tim: "He doesn't pull any punches."
Julie: "That's vivid imagery. It's very effective."
Joe: "I'm going to Chicago. Whose coming with me?"
Mike: "Right on brother."

Tim couldn't bring himself to tell his mom and dad. The idea of him going to Chicago would terrify them. It terrified Tim. He knew his folks would forbid him from going and he wanted to avoid directly defying them, so he kept his thoughts to himself.

Tim assumed the rest of the LIME JUICE would want to join them in storming the convention center's ramparts, but most of them were skeptical at best. The girls thought the whole enterprise was batshit crazy. Sandy didn't understand the strategy, "You're going to disrupt the Democrats, but not the Republicans. How does that make sense?"

Tim tried to explain, "Everyone knows the Republicans are warmongers, but the Democrats have been leading this war so far. Besides, the Democrats are the only ones that have candidates who want to stop the war. We want to convince them to nominate McCarthy or McGovern."

Julie thought that was rich. "As if. The only thing you're going to convince them to do is bash your heads in."

Several guys were considering the trip, but they were waiting to see how things were shaping up. The Republican convention opened in Miami on August 5th. Protests in the Miami Black community of Liberty City were brutally put down. Anti-war demonstrators weren't allowed to get within a half-mile of the convention center. Everyone knew Chicago would be the main event. Mayor Richard Daley, the long-time boss of the Democratic Party machine, vowed zero tolerance for disruptions to an orderly convention. His pronouncements only incited more radical reactions from the protest leaders. Much of the attention focused on the Yippies, who were masters of media manipulation. They threatened to spike the city water supply with LSD. They nominated a pig for President, a real live pig. Both sides were poised for confrontations and some people on both sides seemed to be itching for a fight.

By the middle of August, most of the LIME JUICE had backed out. Warren and Jim said they had to play a gig. The others just honestly thought it was a fool's errand. Al stated it bluntly, "It's not going to change a damn thing, except maybe the contours of your skull."

Joe and Mike were undeterred. Charlie had lots of misgivings, but he felt compelled to do whatever he could to resist the war. As for Tim, he had no idea what he would do. Part of him desperately wanted to back out. He could think of a whole laundry list of reasons not to go. He felt like he had already used up two lives, surviving two issues of *The Chronicle*. His parents would be furious. It wouldn't be easy to get the time off work. He might get arrested. He might get beat up. It might cause problems for him getting into college. He might get on an FBI surveillance list. Then he thought again about the possibility of getting beat up.

218

Tim also had doubts about the wisdom of the whole enterprise. Would creating chaos at the Democratic convention just help secure the presidency for Richard, the Lizard, Nixon? So why in the world would he go? It was because of what he saw on his bedroom wall. Each day he would wake up looking at that wall, and it was the last thing he looked at before turning off the lights each night. He focused on the wall's totality as much as the individual images. The suffering, the celebrations, the struggles, the silliness, the beauty, the barbarism all projected one message to him – *This is the world as it is, all of it. This is life as it is, all of it.* The wall reminded him of the epiphany he had the previous summer in Tucson. Engaging the world is how he wanted to live. He had to live if he wanted to have a life.

Yet, by the middle of August, Tim still hadn't made up his mind about Chicago. He was only seventeen for Pete's sake. Chicago would be the real deal. Both sides were preparing to play for keeps. The protesters converging there would be hardcore. The Chicago police force was hardcore as well. Embracing life didn't have to entail risking his life.

Then, on the morning of August 21st, he woke to news from a tiny republic thousands of miles away that tipped the scale and sealed the deal. It was called "The Prague Spring." He'd been following events in Czechoslovakia since January, when Alexander Dubcek became the First Secretary of the Czech Communist Party. Dubcek immediately began putting in place social, economic and political reforms that the Czech people loved, but bugged the hell out of the leaders in the Soviet Union. All of the Warsaw Pact countries had been under the thumb of their USSR overlords in Moscow since the end of World War II. Dubcek's reforms were bold, including more press freedom, more freedom of expression and freedom of movement. It ignited a Bohemian renaissance that was highly threatening to the Soviet control freaks. On the night of August 20th, over 650,000 Warsaw Pact troops and hundreds of tanks raced into Czechoslovakia and flooded the center of Prague, shutting the whole place down. The people responded valiantly. The images that boggled Tim's mind the most showed thousands of unarmed young people swarming over tanks, defiantly waving Czech flags, and facing down soldiers armed with machine guns. Tim felt humbled by their courage, their chutzpah. How could he be intimated sitting there in Iowa, thinking about facing down the Chicago police department, when these young Czechs were storming tanks? *"I mean, we're talking about a bunch of Chicago cops, not Soviet storm troopers, right? Right? RIGHT?"*

Tim met Joe and Charlie in Steve's basement after work. He told them he would go to Chicago. Joe looked mildly surprised, then handed Tim an envelope and said, "Cool, I guess you can use one of these after all."

Tim opened the envelope and pulled out a badge in a plastic holder hanging on a black lanyard. "What the fuck is this?"

Joe snickered, "It's a press pass. A Democratic National Convention press pass."

Tim looked at it again. Indeed, at the top it said, "Press," and right below, "Democratic Party National Convention, Chicago, Illinois, August 23-28." Below that, on the left, there was a square blank space that looked like it was meant for a photograph. To the right of the blank space were two lines. The first line read, "Name: Timothy McIntyre." The second line said, "Organization: League for International Media Education (LIME)."

Tim struggled to process what he was looking at. "Where the hell did you get this!"

Joe laughed again and said, "A couple of weeks ago I called Josh to see if he and Kayla were going to Chicago. He said of course they were going. Josh just got his notice to report to the Contra Costa County draft board on September 8th, to present his conscientious objector case. He doesn't think they'll approve it. They've been rejecting all the applications. He's refusing to do battle in Vietnam, but he's ready to battle in Chicago."

The thought of Josh being drafted seemed impossible to Tim. "Wait a minute, why can't Josh get a student deferment?"

Joe never met Josh in person, but he wondered about the same thing. "I asked Josh about that. He said he only applied to the one university he most wanted to attend, M.I.T., and he was sure he would get accepted. He was stunned to find out he didn't get in. He's been scrambling to figure out where else to apply, but in the meantime, he's got to appear before the draft board. Josh said he was able to get a couple of press passes. He found out the newspapers in Stockton and Modesto weren't going to send their own reporters, so he secretly submitted press registration requests for them. He could hardly believe it when he got the badges in the mail a couple of weeks later. I asked him if he could get us some badges, but he said there wasn't enough time. He offered to forge a couple of passes for us though, based on the originals he had. Now we just need to add our own photos. We need to go down to Hawkeye Photography Studios tomorrow and get a couple of passport photos."

"So, you have one of these passes too?"

"Absolutely, but Josh wanted us to use two different organizational names, so I'm with Journalism United in College Education (JUICE). Josh thought we could both pose as journalism students, because we look too young to be professionals. I think both organizations sound absurd, but what the fuck, the worst that can happen is we won't get in."

Chapter 18
Sunday, August 25th

Early Sunday morning, Joe, Charlie, Mike, and Tim boarded the Rock Island train to Chicago. An hour earlier, Tim penned a note to his parents, *"Dear Mom and Dad, I'm going to the Democratic National Convention in Chicago for four days. I'm with Joe, Mike and Charlie. We'll look out for each other and we'll be OK, nothing to worry about. We just want to participate in the political process. Maybe I can say hello to Hubert Humphry for you. I love you both, Tim.* The note was meant to ease their minds. The last line was intended to lighten the mood. Regardless, he knew they'd be upset, furious, terrified.

The train pulled into Chicago Union Station mid-afternoon. They disembarked slowly, hesitantly. An image came into Tim's mind of troop ships unloading in England prior to D-Day. The boys were woefully ill-prepared for the trip, with no plans for accommodations. Tim had his canvass Boy Scout knapsack, stuffed with a rain jacket, some snacks and his convention disguise, a white dress shirt, dark slacks, and a tie.

It was a four-mile trek from the train station to Lincoln Park, where they had arranged to meet Josh and Kayla. The Chicago transit workers were on strike, so the boys shunned the EL-train, unfolded their Michelin map, and set out to soak in the city. Marching through the towering urban canyons of the Chicago Loop and down the Magnificent Mile on North Michigan Avenue, Tim was reminded how big the world was and how small his life had been. It struck him how futile it was for him to think he could impact any of it. He felt like a country bumpkin.

Soon after they entered Lincoln Park, they spotted Josh and Kayla sitting beneath their designated rendezvous point - the Benjamin Franklin monument. Josh and Kayla looked dramatically different from the previous summer. Most startling was that Josh had cut his hair. It wasn't a crew cut, but it was cut just above his ears, neatly combed, with a part on the left. He looked downright clean-cut. Kayla's hairstyle was totally different too. Her curly globe hairdo had been straightened into a flip bob that made her look like Mary Tyler Moore on the Dick Van Dyke Show. There were hugs and handshakes all around.

Mike was the first to call out their metamorphosis, "Christ, what gives? You guys both look like Young Republicans!"

Josh laughed, "We're undercover. We thought it was necessary for our stealth mission to get inside the convention hall. You guys already look pretty straight, but we looked like poster children for the revolution. Security would take one look and toss us out on our ears."

Joe was excited about finally meeting them in person. "Man, I've been looking forward to meeting you guys. I feel like we've already been through a lot together, like brothers in arms."

Kayla gave Joe a second hug and said, "I know, we've been so impressed by what you guys have been doing with *The Chronicle*. It's inspired us to keep pushing the envelope with *The Gazette*. So, would this be Charlie?"

Charlie deadpanned, "I guess it was my effervescent personality that gave me away."

Kayla laughed, "Yes, that's the one thing that distinguishes you from these other white bread guys."

Josh spread his arms out to reveal Lincoln Park. "Welcome to the land of peace, love and lunacy. The Yippies have declared a 'Festival of Life' here. A critical mass of serious silliness will erupt in Lincoln Park today."

Mike said gleefully, "Sounds like I'll be in my element. I'll be among my soulmates."

Kayla smiled and shook her head, "I figured you'd feel right at home with the Yippie scene here, Mike."

Young people were flowing into the park from every direction as they wandered through the crowds on their way to the Grant Monument. There was a festive feel to the scene. They passed a large group of people sitting on the grass around an older man with long hair and a long beard, looking like a western version of the Maharishi Mahesh Yogi, who achieved fame as the guru to The Beatles. The furry facsimile was leading the group in a loud, low Ommmmm, while little Tibetan bells were being struck. Charlie asked, "Who's the guru of sorts?"

Josh answered, "That's Allen Ginsberg, the poet. He manages to show up at every counter-culture event, next to every counter-culture icon - Dylan, Leary, The Beatles. I used to think he was pretty cool and I was fascinated with the whole Transcendental Meditation thing, but now I tend to agree with John Lennon, that it's just another illusion, another scam."

Mike jested, "I don't know man, Jerry Ruben said they were going to get everyone to mediate hard enough to levitate The Pentagon. We better not get too close or they might send us up into the clouds."

The atmosphere around the South Pond was more down to business. People were being led through protest training and passive resistance drills, prancing around in unison, dropping down, locking arms, and preparing for police assaults. Some guys wore an assortment of headgear, football and motorcycle helmets, some donned army surplus gas masks. Tim thought it was all a bit much.

As Josh predicted, there was a healthy share of silliness in the air, too. They saw a procession of Yippies carrying the pig they had nominated for President. Small groups of people were sitting around playing guitars, bongo drums and wooden flutes, while others preformed their free-form dances, swinging and swaying, devoid of any discernable choreography or any semblance of rhythm.

They found a spot to make their base camp next to a row of huge arborvitae shrubs. They spread their blankets, sat down, savored the scene around them and reveled in their camaraderie. By late afternoon they needed sustenance. They pooled their funds and discovered their collective cash reserves were only sufficient to provide them with a starvation diet for the next three days. Kayla and Mike set out on a mission to find a grocery store. When they returned from the store, they unpacked a sack with a loaf of bread, a large jar of Jif Peanut Butter, a sack of Ruffles potato chips and four quart-sized bottles of Pepsi. Mike was proud and pleased with their purchases. "This should be enough to get all of us through the next few days.

Josh cautioned, "OK, but we can't risk getting stoned or the munchies will wipe out all of this in one fell swoop."

As darkness descended, the playful atmosphere in the park began to subside and the mood became more tense. There had been a large police presence around the perimeter of the park all day. After sunset, busloads of cops arrived in riot gear and began to get organized. Tim yelled at a young guy walking quickly back from a phalanx of police. He was wearing an armband that said SDS, with a peace symbol. "Hey, what's going on? What do you think is going to happen?"

The guy stopped in his tracks and jabbed his finger towards the cops. "It's total bullshit, man! The city won't give us a permit to camp in the park. Now they're saying the park closes at 11:00 PM and we all have to get out. Fuck those guys!"

Kayla asked, "So what are we going to do?"

The SDS centurion replied, "We're going to bring the war home tonight!"

Mike's jaw dropped and his eyes got wide, "Holy shit guys, this is going to get very real, very fast! Are we ready for this?"

The answer was clear to Charlie, "Hell no! We're miles from the convention and the protests haven't even started. I'm not about to make my last stand here. Besides, these Chicago cops would love nothing better than to use this black kid's head for batting practice. I say we get the hell out of here."

The police line was two rows deep and wrapped around LaSalle Drive. Some protesters gathered on the park side of the street, taunting the cops. At 11:01 PM the police lines moved into the park, grabbing protesters, and pushing them to the ground. Bedlam ensued. Tear gas was fired. Cops donned with gas masks ran through the toxic white clouds swinging their batons. Tim et al. were frozen in place by terror, but when the first whiff of gas hit them, they grabbed their meager belongings, turned around, and raced towards Lake Michigan. They joined hundreds of other protesters as they danced across Lake Shore Drive, dodging the speeding, swerving, screeching traffic. The image Tim had earlier in the day of troops storming the beaches of Normandy was replaced. Now he was thinking of the British army trapped on the beach at Dunkirk.

When they reached the water, they looked back and saw that traffic had completely halted on Lake Shore Drive. The thoroughfare was engulfed in white clouds of tear gas. Cops and protesters were engaged in hand-to-hand combat, spread out across all eight lanes going north and south. They were riveted by the dramatic scene, but they had enough sense to head south towards the Navy Pier. They came to the end of the sandy beach, then they walked along the concrete beach all the way to the Navy Pier. They found a secluded spot to take refuge underneath a cluster of trees in Polk Brothers Park. It was 2:00 AM. They were cold, shaken, disheveled and exhausted. The Chicago police had won the first round. The young neophyte protesters were apprehensive about what might be in store for them in the coming days. It was easier not to talk about it, not to voice their doubts, their fears, their regrets. It was easier to just lie down on their blankets and crash.

Chapter 19
Monday, August 26th

They woke to a spectacular sunrise emerging from Lake Michigan. The calm, mirrored waters were a stark contrast to the previous night's chaos and belied the likely turmoil ahead. After a peanut butter breakfast, the budding subversives enjoyed a leisurely morning by the lake. They freshened-up in the park restrooms, splashing water on their heads and in their pits. In the early afternoon, they pulled out their junior journalist wardrobes. Tim's white dress shirt was hopelessly wrinkled, which didn't look totally out of character for his role. The thin metal prongs on his clip-on necktie were bent, making the preset Windsor knot cockeyed and putting the whole unit at risk of falling off. His black converse tennis shoes had taken a beating while walking down the lakefront, but his pant legs were long enough to cover some of the grime.

It was seven miles from the park to the convention at the International Amphitheatre. The buses weren't running, and they couldn't afford a cab, so they broke up into three pairs and hitched. Tim paired up with Charlie. It took them three rides to get within a half-mile of the convention hall. Their first ride going south on Lake Shore Drive was atypical, a prissy young woman and her two little kids in a Ford station wagon. The second ride was with a middle-aged business man in a suit driving a Pontiac LeMans. He said he picked them up because they were wearing ties. When they said they were headed to the convention, he warned them to beware of trouble from the "goddamn hippies." Their last ride was with three long-haired protesters who were also headed to the convention. They said they almost didn't pick them up because they were wearing ties. The hippies took them as close as possible to the amphitheater, but the streets were closed blocks away from the convention hall and parking was almost non-existent.

They found Kayla, Josh Joe and Mike waiting for them at their meeting point on the corner of Halsted and Root St. Democratic Party delegates were bustling towards the Amphitheater. There was a large police presence, with a smattering of National Guardsmen. Rumors had been swirling about thousands more National Guardsmen on the ready a few miles away. Very few protesters had arrived yet. They wouldn't be coming out in force until closer to nightfall. Charlie and Mike went to case the area, while Josh, Kayla, Joe, and Tim tried to penetrate security with their press badges. The four faced each other, took a couple of deep breaths, and tried to muster up each other's self-confidence. They crossed the street and walked straight towards a gate in the outer chain link fence surrounding the Amphitheater. They flashed their badges at the cops standing around the gate and they were waved through. They couldn't believe it was that easy, but of course, it wasn't.

They boldly strutted up to a row of doors at the front entrance. Once again, they flashed their badges at the police standing in front of each door. Josh was in the lead. As he started walking through the door, one of the cops thrust his arm out and slammed it into Josh's chest, knocking him back a couple of steps. "Where do you kids think you're going?"

While Josh was recovering from the blow, Kayla replied, "I'm a reporter for the Modesto California Bee newspaper and he's with the Stockton California Record. These other two guys are student reporters we just met. We all have press passes."

The burley cop held out his hand and said, "Reporters huh? Let's see what you've got." He grabbed the badge that was hanging from Kayla's neck and closely inspected it, looking up to match the photo with her face. He did the same thing with his other suspects. "The badges look legit, but you kids don't look much like reporters to me. We're making damn sure there isn't going to be any trouble inside here."

Josh regained his composure. "Look officer, as a reporter, I'm supposed to remain non-partisan, but just between you and me, I'm a registered Republican."

Kayla, tried to enhance the ruse. "Not only that, he's going to be inducted into the Marine Corps next month."

The cop was duly impressed. "Good for you, son. I'm so sick of these damn draft-dodging sons-of-bitches. It's great to see a real red-blooded American boy. Go on in there and keep an eye on those pansy politicians."

They smiled at the cops and walked through the main doors home free, or so they thought. Once inside, the delegates were backed up in front of the next security hurdle. Private security guards were standing next to some type of badge screening device, a medal box on top of a metal stand, with a slot to insert the official convention badges. If the badges were accepted, a small light would go off on top of the box. They had no idea what the basis was on which these devices were accepting the badges. They observed the process for a couple of minutes, then Kayla huddled them together to devise a plan. It was a shaky scheme, but if executed as choreographed, it gave Joe and Tim a shot at getting in.

Kayla and Josh had official badges, so they went first. Josh inserted his press pass and the light went on without a hitch. He stepped forward slightly. Kayla was right behind him. She inserted her badge, the light went on, she pulled it out, then looked up at the young security guard, smiled and said, "Hi, I'm a newspaper reporter from California. Would you mind if I asked you a couple of really quick questions?"

He was taken aback and looked uncertain. He glanced around to see who might be watching, then he turned back and saw Kayla still smiling at him. He shrugged and said, "Well I suppose so, but it has to be quick."

Kayla was oozing sweetness. "Great, can I get your name please?"

"Huh, well, I guess so. My name's Bill, I mean William, Schuller."

Kayla leaned in to look at Bill's name badge. "Schuller, so let's see how that's spelled."

As Bill was looking at Kayla, looking at his badge, Josh took the lanyard off from around his neck and handed the badge to Kayla's free hand. Kayla brought her hand behind her back and handed it to Joe, who put it around his neck. Joe inserted Josh's badge in the security box and the light went off.

Joe stepped around Kayla as she asked, "So Bill, can you explain to me how this little badge box doohickey actually works? I've never seen anything like it." As Bill started mansplaining the doohickey box, Kayla stepped between him and Tim, took her Nikon camera off from around her neck and shoulder, and started taking close-up photographs of Bill.

Joe slipped Josh's badge off and put his phony badge back on. He slipped Josh's badge into Kayla's back pocket. She snapped another shot of Bill, then reached behind to take the badge and wrap it around her back again to pass it to Tim. Tim took a step forward to grab the badge, but before he could reach for it, an older security guard walked over and stepped between him and Kayla. "What's the holdup here? We have to keep these lines moving."

Kayla tried to transfer her charm to the older guard. "Oh, I'm so sorry. I'm a reporter and I had a few questions for Bill here."

"You'll have to take your questions elsewhere young lady. Bill has no time for that here. Now move along please." He spread his arms and walked Tim's three companions away from him and Bill.

Tim stood there frozen, watching his co-conspirators get pushed farther away. He looked back blankly at Bill. It was a moment of truth. He could simply turn and walk away, or he could go for broke. There was no time for reflection, for inspiration, or for good sense. Only a flash, a feeling, an instinct that's best described as the LIME JUICE mantra, IGAS. He didn't give a shit. He inserted his counterfeit LIME press pass. A second later, the light went on. He looked up at Bill, who gestured with his head for Tim to keep moving. He pulled the badge out and walked over to his colleagues, who were waiting for him, shaking their heads in disbelief.

Josh had a self-satisfied smile, "I guess I'm a pretty damn good counterfeiter."

The four of them quickly reviewed the plan they had plotted in the park that morning. They knew the McGovern and McCarthy delegates intended to introduce a party policy plank motion that afternoon calling for peace negotiations with North Vietnam to end the war. The imposters' top priority was to advance that motion; however, they also wanted to call out how the City of Chicago was treating the protesters. The four of them dispersed across the convention floor with the goal of contacting each state delegation, using a similar script.

Tim's first stop was the Nebraska delegation. He approached a middle-aged woman wearing a straw hat, an American flag-themed hooped skirt, and a blue blouse with a Hubert Humphrey campaign button. He pulled out a small note pad and a pen. "Excuse me ma'am, I'm with the League of International Media, May I ask you a few questions?"

She was delighted to oblige. "Why of course young man. How can I help you?"

"Well, I was just speaking with the Minnesota delegation, and they've heard that Vice-President Humphrey is open to supporting the Vietnam peace negotiation motion. Is the Nebraska delegation open to supporting it as well?"

The Lady Cornhusker looked incredulous. "Why no, I haven't heard about this, and quite honestly, I find it more than a little surprising. It was my understanding that the President and Vice-President were adamantly opposed to such a motion."

Tim needed to enhance the plausibility of his story. "Oh, you're correct, they were both opposed to it, but the situation is very fluid. I guess they've negotiated some compromises and the current wording of the motion is now acceptable. So, do you think you'll vote in favor of it now that there's such a groundswell of support?"

She thought for a moment, then said, "Well, I've never been opposed to peace, per se. I suppose I would vote to approve the motion if the party can be unified around it.

"Can I quote you ma'am, that you're not opposed to peace?"

"I don't think there would be anything wrong with quoting me on something like that."

"Thank you very much ma'am. Oh, and one more question, would you support a motion supporting peaceful demonstrators' first amendment right of free speech?"

"We all need to support the constitution young man. You can quote me on that too."

The concept was to germinate a narrative, till the field, plant some seeds, grow a consensus, and harvest enough votes to pass two motions. They were going to start some rumors. The kind of rumors that would race through the convention floor like a wildfire. In other words, they were going to lie a lot.

Tim bounced over to the South Dakota delegation. There were three young men standing together with rolled-up shirt sleeves and buttons for South Dakota's favorite son candidate, George McGovern. Tim knew they would be sympathetic to the peace motion, and he wanted to give them something to bolster their pitch to the other delegates. "Excuse me, I'm with the International Media and I'd like to get your reactions to something I just heard. A woman over there in the Nebraska delegation says a compromise has been struck between the McGovern, McCarthy, and Humphrey camps on a peace negotiation proposal. Apparently, all sides are prepared to support the current language. Have you heard about this?"

They looked at each other stunned and excited, then one of them turned back to Tim, "We haven't heard anything about this! I don't think anyone here has heard about it. This is an incredible development! People need to know what's going on. Is there going to be an announcement?"

Tim shrugged, "Beats me, I just report on these things. I think it's up to you folks to decide who needs to know and then get the word out. By the way, you might also want to let people know there's going to be a motion calling for the City of Chicago to respect peaceful protesters' first amendment right to exercise free speech."

Tim left them to mull it over, while he randomly rolled into the Indiana delegation. He was settling into his character, so he confidently approached a group of three men and two women who were arguing vehemently. Turns out, they were debating the Vietnam war. A rotund man in a blue suit was waving his American flag tie in front of himself, proclaiming emphatically, "America has never lost a war and we're not going to now! These colors don't run!" One of the women looked him up and down and responded, "I believe you, Roger. You look like you've never run in your whole life."

Tim stepped into the middle of their exchange, with pen and notepad in hand. "Excuse me, I'm a reporter and I'm wondering if your delegation agrees with the new compromise peace proposal? The Nebraska and South Dakota delegations seem to be on board."

The Hoosier delegates looked at each other in bewilderment. One of the women said to Tim, "What compromise?"

Tim replied with matter-of-fact confidence, "The compromise between the McGovern, McCarthy and Humphrey camps."

The guy with the courageous tie squinted at Tim and said, "Son, if you're going to be a reporter, you're going to need to develop a better nose for horseshit. I'll lay my bottom dollar that there's not any compromise between the damn peaceniks and Humphrey's crowd. Some weasels are making mischief, trying to trick folks into voting for the motion."

Busted! Granted, he didn't call Tim a liar, just a fool, but Tim's schtick had been shit on. He could have recovered from it. He could have been better prepared for provoking some cynical reaction. He could have been nimbler in responding to the pushback. Instead, he crumbled against the first serious challenge to the crap he was purveying. Tim said nothing. He just turned and walked away. He stopped in between the North Carolina and Michigan delegations. For a moment, he tried to decide which group to approach next, but he'd lost his moxie. More to the point, he was embarrassed, ashamed. What the hell was he doing walking around spreading lies? As the Hoosier put it, he was a trickster making mischief.

Tim moved slowly through the Democratic masses, across the grand hall to a point below the NBC News broadcast booth and waited for his co-conspirators. Josh joined him about a half hour later, then Kayla. It was another hour before Joe joined them. Between the four of them, they had contacted twenty-eight delegations. Their story about a compromise peace resolution created a lot of buzz, but they weren't sure if it changed many minds. As they moved between delegations, they talked less about the peace motion and more about the violence outside the convention hall. Most of the delegates had been unaware of how bad the mayhem had been in Lincoln Park the previous night. Many of them were outraged to learn about the tactics being used by the police, the Billy clubs and tear gas. Some said they wanted to make a motion from the floor condemning the police conduct. Tim was most impressed that Joe was able to have a lengthy conversation with the governor of Connecticut, Abraham Ribicoff. The governor was a McGovern backer, so he was already on board with the peace plank. Joe didn't attempt to spring the compromise rumor on him. Instead, he talked about the Chicago police tactics. Ribicoff was scheduled to formally nominate McGovern the following evening and he said he might mention how the protesters were being treated. The pranksters agreed that they had accomplished about as much as they could from inside the belly of the beast.

They hung around the convention hall for a few more hours, long enough to watch the Vietnam peace negotiation policy plank go down to defeat. The peace delegates were furious that debate on the motion had been squashed. They became more vocal and unruly. The tensions manifested outside the convention hall were now being manifested inside. It did not bode well for the Democratic Party's business slated for the following day.

It was 10:00 PM when they walked out onto Halsted Street. The night was hot and muggy, the kind of night that invites subversion, breeds conspiracies, and removes constraints on insurrections. They expected to be greeted outside by another round of chaos, but the streets appeared calmer than the turmoil inside the hall. There were peaceful demonstrators a block away, beyond the chain link security fencing topped with concertina wire. The faux journalist mischief makers beamed big smiles at the private security guards and Chicago cops as they sauntered out through the gate. They wove their way through the demonstrators for a couple of blocks. The thought of hitchhiking through the city at night was a little unnerving. They spotted two hippies pulling out of a parking structure in a 1956 Ford F100 pickup. Kayla flagged them down. They happily agreed to give the kids a lift to Grant Park. The four of them climbed into the back bed of the truck. Riding through the streets of Chicago bathed by a warm breeze, Tim felt like he was flying carefree, massaged in tranquility. It was a welcome respite from the smoked filled cacophony on the convention floor.

Activity on the sidewalks increased as they came closer to the lakefront. When the truck turned from Roosevelt Road onto South Michigan Avenue, they were stunned to see, first hundreds, then thousands of rowdy protesters filling the length of Grant Park, across the street from the swanky hotels where most of the delegates were staying. The truck only traveled a hundred yards further before being stopped at a police barricade, where their shaggy chauffeurs were told to turn around. Tim and his crew took the opportunity to jump out and thank them for the lift. It was tempting to hang around and see what type of fracas might develop, but they had been engulfed in enough intense crowds for one day and it was still a long trek to their meet-up point with Charlie and Mike, a hidden sanctuary they discovered that morning in Lake View Park.

They broke through the mammoth shrubs concealing their campsite and found Charlie and Mike sitting on blankets, giggling, looking up at them with big shit-eating grins. Kayla feigned a disapproving mother, crossing her arms and dropping her chin, "What have you two young men been up to here?"

Mike laughed and said, "We decided to take a day off from the revolution.

Mike and Charlie snickered at each other, then Charlie said, "Yeah, we decided to wait until tomorrow to storm the bastille. We wanted to savor today instead. We had a laid-back afternoon taking in the Windy City."

Tim shook his head and said, "It looks like you've been taking in some herb as well."

Josh groaned and picked up a McDonald's cheeseburger wrapper, "Oh no, you mean to tell me you guys got stoned, got the munchies, then got burgers with the rest of our cash?"

Mike leaned back and roared, "Forgive us father, for we know not what we do."

Tim spotted a half-eaten package of Oreos. "We're screwed! We won't be able to eat for the next two days!"

Charlie smiled and said reassuringly, "Oh ye of so little faith. Do you really think we'd leave you guys to starve? Aren't you familiar with the story of the loaves and fishes? From a little, we can feed many." He reached to his left, pulled his jacket off the blanket and revealed underneath a large cardboard bucket of Kentucky Fried Chicken and a carton of mashed potatoes. Next to it was a loaf of dark brown, homemade bread wrapped in cellophane, four apples and three oranges.

They were amazed and bewildered. Kayla asked, "How in the world could you afford all of this food?"

Mike raised his hands to the heavens, "The spirits of peace and love are alive and well in Grant Park. We just roamed the crowd asking folks if they had any spare change or spare food. One girl had a backpack with a half dozen loaves of homemade banana bread, so she gave us one. Other people gave us these apples and oranges, but most folks just gave us some change. It added up to enough for us to make a run to KFC.

That's not all." Mike reached to his right and pulled his jacket up to reveal a six pack of Pabst Blue Ribbon.

Josh was mystified, "Wait a minute, you might have been given some coin, but how were you able to buy the beer? Even with a fake ID, nobody would ever believe you guys are twenty-one."

Charlie answered, "You're right about that, but we didn't buy it. We hit up a group of guys sitting around a couple of coolers. Rather than give us cash, they pulled a six-pack from the cooler and handed it to us. It was unbelievable!"

They plopped themselves down on the blankets with Charlie and Mike. Mike passed the beers around and Charlie placed the bucket of chicken in the middle. They moaned and groaned with delight as they feasted. They polished off every morsel of chicken and mashed potatoes, followed by the fruit and banana bread. When they were sated, they became overwhelmed with fatigue and laid back on their blankets. Charlie gazed into the night sky over lake Michigan and softly said to Tim, "I called my folks this afternoon and told them we were OK. I asked them to call your parents to tell them you were safe. I thought they must be out of their minds worrying about you."

Tim's mind was jolted awake, *"My parents! Oh my God! It'd been two days since we left home. The scenes of Chicago on TV would have frightened them to death."* He was ashamed that he hadn't thought to call them, but even if he had remembered, he might not have had the courage to call. "Jesus Charlie, thanks for doing that. You're a better man than I."

Charlie chuckled and said, "Yeah, I know, but you can always aspire to be as good as me."

They dozed off listening to the distant roar of battles on the inland side of Grant Park, sirens echoing off the towering hotels and thunderous explosions of teargas and fireworks.

236

Chapter 20
Tuesday, August 27th

    The commotion on Michigan Avenue subsided in the wee hours of the morning, but everyone continued to sleep fitfully. Their second night sleeping on the ground was taking a toll on their bodies, tossing and turning, waking and wandering. They woke groggy, sore, and vaguely anxious. They felt like untested reserves waiting their turn to occupy the trenches on the WWI western front.

    The first few hours were subdued. They kept any misgivings to themselves. Mike and Joe tossed a frisbee. Kayla and Josh took a stroll down the lakefront towards the Museum of Natural History. Charlie read a Kurt Vonnegut novel. Tim took a walk around the Navy Pier. When he returned, Mike was sitting on his blanket, fidgeting, "Man, I can't just wait around here, I'm going to get higher and find out what's happening."

    That made Joe exasperated, "Jesus, Mike, again? Can't you give it a break? It's going to be a long, intense day and we're all going to need to keep our wits about us."

    Mike smiled and pointed up at the Sycamore tree behind him. "No, I mean higher up, as in seeing what's going on over in Grant Park." Mike sprung to his feet and walked to the base of the tree. "I'm going to need a boost." Charlie put down his novel and followed Mike to the tree. He clamped his hands together in front of him. Mike stepped into Charlie's cupped hands for a boost and vaulted up to the first big horizontal branch above him. From there, he moved like a monkey through a web of branches to a spot a good thirty feet up, with an open view looking southwest.

    Joe yelled up, "So, what do you see?"

    Mike replied, "Chicago."

Joe was not amused, "Don't be a wise ass. Beyond just Chicago, what do you see?"

Mike yelled back, "Iowa, Colorado, and I think the top of the Golden Gate Bridge."

Joe waved him off, "Fuck you, I'm going over there to find out for myself." He trudged off across Lake Shore Drive and into Grant Park. He returned an hour later, a few minutes after Josh and Kayla got back from their trek.

Joe reported, "The shit's going to hit the fan tonight. They're going to start by organizing a human blockade in front of Democratic Party headquarters at the Conrad Hilton, then march to the convention center. They're expecting Mayor Daley to call out the National Guard to stop them. It's going to make the past two nights look like dress rehearsals."

Josh and Kayla looked somberly at each other, then Josh looked at each of the others and said, "Kayla and I have been talking about where we go from here. You know, these cops aren't our enemies, neither are the National Guard. They're just having their strings pulled by the powers that be. We came here to stop a war, not to start a war. What we're doing here needs to be about changing hearts and minds."

Joe nodded and took a moment before replying. "You're right, it is about hearts and minds, but not the hearts and minds of those cops or soldiers. At this point, it's not even about the delegates in the convention hall. The fix is in. Humphry's going to get the nomination and he'll likely stay the course on the war. What we need to do tonight is change the hearts and minds of the American people. Let them know that young people aren't going to sit still for this shit anymore, that the war is wrong and it can't go on. Listen, I heard David Dellinger and Tom Hayden at the rally in the park this morning. Dellinger is committed to non-violence tonight. Haden is willing to go along, but he's not sure it'll work. Both of those guys are experienced civil rights protesters. They know how to lead peaceful resistance. We shouldn't bailout now. Let's give it a shot"

Tim wasn't so sure, "I'd prefer not to get shot myself."

Mike asked, "What did Abbie Hoffman have to say, or Jerry Rubin or Rennie Davis?"

Joe shrugged, "The Yippies were off doing their own thing, whatever things Yippies do. Maybe they were debating what their pig nominee's platform should be."

Tim welcomed Joe's dismissal of the Yippie sideshow. "Their centerpiece policy will be to ban bacon."

Charlie was still all in, "I didn't come to Chicago for kicks. It's time we get down to business. I never had a chance to march with Doctor King, but I'm ready to lay my body down for this."

Kayla nodded, "I understand what you're saying Joe, but I think the best thing for me to do is stop pretending to be a journalist and start actually being one. My Nikon's not a prop. I'm going to use it to record what goes down tonight."

Josh pondered for a moment, then he said, "I hope you're right about Dellinger and Hayden knowing what they're doing. I can get on board with passive resistance, but if things turn violent, I'm out."

The conversation elevated Tim's anxiety into the stratosphere, "If things get violent, I'm going to wet my pants, and I didn't bring any spare underwear."

They fortified themselves with the final fragments of peanut butter spread thinly over the last crusts of bread. They evenly divided the one remaining orange among the six of them. Bolstered by protein, carbs, and vitamin C, they set out brimming with the hubris of youth to impress upon the American people the righteousness of their cause.

The view approaching South Michigan Avenue from the lakefront was majestic. The towering buildings surrounding Grant Park on three sides were a magnificent backdrop for the stage on which the drama they were entering would unfold. The players had amassed throughout the day. There were thousands of them, perhaps tens of thousands, it was hard to tell from a single vantage point, that were spread across a vast open air stage. There were no spectators in this spectacle. Anyone there would play an active role. The audience would be tucked safely in their homes, riveted to their television sets, across the country and around the world. When the sun set, it was like the lights going down and the curtains going up in a theater of global proportions.

Tim and his mates hadn't engaged with the protesters for two days, since the Festival of Life in Lincoln Park on Sunday evening, the police blitzkrieg that night, and their mad dash across Lake Shore Drive. By Tuesday, the festival atmosphere had been beaten and frightened out of the crowd. Any casual, recreational participants were long gone. Everyone remaining knew Tuesday night wouldn't be a walk in the park. It would more likely be a thrashing in the park, and in the streets. Tim could see it on the protesters' faces, nervousness, anger, resolve. The cops had similar expressions, with an added dose of contempt and scorn. The protesters were mostly young, but there were older resisters as well. There were lots of hippie types, but many people looked like regular folks, strait-laced, serious, and sincere. A middle-aged man in a sweatsuit was standing behind the crowd, facing the cops lined up in front of the Conrad Hilton Hotel. The man reminded Tim of an adult he had asked for guidance prior to a different confrontation, in a different place, in what seemed like a different life. Tim stood next to him and asked, "What's going on coach? What's the plan?"

The man glanced at Tim, then he looked straight ahead at the Hilton Hotel. His reply spooked Tim. "Just try not to get hurt, kid."

Kayla wanted to circulate freely, to capture whatever went down with her Nikon SLR camera. The boys stuck together, positioning themselves towards the back of the tightly packed masses across the street from the Hilton. Assuming they might get separated during the melee, they agreed to meet back at Lake View Park. They would go looking for anyone who didn't return by dawn, including at the jails and hospitals.

Protesters continued to assemble behind them. Everyone knew the hotel would be the epicenter of any showdown. As the night progressed, the crowd became more anxious, restless, ready to get on with it. Every few minutes, chants would erupt of, "Stop the war!" "Shut it down!" "What do we want? Peace! When do we want it? Now!"

The cops in front of the hotel's main entrance stood stoic in their blue helmets, face shields, and billy clubs held with both hands horizontally against their chests. Tim assumed the cops were scared too, facing such an immense and hostile horde. As police reinforcements streamed in from the sides, the crowd's mood became uglier. Jeers and taunts rose up, "Go home pigs!" "Oink, oink!" The cops continued to stand silent, but you could see the fury in their eyes, their faces reddening, their sneers quivering. Off to the south, just past the park, Tim could see National Guard troop trucks lining up, with soldiers pouring out the back.

240

The demonstrators' aim was to halt any convention delegates from entering or exiting the hotel. The demonstrators didn't have to directly obstruct the entrance. The cops were doing a fine job of that. Their sheer numbers clogged the street and all the side approaches. For the longest time, there didn't seem to be anyone organizing the protesters, giving them directions, taking charge. But after the troops arrived and the cops had sufficient numbers to make a move, a platoon of young men and women wearing bandanas over their faces, and armbands emblazoned with peace symbols began circulating among the crowd, softly but sternly giving orders: "Move into the street and sit down tightly packed together. Link your arms and keep chanting. No matter what happens, resist, but don't fight back. Just don't make it easy for them to move you."

The protesters welcomed the leadership, and everyone complied. Josh, Joe, Charlie, Mike, and Tim linked arms while they were still standing, and slowly shuffled forward with the crowd. From front to back, the throng sat down on the street in a descending wave. The four boys sat and chanted, breaking their arms apart long enough to raise their hands in the air with two fingers making the peace sign. Their adrenalin was pumping. Their hearts were pounding. Their legs nervously tapped on the pavement. They drew courage from each other. The mob's mood was not crazed, it was resolute.

The sit-in chanting had been going on for about a half hour, when a police captain stepped forward with a bullhorn and shouted out, "This demonstration has been declared an unlawful assembly! You are all ordered to disperse and leave the area in the next fifteen minutes! Anyone remaining will be arrested. There will be no additional warnings."

The crowd responded by defiantly chanting, "Power to the people! We will not be moved! Power to the people! We will not be moved!" As the boys chanted, a man sitting about thirty feet to Tim's right stood-up. He was wearing a black suit, the kind priests wear. He stepped over and around the sitting demonstrators, approaching the police captain. They calmly spoke for a couple of minutes, then the man became agitated, waving his arms out to his sides. The captain reacted angrily, shouting something that was incoherent to Tim. The captain started jabbing his finger into the man's chest. Then the captain pointed towards Grant Park, directing the man to leave. The man in black swung around in exasperation, facing Tim with his head down. His right hand covered his forehead and eyes, as if he was overcome with worry. When he raised his head and lowered his hand, Tim was dumbstruck and momentarily disoriented. Tim strained to think, *"I know that man, or someone like him, someone from a different world, and a different time."* For a nanosecond, Tim questioned where he was, when it was. Then his mind accepted who he was looking at. *"It's Father Otto! Our Father Otto. Father Otto from Regis! Father Otto from El Paso and Tucson!"* The same realization hit the other Royals at the same instant. Charlie, Joe and Mike, leaped to their feet and yelled, "Hey Father, Father Otto, over here!"

Father Otto looked at them. It took him a moment to recognize his former charges. He first beamed a big smile, followed by a look of profound dismay. He waded into the crowd towards them. When he was only a few feet away, he stumbled and half fell into Joe's arms. Joe helped him stand erect. Father continued to hold Joe's shoulder with one hand as he reached out to grab Tim's arm with his other hand. He pulled all four of his Royal boys closer to him. Josh continued sitting, looking up at them bewildered. Father leaned in and spoke urgently, "Good Lord boys, what on Earth are you doing here? You shouldn't be here."

Mike replied, "Excuse me Father, but I think we could say the same thing about you."

Father Otto shook his head adamantly. "You boys don't understand. The captain was clear as could be. They're going to sweep everyone out, using whatever force is necessary. It's not safe here. You could get seriously hurt, arrested or both. You're not old enough for this."

Joe responded, "With all due respect Father, in less than a year we'll be old enough to get drafted, to fight, to kill or be killed. I think we're old enough to say something about that."

Josh stood up and took Father Otto's hand. "It's a pleasure to meet you Father. I'll tell you what. How about we all sit down, stick together, and try to look out for one another."

Father had no response. They sat back down and looked straight ahead at the police line in front of the hotel. The cops were putting on gas masks and some were impatiently tapping their clubs in the palms of their hands. Tim heard orders being barked out from the south. He turned to his left and saw a swarm of National Guardsmen organizing a block away. As they lined up four rows deep from curb to curb, they began to fix bayonets on the ends of their rifle barrels. Again, Tim struggled to comprehend what he was seeing. *"Bayonets on their rifles! Bayonets on South Michigan Avenue, in Chicago, in the United States of America!* *"What the fuck?"*

The terror Tim had been pushing to the back of his mind, now overwhelmed him. He started to tremble. He squeezed Joe's arm on his left and Father Otto's arm on his right. Father leaned forward and spoke to the five of them calmly, but firmly, "Now listen to me very carefully boys. I've been through this before, in South Carolina and Georgia. We're going to be arrested. You don't need to cooperate, but don't fight back either. Don't even think of trying to forcefully resist. Just go limp, don't stand and don't let go of one another. They're going to have to work to arrest us. We won't make it easy for them, but there doesn't need to be any violence. Do you all understand? Peace begins with us."

Charlie choked back tears. He started swaying side-to-side and softly singing the civil rights anthem,

> *"We shall overcome. We shall overcome.*
> *We shall overcome, some day.*
> *Deep in my heart, I do believe,*
> *that we shall overcome some day."*

The people around them took up the refrain. Soon, everyone sitting in the street was loudly singing along. The chorus had a soothing impact on all of them. Even the cops seemed a little less annoyed.

That harmonious moment didn't last long. From somewhere behind them in the park, a hail of bottles, cans and fireworks sailed over their heads and crashed into the row of cops standing in front of them. Suddenly, dozens of young men and women emerged from the darkness in the park. They were wearing football helmets, motorcycle helmets, bandanas, and goggles, but no armbands with peace signs. Some were holding baseball bats. They had come to do battle. They congregated at the edge of the demonstrators who were sitting in the street. They screamed taunts and shook their fists at the cops. Another contingent of combatants off to the side, well over a hundred of them, moved in to confront the soldiers.

Tim looked over at Father Otto, then he bowed his head and said to himself, *"Holy shit."*

Time was up. Not the captain's fifteen-minute warning. The cops' time for restraint. They no longer waited for an order. They moved into the street, grabbing people who were sitting down by their hair, arms, and legs, while at the same time wildly swinging their billy clubs. Most of the demonstrators tried to stick with the passive-resistance instructions, but there was something about being beaten with a club that provoked some people to fight back. It also provoked the more militant protesters in the back to charge in and try to rescue those being arrested. Cognizant of the television crews on the scene, the protesters began a new chant, "The whole world is watching! The whole world is watching!"

Father Otto and the boys continued to sit anchored to the pavement, watching those in front of them being dragged off towards paddy wagons. A group of protesters became sandwiched between the police and the hotel. The cops used their batons to shove the protesters against a large plate glass window. The pressure and banging bodies finally broke the glass. The protesters fell through the window onto the hotel lobby floor. The cops jumped through the window and clubbed the protesters while they were lying on the floor.

Guardsmen started shooting tear gas canisters into the park and towards the people sitting in the street. Father Otto reached into the side pockets of his suit coat and pulled out three bandanas. Then he pulled another two bandanas from his pants pockets. "Quickly, fold these into triangles, tie them behind your neck, cover your mouths and noses. When the gas hits, pull them up and hold them over your eyes."

Mike held the bandana in his hand and said, "Wait Father, what are you going to use?"

"Please Mike, just do what I say. I know how to handle this. Besides, priests are really good at doing penance."

A few moments later, a cloud of gas rolled over them. Right before Tim pulled the bandana over his eyes, he saw Father Otto put his head down and place both hands tightly over his face. Their defensive measures were only minimally effective. Their mouths, throats, lungs, and eyes started to burn. They coughed uncontrollably. Their chests tightened and it became difficult to breathe. Josh was sitting next to

Tim. He let out an anguished yell. Tim could feel Josh standing up. Tim peeked above his mask and saw Josh hopping up and down. Then a projectile of some kind, maybe a bottle, or a rock, or a brick, Tim couldn't tell for sure, whizzed by above him, hitting Josh in the side of his head, just above his right ear. Josh stumbled several steps into the grasp of a cop, who was wearing a gas mask. The cop grabbed Josh by his hair, and with his other hand, thrust the top of his Billy club into Josh's stomach. Josh crumbled to his knees.

Mike reached his breaking point and his instincts kicked in. He leaped to his feet. Although he was partially blinded by the gas, he threw himself towards the cop who was holding Josh. Mike wrapped his arms around the cop's neck. The cop let go of Josh in an effort to pull Mike's arms away. Tears were blurring Tim's vision, but he could see four figures that looked like cops moving towards Josh and Mike. Tim stood up at the same time as Joe and Charlie. Tim pulled Josh up to his feet. Joe pulled the club away from the cop battling Mike. Charlie pulled the gas mask off the cop, causing him to start coughing and choking. Tim felt a hand pulling on his shoulder and he saw another hand on Josh. Father Otto yanked them both back screaming, "Get the hell out of here- now!" He let go of them. Then he grabbed Mike, Joe, and Charlie, throwing them back while yelling, "Run like hell and keep running!"

The five boys stumbled along with a crush of protesters fleeing the mayhem, seeking refuge in the park. They managed to stay together while running several hundred yards. Looking back through the eerie white fog of gas towards Michigan Avenue, Tim saw the silhouettes of hundreds more protesters still battling, their numbers overwhelming the cops. Then, emerging through the fog, he could make out the National Guardsmen, in gas masks, bayoneted rifles in hand, double-timing it down the street, past where he had been sitting a few moments earlier. Everyone in the soldiers' path raced away as fast as they could. It was like a plow pushing earth aside while tilling a field. Protesters might be willing to resist a cop with a club, but nobody was prepared to take on soldiers with carbines and bayonets. Tim didn't want to think about Father Otto and whether he would survive the carnage.

It's unsettling to see how much a head wound can bleed. It wasn't until they reached the flatbed truck where protest organizers were making announcements, that Tim noticed blood streaming from the gash, down the side of Josh's head and face, over his shoulder and down the front of his shirt. Josh looked pale and faint. Looking at Josh made Tim feel woozy. He sat himself and Josh down on the grass. The bandana around Josh's neck was soaked in blood, so Tim rolled his bandana up and tied it around Josh's head to stop the bleeding. There were several self-styled volunteer medics around them, wearing armbands with red crosses, tending to the wounded. One of them, a young woman, dropped to one knee next to Josh. She pulled off the bandana on Josh's head. She cleaned the wound with alcohol, applied a 4 by 4 bandage and wrapped it with a roll of gauze around his head. She turned to Tim and advised, "He probably has a concussion. You need to keep a close eye on him. Try to keep him awake. If he becomes delirious or starts to vomit, get him to a hospital."

They continued to catch their breaths as many more demonstrators settled around them. Charlie was still panting when he said, "I can't believe we just left Father Otto back there. We all saw those cops descending on him. He might be dead by now!"

Joe was also upset, "I know, I feel terrible about that, too. But he ordered us to run, and Josh needed our help. How you doing, man?"

Josh moaned, then answered, "It feels like the worst hangover of my life, with none of the fun to show for it. Who attacked me anyway? Was it a cop or a yippie?"

They looked at each other, then said in unison, "Both!"

Charlie added, "You took a hefty dose of National Guard tear gas as well. You must be a notorious hombre Josh, to have all of them after you. Are the CIA and KGB out to get you, too?"

Josh was groggy and looked like he might pass out again. He weakly asked, "Has anyone seen Kayla? I'm really worried about her."

Joe slapped his hands against the sides of his head and looked up, "On my God, Kayla! You're right, we need to go look for her! I hate to even think about her being alone out there."

Charlie was more tempered, "OK, let's think about this, guys. What are the odds of us finding Kayla in the dark, with all this gas, with all these cops and all these soldiers out there? She could be anywhere. I think we should stick to the plan, see if she's makes it back to Lake View Park. If not, it's going to get light in just a few hours. If she's not back by dawn, then we go looking."

246

Protest organizers climbed onto the flatbed truck until every square inch of the platform was jammed. They were frenzied, talking to each other frantically. A few of them had to jump back off to make room when Tom Hayden arrived. In sharp contrast to the agitated group around him, Hayden's demeanor was remarkably controlled and his voice was strangely low key. However, his message was anything but reserved. He grasped the loudspeaker mic with both hands and held it close to his mouth. His words crackled and echoed across the park, "Tomorrow is the day that this operation has been pointing towards for some time. We are going to gather here. We're going to make our way to the Amphitheater, by any means necessary."

The boys were crestfallen not to find Kayla at their hidden rendezvous spot in Lake View Park. They sighed, groaned, fretted, and paced around. Then they pulled their packs from a hiding place underneath the bushes, spread their blankets on the dewy grass and collapsed. Joe and Mike passed out instantly. Charlie and Tim struggled to stay awake, so they could keep an eye on Josh. Despite being knocked senseless and looking like roadkill, Josh had pulled it together and he was now more alert than they were. "I'm sorry I got you guys into this. It was so naïve for me to think we could come here and do anything that would stop the war, that any of this would make a difference. Now look at us, and Kayla's still out there somewhere, injured or in jail, and for what?"

Charlie wasn't having it. "You're a sharp guy Josh, I mean, MIT and all.

"I didn't get accepted, Charlie."

"Regardless, you're a high caliber fella. But I think you got your bell rung back there and it's still drowning out your good sense. First thing, you're not responsible for us being here. Tom Hayden invited us to this party. Second, who knows whether or not any of this is making a difference, or what kind of difference? It's too soon to tell. Doctor King marched, was beaten, was arrested, for years before the Civil Rights Act and the Voting Rights Act were passed.

Josh held his hand up, "OK, I get your point, but ..."

"And third, what if it doesn't make any difference? Does that mean we shouldn't do anything? Does that mean it's not worth trying to stop something that's wrong, just because it might not work? I don't think so. I don't think you think so either." Charlie lay back down on his blanket and closed his eyes. Tim made the same mistake. Despite the medic's directive to stay awake and observe Josh, they were out cold within seconds.

"Good morning boys! I hope you're all having sweet dreams!" Kayla's booming voice startled the boys awake. They were elated to see her. They leapt to their feet and they each threw their arms around her. Josh reacted more slowly. He rolled over and rose on one elbow. That's when Kayla saw the bandage wrapped around his head. "Holy shit! Josh, what happened to you? Did the police do that to you? Those sons-of-bitches!" She dropped to her knees next to Josh and hugged him so hard he was knocked off his elbows and hit the back of his head on the ground.

Mike clarified, "Actually, it wasn't a cop that cracked his head open. Josh was caught between a Yippie's rock and a hard place. Although a cop did bruise his solar plexus with the business end of his night stick."

Kayla held Josh's head with both her hands on his cheeks "You poor thing! Next time I'll know better than to leave you guys alone in a riot."

Joe responded with mild irritation, "We weren't the ones who were alone in a riot- you were. What the hell happened to you? Why didn't you come back here last night? We were thinking the worst."

"Oh yeah, well I'm glad to see none of you lost any sleep because of me."

They sat down around Josh to hear Kayla recount her night. "Man, it was really intense, but I have to be honest, from a photojournalist perspective, it was incredible. I mean it was horrible, but the images were incredible. I shot all six rolls of film. I've got nothing left. There were pitched battles everywhere and I was right in the middle of it, all the rage, the pain, the gas, the blood. I captured masses of protesters surging into police lines; hordes of wild-eyed cops unleashing violence on any civilians in sight; soldiers in gas masks advancing with fixed bayonets into unarmed demonstrators. I've got to get this film processed ASAP. There could be a Pulitzer Prize shot in there.

Josh rubbed the side of his head and said, "I'm going to try to not be offended, Kayla, but some of that blood you were so thrilled to photograph might have been mine."

"Josh, I'm so sorry. I don't want to sound insensitive. It's just that I had to keep my cool, try to stay professional, in order to do my job. The emotions are just hitting me now. I mean I had to fight, too. The cops tried to take my Nikon a half dozen times. I had to knee one of them in the balls to get away."

Tim was more concerned about what was coming next. "Ok, Kayla, we know what you saw. We saw the same shit. What did you hear? You were out there all night. What's going to go down today?"

Kayla took a deep breath, "However bad things have been the last three days, the final act is today, and it's likely going to be a lot worse. The nomination vote is tonight. Everyone agrees the demonstrations need to move from the Hilton to the Amphitheater. There's a big dispute about how to get there. David Dellinger is organizing a non-violent march from Grant Park to the convention center. If he can keep people under control, he's convinced he can persuade the police to let them through. Hayden is convinced any march is doomed. He doesn't think the cops will ever allow it and the marchers will be sitting ducks to be assaulted and arrested. Hayden is organizing a guerilla action. He wants small bands of protesters to flood the side streets and converge at the convention center. The thing is, there are more cops and soldiers pouring into the city. I doubt if anything is going to work."

They sat silently for a minute, then Mike piped up, "Well, what's it going to be, Dellinger or Hayden? I say we go with our man, Tommy. We don't want to be sitting ducks and I think the six of us can serpentine our way to the convention center."

Joe had other ideas. "I'm not so sure. OK, say we make it to the Amphitheater, we've seen what's waiting for us there. The fencing, the razor wire, the barricades will prevent us from getting within two blocks of the convention. Also, the cops or Guardsmen will pick us off immediately if we arrive in small groups. There's strength in numbers. I think we should join Dellinger's march. Even if we don't make it to the convention hall, the march itself will make a statement."

Tim wasn't exactly sure what he was going to say, but he wanted to be on his feet when he said it. He took his time getting up. He put his folded hands up to his mouth as if he was praying and took a deep breath. "Joe, I've admired your opinions since the third grade and I've almost always trusted your judgment. Mike, I admire your courage and your heart. But man, both of you are thinking with your heads up your asses. We all saw how ugly things got last night. Just look at what happened to Josh. You can call me a coward or a quitter, but I'm going home today. I think we all should go home. Maybe what happens here today will help stop the war and maybe it won't. It doesn't matter to me. All I know is that I want to see my family and they need to see me. Your families need to see you, too. Classes begin on Monday. I want to be there. You need to be there, too. We don't need to be in a hospital or the Cook County jail."

Josh turned to Kayla. "I'm going home today, too, Kayla, and I want you to come with me."

Her reply was anguished, "Oh come on man, this is going to be the grand finale. I need to be here. I need to capture this. Besides, our return plane tickets are for tomorrow."

Josh shook his head. "And what are you going to capture the grand finale with Kayla? You've used all your film and I know you don't have any more money. That crowd out there has been here for three days and they won't have much to panhandle for. Yesterday, I said I would stay if the organizers could keep control of things. I don't blame them for the violence, but clearly nobody has control anymore. I'm still not feeling well, Kayla. I'd really appreciate it if you would come home with me. The plane tickets won't be a problem. TWA doesn't charge for changing flights."

It was Charlie's turn to say his piece. "You guys know me. You know there's nobody more committed to stopping the war than I am. We need to take the long view, though. Nothing that happens here is going to stop the war today, or next week or probably not next year. We're going to need to stay strong to continue our resistance. I agree with Tim. We should go home, go back to school, take care of our own business and live to fight another day."

Mike grunted, "Shit, you guys have taken the wind out my sails. I can't fight the revolution without my comrades."

Tim looked over at Joe. "So, what's it going to be Joe, *The Charge of the Light Brigade* or *On the Road?*"

Joe nodded, looked down, then looked up at Tim. He scrunched his face and said, "Damn it, Tim, since when did you start making so much sense? I suppose I'm going to have to let you deprive me of my moment of glory. Let's get the hell out of Dodge."

They lingered there for quite a while longer, letting the summer sun dry the dew off their blankets, strolling along the lakefront, postponing the end of this chapter in their young lives. They walked through Grant Park to drop off Josh and Kayla at the Van Buren Street El station. They said their goodbyes at the turnstiles. It was more emotional than any of them expected. They cried and swore to stay in touch. Joe and Kayla clung to each other a bit longer than their other hugs. Tim suspected something more was going on there. Then Josh and Kayla boarded the train for O'Hare airport.

As the boys emerged from the El station and headed towards Union Station, they saw demonstrators getting organized in the park. Hundreds of National Guardsmen surrounded the perimeter of the park. Tim caught a glimpse of David Dellinger, a balding middle-aged man in a suit and tie, looking like he was carrying the weight of the world on his shoulders. Everyone looked exhausted and grim. For most of them, it would be their fourth day out there. They knew what they were in for, that they would have to sacrifice their bodies again. Tim felt nothing but love for them all.

Chapter 21
Give Peace A Chance

Tim called his mom from a phone booth in Union Station. She cried, told him to come home immediately and to be prepared for a long talk with her and his father. He told her he was genuinely sorry about causing them so much worry. He didn't tell her that he wasn't remorseful about going to Chicago. The train pulled into town at 6:30 PM. Tim's family convened in the den at 7:00 PM. Their talk went through four phases: What in the world was Tim thinking? Which was closely paired with, how could he put them through such an ordeal? What happened in Chicago? Concluding with, what would be required for Tim to redeem himself, regain their trust and salvage his future? As he fully expected, his wings would be clipped for the foreseeable future. His world would be confined to school, work, and home. He was fine with that. He actually welcomed it. He felt like a turtle that needed to pull back into his shell for a while. The hardest part would be the limitations on his time with Sandy outside of work.

Tim wasn't scheduled to work on Wednesday, but he called FoodValu first thing in the morning and was told they could use more help the next day. He relished the opportunity to work. Once again, the FoodValu was his refuge, his shelter from the storm. A truck had been unloaded that morning, so he spent most of his shift stocking shelves. Sandy had been tied down at the checkout counter. They arranged to take their breaks together. She followed Tim into the break room, and when he saw there was no one else there, he turned, threw his arms around her, and started to give her a kiss. She shoved him back and slugged him a couple times on the shoulder. Then they resumed their passionate reunion. When they broke their embrace, she pushed him away again and said, "You're such an idiot, Tim. I've been glued to the TV every night after work. Every time I saw a protester doing something insane, I thought it might be you. Every time I saw a cop swinging his club at a protester, I thought it might be you. Why didn't you call me? What were you thinking?"

"Did you and my mom practice that line together? You both have it down really well."

Monday morning was the first day of Tim's senior year at Regis. Joe picked him up in the GTO. Tim was anxious to find out Joe's status. "So how did it go at home?"

"About as bad as I expected. I might be out of the doghouse by the time I graduate. I'm really glad we came back when we did, Tim. I appreciate you being a chicken-shit and a quitter. Every group needs one. What you lack in intelligence, you make up for in cowardice"

"Gee, what a beautiful thing to say, Joe. I'm touched. It really means a lot."

Pulling into the Regis parking lot, Tim felt surprisingly sentimental. The entire academic year was in front of them, but he sensed it would be fleeting. They arrived earlier than usual. They arranged to meet Charlie and Mike in the cafeteria. They were sitting on a dining table when Tim and Joe walked in. They were glad to see each other, but their greetings were muted, a reflection of their need to tone things down and return to some semblance of normalcy. Tim gave them a slight nod and a casual, "Hey guys, how ya doing?"

Charlie shrugged, "I'm doing OK. I'm thinking about joining the priesthood. It looks like I'm going to be grounded until I'm forty, so I'm going to be celibate anyway."

Joe asked, "What about you, Mike? Did your parents come down on you pretty hard?

"No actually, my parents still don't know I was gone. They were at a fishing resort up in Minnesota last week. They didn't get back until yesterday. It's a good thing they weren't home when Charlie's mom tried to call them."

Tim was itching to get to the business at hand. "We need to get moving, guys. The suspense is killing me." They briskly walked down the hall to the other end of the building and up the back stairs. As they approached the second classroom door on the left, they slowed and then came to a stop. They looked anxiously at each other and took a collective deep breath. They opened the door and quickly entered the back of the room. They stopped in their tracks and looked towards the front. Father Otto was sitting at his desk, writing with his head down.

He looked up at, smiled and said, "Good morning gentlemen, I hoped I'd be seeing you this morning."

They whooped and laughed in jubilation, raced to the front of the room, and surrounded his desk. Father stood, shook their hands, and then hugged each one of them. Once again, they were all teary. Charlie exhaled and said, "Thank God you're OK, Father. We felt so guilty about deserting you back there."

Father looked incredulous, "That's ridiculous, boys. You didn't desert me. I told you to run. I would've kicked your behinds if you hadn't skedaddled."

Joe asked, "So, what happened to you, Father? We've been dying to find out."

Father Otto sat back down in his desk chair. "Well, the first thing I did was try to assist the poor police officer the four of you were assaulting. I managed to find his gas mask on the ground and I helped him put it back on. He was very appreciative. When he went back to work, I took off at a pretty quick clip. After I cleared the demonstration, I could see nothing more productive was going to happen that night, so I went back to the St. Peter's rectory where I was staying."

Tim asked, "What about Wednesday, Father? Did you come home then?"

"Oh no, Wednesday was too important. Our peace message needed to endure until the end of the convention. I went back to Grant Park the next morning with two of my priest friends to join David Dellinger's march. We'd been in touch with Mr. Dellinger for months and knew how committed he was to non-violence. Unfortunately, the police chose a different path. They refused to allow the march to proceed. They began arresting us, using their night sticks very liberally. Regrettably, many of the protesters chose to abandon non-violence. It was a repeat of the previous nights' pandemonium, with tear gas, cracked skulls and broken bones."

Mike asked, "But what happened to you, Father? Were you able to get away?"

"I'm afraid not, Mike. We were arrested straight away. They handcuffed us, put us in a paddy wagon and off we went to a holding pen at a nearby precinct station. I was worried they would hold me for some time and I might miss the opening day of classes. I struck up a pleasant conversation with a police sergeant. He was German Catholic, like me, and sympathetic to my need to return to teaching. So, he let me and my two friends go. Human connections and kindness are very powerful forces, boys. The path of peace can be challenging, though. In the heat of bitter conflicts, many people respond with anger, and violence can seem like the appropriate response. However, surrendering to your passions, like anger and hatred, is merely self-indulgent."

"That's amazing Father," Charlie said, "It sure sounds like it was a good thing we weren't there. I doubt we would have been so lucky."

Father agreed, "I was terribly worried about you boys. It was a big relief to learn you made it home alright."

Which raised a question for Tim, "Wait, how did you know we were alright?"

"Priests have deep ties to their communities, Timothy. I returned here on Friday. I knew you were all safely at home by the end of the day. I appreciate that you were concerned about me, too. Now, the first period bell will be ringing soon. You boys better be off."

Mike and Tim headed for the same first period class. They scampered back downstairs. The hallway was now bustling with students scrambling to beat the bell. They walked by the administration office. Wayne Wagner was standing by the door, legs spread wide in his coach's stance, with his arms folded. Tim chose to ignore him, and Wagner didn't acknowledge them. The boys were two steps past him when Mike turned around and said, "Good morning Mr. Wagner. Have a nice day."

Wagner was startled by the greeting. He looked at Mike suspiciously and replied, "Don't be a smart-ass, Russell. The year's just beginning. I doubt it will end well for you."

Mike tried to reassure Wagner of his sincerity. "I wasn't being a smart-ass, Mr. Wagner. I mean it. I hope you have a good day." They turned away from Wagner and kept walking towards their class.

Joe gave Tim a ride home after school. Tim's mom agreed to let him have her car to get to work. On his way to the FoodValu, he swung by Steve's house to return a couple of albums he borrowed a few months earlier, The Doors, *Waiting for the Sun*, and Cream's, *Wheels of Fire*. Pursuant to standard protocol, Tim entered the side door without knocking and proceeded down to Steve's basement. Most of the LIME JUICE were assembled there, absent Joe and Charlie. They were peppering Mike with questions about Chicago. Typically, Mike would have relished an opportunity to regale everyone with his exploits, but Mike was unusually soft-spoken, and he seemed reluctant to share any details.

Warren called him on it, "What's up, Mike? Why don't you want to talk about it? We were all glued to our TVs last week, watching what was going down, wondering what was happening with you guys. It must have been incredibly heavy."

Julie pressed him further, "Yeah Mike, you seem preoccupied. Something's bothering you.

Jim asked, "Did something really bad happen to you in Chicago?"

Mike hesitated, then he explained, "It's not what happened in Chicago. It's what happened at school this morning. I had another run-in with Wagner, right before the first period on my very first day. I mean, I was doing my best to be civil, but he wasn't having it. He's clearly still out to get me. I don't know how I can survive the next week, let alone finish the year and graduate."

Dean sympathized, "That's really fucked-up, Mike. You shouldn't put up with that bullshit. Maybe you should just transfer to West High and save yourself the grief."

"I've thought about that, but this is my senior year. I don't want to start over at West now. Not to mention that there's some guys there that would love to kick the shit out of me."

Al sat back in the sofa, crossed his legs and shrugged, "Maybe you should buy Wagner off? You could offer to pay off his debts."

Julie asked, "What debts? How would you know about Wayne Wagner's debts?"

Al said matter-of-factly, "I might be just a peon at the National Cigar Store, but I know pretty much everything that goes down there. There's a lot of serious bread that goes through that bookie operation in the back. Wagner loves to play the ponies. He likes to make out like he's some kind of high-roller, but he's no better at gambling than he is at coaching. That fool is in hock up to his ears to Danny Connelly, and man, Danny is the last motherfucker on Earth you want to owe money to."

Mike's ears perked up, "You're telling me Lame Wayne owes money to Danny Connelly?"

Al nodded knowingly, "A shitload, I've heard them arguing about it. Danny gets fed up, but then he lets Wagner wager more bets. I think he's setting Wagner up, so he can clean him out. Lame Wayne either doesn't know what's going to hit him or he doesn't know a way out of it."

Mike relaxed. He shook his head and giggled. Then he looked up and said, "Well, I guess I should have a conversation with my dear old uncle Danny about that."

Al's jaw dropped and he leaned forward, "Fuck me, Danny Connelly is your uncle?"

"Absolutely, he's my mom's brother-in-law. He's actually a great guy, pretty hot tempered though. We get along really well. He's always shown an interest in me. It's been too long since we've spoken."

That Friday, at noon, Mike, Joe, and Tim finished their fish sticks for lunch. They slid their trays into the tall metal tray-racks and headed to their next classes. As they exited the cafeteria's double doors and turned into the hallway, Mike ran head-on into Wayne Wagner. They were both knocked back a step and startled. Mike blurted-out, "Oh Jesus, sorry Mr. Wagner."

The boys braced themselves to absorb Wagner's retaliation. Wagner straightened himself. His mouth was squeezed tightly shut. He took a deep breath. A pained slit of a smile emerged, and he replied, "That's quite alright Michael, I mean Mike. No harm, no foul. Are you alright?"

Mike smiled back slightly and said, "Yeah, yeah, I'm just fine. Thanks."

Wagner wanted to engage more, "So tell me Mike, how are your classes going so far?"

"Oh, just fine, thanks." Mike paused for a moment, then he added, "Actually, I'd like to take American Government from you next semester – if that's OK?"

"That would be just fine, Mike. I'd love to have you in my class. I'm sure you would do very well."

Mike's smiled broadened and he just said, "Cool."

The three boys started to walk away from Wagner. Mike turned around and cheerfully called out, "And Wayne, I hope you have a very nice afternoon."

Over the following weeks, Tim settled into his new monk-like lifestyle. Being limited to floating between home, school and work brought him peace of mind. The reduction in distractions left him more time for his school subjects. He read more books and listened to more music. There had been an flurry of album releases destined to become classics, Jimi Hendrix's, *Electric Ladyland*; Joni Mitchel's, *Song to a Seagull*; Neil Young and Creedence Clearwater Revival's self-named albums; Aretha Franklin's *Lady Soul;* The Rolling Stones' *Beggars Banquet*, The Byrds, Van Morrison, Miles Davis, The Mothers of Invention, The Kinks; and of course, the Beatles, who continued to be prolific with hit singles, *Lady Madonna*, *Hey Jude* and *Revolution*, leading up to the release of their double *White Album*. It was difficult for Tim to take his headphones off long enough to come up for air.

Tim also took a hiatus from politics. The timing was fortunate, because in the aftermath of the Democratic National Convention fiasco, Richard Nixon took a huge lead in the race. The country's political wounds continued to deepen. The body count in Vietnam continued to rise. The cultural divides widened. Tim knew he would re-engage at some point, but he needed to do some personal work and take some time to reflect on the infinite mysteries of the universe.

It was Wednesday, October 30th. Tim had gotten up at 4:30 AM to go unload a semi-truck at the FoodValu. They were shorthanded, so it took longer than usual. He called his mom and she agreed to let him take her car directly from work to school. He left Regis at 3:15 PM, went home and had his mom drive him back to work. The store closed at 10:00 PM. Sandy gave him a lift home. He heated some leftover lasagna in the oven, took his plate and a bottle of Pepsi into the den and sat down on the sofa next to his mom. The Tonight Show starring Johnny Carson was just coming on. They enjoyed Johnny's monologue without comment. When the first commercial came on, his mom reached over to the end table next her and grabbed a manilla envelope. She handed it to Tim saying, "This came for you today. It's got a

California return address. Thank goodness it doesn't appear to be one of those radical newspapers you used to get."

Tim looked at the envelope without opening it. "It's from my friend Kayla, a girl I met in Tucson. I'm going to go crash now, mom. It's been a long day- love you."

He plodded up the stairs to his bedroom, closed the door and put his newest album on the stereo, Simon and Garfunkel's *Bookends*, a beautifully poignant record well-suited for his reflective mood. He lay on the bed with his back against the wall and opened Kayla's envelope. There was another sealed envelope inside and a loose white sheet of paper folded in half. He unfolded it and read:

> *Dear Tim,*
>
> *I hope you are doing well. Joe and I have been writing each other. He tells me you boys have had to cool your jets since Chicago. That's probably a good thing. You should savor your Senior year, or at least survive it.*
>
> *Josh is back in school. He finally got admitted to UCLA, just in time to get a student draft deferment. It was a huge relief! Rebecca and I really miss him though.*
>
> *I decided to postpone college because I got an incredibly lucky break. I've landed a job as a photographer at Rolling Stone magazine. I'm anxious to do well. It blows my mind how much I'm learning! Most of my assignments have been in the Bay Area, but I'm going to get lots of opportunities to travel soon. Maybe I can come to Iowa sometime and cover the next new wave of hot Iowa Rock and Roll bands, the Hawkeye invasion.*
>
> *I thought you might like these photographs from Chicago. There's no photo that can really capture what went down there.*
> *Peace,*
> *Kayla*

Tim pealed open the fold on top of the second envelope. There were four 11 x 7 glossy color prints inside. The top one showed Tim sitting with his legs folded on the grass in Lincoln Park. There was a circle of hippies dancing behind him. Tim's face was raised upwards into the sun, as he blew bubbles into the air. The sunlight was hitting the bubbles like a prism, reflecting spots of light onto his face. The next photo was taken inside the International Amphitheater. The shot was taken looking through the crowd at Tim, in his dress shirt and tie, pen and paper in hand, engaged in a lively discussion with the stars and stripes delegate from Indiana. The third photo was Tim standing in Lake View Park. He was facing Lake Michigan, his back to the camera, his arms outstretched, with his head tilted towards the sunlight and the brilliant blue sky.

The fourth shot made Tim gasp. It was taken from a distance. Kayla must have used a telephoto lens. There they were on the left, Josh, Tim, Charlie, Mike, Joe, and Father Otto, sitting in a row on the street, their heads down, eyes closed, bandanas over their faces, Father's hand over his mouth and nose. All of them had one arm raised, with their hands making the two-fingered V for peace sign. In the background, an ominous cloud of white gas was rolling towards them. On the right, a line of policemen stood facing them, blue helmets, gasmasks, and billy clubs held with both hands high across their chests. Tim flipped the print over and found Kayla had written, *"I think this is the shot that got me my job."*

Tim scooted off the bed and walked to his desk. He rolled up small pieces of Scotch tape, placed them on the back corners of the four prints and randomly stuck them on the wall, on top of the other photos. Returning to bed, he sat up with his legs straight out and his feet crossed. The Simon and Garfunkel song, "America", was playing:

> *"Kathy, I'm lost", I said, though I knew she was sleeping*
> *I'm empty and aching and I don't know why*
> *Counting the cars on the New Jersey Turnpike*
> *They've all come to look for America*
> *All come to look for America*
> *All come to look for America"*

It was right there in front of him, America, the world. His collage now extended across three walls. There were wars, assassinations, celebrations, musicians, painters, politicians, protesters, movie stars, athletes, rebels, warriors, adventurers, the devout, the profane, suffering, joy, loathing, and love. But his relationship with those walls felt different now. He no longer contemplated them with detached curiosity. He felt a new familiarity with them. Scattered among the photographs of that world were images of his world; an advertisement for The Sharks performing at the YMCA; a photo of Donny Stevens in his Marine uniform; Eddie Frazer's obituary; *The Lime Juice Chronicle* front pages and masthead; the Sweeny lumber yard in flames.

Overlaying all of it were the four images of a young fella he was still getting to know. Tim McIntyre, injecting some joy into the atmosphere. Tim McIntyre, embracing life, soaking it in. Tim McIntyre, engaging the debate. Tim McIntyre, holding the line. These new depictions were a welcomed counterbalance to the images that had been taped inside his head and stapled on his heart. Tim, the loser. Tim, the fuck-up. Tim, the coward. Tim, dubious and clueless. It was all accurate. One version no more valid than the other. They all composed the mosaic of his life to that point.

Seeing himself taped up there amid images of those turbulent times provoked some serious soul searching. He had to confess that his decisions, his actions, had been driven by more than a devotion to just causes. They weren't the result of him being buffeted by momentous events. It was more about him, what he wanted, what he thought he needed. He hadn't been searching for himself. He'd been molding himself into who he wanted to be. He wasn't following a script. He was writing his own story, and he needed to accept responsibility for wherever the plot took him. One thing for sure, there was plenty of room for improvement, starting with being a better son.

It would be 1969 soon. He hoped things would start settling down. They had to. He was running out of space on his wall.

Epilogue

Some of what followed this story you already know. Richard Nixon's early lead in the 1968 presidential race steadily shrank. It was primarily because he was Richard Nixon. Humphrey revised his position on the Vietnam War as the campaign progressed, but it wasn't enough to mend the divides within the Democratic Party. Civil rights issues were even more problematic for the Democrats, as the Republican Party's "Southern Strategy" aimed to appeal to disaffected white Dixiecrats who opposed integration. Nixon won the election by only 0.7 percent. "Tricky Dick" lived-up to his brand. His presidency ended in disgrace. Nixon's Watergate scandal was long regarded as a low point in US politics. However, by current standards, Nixon would look like a noble statesman. Today, some political leaders believe the lesson from Nixon is to avoid disgrace by divesting yourself of shame, and under all circumstances, at all costs, refusing to do the right thing.

1968 ended by being the deadliest year of the Vietnam War, with 16,899 US casualties. The war continued for seven more years. It ended in 1975, as a humiliating defeat for the United States. Over the course of the war, 58,220 Americans died, 851 from Iowa. It was officially defined as a "Conflict," because "War" was never declared by Congress. America experienced a long national hangover after the war. For many, the trauma would last a lifetime. Over 125,000 Vietnamese refugees immigrated to the United States, making valuable contributions to American society and culture. More than 150,000 Americans visit Vietnam annually. The foreign policy lessons from the Vietnam War have been forgotten. Following the attacks on 9/11, the US made many of the same mistakes.

The struggle for civil rights and racial justice in America continues. Racial politics continues to generate many hot-button issues. However, progress should not be ignored. Today, ethnic minorities reside all across Waterloo, including African-Americans, Hispanic-Americans, Asian-Americans, Arab-Americans, Bosnians, Canadians and even Minnesotans. The Mayor of Waterloo is Afican-American.

Older people touting the superiority of the music from their youth rests in the pantheon of old geezer cliches, right next to "Get off of my lawn." That said, there is no doubt that the music industry has undergone dramatic changes. The major record labels have withered away and anyone can produce a decent recording on their laptop. Musicians can barely make a living selling their recordings, but this has revitalized live performances. Regrettably, Auto-Tune has driven some of the humanity out of music. It was often stated and deeply believed that "Rock and Roll will never die." Well, if it hasn't expired, it's certainly on life support. More recent musical genres have brilliant artists, and every period of music includes a bell curve of quality, but there's general agreement that the conditions that existed in the 1960s and 1970s fostered an unparalleled degree of musical creativity and dynamism. Much of the music since has not been as good - and by the way, get off my lawn.

The characters and events in this story are fictional, imaginary, not real, made up. Any resemblances to real people or occurrences are purely coincidental. If you think you know the real people that these characters are based on, you are wrong. Please do not pester these people to confess their association with this story. Some of them might relent and acknowledge that they are, in fact, the characters you suspected them to be. Some might even insist that they are a character in this story. Don't believe them. They might want to expound beyond what has been written here, to share more details, more background information, more context. They might challenge the accuracy of how the story has been told. They might want to give you their version of events. There's nothing that can be done about that. Despite what you might hear from others, this is what happened.

Father Parker suddenly left his position as principal of Regis High School in March of 1969. There was never an official explanation.

263

It's unknown whether he resigned or was removed. Rumors flourished. Dean heard from a reliable source (his older sister who worked in the front office) that Father Parker was admitted to a facility that specialized in treating priests with substance abuse disorders. His successor as principal of Regis High School was Father Otto.

In a gambit to escape crushing financial pressures, Wayne Wagner took out a second mortgage on his home to start a side-business selling waterbeds. The business failed six months later, forcing him to declare personal bankruptcy. Wagner abruptly quit his position at Regis in the middle of the 1970 spring term. His last known address was in Oden, Arkansas.

Jim and Warren continued to pursue musical careers. Together, they formed and dissolved several bands. Warren married and had two children. He ceased performing in 1978, so he could spend more time with his family. He became the program manager at an FM radio station in the Chicago area. Jim stuck with music and eventually settled in Nashville, where he became a successful song writer. He occasionally tours with nationally known performers.

Julie and Mary attended universities on opposite coasts. Julie became a clinical psychologist practicing in Walnut Grove, California. Mary studied interior design and became a buyer for Pottery Barn. After years without any communication, Julie and Mary re-connected at the Regis Class of 1969 twenty-year reunion. They've been together ever since. In 2009, Iowa became the third state in the union to legalize same-sex marriage. Julie and Mary returned to Iowa from California and were married on June 20th, 2010.

Steve Janzen remained close to home and eventually became the owner of a True Value Hardware store. He married, had three children, divorced and remained a devoted father. Steve continues to be the "Glue guy," for all the remaining LIME JUICE in the area. He organizes softball teams and hosts monthly poker games. He astutely follows politics and has been a Democratic Party precinct captain during several Iowa presidential caucuses.

Larry O'Malley attended North Iowa Community College. He left school after one year. His United States Selective Service lottery number was 47. He was destined to be drafted and quite possibly be compelled to serve in Vietnam. Larry dropped out of sight. He supported himself by selling marijuana. In June of 1977, Larry died of a heroin overdose.

Al Gravano was drafted into the Army in August 1969. He served a tour of duty in Vietnam and was honorably discharged in 1971. Al attended the University of Iowa, with support from the G.I. Bill. He received his J.D. law degree in 1978. He has a successful criminal defense practice in Des Moines.

Dean Klein enlisted in the Navy, as an alternative to being drafted into the Army or the Marine Corps. He served the bulk of his service at the US Naval Base, Guantanamo Bay, Cuba. After discharge, he attended Iowa State University and graduated with a degree in Business. Dean is a commercial real estate broker in Austin, Texas. He's been married twice, has five children, three step-children and eleven grandchildren.

Mike Russell attended the University of Iowa for one semester. In the first Selective Service Lottery on December 1, 1969, Mike's number was 286, assuring him that he would not be drafted. After dropping out of the University, he moved to a farm commune near Taos, New Mexico. Two years later, he enrolled at the University of Colorado, Boulder, where he eventually earned a Master of Social Work degree. He has spent his career working with homeless youth in the Denver area. Mike has never married.

Sandy Anderson attended nursing school in Minneapolis. She worked in the cardiac units at a couple of Twin City area hospitals. She married a Family Medicine physician and they had two children. In 1998, Sandy died suddenly from a brain aneurysm at the age of 47.

Charlie Cummings was awarded a full scholarship to attend Oberlin College. He went on to graduate from the Ohio State School of Medicine. He is board certified in Internal Medicine, with a sub-specialty in Infectious Diseases. He practices at the Cleveland Clinic and periodically volunteers for medical missions in developing countries.

Toni Cummings attended Howard University and graduated with a degree in International Studies. She went on to earn an MBA from American University. She works for the World Bank and lives in Geneva, Switzerland. She married a Frenchman. They have four grandchildren.

Josh graduated from UCLA with a degree in Philosophy. He worked for a couple years as a paralegal for Los Angeles County Legal

Aid. Josh moved on from his youthful dalliance with paganism and followed his father's path. He went back to school and obtained a PhD from the Claremont School of Theology. He's a professor at Loyola Marymount University in Los Angeles, where he met and married his wife, a chemistry professor. They have four children.

Kayla had a long career as a professional photographer, working for a variety of publications and then freelancing. She's an avid runner and has completed fourteen marathons. She married an electrical contractor. They had two children. They live in Danville, California.

Joe Snyder earned a Master of Fine Arts degree from Northwestern University. After graduate school, he joined the Peace Corps, teaching for two years at a remote Himalayan school in Nepal. He backpacked the world for the next two years. Returning to the US, he worked as a carpenter and a woodworker. He married a woman from Senegal, and they had one daughter. He lives in Bend, Oregon, where he custom builds acoustic guitars. He is actively involved with environmental organizations.

Tim McIntyre's senior year was relatively mundane, but his life didn't settle down for long. He decided to forego a career with FoodValu, and enrolled at the University of Iowa in the fall of 1969. A few months later, he learned his draft lottery number was 144. It was uncomfortably low, but proved high enough to keep him out of the military. His college years were tumultuous, marked by his participation in increasingly intense anti-war demonstrations. He sampled a variety of courses. He stumbled into an introductory class on computers. He was surprised to find he had an aptitude for coding. Despite many distractions, he managed to graduate in 1974 with a degree in Computer Science.

After graduating, Tim took a year-long road trip around the country. When his student loans started coming due, he landed a job with Honeywell in Minneapolis. Three years later, he was recruited to work for a start-up software company in Bellevue, Washington. He worked in the Seattle area tech industry for the following thirty-five years.

There were several failed relationships along the way. Then Tim met Lisa in 1980, while they were both volunteering for the Ted Kennedy presidential campaign. They married two weeks after Ronald

Reagan defeated Jimmy Carter for the presidency. They had one son, Sean, and two daughters, Rita and Lucy, both named after Beatles songs. Lisa remained active in politics and served in the Washington State legislature for many years.

Along the way, Tim endeavored to be a better person, occasionally failing. He wanted to continue learning, to become wiser, to look at himself and the world honestly and without fear. He grappled with the great questions of why it is, and why me? He had a couple of existential crises. Then, he made peace with the universe, its unfathomable vastness, and the magnificent improbability of human beings.

Tim regularly returned to Iowa, primarily to visit his parents while they were still alive. He also liked to reconnect with the remnants of the LIME JUICE. Regardless of how long it had been since their last encounter, they quickly fell into their old patterns, like flipping shit at one another and calling bullshit on the powers that be. They looked back on their adolescence fondly and relished recounting how foolish they had been. They wished they had known then what they learned later, but then again, that's the point of getting older. They all agreed that youth is often wasted on the young.

Playlist

If stories had soundtracks, this would be that:

Artists	**Albums/Songs**

1965

1.	Herb Albert's Tijuana Brass	"A taste of Honey"
2.	The Beatles	*Help*
3.	The Beatles	*Rubber Soul*
4.	John Coltrane	*A Love Supreme*
5.	The Byrds	*Mr. Tambourine Man*
6.	Bob Dylan	*Highway 61 Revisited*
7.	Bob Dylan	*Bringing It All Back Home*
8.	The Supremes	"Stop in the Name of Love"
9.	Lovin' Spoonful	"Do You Believe in Magic"
10.	The Zombies	"She's Not There"

1966

1.	Simon & Garfunkel	"Sound of Silence"
2.	Simon & Garfunkel	"Scarborough Fair"
3.	Mammas & Papas	"Monday Monday"
4.	Cream	"I'm so Glad"
5.	Lovin' Spoonful	"Daydream"
6.	Beatles	*Revolver*
7.	Bob Dylan	"Rainy Day Woman"
8.	Beach Boys	"Wouldn't It Be Nice"
9.	Donovan	"Season of the Witch"
10.	The Byrds	"Mr. Spaceman"
11.	Stevie Wonder	"Up-Tight"
12.	The Temptations	"Gettin' Ready"
13.	The Rascals	"Good Lovin'"
14.	Paul Butterfield	"East-West"
15.	Sam & Dave	"Hold on I'm Coming"

1967

1.	The Beatles	"A Day in the Life"
2.	Jimi Hendrix	*Are You Experienced*

3.	Cream	"Sunshine of Your Life"
4.	Jefferson Airplane	"White Rabbit"
5.	The Doors	"Light My Fire"
6.	The Byrds	"Rock and Roll Star"
7.	Aretha Franklin	"Respect"
8.	The Who	"I Can see For Miles"
9.	The Beatles	*Magical Mystery Tour*
10.	The Moody Blues	*Days of Future Past*
11.	Bob Dylan	*John Wesley Harding*
12.	Rolling Stones	"She's a Rainbow"
13.	Donovan	"Mellow Yellow"
14.	The Turtles	"Happy Together"
15.	Procol Harum	"Whiter Shade of Pale"
16.	Traffic	"Dear Mr. Fantasy"
17.	Marvin Gaye	"Ain't No Mountain"
18.	The Rascals	"Groovin'"
19.	The Rolling Stones	"Ruby Tuesday"
20.	Albert King	"Born Under A Bad Sign"

1968

1.	Kooper, Bloomfield & Stills	*Super Session*
2.	Miles Davis	"Nefertiti"
3.	The Beatles	*The White Album*
4.	The Rolling Stones	*Beggars Banquet*
5.	Jimi Hendrix	"Voodoo Child"
6.	The Band	"The Weight"
7.	Cream	"Crossroads"
8.	Big Brother and the Holding Co.	"Piece of My Heart"
9.	Aretha Franklin	"Chain of Fools"
10.	Otis Redding	"The Dock of the Bay"
11.	Steppenwolf	"Born to be Wild"
12.	The Moody Blues	"Ride My See-Saw"
13.	Creedence Clearwater Revival	"Susie Q."
14.	Traffic	"Feelin' All Right"
15.	Deep Purple	"Hush"
16.	Joni Mitchel	"Michael from Mountain"
17.	Canned Heat	"On the Road Again"
18.	Jose Feliciano	"Light My fire"
19.	Simon & Garfunkel	*Bookends*

270

1969

1.	The Who	*Tommy*
2.	The Beatles	*Abbey Road*
3.	Led Zeppelin	*Led Zeppelin I & II*
4.	The Rolling Stones	"Gimme Shelter"
5.	Neil Young	"Cinnamon Girl"
6.	Creedence Clearwater Revival	"Bad Moon Rising"
7.	Creedence Clearwater Revival	*Bayou Country*
8.	Bob Dylan	*Nashville Skyline*
9.	Frank Zappa	"Peaches En Regalia"
10.	Joni Mitchel	*Clouds*
11.	Santana	*Santana*
12.	The Temptations	"Through the Grapevine"
13.	Jethro Tull	*Stand Up*
14.	Quicksilver Messenger Service	"Who Do You Love"
15.	Blind Faith	"Can't Find My Way Home"
16.	Jeff Beck	*Beck-Ola*
17.	Grateful Dead	"Mountains of the Moon"
18.	Joe Cocker	"With a Little Help From My Friends"
19.	Moody Blues	*Threshold of a Dream*
20.	James Brown	"I'm Black and Proud"
21.	Pink Floyd	"Sysyphus I, II, III"
22.	Johnny Cash	"I Walk the Line"
23.	Crosby Stills & Nash	*Crosby, Stills & Nash*
24.	Jefferson Airplane	"Volunteers"

Acknowledgments

This story was made possible because of the people who made my story possible, particularly my wife, H. Leslie Steeves, and our daughters Fekerte and Anna.

My life-long friends Dr. Bill Girsch and Kathy Girsch motivated me to get off the dime and get about putting my fingers to keyboard. Kathy's brilliant stories stirred me to action. Bill created the beautiful cover design.

I was spared humiliation by those who endured reading early drafts of the story. In addition to Professor Jim Earl's meticulous editing, his insightful questions prompted lots of reflection and led to significant improvements.

Dan Armstrong of Mud City Press provided professional formatting, and his guidance was instrumental in helping me bring this project to fruition.

Lastly, this story was inspired by my friends from Waterloo, who together with me, experienced the joys and turbulence of that place and that time. Their enduring memory always makes me smile.

Made in the USA
Monee, IL
10 July 2023

38547626R00166